MILL TOWN

Also by **P.D. LaFleur**

In the Company of Strangers

Vengeance Betrayed

P.D. LaFleur

MILL TOWN

RGI
Press

Punta Gorda, Florida

RGI Press
Suite 1139, Box 261
1133 Bal Harbor Blvd
Punta Gorda, Florida 33950.

This book is a work of fiction. Names, characters, businesses, organizations, places, events and incidents either are the product of the author's imagination or are used fictitiously. Any resemblance to persons, living or dead, events or locales is entirely coincidental.

ISBN (13): 978-0-9792597-1-5
ISBN (10): 0-9792597-1-1

Author website: www.pdlafleur.com
Cover design © Vivid Invention (vividinvention.com)
Author photo © John Zawacki (JZStudios.com)

PRINTED IN THE UNITED STATES OF AMERICA

Second Printing

RGI
Press

For RJ

PROLOGUE

Whether people leave the place where they grew up, or stay in that one spot through their adulthood as I did, there is some longing to romanticize that place. The neighborhoods were 'small and quaint', or the streets were 'broad and busy with the noise of traffic'; the waters 'babbled cold and shallow across the stones', or they 'rushed headlong through town, deep and dark on their way to the sea'. Maybe it's just a primal need for the familiar. I don't know.

I remember my aunt Alice telling me once, after I helped her move from her home into a small senior housing apartment, that she missed knowing where everything went. Now, there would be new places to put things and she would have to learn them all over again.

That's how I feel about Apsley. I've been here my entire life, and that adds up to almost fifty years. Living here is comfortable, like a worn leather jacket that ought to be tossed out, but you keep it anyway. Maybe I just don't like surprises. And like my aunt and her house, I know where everything goes in Apsley, except, sometimes, for myself.

There's an old French adage: Tell me whom you haunt, whom you have as friends, and I'll tell you what you are. I believe it's my collection of friends who make me feel like I belong here, who define me. I've known most of them since I was just a small child. I still hang around with them, still see most of them regularly to play cards and drink beer.

It was one of those long-time friends, Max Zenga, who told me I ought to write this story. "Dave," he said one day over a cup of coffee a few weeks after this episode was over, "you should put all this on paper so people remember what happened." In some ways, I wanted to put the whole thing behind me and just move on. But Max was right; we needed to remember.

In any case, I'm describing here what I believe to be accurate. I can't be certain if what I depict is as precise as it ought to be because it comes from my mind with all its bias, from memories that sometimes lie to me bald faced, and puff up or deflate what really was.

Perhaps I should share the passion of true historians who capture as many accounts of the same places and events as they can so that some balance might occur that results in a better portrayal and a more honest report. For now, mine is the only version, true or bent to some part of my will. This is the town and these are the events I remember.

Apsley is a small town by American standards. Its population is certainly growing, but it is not so substantial that it deserves to be described as anything more than a small town.

It owes its existence to geological phenomena that resulted in a winding river coursing through a valley that sat only forty miles from a city. The river gave Apsley its power and the city gave it a place to send the goods that it produced. Apsley was just meant to have factories.

There were some farms on the outskirts of town and they

supported dozens of families by growing crops, but by and large, Apsley lived, and eventually almost died, on its mills.

I am sure that some people here thought that Apsley could become bigger and more important than it was, even a city someday. But that never happened. The factories that made fabric and shoes and tools and rubber boots aren't working any longer. When they closed, the proximity to the city made Apsley a bit more attractive to commuters who wanted a less expensive suburban lifestyle, and that's where the only real growth has come from. Most of the farms are gone now and the land now has bigger houses and streets with names like Windward Place and Charter Way.

When I was younger, though, Apsley was still a place to work and live, and most of the men left home in the morning with a lunch pail and a thermos. Most of them walked to work, and almost everyone's father served in World War II or Korea. It wasn't poor by our narrow standards, but it was far from rich, and we knew that. The real wealth stayed closer to the city, and we got to see the real wealth when we drove through those towns on the way to the city. The air was cleaner, the houses were bigger, and the cars in the driveways were newer and nicer.

We also knew that there were poorer people than us. To those of us in Apsley, the real poor lived in Eastland, about ten miles away and that much further from the city. That town was rustic beyond repair. In Eastland, there was only one small mill and most of the jobs were tied to the land. Except for a few of the farmhouses, the houses there were smaller and closer together. People from Eastland thought Apsley was pretty hot stuff. At least we had a movie theater and a courthouse and a small branch hospital.

It's not so different today. Eastland is still there, and compared to Apsley it still looks down at the heels. There's some talk that the train tracks from the city are going to be restored all the way to downtown Apsley, and the commuter service will make Apsley and Eastland more accessible and attractive. House prices are still reasonable around here, but quick access to the city would mean big things for us here. Some of us think that's a good thing, but there are still a lot of folks here who like things the way they are.

I own a few pieces of property in Apsley, all of them converted into apartments. My rents are lower than most, maybe even a little lower than they ought to be, but I pick my renters carefully and I'm not afraid of weeding out the inevitable slobs and the non-payers and the loud drunks. My buildings are old but they're all well taken care of. I keep them painted and they all look good. Before my divorce six years ago, I lived in a handsome single-family home with a two-car garage and almost an acre of land, and now I'm in one of my own little apartments near the center of town; it might be a comedown for most people, but for me it's not such a bad way to live.

The stories I remember from my youth in Apsley are stories of playing baseball and riding bicycles and swimming at the town pond. I knew just about everyone around my age in town. Many of them drifted off to other places, but there remains in town a bunch of us who grew up together and never left. They are still my friends and we still speak in a sort of shorthand that outsiders find a little unusual and even uncomfortable. We know the same streets and shortcuts and we had the same teachers and knew the same coaches and policemen.

We also share the same sad memories, of the people who suffered, who were disgraced, or who were murdered. There weren't many of these . . . murders. I can only remember a handful in Apsley in my lifetime. The most recent one was about seven years ago when a woman was smothered with a pillow as she slept. One day, the husband came home drunk and an argument with his wife erupted. The husband apparently lost the argument but had the patience to wait until his wife fell off to sleep that night. I remember the headline from the local newspaper: 'Local Woman Slain by Husband—Accused Said to Be Angry'. Things have been quiet on the Apsley murder scene ever since. I've forgotten some of the others, though if I sat down with a few friends we could recall every single one in the past fifty years and most of their details.

One murder from twenty-nine years ago still stands out like a haunted lighthouse flashing relentlessly and warning of dodgy shallows and perilous shoals. It's the one we . . . my friends and I . . . were closest to, and the one we were most affected by, and the one we really don't like to talk about.

Then, in the autumn of last year, everything changed. That murder case was taken from its quiet place on a back room shelf, undisturbed for decades, and brought forward for all of us to see in all its horror and under the bright light of a brand new day. It was the only murder in Apsley that remained unsolved. There are some people here who wish the memories were allowed to decay into dust, unfit for resurrection, and who feel its emergence exposed a less dignified side of our town and the people in it. If sleeping dogs ought to be left alone, they'll tell you, maybe the murder of Catherine Marchand should have been left alone as well.

But then, Catherine's twin brother would never have come back to town to try to reopen the case, and we never would have found the truth of how and why his sister died, and we would not have met the people we did.

In the end, I think that's all good. In the process, we've learned a lot about each other and what makes us who we are. Tough as it was, we got through it. In a way, it makes us proud of our town and the people in it. But it also showed us that, in the end, dignity doesn't matter very much. Honesty does.

ONE

Monday night in early autumn

Whenever the cards fell this way, George Wessel felt tightness in the center of his chest. They were just too good, better than he felt he deserved, and he convinced himself, as he usually did in such circumstances, that he'd blow a sure chance to win the hand. Self-confidence was not a familiar feeling to George. George would have been content to be dealt mediocre cards so he'd have only a mediocre chance of winning.

"It's up to you, Georgie." I was holding the kinds of cards that George usually expected. Nothing promising, but I'd probably take a chance and bid three anyway. This was only a game of pitch, and should not have been the source of such tension in George's life.

"Are you going to go four?" Gordon Jefts asked the question and George looked up, hating the pressure. A few seconds ticked by and a bead of sweat trickled down from George's ear and down the dimpled flesh of his neck. He looked over to me, feeble, as he tried to estimate my chances of making a three bid. My expression, apparently, yielded no clues.

"C'mon, George." It was Max Zenga trying to move George along this time. It was Max's deal and George knew that Max would take the hand for three unless he bumped up the bid. He studied his cards once more and chewed the corner of his lip before reaching his decision.

"Pass," George finally said in an exhale. "It's up to you, Massimiliano," George said, using Max's given name. George lifted his glass and took a sip of his Diet Sprite, relief written on his face.

Max immediately played his first card, the Ace of hearts, and George had to toss his only heart, a ten, onto the pile. "Thank you very much, Georgie," he said as he swooped up the cards and laid his Queen of hearts on the table. Max pushed his baseball cap high on his head as he reeled off his lead cards. It was over quickly and he made his hand easily.

"Christ, George," said Max as he shoveled the cards to his left for the next deal. "Why didn't you take it for four in clubs? You had the ace, jack and eight. Lady Luck was sitting right there on your lap and you still didn't bid."

George just shrugged his sloped shoulders. He didn't like being the center of conversation and he knew that Lady Luck didn't even know his name.

This was Monday night at Dean's Town Tavern. Five friends showed up to play cards tonight and occasionally watch a little football on TV in between. The volume on the new plasma set was turned down low and it served tonight more as backdrop, like an oversized lava lamp that swirled with the team colors. A few others, all regulars, sat at the bar.

"Any news on the lottery winner yet?" It was Max. "Six million's a lot to let sit there. You guys are pretty well plugged in; any rumors flying around?"

Max scanned the faces of his four companions: I shook my

head no; I hadn't heard a thing. Gordon Jefts adjusted his cuffs; Bob Hayes and George Wessel just shrugged.

A winning ticket worth nearly six million dollars was sold three weeks earlier at Eubanks' News Stand on Main Street and no one had yet stepped forward to claim the winnings. The conversation at Dean's drifted along through the usual fantasies of sudden wealth. New cars, new houses, and lots of travel were the usual dreams.

"Hey, guess who I saw last Friday." It was Bobby Hayes, the undertaker. Bob usually looked the part of the undertaker . . . always clean, ever neat, each hair in place . . . but he enjoyed his time out with his friends when he could trade his charcoal suits and stiff white shirts for a well worn sweatshirt and faded jeans.

"Was he breathing?" Max asked.

"He wasn't a customer, if that's what you mean." Bob took his time shuffling the cards and waiting for the tension to build.

George broke the silence. "So who'd you see?"

Bob cracked a half smile that came with inside knowledge and allowed for three beats of silence before he spoke. "Phil Marchand."

All eyes were on Bob waiting for elaboration. This was rather significant news to the group. Max said, "Phil? I haven't seen him since he moved away."

Bob's card shuffling came to a stop and all eyes were on him.

"How was he? What was he doing back here?" George's curiosity was quick to express itself and his were the two questions that everyone wanted to ask.

"He looks fine. Said he's planning to move back to Apsley."

"He's moving back?" It was George again. "Why?"

"He quit his job as CFO for some big financial company. Plus he's going through a divorce." Bob Hayes was always a good source of local news. His funeral home sat near the center of Apsley's downtown and Bob enjoyed chatting it up with anyone who stopped by. Unless he had a funeral or a viewing going on, he was always available for a drop in visit.

"No kidding." Gordon Jefts chimed in. Gordon had a law office over the drug store at the town's square and prided himself in knowing the comings and goings of almost everybody in the area, and the news about Phil Marchand was a bit of a coup for Bob Hayes. Unlike Bob who eschewed formal wear on his nights out, Gordon always looked like a combed, pressed and starched lawyer ready for appearance before clients or the court. His only concession this night was removing his Ferragamo tie. The crisp pale blue custom shirt was opened at the collar but remained fresh and unwrinkled; the French cuffs were embossed with a gothic 'J' and held together with gold knots.

George said, "Phil's married to a real society dame, isn't he?"

Gordon Jefts cut in. "Duh. Georgie boy, have you been watching TV reruns again? 'Society dame?' I haven't heard that since Paul Drake used the term on Perry Mason."

George was sufficiently abashed and Bob Hayes saw his discomfort. George was always easy to pick on and Bob was usually his protection. He stepped in. "Her grandfather started Marlowe Pharmaceuticals in North Carolina. She's got to be worth millions."

The door to the tavern opened and a cold gust cut the air and washed over the table. Kenny Gladwell removed his jacket and gave a small wave to the group. A few chairs moved to let him drag over another chair and join the group. "What's up, amigos?"

Max filled him in on the breaking news. "Bobby tells us that Phil Marchand is moving back here."

Kenny was about to sit and stood back up abruptly. Ken had a long way to go, for he was six-foot-six and had the lean build of a cyclist or a mountain climber. "Anybody ready for a beer?"

Max responded with a vigorous nod. You didn't have to ask Max twice. "If you're buying."

The rest had nearly full beers and motioned to Ken that they were fine for now. When Ken went to the bar to place his order, Gordon Jefts said in a low voice to the group at the table, "Kenny's not too happy about Phil moving back."

I knew that Phil Marchand and Ken Gladwell mixed like oil and water when they were kids, but it had been almost thirty years. "That's old history."

"I wouldn't bet on it. Did you see his face when Max said Phil's name?"

Ken returned to the table and slid a beer in Max's direction. He raised his bottle, said "Cheers", and took his first sip. He wiped his lips and looked around the table. All eyes were fixed in his direction. "What?" He looked at everyone. "You mean Phil Marchand? It'll be good to see him again." His table mates weren't convinced.

"You hated his guts." Max was always the most likely to speak bluntly.

"OK, so Phil Marchand is the kind of guy who was born on third base and thinks he hit a triple. I didn't like him very much back then, and unless he's changed, I probably won't when he comes back. So what?"

That put a quick end to any thoughts of conciliation and a few of us glanced over to the TV set, none of us really interested in the score, more as a way to let the bile float away on its own.

George still had questions for Bob Hayes. "What about Phil's kids?"

"He's got two," Bobby said. "One's in medical school in New York and the other one's a dancer living in San Francisco."

"Good place for a dancer," Max added. "Probably a drag queen."

"So what?" Gordon Jefts was looking at his cards as he asked the question but then challenged Max with a stare. "You sound like a homophobe." He folded his cards back up. "I'll bid two."

It was my turn to bid. "Three." I didn't say much, even though I was Phil Marchand's best friend when we were kids.

Bobby said, "Phil was asking about you, by the way, Dave. I'll bet he gives you a call. He flew back home and he's driving back up here. Probably be here before the week is out."

"It'd be nice to see him," I said, barely looking up from my hand, which was an assortment of crap. I was hoping someone else would take it.

"It's by me." Kenny Gladwell sat back in his chair.

"Pass." George Wessel, the risk taker.

"Four," Max came through. He always took the biggest chances.

"All yours, Max," said Bobby Hayes.

Max Zenga took every trick of the hand and moaned, "No jack? Screwed."

"Nothing ventured, nothing gained." Gordon Jefts scooped the cards up from the table as George made a note on the score pad.

"So where's he going to live?" It was Ken Gladwell's question, delivered off-hand, as if he didn't care. "Maybe Dave here has a place open."

Oh, right, I thought, knowing as my friends did that my apartments weren't exactly executive class. "There are the new condos at the other end of Main Street. What do they call it? Pompicott Village? They'll probably have something for him."

"They're getting primero dineros for those places," George offered. "Top dollar." As if the others didn't understand that 'primero dineros' might mean 'expensive'.

Gordon Jefts added as he dealt the cards, "Phil can afford it. If he was CFO for a big financial company, he probably made a half a mil or more a year there."

In Apsley, as in most places, that was a lot of money. This was a blue collar town with its roots in shoes and textiles, now long gone. There were a couple of smaller high tech firms with offices in town now, but most of their big earners would live somewhere else. Apsley housed worker bees.

"Is he going to work someplace around here? It's not like there are tons of big jobs in Apsley." George wanted all the details.

Bob Hayes answered. "I'm sure he has a big enough bankroll to retire, but who know? Maybe he'll buy a business. He's still young."

"What about his divorce? That probably cost him a bundle." George Wessel owned a laundry and dry cleaning business in town. His finances, while not robust, were solid by Apsley standards. He had a beautiful older home with a small mortgage, and his children all went to college and graduated with only small college loans. That didn't keep him from worrying about money every day.

Bob Hayes offered the sense that Phil Marchand's soon-to-be ex-wife would likely be out-earning Phil, just on her dividends from the family fortune. "Not that he said anything like that, but Phil didn't exactly look broke when I saw him."

George Wessel wasn't through with his questions. "Why come home, though? I mean, if he's been living the good life for all these years, why come back to this place?"

There was no answer from anyone to that question. Cards were picked up, bids were presented and the game played out before another word was spoken. Max Zenga suggested the answer that was on everyone's mind but that had as yet remained unspoken: "His sister. Maybe he wants to figure out what really happened to his sister."

This was followed by prolonged silence as we chewed on the thought. The sister in question, Catherine Marchand, was Phil's twin, high school cheerleading captain, queen of the prom, and all around beautiful young woman twenty-nine years ago when her battered body was discovered at the base of a tree near Squash Pond behind the old high school. There were a lot of theories regarding the possible motive and the likely suspect, but not enough evidence to put anybody away. The murder was never solved.

Gordon Jefts broke the silence. "I remember her wake. And her funeral." There were nods around the table as we each recalled the events. "It was a bitch, I can tell you."

"We were all there, Gordon," Bobby Hayes noted. "I was just starting to work part-time at the funeral home when it happened."

George was curious. "Did you have to . . . do the embalming?"

"No. The boss wouldn't let me even look at her when they brought her in. She was real bad and I don't think he wanted me hanging around while he was trying to put her back together. I was about eighteen then, and she was what, maybe seventeen?"

George put the common sentiment about the murder on the table. "People said it was Malcolm Prudhomme who did it. They still do. You can even see it today. When Malcolm walks downtown, most people don't even say hello."

Malcolm was a local eccentric with a long history of alcoholism and suspected pedophilia. Over the years, Malcolm Prudhomme could be found in the stands at little league games, or on the sidelines at school athletic contest, even though he was unmarried and childless. No one could even remember if Malcolm ever drove a car. He was always seen walking and always with his head tilted down. His teeth were twisted yellow stubs and no one could remember him ever cracking a smile.

People had a difficult time understanding Malcolm because he mumbled so badly. He wore smudged sunglasses most of the time, even when the sun was down. There was no shortage of suspicions when Malcolm's name arose in local conversations; he was certainly peculiar, and perhaps aberrant, although no one at the table this evening had a personal experience that might verify any serious allegations. Now in his seventies and walking sometimes with a cane, he was largely confined to the run-down family home near the top of the tallest hill in town. Occasionally he'd be seen shuffling along the sidewalks downtown, always alone.

I offered my own thoughts. "Malcolm's a strange bastard, no question. He always hung around at the girls' basketball games sniffing around. But no one could connect him to Catherine's murder. Even Chief Moncton said so."

There were nods all around. The Chief of Police at the time, Alfred Moncton, placed Malcolm Prudhomme in his sights as soon as Catherine's body was found. Malcolm insisted he was innocent but was still subjected to hours of interrogation, including plenty of threats, but to no avail. There simply was no evidence to keep Malcolm in jail, and the police reluctantly told Malcolm to go home.

Ken Gladwell tried to get off the subject. "So who's going to bid on this mess?"

The hand was played, this time with Bobby Hayes taking the hand.

George Wessel tried to steer the conversation back to Catherine Marchand and the returning brother, Philip. The story was too rich in history and in the lore of the town for him to put the story away and out of sight. "That year that Catherine was murdered, there was another tragedy, remember?"

Everyone did but said nothing. We all recalled the morning in May of that same year when Doug Dumont was found hanging from a tree behind a neighborhood saloon on Elm Street.

"That was a suicide, Georgie. Catherine's case was a little different." Max was among the group who skipped class that day when they spotted Dumont's body suspended from an oak tree. "They found a note and everything with Dumont."

"Yeah, but," George went on, "Malcolm was somehow connected, wasn't he? I heard that Dumont hung himself because he'd been fooling around with Malcolm."

Max tried to shut down George's persistence in maintaining the same conversation.

"Can it, Georgie. It was a bad year. You're such a ray of fucking sunshine, George. Just play some cards, OK?"

Gordon Jefts stretched his arms out and made a move to rise from his seat. "No more for me, guys. I've got a court date tomorrow morning and I need to get some sleep."

That started a few more suggestions that the card game come to an end. I reached for my jacket and Bob Hayes reached for his at the same time. George made his exit, saying he needed to be at the laundry at eight and had some paperwork to do before he went in. Gordon Jefts was already in his Burberry trench coat and standing by the door.

Ken and Max moved to the bar where they sipped their beers. I was glad to get away.

Bob Hayes and George Wessel walked to their cars and drove off. Gordon Jefts and I made our way along East Main Street in the evening chill towards our respective homes. The moon was approaching full and cast a soft and comforting glow. We lived only a few doors apart; me in an upstairs unit of one of my apartment buildings, and Gordon in a high-ceilinged loft apartment over a retail store a block further along.

For me, living in an apartment close to downtown was a necessity, due to a bad divorce and a few financial setbacks. For Gordon Jefts, a loft apartment had a certain cachet. It was the sort of place a successful, single lawyer would have if he lived in a city. All that was missing here was the city.

Our walk took us past a row of derelict duplex houses built over a century ago to house factory workers. Several factories stood just a bit further along the river. One of the houses was already slated to be torn down, the others yielding slowly but relentlessly to gravity as they made their way to the same conclusion.

This area was known in Apsley as 'tannery row', the place where raw hides were tanned into shoe and belt leather for ninety years, beginning a century and a half ago, and where the effluent ran into the river and turned the waters sometime green, sometimes pink, always deadly. Within a year of the last tanning factory's closing, the river looked positively pristine and today it is almost swimmable.

The Kerrigan Mills further along the river described clusters of connected brick buildings, some of which were already bought from the Kerrigan family and being redeveloped into condos and commercial space. I had my eye on one of the smaller buildings in the Kerrigan Mills complex.

"You never considered buying those houses and doing them over, did you Dave?"

"Not really, Gordon, but I may want to talk to you about buying part of the Kerrigan Mills."

Gordon turned quickly and said, "You knew I was handling the Mills?"

"It's a small town, Gordon."

Gordon liked to think of himself as an insider, even a power broker, but word travelled too fast to have many secrets here. He fairly grumbled when he said, "There's a lot happening there right now but maybe we can talk about it. Are you sure you want to get into the commercial side? You'd be risking a lot with even a small piece of the Kerrigan place."

"It's just a thought, Gordon."

We walked for a while without speaking, the thinning canopy of the maples ruffling in the cool breeze.

"So Phil Marchand returns, Dave. Who would have guessed?" Gordon Jefts' words broke the silence but my mind was already deep into the subject.

I gave that some thought before answering. "I think maybe I would have guessed he'd eventually come back here if I thought about it long enough. When his family moved away, they weren't over Catherine's death. Maybe it's been gnawing at him ever since, even though he's been a thousand miles away."

"I don't know how I'd react after all these years, but if you wanted to talk about a cold case, this is it. No evidence that ties to anyone. No witnesses ever found. Even Chief Moncton is dead now. Who does he talk to?"

"They must still have the evidence in storage someplace. Maybe there's an old retired cop around who worked on the case. Maybe he'll hire some forensic people to dig into things. I don't know."

"You and Phil were good friends."

"It was a long time ago. I haven't heard from him since he moved away."

On the sidewalk in front of my place, we stopped, and Gordon said, "Ken didn't seem very happy about Phil coming back here. I didn't imagine that."

"They didn't get along when we were kids and I guess absence didn't make Ken any fonder."

"Yeah, but I think Ken wasn't happy about anything tonight. He's got a lot to deal with right now."

I hadn't heard anything about this and my face must have shown my puzzlement.

Gordon shook his head. "I shouldn't be saying anything,

Dave." How many times had I heard these same words from Gordon? Maybe Gordon should not but I knew with the certainty of experience that he would anyway. "It's just that I've heard some things about Ken's life that would make anyone a little upset."

"Like what?"

"I hear that things at home aren't going well, that's all." Gordon knew something he wasn't telling but I backed off from following up with any questions. This was the kind of subject matter that our sidewalk discussion couldn't help.

"Fair enough, Gordon." I put my hand out and we shook. "Good luck tomorrow in court."

"I'm not really going to court tomorrow. I just wanted to get out of there tonight."

I raised my eyebrows to ask the obvious question.

"I just felt a little crappy about all this talk about Catherine Marchand. George didn't want to let it go."

"Well, Georgie really enjoys a good car wreck."

Gordon nodded. "I think he just enjoys seeing other people suffering instead of him."

I brushed off the thought. George was too easy to pick on but he was harmless. "C'mon Gordon, you're being too tough on poor George. He's always there when you need him, you know that."

"I know, I know. It's my issue, not his."

I patted Gordon on the shoulder as he turned towards his building's front door. "Take it easy," I said, knowing precisely the response that would generate.

"I'll take it anyway I can get it."

I reached my front door, found my key, and turned the doorknob and let myself in the front hallway. At the second floor landing I used another key to go into my humble apartment. When I bought the building eleven years ago, it was a large two-family house. I turned it into four apartments and did all the work myself. I was proud of the work I did. I just never expected at the time that I'd be my own tenant.

Six years ago, my wife of eighteen years announced that she was leaving me. More to the point, she said she was filing for divorce and I was to leave the family home. Gail wanted to stay in the house with our two sons. I was shocked and speechless at the announcement.

She hadn't been in love with me for years, she said. I knew later that I should have seen this moment coming. The night classes at the state college; the unusual late nights when she didn't get home until midnight, even though class ended at nine and the school was only sixteen miles away. I even missed the most explicit and cruel clue: the crude odor of musk in our minivan, the same one we used to transport our sons to and from school and baseball practice, and trips to our vacation cabin.

So here I was, living alone upstairs in an apartment building while my former wife lived in the home we bought together in happier times and in another part of town. It wasn't so bad, especially since my sons still spent occasional weekends at my apartment. I didn't know what Gail was up to on the weekends, nor did I care, now that the wounds were scarred over. I just lamented, in advance, the losses I'd suffer in the next year when our younger son graduated from college and moved away for good. Like his older brother before him, he wanted to put some serious distance between himself and Apsley. He wouldn't be coming back for weekends any longer, and I already anticipated the pangs of separation.

I walked into the bathroom, used the john, and sat down at the kitchen table where I poured myself one last beer before going to bed. I liked my late nights alone now, using the time before bed to give some consideration to the events of the day just passed. Tonight, my thoughts were fixed on Phil Marchand, the interconnections to him and his sister, Catherine, and the strange human being that was Malcolm Prudhomme.

I could recall clearly the face of Catherine Marchand. There were plenty of good looking girls in school, but Catherine had a certain way about her that made her particularly attractive. She had that low voice, and a way of walking that was, well, just plain seductive. She didn't have a steady boyfriend but 'played the field,' if Apsley could be said to have a 'field' in which to play. At least that was the public observation and one that Catherine cultivated. For better or worse, I knew better.

I closed my eyes for a moment, recalling how she was a perfect masturbatory fantasy when I was in my early teens. I shook my head at the thoughts that ensued when Catherine actually began to pay attention to me. It was heady stuff.

I knew Catherine from a very young age since Phil Marchand was one of my best friends going back to age ten or eleven. Other kids would occasionally tease Phil about what it must be like to live in the same house as Catherine, the goddess.

When her body was found, just before sunset on an autumn day, beaten to death, I was over at Phil's house listening to music on his new stereo. The police came to the door and a sobbing Mrs. Marchand asked me in a rush to go home, that there was a 'family problem' and things would be better if I wasn't there.

The days after were crystal clear, even twenty-nine years later. Word traveled through Apsley faster than the newspapers could print and deliver the story. The place where her body was found was well known to nearly everyone in town. Squash Pond lay some three hundred yards behind the high school, surrounded by thick woods of pine and ash and oak, and accessible by pathways worn smooth by youngsters wanting a shortcut to go home after school, or to play hockey on the pond in the winter, or to go fishing in the summer.

It was a somber time and rumors flew in every direction, many of them aimed at Malcolm Prudhomme. But even that seemed like a long shot. For all his creepiness, Malcolm didn't appear to be the violent type, and Catherine was subjected to a vicious and determined attack.

I checked my phone answering machine . . . nothing . . . set my alarm clock and checked my calendar for tomorrow. Except for an early appointment with an electrician, my day was unplanned. I pulled the sheet over my legs and before I reached the memories about Catherine's funeral, I was asleep.

TWO

Tuesday

She turned the corner at a trot and continued along the side of the road in the general direction of home. Ahead of her on the right was the grass of the sloping meadow. The air was thick with the dusky aromas of autumn and she relished these quiet solitary minutes early in the morning. Her house was filled with sounds of clattering dishes and morning radio and her younger brother's grousing about the unfairness of his homework assignments. The silence as she ran gave her the opportunity to think.

Unlike most of her friends at Apsley High, Samantha Zenga didn't clutter her solitude with iPods and earplugs. Instead she listened to the robins, now getting ready for their annual flight south, and the intermittent barks of the neighborhood dogs. She cut to her right and left the dry pavement for the meadow. The grass was long but most of it was bent to the ground where foot traffic led to the path ahead of her. To her left and through the clumps of pine and oak and thick brush was Squash Pond. She inhaled the marshy odor coming from the pond and felt the dew splattering the backs of her calves as she continued.

This morning her thoughts were on her upcoming birthday and the prospect of getting her learner's permit. With some good grades, rational behavior and some sweet-talk, especially to her father, she just might get a car of her own within the year. She had the grades and she was generally a "good kid" (she'd heard her parents describe her this way to their friends). Top that off with a father who adored her, and she could envision the car in her driveway already. She had few conditions; it simply had to be something sporty and have a good sound system. She smiled at the notion and kept running.

Ahead of her were the shadows of taller trees and dense overgrowth. On the far side, the path opened up again and she'd be at the end of her street. The trees had lost many of their leaves, but oaks tended to hold on longer than most. The rusting foliage formed a canopy and the early morning sunlight only reached the ground here in flecks.

That's when she felt them. They were hidden from view but they were there just the same. Eyes.

She looked over her shoulder to the left and tried to scan the thick clumps of trees and brush and ferns that sat motionless in the shade, still wrapped in wisps of morning fog, but saw nothing untoward. She didn't bother looking right; she knew with no other proof that the eyes were at her left side. She picked up her pace a bit and focused on the path ahead. Eighty yards in front of her, more or less, lay the pavement and the sunshine.

Her breathing rate increased and she threw herself into a full blown burst as she reached the last fifty yards, feeling her heart pumping and some cramping in her thighs and calves.

As she raced into the street and into the direct sunlight, she thought she heard noises in the thick underbrush behind her.

No turning around now, she pumped harder and faster and knew that whatever was back there was still back there and not at her heels.

She never slowed, focused like a laser on her house four doors away. She continued to kick hard and fast until she reached the wooden deck and the back door of her house. Out of breath and anxious to enter the safety of her home, she reached for the door handle when she heard a voice. "What's the big rush this morning?"

It caught her by surprise. She stopped abruptly and looked in the direction of the questioner. At the end of the deck sat her father in a deck chair, snatching a smoke before heading off to morning coffee with his friends.

"Nothing, Dad. Just trying to get the blood pumping." Samantha Zenga's breath was coming in pants and she turned the handle. She'd just as soon not share her fear. She had seen nothing, heard not a distinguishable sound as she tromped along the path except for her own footfalls. Telling her father that she "felt" a pair of eyes on her during her morning run would only alarm him and make her feel like a jerk. Weak and afraid.

"Well, hurry up and shower because Max Zenga's bus will be leaving in fifteen."

She smiled at him and said, "If you guys leave before I'm ready, I'll never speak to you for the rest of my life." She opened the door and dashed up the stairs, ignoring her mother who was pouring orange juice at the counter, and her thirteen year old brother, who was gulping his cereal at the kitchen table. She took the stairs two at a time and was standing under the hot shower in seconds. She tried to re-experience the sense she felt minutes before along the path, but could not. "Silly" she thought to herself. "Who's going to be hiding in the woods at 6:30 in the morning except for maybe a chipmunk?" She dried, dressed, snatched an orange juice and a slice of cinnamon toast from the counter and pecked her mother on the cheek before grabbing a knapsack with her books and homework and dashing out the door. She was ready in twelve minutes.

In spite of the sunny start, the morning promised some rain and Malcolm Prudhomme thought he felt a few drops on the back of his neck, even though he was under the cover of the oaks. He dismissed the sensation and maintained his focus on the young girl running in his direction. He rubbed himself through his trousers, felt the swelling in his groin. She's so adorable, he thought. Young and fresh and with such smooth skin. She runs so fast and her ponytail flies up with every step. He closed his eyes and allowed the mental image to wash over him, the rippling leg muscles and the slim buttocks. He continued rubbing.

He had been taking an early morning walk after a sleepless night when he heard her footfalls. That's when he moved from the path into the trees. He watched her turn the corner. She passed just a few feet in front of him and he listened to her breathing, almost hearing her heart beating. Her footfalls were muffled in the carpet of grass and moss and leaves and soft soil. He inhaled the aroma. Fresh sweat that had not yet soured or fouled that glorious odor, the unmistakable and seductive scent of a young woman. That's what truly excited him and he rubbed and squeezed.

As she passed close by, she abruptly increased her speed and he watched her exit the shade and approach the street, now pumping at full throttle. No one else was around. In the silence and the solitude he unzipped his fly and put his hand inside. Still not fully hard but warm and beginning to grow. It had been a long time since he felt this way. It was the smell of her.

He stroked but remained flaccid, persisting for a few moments until he had to acknowledge the futility of his efforts. He cursed, spat on the ground and zipped up his fly. The mist was definitely turning to rain. In a minute, he stepped out of the trees and the undergrowth and on to the path. In another fifteen minutes, he entered the side door of his decaying house and sat at the kitchen table, still clad in his windbreaker. He took off his damp and soiled baseball cap and poured himself a cup of leftover cold coffee.

Max Zenga always had coffee at Dunkin' Donuts at eight o'clock, rain, shine or blizzard. There, he sat and made small talk with Lou Pellerin from the police department.

As usual, by the time Max arrived, after dropping his son and daughter off at school, Lou Pellerin was already there in the booth. Lou had been promoted to Assistant Chief of Police a few years ago, and also served as the department's unofficial detective. It meant that he kept fairly regular hours. It didn't mean that he eschewed jelly donuts today any more than he did when he first joined the force and his girth confirmed it.

"Lou, you whale," Max said in greeting. "You ought to know better." That was a barely veiled reference to Pellerin's predecessor as Assistant Chief, Jacko Moriarty, who died of a heart attack in the course of chasing down a group of teens drinking at the sand pits. Jacko, like Lou, wasn't as svelte as he'd been when he joined the force years earlier, and a jelly donut was part of his daily regimen.

"Shut up, Max, and sit your skinny ass down."

The pair of them cursed each other and rarely failed to find some petty flaw in the other on which to dwell. It was male camaraderie at its finest.

"If this rain keeps coming, Max, you're going to be shit out of luck today." Max Zenga ran an excavation and landscaping business. The job he'd been working on, installing septic tanks and leach fields for a pair of new homes, would be dirty and tough in this weather. "You'll just have to go home and beat the wife, then. That's what you usually do on rainy days, isn't it?"

"If this rain screws up the job, I've got some welding I've got to get done for a guy in Marlton." Max was adept at many jobs and always had a steady stream of business. He had a shop and repaired heavy equipment at his garage and didn't lack for customers.

"It's supposed to quit soon, so you should be fine. But tell me, what the hell is up with Phil Marchand."

Max turned to Lou at once. "You got radar or something?"

Lou Pellerin watched the reaction before saying, "He's moving back to Apsley. Just separated from his old lady and is coming back here. That's what I hear?"

"You're freaking amazing, Lou." Max put his coffee down. "And here I thought I was the one with the news."

Lou filled him in. "Phil Marchand is getting a condo, one of the new ones down at the lower end of Main Street. He'll probably be here within a week. Left a big job in North Carolina with a bundle of money. His wife doesn't want a divorce, is what I heard."

"So if you know everything about him, why even ask me what's going on? Sounds like you got it wired."

"I'm asking because I want to be prepared, that's all. Right now, all I know is what I heard plus what I can dig up through channels. What I want to know, and what I'm asking you, is why is Phil moving back? Apsley isn't exactly the center of the universe."

"You got that right. I'm driving a six-year-old Mercury and Phil's probably driving a BMW."

"Mercedes, S-class."

Max almost coughed out his coffee. "What the hell, Lou, why are you asking me anything at all? You got Phil Marchand all figured out."

"But why? Why is he coming back here? That's my question."

"Who gives a crap? Guy moves away. Guy splits from his wife. Guy moves back to his old hometown. Case closed."

Lou's response was less than kind. "Max, you move dirt for a living and I don't pretend to know how to do that, OK? I ask questions for a living, and I do it for a reason, so don't try to second guess me."

Max could feel the blood rising in his neck and face. "I don't give a rip, Lou. Maybe it has something to do with his sister; who the hell knows? Just don't pretend that you have something mysterious going on and everybody else is just clueless. If you're getting your shorts in a knot because of an old murder case, that's your problem, not mine."

Lou hated being predictable. He stared at his coffee cup for a moment before he went on.

"OK. It does have something to do with his sister. I'm just wondering if Phil's going to come into town and use his money to hire some high-priced lawyers and private detectives and just stir up trouble. Shit, Catherine Marchand was killed a long time ago and I hate to see old scabs reopened. That's all."

Max said nothing. He recalled that the air was filled with accusations and finger pointing and failure when Catherine's case was put on a shelf and tagged 'unsolved'. No one wanted a replay of those times. Many of the people who were involved in the investigation were dead; the only person ever suspected of the crime was now a feeble old man.

"Well, so what if he wants to find out whatever he can. It's a free country, Lou, and this is his sister we're talking about."

Lou considered that before he answered. "It just muddies up the waters, that's all. It's such a cold case that there's not much we can do. I just don't want to be spending all my time and the department's time on something like this."

"Maybe he just can't let it go. If it was my sister and I never found out what really happened, I'm not sure what I'd do."

Pellerin shook his head. "Maybe you're right."

Max started to get up from the booth. "Look, Lou. I have to get going." After they said their goodbyes and Lou Pellerin was getting in his car, Max motioned to him to roll down the window.

"Have you talked with Dave Blondin about Phil yet?"

Lou shook his head. "No. Should I?"

"You're too young to remember this, but they were best friends, that's all. Phil would probably get in touch with Dave if he moved back here."

"Thanks, Max. I'll keep that in mind."

Max turned around to walk back to his pickup when he decided to ask a leading question. "Lou, by the way, how's life with the new Chief?"

Lou used a conspiratorial voice when he spoke, looking left and right quickly, making sure no one else was within earshot. "I didn't want to say anything in there with other people around, but I've got my doubts."

"Why do you say that? He seems like a nice enough guy."

"Maybe. But he's like, a city guy. Not a native, know what I mean? He needs to get the lay of the land before he starts barking out orders to the rest of the guys."

"The new Chief, Jerry Wetman? He's barking?"

"It's just his way, that's all. I'm not making any judgments yet, but you just wait and see."

"Lou, just because he got picked over you ..."

"Don't give me that bull. It was politics and you know it. If I had one more vote on the Board of Selectmen, I'd be Chief right now."

"But it didn't happen that way. Lou. How old are you anyway?"

"Forty-one."

"So, you're still young to be a chief, even in a small town

like this. You gotta lose the attitude, buddy. Let this guy do his thing and when he retires in a few years, you-da-man! You just wait and see."

"Maybe. I'm not so sure."

"I'll put money on it." Max gave him an assuring pat on the shoulder and they each headed to their day's jobs.

I like to mark the advance of the seasons botanically. The asters and the chrysanthemums this morning were tall and still blossoming, and leaves cluttered the sidewalks and gathered in the hollows and corners beginning their inevitable journey into dust. The foliage that was fiery red, yellow and orange ten days ago was muted now and past its peak, as if the brightness control knob was turned down. The sun was hidden behind clouds this morning, and occasional rain spit down from time to time. It was nearly time to take the gloves and scarf from the shoebox in the front closet and stow them nearer at hand.

As I did every year since I was a boy, I wanted to play hooky before the truly bitter weather set in. I had scheduled a visit over coffee with a newly licensed electrician this morning to talk about the kind of work that arose in my apartment buildings from time to time. Young, eager tradesmen generally took the small jobs, like mine, that the more experienced ones disdained. With some reluctance, I showed up at Lafferty's Diner. I didn't have much work for him at the moment, but also told him that he ought to contact a few other people in town who, like me, were in the market occasionally for a good, hustling electrician. I gave him four names, accepted his thanks, and went off for the day.

I knew I needed to do some work in the laundry of my six-family building on Oak Street and install a new range in the vacant third floor unit of that same building. Instead, I decided that for the rest of this day I'd do only what I wanted to do, and nothing of what I ought to do. Never put off until tomorrow what you can put off until the day after tomorrow; I heard that once and decided the adage suited my mood. I hopped into my pick up truck, a rust-stained relic with a questionable muffler, and picked up a newspaper downtown.

Around nine, the light rain seemed to have abated and I walked along Apsley's Main Street towards the public library at the town square. I walked into the library and headed straight for the reference area where I knew I'd be bound to find some of the documents and records for the time I wanted. The conversation at Dean's Town Tavern last night begged for confirmation. I wanted to check the newspaper and records for that time to refresh my memory, even though it was unpleasant.

I first found the Apsley town reports and pulled the book for the year I sought: Twenty-nine years ago, and the pages were dog eared. I sat alone at the long table in the center of the reference room and flipped through the pages until I found the entry I wanted: "October 17, Catherine Joanne Marchand, age 17 years, 1 month and 14 days. Cause of death: Multiple trauma (Homicide)."

That was the entire entry. I'd forgotten the exact date. I removed a piece of paper and a pencil from the desk and jotted down the information.

I wanted to pull up the newspaper accounts and at the microfilm desk, I read the instructions. Nancy Easter saw me and came over. "What can I get you, Dave?" Nancy was my age, and we even dated once or twice in high school. Nancy had been the reference librarian here for years.

"Can I take a look at the local papers in the archives? I'm just looking up a few things."

Nancy Easter always intrigued me. In high school, she was considered aloof. She was, after all, a beauty back in high school, with an extra helping of brains. Her hair was thick and chestnut brown, held up this day in a bun with a few wisps at each ear. Probably a rinse kept her hair that color, but it worked for me. With a neck that was porcelain and long, she also had wide-set eyes of the deepest blue, with silver flecks.

Nancy Easter was not the fantasy material for me that Catherine Marchand was; Catherine was downright voluptuous, while Nancy was taut of body and just as tight in attitude. This morning Nancy wore a gray wool skirt and an off-white silk blouse, reminding those who saw her that she remained as fit and as trim as she was decades earlier.

She pulled a cartridge marked with the dates covering the ones I wanted and said, "I'll get you started. It's pretty easy once you get in."

After a few minutes of searching, I was reading newspaper articles from the days in question. There were several and I wanted to read them at home, so I asked for Nancy's help to print them.

Nancy noticed the documents I wanted copied but didn't say anything at first. When she finished showing me how to use the microfiche printer, she said, "I see you're looking into some old memories, Dave. Doing some detective work?"

I tend to be a private person, at least as private as a person can be in a small town, but I'd known Nancy since we were kids. And of course, she knew all about the murder of Catherine Marchand. She, like Catherine, was one of the "five princesses", the local nickname at the time for five young women at Apsley High of remarkable talent, intelligence and good looks that everyone recognized as uncanny, truly astonishing in such a small community. "Not exactly, Nancy," I said. "I thought I'd refresh my memory, that's all."

"With Phil Marchand coming back to Apsley, I figured you'd be his sidekick, sort of like Holmes and Watson." She smiled at her own remark. "You being Holmes, of course."

I smiled back. "I haven't talked to Phil since we graduated, and I'm not even sure that Catherine's murder is why he's planning to come back."

"Oh, come on, Dave." Her mood changed on a dime and she got serious. "Tell me why a success story like Phil Marchand is moving back here if he's not interested in stirring things up. This isn't exactly the center of the universe, and unless Phil Marchand has changed entirely, I doubt he's just looking for a quiet place to retire."

Whatever I did or said struck a nerve in Nancy Easter that I didn't want to irritate. I wanted to get my copies and leave.

"I have no idea why he's coming back, Nancy. You may be right, but I don't really know."

"Sometimes it's better to leave things alone."

The copies were done and Nancy picked them up and held the packet of papers close to her chest. She wasn't done and I couldn't escape just yet.

"If Phil comes back and starts snooping around, there's no telling what ugly stuff comes out. If you ask me, it's like picking at an old sore."

I had not asked her and I was bewildered by her emphatic posture and strong remarks. Over the years Nancy was pleasant enough, if not effusive in her occasional dealings with me. Today, I apparently irritated a raw nerve and I just wanted to take my papers and leave.

"OK. Can I have my papers?" Nancy appeared annoyed that I had no interest in continuing the conversation.

She handed me the pages and said, "Nineteen pages. So it's three dollars and eighty cents."

I counted out four singles and said, "Keep the change, Nancy. And thanks." She accepted the money but wasn't anxious to release the papers; for a moment, I thought she wanted to spew a bit more. Nevertheless, she handed me the nineteen pages, I took them, and left.

I gave some thought to Nancy and her reaction as I left the library and walked back to my truck. She was one of the brightest people I could remember in high school, and she had a scholarship to Columbia. Everyone in Apsley figured she'd go to New York and never come back. Then, before a year had passed, she was back in Apsley.

I never heard why, even though there were a few rumors, some of them ugly, and Nancy eventually went to a community college. After she graduated with an associate's degree, she got a job at the Apsley Public Library and never left. She never married and rarely dated anyone as far as I knew.

Nancy was one of the superstar students, athletes, geniuses at Apsley High. The cluster of young women there at the time was considered a remarkable coincidence of talent, beauty and brains, an aberration and cause of much conversation in and around the community: Nancy Easter, Lourdes Freitas, Tina Kerrigan, Catherine Marchand and Elissa Summers. People in town familiar with that era remembered their names just as they remembered the names of the backfield from the school's state champion football team a few years later. No other such phenomenon, female or male, occurred here before or since. Of course, a few came along here and there, but not in such dramatic convergence. "Destined for great things," was a phrase I remembered hearing about them on more than one occasion.

I wasn't sure, but I thought that Phil Marchand and Nancy Easter dated a few times, maybe even for a long time, and perhaps her memories of Phil were less than grand. That might explain Nancy's sudden change of mood a few minutes ago. I couldn't imagine anyone carrying such a torch for so long, but I knew other cases where grudges were borne for decades. I considered Ken Gladwell's sudden antagonism as soon as Phil Marchand's name was mentioned last night. Maybe this was the same kind of thing. "Too much for me," I sighed as I zipped up my jacket and kept walking.

It was still early and I still had a lot of indolence ahead to enjoy. I drove to the grocery store to pick up a few essentials, after which I planned a quiet and solitary afternoon of reading and listening to jazz in my apartment. A cup of hot tea and honey would complete the scene and I was looking forward to being alone. The grocery store was on the fringes of the town and, being the only market of any size in the area, captured most of the food shopping business in Apsley. In my carriage I placed a quart of skim milk, a box of macaroni and a jar of tomato sauce.

I needed some hamburger and was making my way to the meat counter when I saw Tina Gladwell in one of the aisles. Tina was picking out a few items and putting them in her basket. I nearly missed seeing her since her head was covered in a silky floral scarf and knotted below her chin. She was wearing dark glasses and seemed preoccupied. I stood at the end of the aisle twenty feet away and said, "Hi Tina. I almost didn't recognize you."

She turned in my direction abruptly and dropped a can of vegetables on the floor. She held my gaze for just a moment and I saw that the left side of her face was bluish and bruised. "Tina, are you alright?" She tilted her head down and turned away, walking quickly, almost running away from me and towards the front of the store. I left my cart where it was and followed after her but by the time I reached the front, she was gone. Maybe to the ladies' room, maybe out the door.

Puzzled and disturbed by Tina's appearance, I returned to my cart, finished shopping and went home. But the image of Tina Gladwell stayed with me. Something was wrong and I thought back to Gordon Jefts' comments last night. Maybe there was more to the Gladwells' problems than I realized.

On my way back home, I pulled in front of the Apsley Cleaners to pick up my one suit that was being dry cleaned. The bell over the door jingled when I came in. George saw me and called me out back.

"What's up, Georgie?"

"Oh nothing, Dave. Just wanted to say hi. Plus, I wondered if you heard from Phil Marchand yet."

"Nope. Not a word. I don't know if he's even got back to town yet. I'm sure he'll be stopping in when he gets here."

"It'll be good to see him."

"Yeah. By the way, I saw Nancy Easter this morning. She was acting strange and she's about as happy about Phil coming back as Ken Gladwell was last night. What's up with her?"

"No idea. I haven't seen her for a while."

"Look, George, I've got some groceries to get back home so I'll catch you later."

I dropped the groceries and my suit back at my apartment and drove over to the Kerrigan Mills where I wandered around the property getting a feel for the work that was being done there. If the developer did it right, the back of the building would be a fabulous place for some kind of retail on the first floor and condos above. The view to the river below was worth plenty.

I walked around the entire property and paid particular attention to the older front section where Tina Gladwell once owned and operated a health club. So far, I hoped, there were no takers for this part of the complex. It had no river view and would draw less attention from potential investors. The section attached to the rear, the part that was used as a loading platform, was being refurbished but its view of the river below would command a much higher premium than I could ever expect to afford. With some good number crunching and some luck, I just might be able to pick up the less desirable front space and do well with it. It was a big gamble for a little guy in real estate like me, but the time felt right.

The rain was spitting off and on all day. At this time of year, the rain was not icy but it still chilled Bob Hayes to the bone when he went to his front yard to retrieve the mail. Bob's plans for the day included raking the leaves from the front yard of the funeral home, but the rain put a stop to that. Instead, he did a top to bottom cleaning and reorganizing of his show room. Bob had installed new track lighting last month and he wanted to show the array of caskets in the best possible light.

He was reaching into the mailbox when he heard his cell phone ring. It was always attached in some manner to his person, this time in the pocket of his jeans. In his business, he had to be ready to take any and every call. There were few repeat calls in his line of work.

This one came from the regional hospital in Marlton. Earl Carver died and the family asked that the Hayes Funeral Home take care of things. Earl's family was well known to Bob, and Earl himself was Bob's hockey coach in high school.

Bob put on a fresh shirt and pair of slacks, then went to his garage and made sure he had his body basket and some clean sheets in the back of his van. As he drove down Main Street, he saw George Wessel walking out the front door of his business, Apsley Cleaners. He tapped his horn and George seemed to jump six inches before he turned and recognized that it was Bob. Bob lowered his window and called out, "Hey Georgie."

George Wessel smiled when he recognized Hayes and gave a small wave.

Poor Georgie, thought Bob Hayes. A walking advertisement for hemorrhoid medication. Bob would acknowledge, though, that George's steady weight loss made him a new person. Referred to as "Bottle Ass" Wessel since high school, George was looking lean and fit lately. His diet and exercise regimen were making a difference.

Bob continued on his way to the hospital and his appointment with Earl Carver. He'd make the pick up and call the family on his way back home on his cell phone to set up a meeting. Chances are they would want a wake on Wednesday and a funeral Thursday. He made a mental note as he drove on.

THREE

———————

Wednesday

"**L**ook, Dave, if you're not used to this, it can be pretty gross."

I eyed the naked frame of what once housed Earl Carver. Dead at eighty-nine, his remains were a frail assemblage of bones and skin and this was not the strapping Mr. Carver I remembered. When my friends and I were in high school, Earl Carver was the hockey coach, loud, aggressive, and tough. He played semi-pro when he was a boy growing up in Canada but never had the full collection of skills it took to make the big time. Never beefy, Carver was lean and fast.

He'd lace his skates up with the rest of the kids before practice and then take the puck around and through them with a series of pirouettes, dekes and feints. He taught his athletes how to check, how to slow down the opponent by using their entire bodies. His demonstrations were devastating and would take the breath out of his charges. Now, on a stainless steel table, here was what was left of the coach. Probably less than a hundred pounds.

"No, Bobby. It's OK. I'll just look away if I have to." I grabbed a chair at the desk and turned it around so I could communicate with Bob while avoiding a direct view of Earl Carver.

"Your call, Dave. The longer I wait, the longer it takes to mold him back into something his family and friends will recognize at the wake."

Bob moved a cart holding an electric pump and some plastic tubing closer to the stainless steel table. He carried a tray of polished stainless steel surgical equipment from a counter and set it on a shelf attached to the cart.

His movements were smooth and swift and he talked while he worked. "So what do you think about Phil Marchand coming back here after all these years?"

"I'm not sure what to think, Bob. I haven't talked to Phil since he moved away."

"Well, I didn't say anything when we were playing cards the other night, but I think Max Zenga was right. When Phil stopped by here, I got the impression he was going to try to figure out what really happened to his sister. He's not working, has plenty of dough, and all the time in the world."

Bob reached for a scalpel from the tray and I moved my attention to another direction. I never minded dissecting frogs in biology lab, but this was Coach Carver.

"He was sort of probing, you know? Asking what I remembered from that time. I told him I wasn't even involved in his sister's funeral except to open the door at the wake. Besides, that was years ago. I was just a kid."

"We all were. But maybe there's something you can help him with."

"Like what?" Bob was working steadily and almost silently.

"When Catherine died, you remember all the rumors, and you saw every single person who came to the wake. Maybe there's something that stands out. Maybe you saw something that can help."

Bob was concentrating on his embalming tasks but was proficient enough to maintain a conversation simultaneously. "You mean the people who came? There were hundreds. Kids, parents, friends of the family. I can't remember all of them."

"No, it's not that. But did anything strike you as really odd? Did anybody act really strange?"

"Not that I remember off the top of my head. I remember that Catherine's casket was in the big room at the back. I set up chairs in every sitting room because we knew the crowd was going to be big. But anything odd? Not that I remember."

I turned back cautiously. "How did Earl die, by the way?"

Bob never looked up, his concentration entirely focused on his work. "Earl? He's almost ninety. The death certificate says multiple organ failure. His parts just gave up."

Bob untangled the plastic tubing that hung on the cart and I looked away. I heard him flip a switch and the pump made a droning sound.

I didn't want to watch the whole thing but I could see the legs and feet of Earl Carver begin to take on a rosy bloom as the embalming fluid made its way through the cadaver.

"You know, Dave, I just saw Earl Carver about a month ago getting a newspaper downtown. We talked for a few minutes. He looked pretty good then."

I picked up a funeral director trade magazine from the desk and began skimming through. The lead article described how to best clean a decedent's finger nails "as the hands, of men especially, are often overlooked when preparing a body for viewing." Great stuff, I thought.

"I don't know how you do this job, Bobby."

"It's all in what you get used to, Dave."

"But dealing with death all the time." I looked for something else to read as I waited for Bob to finish.

"In your business, Dave, you have tenants who either can't afford a house or don't really want one. Eventually, they all move out and somebody else moves in. In my business, I'm dealing with people who rented their bodies for maybe eighty or ninety years, hopefully, and then they're gone. We're all renters here. No matter what we own or how much money we've got. In the end, we don't really *own* a damned thing."

Bob tripped a switch and the pump stopped. He went to the sink, removed his latex gloves, washed his hands and arms, thoroughly I saw, and said, "It's almost eleven and I need a cold beer. Want one?"

I was glad to hear that there was an opportunity to leave Earl in the embalming room and its attendant smells and sights. The thought of a cold beer was welcomed.

We went to his kitchen and Bob pulled a pair of cans from the refrigerator. We sat at the kitchen table and popped the cans open.

Bob took a long swallow. "You know, Dave, it's funny, but I don't think I'm dealing with death. Not the way I think you mean."

"Right, Bob. Earl in the other room might disagree."

"No, I mean it. Death, the actual dying part, has been taken care of before I show up. I do some cosmetic work and then I do the pomp and circumstance of a funeral. I work with the florists and the churches and the cemeteries. I make sure there's a grave marker later on. I've probably handled a few thousand dead bodies, but that's after the fact. But I've never seen a person actually die. Never."

"I saw two. My grandmother had an aneurism and we sat with her at the hospital until she finally died. It was very quiet. And I saw a guy get thrown from a car in an accident on the highway about twenty years ago. He must have flown fifty feet before he hit the pavement. By the time I got to him, his eyes were opened, and he looked me right in the eye. Then he twitched a lot. The ambulance came a few minutes later and tried to revive the poor guy, but he was gone."

"See? You've really seen more death than I have. Even when I was in the service and I was a military mortician, all the suffering was already done."

I shook my head. "I'm not sure I could handle that, Bob. Gruesome."

"It wasn't fun, but at least I didn't have to be in the middle of the battle. Too much chaos for me. By the time I was sent in with a few other guys, the noise and confusion was all over."

I had enough of the discussion. Never one to fear death, I nevertheless did not enjoy complete immersion in the subject. I sucked the last bit of beer from the can, thanked Bob, and started for the door. I was stepping onto the front porch when Bob asked the question: "What did you stop by for anyway, Dave? I get the feeling something was on your mind beyond just Phil Marchand?"

I considered not saying anything. A few seconds of silence passed before I looked at Bob and said, "Yeah. I wanted to talk about Ken Gladwell. You and I are probably the best friends he has, and something's bothering me about him."

Bob held the screen door open. "How so?"

"It's Ken and Tina. Is there a problem with them?"

Bob took a step back. "What do you mean?"

"I saw Tina yesterday at the grocery store. Dark glasses, a big welt on her cheek. I asked her how she was and she just waved at me and turned down another aisle. I'm pretty sure she just walked out of the store and left."

Bob turned his attention to the sky and was silent for a moment.

"It looked to me like she'd been slapped around."

"Tina didn't say anything?"

"She just turned away and kept walking. Fast. We all know Kenny has a royal temper. You've seen him blow up before."

"I did Eric's funeral, remember?"

How could I forget that horrid episode? Ken and Tina Gladwell's only child, sixteen year old Eric, parked his car in the garage, closed the door, and committed suicide by carbon monoxide. That was almost seven years ago.

"Ken went nuts and Tina was like a zombie. If there was any couple that reached a breaking point, it was them."

I recalled that Ken spent most of the viewing sobbing loudly. Tina sat stone still, cold as ice, never acknowledging any expression of condolence from the hundreds of visitors. "Ken's never been the same and neither has Tina."

Bob said, "Ken's always been right near the edge, wherever the edge has been. He seems better now, but Tina, I think she's been reliving the nightmare since Eric died, and Ken doesn't seem to be any help. I don't know if they'll ever be the couple they were. Maybe they shouldn't be a couple."

That seemed to me an unusual observation. Ken was emotional, high-strung, and very expressive. He didn't hold back. Tina didn't become a recluse, but it was rare to see the two of them together out socially ever since Eric died. But maybe Bob was right and all these problems eluded my sight because it was too close in view. Maybe Ken and Tina handled things so differently that they could never bridge the chasm that Eric's death opened up. I'm no psychologist, but it seems to me that the loss of a child would certainly have a devastating effect on any family. I couldn't imagine losing one of my sons and could only speculate as to the depth of the loss that Ken and Tina Gladwell experienced.

Still, the question of getting physical gnawed at me. "But hitting his wife, Bob? I hope I'm making a mistake because that doesn't seem like Ken. Have you noticed any changes lately?"

Bob didn't respond but looked at his watch and his face assumed a frown. "I've really got to get back to Earl, Dave. The viewing starts at five. If you hear anything else about Tina and Ken, let me know."

Bob let the screen door close. I thought Bob's reaction was odd and walked down the steps and headed back to my apartment.

I took my time walking back home. There was a lot on my mind and I wanted to mull it over. In the end, I decided I didn't want to put myself in the middle of things. If Ken and Tina Gladwell were having problems, I could speak to Ken, tell him that there was talk about physical abuse, tell him to knock it off, if in fact the rumor was true, but then leave it at that. I wanted to be a friend but not a confessor, and I wanted to put some distance between myself and any conflict that Ken and Tina Gladwell were going through.

I also thought I'd put some distance between myself and the entire Phil Marchand scenario. Too many years had gone by and getting involved in this thing again would only scratch old wounds raw. What was to be gained? I might have been Phil's closest friend when we grew up, but that was years ago. I wanted to visit with Phil, sure, and maybe reminisce about old times. I would just as soon stay clear of any problems Phil might stir up. This was Phil's issue, and I had my own problems without looking for more.

George Wessel generally and genuinely enjoyed his job. The business of cleaning clothes had been good to him and his family. He started in the business when he was twenty eight after a few years as an insurance adjuster. That job had taken him all over the country dealing with the consequences of catastrophes, but he had a young family and wanted to stay closer to home. He bought the business from Murray Skillman when Murray's wife died and he moved across the state to be closer to his kids.

The early years in the dry cleaning business for George were rough and there were many times when he and his wife, Carla, had to decide which payments would be made and which deferred. On more than one occasion, George and Carla had to approach the bank for temporary loans to get them over various financial humps. Once, a key piece of machinery went on the fritz and the cost of repairs nearly forced them into closure, but they managed to squeeze by.

Those loans were now a thing of the past. Today, George had the same business, newer equipment, and even a satellite storefront in Eastland. Three years ago he branched out into coin operated laundries and the three locations he had in operation were providing a healthy cash flow.

He didn't want to grow the business too quickly but he had an excellent manager in Eastland who would become part owner over time. His employees adored George and in ten years, he could turn over everything to his manager and collect a reasonable, if not lucrative retirement.

Carla was his rock, the one person who kept faith in George during those difficult times. He was looking forward to the day when he and Carla could spend more time traveling and seeing the world. Financially, they should be in good shape when the time came. There was even some discussion at the bank that he might be asked to serve on the board of directors, quite a change for the man who went there, hat-in-hand, only a few years ago just to stay afloat.

George liked his morning routine, even though he'd recently dropped a tasty but dangerous part of it when he adopted his new diet and cut out the Texas-sized muffins. Instead, he had two slices of rye toast at home with black coffee and a glass of V-8. He also made coffee at work and had another cup there. At ten, instead of another muffin, he'd have an apple and a cup of tea. In nine weeks, he was down thirty-one pounds with still a lot more to go.

He grabbed his mug of black, unsweetened coffee this morning and looked over the previous day's receipts. He also checked an envelope that he kept tacked to the corkboard outside his office where particular problem cases were referred to him. Customer complaints were rare but seemed to occur when the garment was particularly treasured. Most mornings, the envelope was empty, but this morning he found a slip from an employee about a nasty stain on a woman's suit that simply resisted every effort to remove it. He made a mental note to check this out later on and kept the note on his desk.

The store would open in another twenty minutes and George turned on his police scanner that he kept on a shelf above his desk. He walked through the shop and said hello to his counter clerk, Betty Forman. She was the last person left over from the days when Murray Skillman owned Apsley Cleaners, and she probably should have retired nine years ago when she was 65. But she knew every customer by name and since her husband was confined to a nursing home, her job was her social life as well as her source of income.

"Hi George," she said, putting her purse under the counter and out of sight. "My but you're looking like you're wasting away. How much have you lost?"

"Not enough, Betty. I still have a lot more to lose."

"Well, you'd better start sending some of your trousers out to the tailor because they're bunching up at the waist on you."

"I have a couple pair going out today, as a matter of fact. And thanks for noticing."

"I notice everything, George. You ought to know that by now." Betty was right. Little slipped by in Apsley without Betty having some knowledge of it. Without being nosy, she managed to hear just about everything that passed for local news.

George watched her set up the register before she walked

back to pour herself a cup of coffee. She'd unlock the door at nine, exactly. "Betty, so what's going on?" This was always the best way for George to get a sense of things well before the newspapers were delivered.

Betty's face was a spider web of fine lines and deeper wrinkles, every one earned in a lifetime of hard work and the joys and sadness of experience, every furrow holding bits of knowledge and wisdom gathered over decades of toil and steadfast interest in the people and events around her. She took a swallow and laid out her counter as she answered. "Well, there's still no word on who won the lottery jackpot on that ticket from Eubanks' News Stand, if that's what's on your mind. Almost six million and no one has made a claim yet."

"I'll bet whoever won has got some CPA working on it. Get all his ducks in a row before he goes to get his check."

"That's my guess. And the new Chief's settling in with his wife in a rented house on Maple Street. Probably stay there for a year while he looks for a permanent house."

"How are the new Chief and Lou Pellerin getting along?" The local scuttlebutt suggested that there were some trying moments in this new relationship. Jerome Wetman, a former city detective, was chosen over local boy Lou Pellerin, and bad blood wouldn't be unexpected.

"Lou Pellerin was always such a nice boy. I know some people think he's probably a little young for the Chief's job, but I hope he gets it someday. Outside of that, I haven't heard much. But you're the one with the police scanner; I should be asking you these questions."

"Oh, Betty, it's just become a habit. And besides, they don't talk about that stuff over the radio. Believe me, the chatter over the scanner is minimal, and most of it is pretty boring."

"I'll say. It's been dead lately around here."

"Maybe that's a good thing."

"There's a difference between quiet and dead, George. If the level of newsworthy information is any indication, then Apsley is on life support and ready for hospice."

"You're probably right, Betty. But there's something nice about there being no news. It's . . ." George was reaching for the right word.

"Predictable?"

"That's the word, Betty."

"Well, I've lived here all my life, and there are some people . . . a lot of people . . . who sit around and complain about how things have changed."

Betty took out a bottle of Windex while she talked and gave the counter a few squirts. "They talk about the good old days, as if there was no poverty and no crime and nothing bad ever happened. They'd better get used to the idea that things are going to change no matter what they think or do. Pretty soon, those old fogies are going to be dust in the ground, and no one is going to give a hoot what they think. We're all going to leave this world, George, and we're dead a long, long time. I'd rather not complain and just enjoy the life we've got."

Betty never stopped moving when she talked. All the while, she was wiping the counter, sorting laundry tags, putting pens in a box, lining up her paper clips and rubber bands.

"And, by the way, George, speaking about being dead a long time, there's some talk that the police will have to take another look at that Marchand girl's murder now that her brother is moving back here."

Both of them turned to hear a rapping at the front door. Betty checked the wall clock and it read 8:58. She set her coffee down and said, "Oh, I'll get that." She looked at the front door and saw Emily Donahue standing there with an urgent expression. Betty used her key and let Emily in. The bell over the door jingled.

"Good morning, Emily. My but we're out early today."

Emily looked rushed. She placed her claim slip on the counter as she spoke. "I've got so much to get done today. I've got a job interview at ten thirty and I need the slacks that I dropped off for dry cleaning. That's my best pair." Emily was already fishing in her purse for the money to pay for the cleaning.

Betty took the slip and searched for the slacks. In a moment she reappeared and started ringing in Emily's charge. "Where's the interview? I thought you had a good job at the market."

Emily was an assistant manager of the produce department at the supermarket where almost everyone shopped.

In a conspirator's voice, Emily said, "It's with Mike Moura, the lawyer. He's looking for another secretary at his office. But I haven't said anything at work, so don't say anything."

"Not a word, Emily."

"I mean, I like my job at the market, but the hours are crazy, late nights sometimes and a lot of weekends. I'm looking for the old 'nine to five' if I can get it."

"I don't blame you." Emily was out the door and Betty had another nugget of information about the goings on in Apsley. She was true to her word and wouldn't say a thing about Emily's interview. Not a flannel-mouth like that waitress over at Lafferty's Diner who leaked personal information about every conversation she overheard to anyone who'd listen. Betty was someone to trust.

George reappeared at the front with the stained suit. He held it under the light at the front of the store to get a better look. Sure enough, the lapel had a brownish shadow that extended several inches. Curious, he showed Betty. "What do you think?"

"I saw it yesterday. Looks like some kind of oil stain to me, like salad oil. It's not anything else I can think of."

George looked again. "It should have come out if it was just that. I'll check it out. Could you call the customer . . . the name's on the slip here . . . and tell her we're still working on it?"

Phil Marchand changed channels on his radio as he motored along the turnpike. He still had seven hundred miles ahead of him but he was feeling refreshed this morning. He turned to a straight ahead jazz station and listened to John Coltrane and Duke Ellington collaborating on some classic jazz pieces. The magic of the music captivated him and he wondered why so many stations were opting instead to broadcast only smooth jazz. To Phil, smooth jazz was little more than elevator music. Improvisation and creativity just weren't there.

His clock read 9:35 and most of the day's traffic was already at work. Most of the other vehicles on the road were tractor trailers. He felt like he could drive for another nine or ten hours but decided to pace himself. He knew he needed frequent rest stops. He was driving alone and he didn't want to jeopardize himself or anyone else on the highway by pushing too hard. In his head, he calculated that he'd reach Apsley by Thursday afternoon, tomorrow, by early evening. His attention was caught by a sign for the major interchange ahead; he looked at his fuel gauge and decided he'd fill up there.

Also ahead was an adventure, of sorts. In a few days, he'd be back in the small town where he grew up. He thought about the cliché "You can never go home again." Was it Tom Wolfe? Thomas Mann? O. Henry? Somebody, he thought, apparently said it first. In Phil's case, he was using this journey as a way to focus his energy on an issue he'd never come to accept. Who killed his sister?

He remembered Apsley and the good times he enjoyed, but the singular event of Catherine's murder defined much of the rest of his life. It meant an emotional and physical upheaval in the family from which it could not ever recover. The dynamics changed irrevocably. It caused a physical relocation far away to escape the memories which nevertheless continued to haunt him and his parents. It colored his perception of the world and made him less likely to invest himself unconditionally in any person or task. More prudent, he decided, was to hold a little bit of himself back.

His marriage lasted longer than most. Jacqueline met Phil in college in Arizona and married, perhaps too quickly. She was quick-witted and not at all the remote aristocrat he might have expected when he learned of her family's wealth and position in southern society. They raised two sons together while Phil made his way though a succession of jobs and promotions.

With Jacqueline's considerable family money, there was little reason for Philip Marchand to keep working and even less reason for him to work so aggressively and relentlessly to climb the rungs of the corporate ladder. His pride was part of the reason. He didn't spurn the good things in life that Jacqueline's assets afforded, but the fact that he was responsible for earning a significant income made life more pleasurable.

He brushed a lock of hair from his forehead as he approached the exit he wanted. His hair was longer now since he left the world of three piece suits and silk ties, and it waved thickly over his ears and down the back of his neck. Some gray had crept in over the past few years, but it remained concentrated at the temples, a fact that made Jacqueline comment on his good fortune. "You are aging so well, damn you," she said, with only a shred of humor. "You barely gained five pounds since we got married and the gray in your hair only makes you look more distinguished."

He appreciated the remark and pandered just a little. "You look prettier now than you ever did, Jacqueline. Time has been good to you."

If there was a touch of jealousy in Jacqueline Marchand, she gave no indication. Her only response was, "Time may be a great healer, Philip, but it's a lousy beautician."

He wondered about Jacqueline and hoped she'd understand, if not now, then eventually, the reasons for his abrupt demand for a separation and divorce. She was shocked, to be sure, when he made his announcement three weeks ago over dinner. She was just as shocked when he told her later of his plans to leave the area soon, that he was heading to Apsley and would reopen the case of his sister's murder. He left little room for discussion and told her he'd agree to any financial arrangement her lawyer devised. Then, he was gone.

FOUR

The same day

Lou Pellerin drove to the station still grumbling about yesterday's conversation with Max Zenga and the fact that Max was even less understanding this morning.

"You're going to have to buck up, Lou," Max told him over coffee this morning. "Stop whining and just do your job."

Lou Pellerin was certain he'd be appointed Apsley's new Chief of Police and the fact that he was bypassed, and for an outsider, bothered him deeply. After all, he was born and raised in Apsley, had almost eighteen years experience on the Apsley force, carried the blessing of the previous Chief, and, despite his relative youth . . . he was only forty-one . . . felt fully prepared to take over. He'd taken the civil service Police Chief Qualifying Exam two years ago and did very well. He was the only applicant for the job from Apsley. These were all checkmarks in the "plus" column for those who would make the hiring decision.

The Board of Selectmen did open up the position to outside candidates. This was not considered unusual, especially when there was only one internal candidate. Across the state, several hundred men and women had the appropriate credentials, including a passing grade on the Chief's Qualifying Exam. Many of them, though, were from the bigger cities and towns where the pay was higher, the prestige greater, and the opportunities more extensive. Most observers thought it unlikely that an experienced law enforcement professional would toss a hat into Apsley's ring.

The decision did generate discussion and some divisions. "It's time for new blood" was countered with "We ought to promote from within the department."

Lou Pellerin didn't like the decision to open up the job to outside candidates, but only because it would delay his start date as Chief. He never felt his selection was threatened.

The Board of Selectmen even had some 'outsiders' on the panel, people who weren't born and raised here. While this might have been heresy just a generation ago . . . and still was considered heresy today in some quarters of Apsley, there was no turning back. "I remember when Leo Fuller (or Martin Cardwell, or Hastings Pierce) was on the board back in eighty-nine (or seventy-six, or sixty-four)," one might hear. "There was a guy who really ran this town the right way. But with all these immigrants from the city and the suburbs moving in, there's no more tradition to things anymore. Things are just plain different now."

As Pellerin's luck would have it, an outsider not only applied for the job but was offered the position and then accepted. "Fresh blood," was mentioned as one reason at the Selectmen's meeting. "Good credentials and great experience," was another. Thus, Jerome Wetman, in a three-to-two vote, was named the new Chief for Apsley and a defeated, depressed Lou Pellerin was consigned to be the assistant to the new Chief, knowing in his heart of hearts, that the Selectmen made a bad choice.

After a light lunch and a brisk walk in the light rain, George Wessel sat at his desk and placed his next project, a woman's blouse with a floral pattern, in front of him. The tag pinned to the blouse indicated that it belonged to Tina Gladwell, and George knew from experience that she bought expensive clothes. He adjusted the neck of the desk lamp so it lit up the stain on the blouse. Then he took a magnifying glass from his top drawer and looked at the stain closely. He picked up the blouse and put it to his nose. There was some lingering odor, almost a perfume that centered on the stain. It was some sort of make-up but it wasn't just your everyday pancake foundation that he was used to seeing.

This was almost like a grease stain, and he'd seen it before. It looked to George like stage make up. But dark brown and blue? And around the neck of an expensive blouse? Tina Gladwell? It didn't make sense.

George looked at the fabric label on the inside seam of the blouse. It was silk and made in Italy. Then he poked around in a shoe box that he kept on the corner of his desk. It contained several small bottles, all marked with different chemical names, and most marked "poison". He selected one and used an eye dropper to place a small dot of the liquid on the inside hem of the blouse. He waited a few seconds and saw no damage or change in color. He placed a few drops on the stain itself and used a Q-tip to swab it over the area.

In moments, the stain lightened and nearly disappeared. He pinned a note to the blouse and left it in a bin for re-cleaning. Tina could pick up her blouse and never know the trouble that it caused George and his staff. The blouse would look as good as new.

* * *

Evening approached and the highway traffic thinned out. Under other circumstances, he'd have preferred driving straight through, but he was exhausted.

Philip Marchand pulled into a parking lot of the Holiday Inn, the first hotel he saw, and checked in. Tomorrow, he thought as he walked to his room and tossed the overnight bag on the bed, tomorrow I'll get to Apsley and start the next chapter of my life.

He rummaged through the bag for his toothbrush and toothpaste and then proceeded to take a long shower, letting the steam fill his nostrils and cloud the small bath. He'd get to Apsley before the end of the next day, check in to a hotel there, and in the following days he'd pay some visits. First to the police department to introduce himself and let the Chief, whoever he was, know that he'd be asking for his help. He wanted to stop in to see Bob Hayes at the funeral home and then locate Dave Blondin, the best friend he'd had in Apsley.

He hadn't talked with Dave since he graduated from high school and moved away, but he had a sense that he'd reconnect seamlessly. They had been through their pre-adolescent and teen years together, and those memories don't just disappear. They became blood brothers when they were eleven. They went to scout camp together. They learned about masturbation and sex and smoking cigarettes and drinking beer and girls and breasts and body hair and all that great stuff together.

Marchand recalled that Dave was at his home when the police arrived on the evening that changed everything. He was there when his mother stepped into the bedroom and said that Dave should go home, that there was a problem, a family emergency. Phil thought at the time that there might be a problem with his elderly grandmother in Florida. After Dave left, Phil recalled that his mother and father came into his bedroom and sat down on the edge of the bed together. Their eyes were red, their cheeks wet with tears. He remembered the words exactly as his parents spoke them, just as if it all happened yesterday.

"Catherine's gone," his mother said, her voice rising, her hands clenched around a wad of tissues.

Gone? Phil wondered what that meant. Did she run away? Where had she run? What was going on?

"The police were just here, Philip." His father spoke. His voice was halting, his words chopped. He was obviously trying to maintain some control and it was a struggle. "Philip, your sister was found in the woods tonight. Out by Squash Pond. She was dead."

Dead? Catherine? Couldn't be. She was OK at school today. She's had an upset stomach, but she wasn't that sick. What do you mean?

"Somebody killed her," his father continued before Philip had a chance to ask any questions. "The police . . . they don't know who did it."

Phil finally found his voice. "Dead?" The whole idea was surreal, the room suddenly cramped and stuffy. "Dead," he said again? His throat was constricted and dry.

"Murdered," his mother shrieked. "Somebody murdered our little girl."

"Son, the police are going to come back in a little while." His father rubbed his brow. "I think the Chief himself. They have some questions for us." His father's eyes wandered aimlessly around the room. He was holding things together until his lower lip began to tremble.

"They said we can't see her right now. Our little girl."

He started to sob and tried to choke back the tears.

Phil's mother reached over and hugged Phil as she wailed, "My girl . . . my Catherine. Your sister's gone. Somebody beat her to death. Oh Lord!"

To this point in his life, Phil's existence was marked by a

school calendar. His days were fairly predictable, his summer vacations always including at least a week at the lake, his course through life charted to follow a routine that included his mother, father, Catherine, him and some friends. His sister was the queen of the junior prom, the homecoming queen just this past weekend, the captain of the cheerleading squad. She'd applied to Harvard and Yale, for crying out loud.

Phil was the class vice president, an honor roll student, and like Catherine, a member of the National Honor Society. This sort of thing didn't happen to the Marchands. This was not supposed to happen.

It was at this moment, when his parents hugged him and cried, that Phil experienced a maelstrom of thoughts, about Catherine, about what might have happened to her, about the pain she could have suffered, about the pain his parents were suffering, that he saw every event and emotion pointing him in an entirely new direction. His life, he saw clearly, was destined to change dramatically, and he was not looking forward to this at all.

In truth, the event was a toxic explosion for the family with a cloud of noxious fumes that never left. After the funeral and Catherine's burial, the vapors lingered and found their way into every crevice of their collective lives. Even with the family's subsequent relocation across the country, the miasma clung to them like a pea green haze. Words rarely passed among them without some sense that the reason for speaking had something to do with the loss of Catherine.

"We're going to visit your grandmother in Florida for Thanksgiving," was thenceforth loaded with the legacy of the lost soul of Catherine; she would not be there.

Cameras were stowed away, no record sufficient for a family of three that would not immediately remind them that they'd once been very happily four. The stereo was silent, books sat on shelves unread. His mother resigned from her job and retreated into silence; his father continued to work but was a hollow man, an empty suit.

Philip proved more resilient that either parent. If his loss was at least as deep, he could sense that the wound was scabbing over with time and distance, even though the scar would be ever acknowledged. Neither parent could get that far. Both would die young, never recovering from their loss.

Now, he remained the only living relic of that horrifying evening in Apsley. So much had been made of the word "closure" that Marchand was reluctant to use it. Nonetheless, he felt driven to find out what happened that day at Squash Pond, and especially driven to find out who caused the death of his sister and the ultimate destruction of his family. He thought, if not me, who?

FIVE

Thursday

I was enjoying a spot of solitude in a booth at the diner where I had eaten a late lunch and finished a book I'd been meaning to read. I had just closed the book and set it aside when Gordon Jefts walked over and took a seat opposite my own.

"So what's up, Gordon?"

I liked Gordon Jefts in spite of his practiced affectations. Max Zenga considered Gordon a busybody, and Ken Gladwell thought that Gordon was too polished for his own good, a dilettante with no good reason to be.

Gordon, in truth, could be a worrywort, and a nosy one. In that respect, he was much like George Wessel. But where George was almost flagrant in his insecurities, Gordon hid his well. Gordon Jefts relished intrigue, always in short supply in Apsley, and liked being the first one to know anything of importance that was going on in town, even if his definition of important had a low threshold.

Nevertheless, I forged a bond with Jefts over a lifetime that transcended the considerations of our other friends. Gordon began as a generalist in his legal practice but gravitated over time into real estate transactions. He handled most of my work when it came to updating leases or the rare eviction, and I found Gordon to be honest in his dealings, capable in his advice, and reasonable in his fees. Plus, the Jefts clan was one of the oldest and most distinguished in the area and numbered among its ancestors more than one state representative, a few judges, and a prominent mill owner. This gave Gordon the kind of connections that had value in a small community. If Gordon was annoying from time to time, it was a small premium to pay.

Gordon wore his raincoat and carried a to-go cup of coffee.

"What are you doing here alone, Dave? Reading?"

"I just finished and I'm heading out to pick up some stuff at the hardware store."

"I'll walk with you if you don't mind."

"OK by me, but it's cold and wet outside and I hope this is a brief conversation."

I held the door open for Gordon and we stepped out into a cool mist. The rain earlier in the day left some puddles and Gordon had to dodge and weave to avoid ruining his shoes. I had no such problem with my work boots and Gordon was alternately on my right, then my left, as he struggled to stay dry.

"It will be. I just wanted to ask you about Malcolm Prudhomme. He was in the office and that struck me as odd."

"Really? Does he need a lawyer?"

"He's got one. Mike Moura has him, but I'm not sure why. Mike usually does pretty basic stuff like wills and trusts and estates. He doesn't usually do defense work."

Mike Moura was a younger attorney who shared some space with Gordon in an office downtown. Their practices were independent, but sharing space and a receptionist saved on the expenses.

"What makes you believe that Malcolm is in the market for defense counsel?"

A mass of dark clouds were gathered and I heard a low roar of thunder in the distance. This on and off weather would be the order of the day.

"Well, it's just that his name has come up a few times lately and I figured with Phil Marchand coming back to town . . ."

I didn't bite right away and let the vapidity of Gordon's conclusion hang in the mist and drop with a thud.

"OK, Dave, maybe I'm just nosy. I could smell Malcolm from inside my office as soon as he walked in. That guy is one rank dude. Plus, it just didn't add up. I thought you might know something. You're really plugged in to just about everyone in Apsley."

"Nope. I'm sure Malcolm has his reasons for going to see Mike, but I don't know what they are."

We reached the corner and waited for the light to change. "So, there's nothing going on with Phil and Malcolm?"

Gordon had all the instincts of a conspiracy theorist

"C'mon, Gordon. You're fishing, and you're a lousy fisherman. Just leave it alone. Maybe Malcolm . . . what the hell, I'm starting to speculate and I don't even give a damn! Just handle your own clients and keep doing a good job. There's no reason for you to nose around Malcolm's business. You've got enough to do."

So did I. I'd been letting some little repair jobs pile up, and if I didn't get my ass in gear soon, I'd be playing catch-up for weeks. We crossed Main Street together.

"I guess you're right, Dave. Look, I probably went overboard and I'm sorry I wasted your time."

I stopped when we reached the other side. Gordon deserved to be chastened, not crushed, and he was suddenly looking and sounding like a whipped puppy.

"Gordon, talking with you is never a waste of time. But I

will need to talk to you about some of my own stuff soon. I need a variance to do some work on an apartment building on Central Street, and maybe you can handle that for me. And I've been thinking more about that Kerrigan Mill building. I want a piece of that if I can get it."

"Most of the mill has been taken already. What piece are you looking at anyway?" Gordon's mood improved with the change in subject, but I read some unusual caution in his expression as soon as I mentioned the old mill.

"The space in front where Tina Gladwell used to have her health spa and gym. Is that still available?"

"Yeah, maybe. I'll check it out. Maybe we can get out of the office and get a beer while we talk."

That sounded fine to me and we parted ways, Gordon back to his office and me to the hardware store for some supplies. I worried about Gordon sometimes, and here was a good reason why. He was sometimes too inquisitive for his own good, and in Apsley there were plenty of busybodies already. Better to just let the professionals handle the scurrilous rumors and stick to lawyering.

Later in the day, the rain and clouds moved out. When dusk arrived and the season's darkness began to cloak the town, I walked up the flight of stairs to my apartment, opened the door and placed my small bag of groceries on the counter. I draped my damp jacket on the back of a kitchen chair and took a jar of pasta sauce from the bag. I put water and salt in a pot and was reaching for the spaghetti when I saw the message light blink on my phone. A tenant complaint? A roof leak? I pressed the play button.

"Hey Dave. Ken Gladwell. I'm still at work but can we meet for a drink down at Dean's later on? Say around 6:30? I got something I'd like to talk to you about. It's kind of important. I hope I see you there, buddy."

I couldn't detect much from Ken's call, but it was rare for Ken to call like that. I sliced some tomatoes and mozzarella and checked my watch. Just after five. I'd have time to cook and eat my dinner and maybe catch some of the television news before I went over to Dean's Town Tavern to meet Ken.

George Wessel had a curious side, and that was another reason why he liked having Betty Forman working for him. To George's question about Nancy Easter, though, Betty was uncharacteristically reserved. George had been thinking over his conversation with me about Nancy, and he hoped he might learn something.

"Let's just say that she went through quite a bit after she left Apsley and went away to school."

That answer only whet George's appetite.

"But she was one of the smartest kids in school. There were rumors going around that she got pregnant in college, and that's why she dropped out and come back after less than a year."

Betty made it known by body language and facial expression that she didn't want to get into the details.

"Sometimes it's just better to let people have their reasons."

On an intellectual level, George accepted that. On an emotional level, he wanted to know everything.

"But why would . . ."

Betty turned around quickly from her task of aligning every pencil and paper clip on the counter and looked George in the eye. "George, leave it alone."

Just before closing, Gordon Jefts came into the cleaners to pick up two suits and five shirts. He'd just paid Betty when George saw him and called from the back, "Got time for a quick one, Gordon?"

"Let me drop this stuff off at my place and I'll see you there."

When he was gone and Betty hung the 'closed' sign on the door and had the keys in her hand, she turned to George. "You just have to know, don't you?"

"What?"

"You see Gordon come in, Nancy Easter's cousin and another busybody if I ever saw one, and all of a sudden you need to spend some quality time with him. Just remember, George: Nobody likes a gossip."

With that comment, she turned the key in the lock, took her coat from the rack on the wall, and walked home.

George was chastened, but that didn't stop him from wanting to know about Nancy Easter, and he walked to Dean's, ordered a Diet Coke and waited for Gordon to show up.

After some shallow chit chat, George asked the question he'd been holding inside.

"Nancy?" Gordon's brow furrowed at once and George wondered if he's struck a nerve just by mentioning Nancy's name.

"She seems, I don't know, like she's on edge lately."

"Maybe she has good reason to be, George. Why the sudden interest?"

George shrugged his shoulders as if his question was innocent curiosity.

"If you grew up with her parents, you'd be on edge too, or in an asylum."

George was all ears, waiting for a good story.

"She's my second cousin, you know. Her mother and my grandmother were sisters."

George knew that part and wasn't interested in all the background, but it did reassure him that what he was about to hear was likely to be true.

"She was sort of a loner in high school, wasn't she?"

"Some people called Nancy a snob, but she was just shy,

George. And smart. She was reading Plato when she was a sophomore in high school, for crying out loud. At Columbia, she got into upper level classes and still got all A's her first semester."

George took a risk by dropping his only tidbit into the conversation, something he'd heard years ago and only in the form of a rumor, as if he was fully aware of Nancy's background. "Then she got pregnant."

Gordon turned quickly to George. "You know about that?"

George nodded solemnly. "Sure. I've known all about it for years." Speak in declarative sentences, he told himself. That's the ticket. He had no idea that he could pull such a convincing, straight-faced con, and this gave him such an unfamiliar sense of power he thought he'd wet his pants.

"Well, then you know about the botched abortion, then."

At that revelation, George almost choked on his soda and his sense of compassion rose from his core. Remorse started to settle in with a vengeance and he just wanted the conversation to end.

"They had to remove her uterus. After a week in the hospital, she came home to Apsley."

"Thank goodness she's OK now." George used up every last shred of confidence in his soul in the past thirty seconds and felt like a fraud, a worm.

"Her parents were old school, ultra religious. Her father wouldn't think of letting her go back to college after all that, but her mother convinced him that the community college was OK. At least she could live at home. For somebody who had a great future ahead of her, it was a huge comedown."

Gordon wasn't quite finished. "Nancy's father insisted that her sterility was God's punishment for her sins. Imagine how that would screw a person up."

Gordon drained his beer but George couldn't finish his soda.

"Look, George, I had no idea you knew about Nancy. I'm glad you never spread it around."

"Oh, sure, Gordon. No problem. See you around." He left Dean's in a rush and drove home, preoccupied and filled with self-reproach. Now that George had the kind of inside information that eluded him so thoroughly in the past, the question that nagged at him was, what could he do with it?

Phil Marchand looked down at the dashboard clock. Just after six and already near full dark. The moon was full and followed him over his left shoulder, throwing dim shadows in his path. A band of thick clouds moved quickly across the sky and the moon was soon just a faint blur. The rain began with a drizzle and stayed that way except for one brief downpour. The whap-whap of the wiper blades obscured the music on his radio and he eventually turned it off. The outside thermometer was dropping and getting close to freezing. He wanted to get to Apsley earlier but he'd found himself exhausted all day during the drive and took frequent rest stops.

As quickly as the rain appeared, it left and the clouds scudded east. The lunar glow reappeared and patches of fog swirled like wraiths without direction. There were few streetlights this far out of town but instead the area was flat and mostly farmland, though the farms were fewer now than he remembered. He passed a farmhouse and saw lights on inside. This was not an area that big agri-business had sought just yet. Here, men still drove their tractors from the barn to the field and back again at nightfall.

Some of the kids he played with were working sons and working daughters of farmers. They were the ones with coarse grit embedded in their calloused hands, who fell asleep in school during harvest season and couldn't play school sports because they had chores to do. Eventually, as they got older, the farmers' kids tended to be the earliest to drop out, or to keep to themselves while they worked toward graduation. They weren't part of the after-school social scene, and some of the townies poked fun at the hayseeds, as if Apsley was a sophisticated sanctuary of right-thinking, blessed souls.

Phil envied the farm kids in many ways, though. He recalled being in their kitchens with their enormous dining tables where there was always room for one more. He enjoyed their dinnertime conversation, their good humor, and their seriousness of purpose. He envied their connection to the earth and the weather, the way they could almost smell the coming rain and taste the substance of the soil. He wondered if he'd recognize the farm kids of his youth, or if they'd remember him.

He recognized the feelings of nostalgia and willingly succumbed to them. They may be fruitless and a little painful, he thought, but he decided to let them wash over him for now. The task he placed in front of him was serious enough and would command his attention sufficiently to dispel those feelings soon. Now, he thought, was not the time to cast them out.

Across the fields, lightning could be seen occasionally flashing in the distance. He waited for the sound to arrive but it never did. In a few minutes, he'd reach the fringes of the valley that held Apsley and he spotted a misty halo of streetlights rising like a vapor into the sky a few miles straight ahead. As he drove on, he saw that Apsley had yet to see the effects of a relentless spread of its boundaries, and for this he was pleased. While there were new homes being built, most of them were still closer to the center of town. During his recent visit, he believed the community retained some of its personality, its appreciation of its characters, its relative innocence and he hoped his presumption was accurate.

He didn't resent all development and its associated troubles, like the congestion of traffic and the anonymity of larger communities, and indeed some of the wealth he had amassed was the result of such developments elsewhere. He might even want to get involved in some development projects here after he settled in. In spite of the terrible events that occurred on the small stage that was Apsley, a big part of him wished the town to cherish its smallness as a precious gem and resist the siren song of growth.

Ahead was the rock-bottomed river that gave the town its original reason for being. It had been channeled in places a century or more ago to turn the water wheels that powered the mills that ran the machinery. At some machines, workers stitched shoes, at others they used lathes to fashion tools, and at even more they wove belting. The water wheels stopped spinning decades ago and rotted in place until all that remained were the rusted metal braces and axles that once supported them. Then the workers disappeared as the jobs moved first south where labor was cheap and then elsewhere where it was even cheaper. Even at the time Marchand lived there, some of the mills were being vacated and fell into disrepair. Others, those built of thick brick walls, were, he hoped, still standing, even if they now housed quiet offices instead of the rumbling whirr of heavy machinery.

He crossed the bridge that spanned the river and slowed to approach the center of town. Gone from Main Street were the simple green lamp posts and their warm golden glow. The replacements were stainless posts with massive lamps that apparently prevented crime while they sanitized the streets of their comfort and personality. Most of the storefronts were unfamiliar to him as he glanced left and right, but at least most of them were full. A few, he saw, were discount shops and he passed a pawn shop, something he didn't expect to see, and he wondered if the town was feeling the economic and social pain that damaged so many other mill towns. There were no grocery stores or small markets like the ones he remembered: the Fish Basket, Martin's Variety, Kennedy Butter and Eggs. With supermarkets everywhere, he really didn't expect many to survive anyway.

In too many towns like Apsley, vacant shops infected and blossomed like spores until the downtowns died. Big box stores on the outskirts of many communities didn't help, but except for a single supermarket, he didn't see any signs of them as he approached Apsley. Ahead on his right was Apsley Cleaners, and he smiled to himself as he recalled chubby George Wessel. He'd be sure to stop in to say hello soon.

Beyond the next intersection was a large familiar sign of a chain motel that housed a modest but clean collection of rooms, and he flipped his signal to enter the lot and check in. He was exhausted and looked forward to a good night's sleep.

I watched Ken Gladwell pull up in front of Dean's and walk into the bar, but decided to wait for a few minutes before meeting him. He usually walked with purpose and confidence, still slim, and athletic, but Ken wasn't moving like a leopard tonight. He looked more his age, when most men were feeling the inexorable arthritis in their joints and probably carrying more pounds than they should.

Instead, I decided to go to the library and poke around the stacks for a few minutes. Let Ken get a belt or two inside him before I showed up.

I saw Nancy Easter checking something on her computer screen and said hello. She looked up at me and nodded. Whatever she was studying on the screen had her attention.

I saw some of the city editions of the paper and flipped through them looking for anything interesting to waste ten minutes when Nancy approached me.

"Dave?"

"Hey Nancy."

"About the other morning, I want to apologize. I sort of snapped at you, and I'm sorry."

"Not a problem, Nancy."

"No. It is a problem, and I shouldn't have acted that way. Just stressed I guess. A lot on my mind. I'm sorry." She held her hand out. "Friends?"

"Friends." I shook it and it was the warm and smooth skin of a much younger woman. If I had any concerns about why she was so upset when I was in here before, they were all dissipated now.

"What brings you in tonight? Just escaping the cold?"

Nancy was standing fairly close and I could catch a hint of Estee in the air around her. I always marvel how a particular scent on one woman could have a totally different affect on another. Something about body chemistry, I guess. On Nancy, I liked it.

"I'm meeting somebody downtown and I'm a few minutes early. So I thought I'd catch up on what's happening in the real world." I held up the city's major daily.

"Hey, we've gone big time here. If you want the Washington Post or the New York Times, we even have those."

Her smile was still alluring. A dimple on one cheek and those blue eyes with the silver flecks.

I was trying to think of something clever to say but Nancy's name was called and she went to help someone at the counter.

I spent a few minutes of idle time scanning the pages and wondering about Nancy Easter when I realized I'd been there for almost fifteen minutes. I walked over to Dean's to see Ken.

As long as I knew him, Ken had his mood swings. One day he'd be chipper and ready to horse around; other days he'd be sullen and somber and ready only to snarl and claw like a cornered cat. Being a friend of Ken's was almost like work, I thought, and sometimes it just wasn't worth it.

There were times when, after an outburst by Ken over some perceived wrong, I would simply walk away and stay away from Ken for awhile. A few days would pass before Ken would call and apologize; I always accepted, even knowing that something else, some new wound, would someday again injure Ken and the process of rage and recovery would happen once more.

Ken was smart enough in high school to get a National Merit Scholarship and he took advantage of that by getting a degree in three years in mechanical engineering and a masters two years after that. From there, he joined a design firm where he became a partner by the time he was thirty-three.

If I had to guess, I'd say that Ken was bipolar, a diagnosis that had become popular. I even mentioned this to Ken in a private moment, to which Ken responded "Psycho-babble!"

I could see as soon as I walked into Dean's that Ken was already into a serious drinking session and slurred his words. "C'mon, Dave. Be a friend. I'm going to be pounding down a few and I'll bet I need a ride home. Whaddya say?" He was still dressed in his business suit but the knot of his tie was loose.

"What's going on, Ken?"

"My lovely wife left me a note on the counter when I got home. Said she was going to her Mom's house. Tina says she wants a divorce and I'm supposed to get my shit out of the house by Sunday. Good stuff, huh? Twenty-four years and Tina says 'No more, Kenny. No more.'"

I suspected that there were some problems, but the news still stunned me.

Drinks arrived and Ken slurped half of his in one swig. He was hunched over the bar and I could see the anguish in the slack skin of his face and the dark crescents under his eyes. I motioned to the corner booth where we could have a little more privacy.

When we were seated, I said, "We've been friends since we were what, six? Seven?"

He said nothing but his head bobbed slowly up and down. His reflexes were slowed by the alcohol and his eyes had a dull cast.

"I want you to talk to me."

I wondered if Ken was ready and decided now was as good a time as any to start pressing. It might be an unfair fight given his current state, but I went forward anyway.

"Have you been physical with Tina?"

Ken looked like he'd been slapped hard.

"C'mon, Ken. It's not just me who's asking. A few of the other guys have noticed, too."

Ken shook his head and every sign of drunkenness was gone. He leaned towards me and hissed his response. "Screw you, Dave. I never hit Tina and that's a fact. Never." His eyes, swollen with grief just seconds before, were ablaze.

I told him about seeing Tina at the grocery store.

"I'm telling you I've never hit Tina. OK, once, about five or six years ago, we had a big blow out and I shoved her. But she didn't fall, and she didn't get hurt. That's it! Twenty-four years!"

I was at a loss for words. I'd felt secure enough to accuse my friend of committing physical spousal abuse and of letting my friend know that others shared that perception. But the tone and severity of Ken's denial wasn't just a knee-jerk reaction. What was going on?

Ken wasn't going to give me time to get my act together.

He stood up from the booth and stared down at me, glaring. "I was going to ask you if I could bunk in with you for a while, at least until I get some things sorted out. Am I crazy for asking?"

Ken had been there for me when I needed him and there was no way I was going to say no. We don't make and keep friends by denying them aid when they need it. I said yes.

Ken nodded his thanks, grabbed his jacket and left.

Homecoming at Apsley High School was a big event on the social calendar. Catherine Marchand's last Homecoming began the evening before the annual football contest with a local rival. That year, it was Eastland.

At the Homecoming Smoker held at the Masonic Hall, the high school football team members were treated with soft drinks and snacks. The coach was introduced, said a few encouraging words, and expressed the hope that this year, Apsley would emerge victorious. "After all," he said, "we owe it to the town to do our level best."

The coach's words rang hollow. Eastland generally fielded a tough team, perhaps the grittiest team in the area. In the prior five years, Eastland captured two state titles in its class. Apsley would do well to make it a competitive match. The Apsley team had fallen on difficult football times. Last year's team won three and lost six. This year's squad was already 0-3 with the distinct possibility of being 0-4 by sunset tomorrow.

The cheerleaders performed a few rousing cheers before everybody in the room under the age of twenty one were ushered away and sent back home.

When the youngsters were all gone from the hall, the bar was opened and the adults stood around and relived the old days when Apsley was even smaller, but the football teams better. The people there, more to the point, remembered well when all the local mills were running at full throttle and the hum of heavy machinery permeated the downtown.

That year, some of the ancient magnates were still around, some frail and failing. Coleman Burgess, founder of General Belt was master of ceremonies, a post he'd held for at least a quarter century. Emmanuel Elfman, owner of the Baker & Harding mill was there, feeble in his dotage and just a shadow of his former feared persona.

Fulton Jefts and Lyman Forbes were, as usual, seated together and still bitter over the loss of their manufacturing trade to the Sunbelt states. They hadn't even been able to unload their investment in heavy machinery that sat and gathered dust in their abandoned factory.

Warren "Bo" Kerrigan was there, a younger but no less imposing figure in the town's manufacturing history. His mills were likewise being threatened by the move to areas with cheaper labor, but he'd made his bargain. In a private, as yet unannounced deal, he would sell his interest in his firm to a company a thousand miles to the south. His machinery would fetch a handsome sum, even if his mill eventually closed its doors and terminated the employment of almost two hundred workers. There were few soft spots in the heart of Bo Kerrigan.

It was Bo Kerrigan who was asked by the high school principal for the use of some extra space in his underused factory for the storage of out-of-season athletic equipment. The school was cramped for space. Bo Kerrigan agreed, but only after Tina, who was active in several sports, pleaded with him.

The talk at the smoker this night centered on Apsley's pride, represented earlier in the evening on the cheerleading squad. "They're all princesses," Coleman Burgess said in his remarks, "and they make us so proud."

Indeed, he was correct. All of them, nicknamed the "five princesses" were bright and beautiful. They were accomplished, and one, Tina Kerrigan, was already accepted at her mother's alma mater, Smith.

Tina, willowy and freckled, was as accomplished on the flute and piano as she was at basketball where she was Apsley's center, leading scorer, and a league all-star.

Lourdes Freitas was another. With flawless mocha skin and almost oval eyes, she was as exotic as Apsley might produce. State champion at the previous spring's math meet, she was all-state in softball and a whiz at chemistry.

Elissa Summers was only a junior and as slender as a rail, a ballerina who'd performed with the city ballet company in its annual Nutcracker event. Elissa already had several poems published in a state journal.

Nancy Easter won the grand prize at last year's science fair. She started a philosophy club at the high school and read Kierkegaard, Kant and Hegel. A beautiful young woman with an astonishing IQ.

And Catherine Marchand, striking beauty with a powerful alto voice that echoed at every performance. She soloed regularly at her church and in the school choir and was likely to graduate first in her class. She'd applied for early acceptance to several top rated schools, and her grades and recommendations would serve her well in that regard.

"You just watch these young fillies," Coleman Burgess said after the cheerleaders and football team were gone. "People in Apsley are going to be talking about them for years. Phenomenal, that's what they are."

SIX

Friday morning

Jerome Wetman didn't look like a Chief of Police. He was shorter than he should be and as thin as a whippet. His eyes were beady and dark, and he wore his thinning black and gray hair in a bad comb-over. In his previous job, his nickname was "Weasel," and this bit of information reached Lou Pellerin from a friend with some connections in the city police force where Wetman was a long-time detective.

"He's a pain in the ass and doesn't necessarily believe that the rule book was written for him, but he's a damned good cop," Pellerin's contact reported. Worst of all in Lou Pellerin's mind, Wetman didn't come from Apsley, and had only been to the town once fourteen years ago to attend an antique car show at Mason Park.

When Wetman was appointed Apsley's new Chief, the Board of Selectmen gave him a few weeks to wrap up his job in the city, find a place in Apsley and start work. To their collective surprise, Wetman offered to start right away. His current employer required no notice, he said, and he and his wife were anxious to move to Apsley so he could begin this new phase of his career. If the Selectmen didn't object, he'd like to start the day after tomorrow.

"But the contract," one of the Selectmen said. "We have to work out the details."

The Apsley Town Counsel immediately offered that the new Chief's offer to work without a final contract was highly unusual.

Wetman had a low regard of convention, and his regard for lawyers was not much higher. "Is it legal," he asked the attorney?

Town Counsel was rarely put on the spot like this. He liked to get the question, do some research within the quiet and protective walls of his office, and return to the next meeting with an answer couched in sufficiently convoluted language to justify his fee. He stumbled over a few words before admitting that there was nothing illegal with Wetman starting the job before an official contract was signed.

"Then it's not a problem," Wetman said. Besides, he assured everyone in the room, he had great trust in the honor and integrity of the Selectmen and didn't anticipate any problems. They could work out the details over the next few weeks.

Word of Wetman's appointment ricocheted through the town like a pistol shot and continued to echo even two weeks later. This morning, with the light rain from yesterday turning to ice overnight as the temperature dropped, Max saw Lou standing in front of the donut shop. Lou Pellerin was at the doorway shifting from one foot to the other in the bitter cold. "I'm telling you, Max, this guy's a mistake." Lou Pellerin fairly accosted Zenga when he arrived. "Wetman's a city guy, Max. We needed someone who knows this town and the people in it."

Max was exhausted trying to provide some consolation to

Lou and felt that Lou needed to finally accept the fact of the decision and move forward. There was no sense in just being a crutch for Lou's whining. "Let's go inside, Lou. It's freezing out here."

"Plus, you've seen the guy; he just doesn't look like a chief. I mean it, Max. Do you think this guy looks like a chief?"

Max Zenga looked at his friend and saw what he meant. Lou Pellerin was as big as a doorway and wore a buzz cut. If his diet of jelly donuts had added some inches around his middle, those inches were solid ones. He could take a stroll along Main Street and recognize almost everyone he encountered. But it was time to move Lou along.

"Whatever, Lou. You're probably right. The guy looks like a little weasel, just like you said. But they made their decision, Lou, so what are you going to do? It's done. They did it by the book, and they voted in public. How long are you going to let this eat you up? What are you going to do, Lou? Quit? Look for a job someplace else? Get pissed off and take a job directing traffic in Eastland?"

Lou didn't want to hear this, especially from someone like Max. He sat in the booth stone faced and stared at Max with a combination of disappointment and resentment.

"Lou, someone had to get the job and it wasn't you. You either have to keep doing your job the best way you can, or just quit. Retire, or do something else. That's what you're up against right now."

"Bullshit, Max. I don't have to make it easy for some little prick to just walk in and take over. I've been here my whole life. I know this town and everybody in it. If Wetman thinks he's going to have it easy here . . ."

Max held up his hand and motioned for Lou to stop. "That's not the way you work, Lou. You'd be hurting the town and everybody in it. Remember, this new guy needs you. He probably wants to do a good job just like anyone else, but he's going to need you. Give him a chance. Maybe he's an asshole, but maybe he's not. He might turn out to be the best chief we've ever had here. One thing is for sure: He's going to have to learn a lot in a very short time about Apsley, and you've got to be his right hand man. Look, just the other day you were talking about Phil Marchand and how you and the chief were concerned about his coming back. What gives today? Either you're on his side or you're not, but if I were you, I'd be on his side."

"That's a bunch of crap, Max. We both know it. I don't have to help him if I don't want to."

Max shook his head. "Lou, just because you lost the ballgame doesn't mean you quit playing baseball. Give the guy a chance. Cut him some slack. And look, Lou, I'm tired of your complaining. No more of this, OK?"

Lou just rose from his seat and walked out.

That's when I happened to step in. Lou Pellerin, who never failed to say hello to me, or to most people, just swung the door open so hard that it nearly hit me in the smacker. I managed to catch the door in time and thought about saying something to Lou, but he looked like a man possessed. Max Zenga waved me over to the booth.

"Lou is, shall we say, a little pissed this morning."

I ordered a coffee and took a seat with Max. "I guess. Maybe he needs a little time to cool off."

"Then this is the right morning for that. It's freezing out there."

"Is he still pissed about not getting the Chief's job? Do you know this guy that was picked? This Wetman?"

"Not really. Just what I've heard. I guess he did a heck of a job with his interview, has a ton of experience, just got married for the second time about six months ago. I think he's in his mid fifties. That's about it."

I sipped my coffee and blew across the top of the cup to cool it off. "How old is Lou, anyway?"

"Forty-one. Why?"

"Well, if this new guy does a decent job and Lou keeps his nose clean, he'll probably be get promoted the next time around. Maybe five years. Doesn't seem like a forever thing, know what I mean?"

"Try telling that to Lou. To him, picking Wetman was a slap in the face. He thinks because he's been here a long time, he ought to just get awarded the chair. But I agree with you. If he uses the next couple of years to polish himself up and learn a few things, then he'll probably be chief in just a few years. But I don't want to be the one to suggest that to him right now. Let him cool off a little."

There was a little commotion coming from the front door of the shop and both Max and I looked up at the same time. "Dad! Dad!" It was an obviously upset Samantha Zenga, Max's daughter, dressed in sweats and running to he father's arms.

"What's the matter, Sammy?" Max was genuinely concerned. Today was a teacher's conference and Samantha had the day off from school. When Max left the house a half-hour ago, Sammy was just getting out of bed.

"It was so creepy, Dad." She kept her voice low, making sure people weren't paying her too much attention.

"What was?"

"I was doing my run this morning like I usually do, and I cut through the field near the pond. And I felt like someone was watching me, hiding. Dad, I've felt this guy watching me a few times already, know what I mean? Like I can feel his eyes on me? And I stopped and went back. And it was that weird guy you told me about. He was behind some bushes and he was . . ." She made a motion with her hand. The meaning was clear to me and I'm sure just as clear to Max.

"C'mon. Sweetheart, c'mon home." Max put his arm around his daughter's shoulders and started walking with her to his car.

I walked out with him and waited until Max had his daughter safely inside his vehicle before talking. When he turned back to me, there was fire in his eyes.

"It's that fucking Malcolm, Dave. No way he's going to be doing this shit around my kid." In a minute, Max was speeding off towards home and I wondered what was in store for Malcolm when Max found him.

Chief Jerome Wetman was still getting used to working in Apsley and sitting behind his desk, flipping through a stack of paperwork. He looked over at his calendar and then picked up a stack of papers, riffling through them. Then another stack. Finally, he looked in his wastebasket and pawed through several scraps of discarded papers, searching. He buzzed the office of the Assistant Chief, Lou Pellerin, and asked him to come to his office. When he arrived, Lou rapped on the door jamb to announce his presence.

Wetman glanced up and kept searching. "Thanks for coming in. Would you check to see where the results are for yesterday's pistol range practice? I don't see them in my in box and I've looked everywhere."

Pellerin stayed at the door and said. "Chief, it was raining yesterday."

"Yeah right. I remember. But where are the results?" Wetman continued rummaging through the papers on his desk.

Lou Pellerin took a few steps into the office and explained. "The guys couldn't go down to the range in that kind of weather, so they'll probably go down today or next week."

Wetman stopped abruptly, sat back in his chair and shook his head as if to chase the cobwebs out. He looked up at Pellerin and spoke very slowly. "It was raining yesterday and therefore the law enforcement officers of the town of Apsley did not care to conduct their required shooting range assignments? What am I missing here? There was nothing on the radio this morning and I didn't see any signs when I drove into work yesterday?"

"Signs, Chief?"

"Yeah. Warning signs. Warning bad guys not to commit any crimes in Apsley until the weather cleared."

"But, Chief..." Lou thought better than to defend the lack of shooting practice results.

"Do they also fail to perform their required training in very cold weather? Or very hot weather?" Wetman opened the top drawer of his desk and poked around. "Hold on, I'll bet I've got it figured out. There must be a roll of quarters in here somewhere."

Lou felt the Chief's sarcasm but had to ask anyway. "Roll, Chief?"

"Yeah. Where did the old chief keep his rolls of quarters?"

"Chief?"

"If these guys don't want to go shooting in bad weather, I figure that maybe the old chief used to drop off the guys with their own rolls of quarters at the mall and tell them to go into the arcade and play video games. Good shooting practice. Nice and dry. Even air conditioned."

"Chief."

"What?"

Lou knew he couldn't argue. Wetman was right. "I'll tell them."

"Yes you will. And you will be emphatic when you speak with them. The results will be in my in-basket by the end of the day tomorrow. And your results are going to be coming in, too, right?"

"Right, Chief." He was just about to leave the Chief's office when Wetman asked him to also tell every officer that their weapons were going to be periodically inspected by the Chief or the Assistant Chief to make sure they were clean and in perfect working order.

"I saw one weapon yesterday that had a rust spot on the trigger guard. That doesn't cut it. If a weapon is found not to pass inspection, it will be taken from the officer who will be re-assigned as a crossing guard, because that's all that officer will be capable of doing."

"Yes Chief."

"And by the way, they ought to understand that pistol practice will be as scheduled, whether it's ten below zero and they have to wear a heavy parka, or it's pouring rain, or sleeting, or windy."

"Right Chief." Lou finally felt it was safe to leave and turned around to make his way to the squad room. He was fuming inside but maintained control.

"Thanks, Lou," Wetman said as he left. "And let me know when you're heading to the range because I'll get my own practice in at the same time."

Pellerin stopped and said "Yes, sir," appropriately chastened. At the same time, as he went on his way, he recognized something in Wetman that caused him some measure of pleasure. He'd never seen any Chief in Apsley take the job this seriously; he'd never seen a Chief take shooting practice; and for the first time, Wetman called him Lou.

Late in the afternoon, I was sitting at the bar of Dean's Town Tavern, waiting. I'd received a phone call an hour ago from my old friend, Phil Marchand. "Can we get together later on?" Phil had arrived the night before, checked into the motel and wanted to share a beer with his friend.

Phil Marchand walked in, a few minutes late, and took off his coat and scarf. "Holy shit, Dave, what's with this weather? Don't you have any pull around here?"

I walked over to Phil and gave him a bear hug. It was good to see my old friend. We took seats at the bar where Marchand ordered a beer and we took good looks at each other. The jokes and complaints that accompany reunions followed. Relative weight gain and hair loss were addressed, and after just a few minutes, I felt Phil had never left Apsley. We were connecting just like we did decades ago.

After two beers apiece, we decided to order burgers and took a booth to continue catching up with each other. With little prodding, I got Phil to talk about his life since leaving Apsley decades past.

Marchand's mood grew somber and he spoke slowly and with less animation.

"You knew my family, Dave. You remember how involved with the church my father was. It was part of his life, and he did his best to make it part of mine. Church every Sunday, youth groups, all the things he thought I ought to be doing. I guess he thought it would make a permanent impression on me.

"After Catherine was killed, though, I got this sneaking suspicion that there wasn't this compassionate Jesus looking over his flock, taking care of everybody. Instead, there was a big fat nothing out there. No comfort, no solace. I remember that it came to me like some revelation, some cosmic awakening. It hit me like a thunderbolt. 'What the fuck is going on?' I thought. 'This isn't supposed to be this way.'"

I agreed. "I remember. It was an awful time. If it helps at all, I felt the same way."

Phil went on. "Of course, my mother was devastated when Catherine was killed. She's quit smoking three years before and then took it back up with a vengeance. Two, three packs a day. Stopped talking to friends, stopped going out, quit her job. She started looking like an old lady. You saw her going downhill even when we were still here in Apsley, right?"

I nodded. Mrs. Marchand was a hollowed shell the last time I saw her, just before the family moved away.

"As bad as my mother was, though, Catherine's death really crushed the life out of my father. This was his little girl, his pride and joy. The fact that she died was bad enough. The way she died threw him right over the cliff. He was walking around in a fog. He just sat in his chair and stayed there.

"Life at home was pretty good when it was a family of four, but three just didn't make it. About a month after the funeral, my parents and I took a ride to the cemetery. We gathered around Catherine's grave. The grave marker had just been put in place and we said some prayers. Afterwards, we came home and everything was silence. Like I said, three just didn't make it, and I was the odd man out.

"No one was talking and I walked out the door and took a walk. And ended up at the top of the hill near the railroad trestle and I remember I just looked around and saw the downtown, and the edge of the woods, and the river. Everything looked so beautiful. The rooftops and the streets and I felt so completely at home. And then, just like a lightning flash I decided that I had to get out of here, to get away. Like I belonged, but still had to leave.

"I think my folks felt the same way, but we never talked about it. Even though our family was here for three generations, the weight of what happened was too much. If we stayed here, it would just be with us forever, the history, the whole place, and it would just keep repeating."

I reminded him, "You really closed yourself off, Phil. Then, right after we graduated, you moved away."

"My father wanted to leave sooner, but my mother convinced him they should stay until I was done school. But he had another job and another house already taken care of a long time before my graduation.

"Anyway, we moved and I hardly remember ever setting foot in the new house. I couldn't wait to get away to college. I went that fall and got a little fucked up. A little weed, a lot of angst. On top of everything, I tended to get political. At least I wanted to be. I marched in a few rallies, read as much as I could about what was going on in the world. But I couldn't get my head together.

"A lot had to do with my sister and what happened. I tried a couple semesters of philosophy and psychology, but that didn't work. I wrote some bad free-form poetry and painted some bad art and played bad guitar. I dropped out of school and moved away.

"I ended up in Jerome, a small town stuck on the side of a mountain in Arizona. Imagine you're Alice in Wonderland and you're following the little white rabbit. Jerome was that rabbit hole. Lots of cannabis, a little acid, a bunch of freaks with plenty of talent and a little bit of money.

"Jerome was actually a ghost town. Empty houses, empty schools, an empty fire station, an empty jail. All given up for lost except for a few zoned out souls who moved in and stayed. And it happened to have great weather to grow good dope.

"We had a metallurgist and a coal miner, a disbarred lawyer, a fucked up college professor. There were two Indians who argued about their credentials as shamans. One had a feathered headdress that was made in China and another had a whole set of clothes that he claimed was stitched together from the hides of javelinas that he killed with his bare hands and skinned."

My experiences at the same age were much more traditional and I could only imagine what this must have been like for someone raised in a place like Apsley.

"I took up with a Scandinavian earth mother from Vermont. She was on the run from the law in at least twelve states, grew her own food and didn't shave her legs or her underarms. She stank like a wet dog, but she just loved lots of powerful sweaty sex. She'd grab my crank and suck it down to her tonsils, then crawl on top of me and plunge herself down. Christ, it was unbelievable. My loins, as they say, were on fire, and I could do it six times a day. And lots of times I did."

"I'm proud of you, buddy." I was enjoying this part of the story.

"But in about eighteen months, I was done. The sex was great, but the place was changing. At first, it was just a carload of tourists stopping by to look at one of the great ghost towns of the old west. Then it was a couple cars a day, until Jerome became a destination.

"My earth mother saw all this and complained just like the rest of us. But one day she changed as if a tornado had blown through the doorway and reconfigured her brain cells. Before you know it, she's a fucking capitalist. Then everybody else starts to jump in on the action. She started banging out cheap earrings, another guy brought in a bunch of knock off Navajo blankets, and the professor opened a bar and gouged everybody that happened by. So much for being true to one's values.

"So I left Jerome and went to Flagstaff, found a real job and started taking classes. I was still hoping that I'd find some place where magnificent magic would appear, but I grew away from that part of my life. I didn't believe in some great man in the sky, but I didn't have anything else in its place. I just lived, and then I worked, and then I studied. I was a business nerd, and then a real apostle in the one true church of profit and loss, and mostly profit. And I found out I was very good at it."

Phil paused and took a long drink, present in body but far away in spirit, probably on the rocky crest of an Arizona mountain again. He sat back in the booth with his eyes closed. When he opened his eyes and looked at me, for the first time I saw the limp satchels under his eyes and the sallow cheeks. Phil Marchand didn't look well.

I must have been staring for he asked, "What's up, Dave? What's on your mind?"

I stuttered a response. "I was just wondering why you'd come back here after all these years?"

This changed the tone of the conversation and we leap-frogged decades ahead from his college days.

"I knew a long time ago that I had to leave Apsley, but this little town never left me. I loved it when I was growing up, and part of me still loves it, even though I keep getting lost since I've been back. New streets, old landmarks gone. Even my grandmother's house is gone. I guess it's just a romantic thing."

His tone changed, became more serious. "I've been preoccupied with Catherine's murder, even when I was busy someplace else with my own family. It's been like an ache. I've needed to come back for a long time."

"And you think you can accomplish something with your sister's case?" Ever since Phil's name came up in conversation at Dean's, this was the central question. Maybe I'd get the central answer.

"The Germans have a word 'Heimweh'. It means the sense of longing to go back to your home, but it also means the impossibility of doing so. Maybe I won't get anywhere, but I'm going to try."

"And do you have any idea what you're looking for?"

"Not a thing. It's just an unfinished chapter. I figured I could take a fresh look at the case, talk to the police, even hire a detective if I had to, and maybe find something that was overlooked the first time."

I told Phil about the photocopies I made at the library. "I've got them at my place. I'll have them the next time I see you and I'll give them to you. Might give you a little head start. I know reading the stuff after all these years brought back a lot of memories for me."

I thought this might be good news to Phil, but he dismissed the work that I did at the library with a wave of the hand.

George Wessel walked in at that moment and saw us. He came up to the table and said hello, taking a seat at the edge of the booth on my side. In another day, he'd have had trouble shoving his bulk into the seat, but his weight loss and exercise regimen were having an effect. He moved in easily. Phil spoke first.

"George! You look terrific. Long time." Phil's hand was out and George shook it.

"Phil's right, George," I said. "You are looking so . . . what's the word . . . buff? How much weight have you lost?"

George just waved us off but he blushed at the compliment. "Aw, c'mon, I've still got a ways to go."

"No, George. I mean it. You're looking great."

"Thanks." He was almost blushing. "I just got back from watching my grandson play pee wee hockey and saw your truck out front so I thought I'd stop by and have a beer with you guys. It's not on my diet, but what the heck."

Phil asked, "Remember George when we were in high school and you weighed what, two-fifty?"

George nodded. "About that."

"And in that big game against Eastland we were behind when you hit that guy so hard the ball went out of his hands and straight up into the air. I'll never forget that."

Now George was definitely blushing.

"You were kind of a quiet guy back in school, but when the chips were down, Georgie, watch out. You picked off that ball in the air and ran right into the end zone to win the game. That was super!"

I echoed my friend. "He's right, George. In crunch time, you were always the one who came through."

"It was a long time ago, guys." George was embarrassed by the attention but still grinning that his moment of glory would still generate some excitement.

Apsley had been down 14-8 in the final period, and most observers expected another Eastland win. But a pair of defensive moves by the Apsley line pushed Eastland back to its thirty-five when the Eastland quarterback attempted a pass. He dropped back and looked left and right for a receiver. Then George broke through and thumped the quarterback cleanly just as he released a pass and the ball squirted high in the air, straight up. The QB was flat on his back and a hush came over both sides of the stands. George stood alone under the ball, waiting for what seemed an eternity for it to come down. He caught it and rumbled the rest of the way over two Eastland defenders for the tie. A point after kick made it 15-14 and the buzzer sounded. George was the town's hero.

I said to George, "Phil was just telling me about his life after Apsley. I'd like to fill him in on everything that's happened here since he's been gone, but that would take about seven minutes and I don't have that kind of time."

George chuckled, his belly still loose enough to jiggle. "He's right, Phil. It's still a quiet place with not much happening, but I kind of like it that way."

"Tell me about the new Chief, George. Have you met him?"

"I just met the guy this afternoon. He dropped off some shirts and a couple suits. Seems like a nice guy. Kind of short, wiry little guy."

Phil was looking for more detail. "I mean, what kind of a guy does he seem like to you? Is he friendly? Pompous? You know what I mean."

"I'd say very regular. Maybe a little on the intense side. Not nervous so much, but he strikes me like a guy that's always paying attention. But hey, give the guy a chance to make his way around town. He and his wife haven't even moved all their stuff into their apartment yet."

Phil nodded. "I've got to go meet him soon so it's always good to know a little bit about somebody before you meet him. Thanks, George."

With that Phil rose, said his goodbyes, and told me he'd call me tomorrow. George took his seat and waited until Phil was out the door before he leaned in conspiratorially. "It's good to see Phil, but I need to talk to you." He was anxious about something. "It's about Tina Gladwell. There are some rumors going around, but I don't think that Ken is hitting her at all. It's something else. Something's a little weird, if you ask me."

"What makes you say that?" Someone at the bar had put some coins into the jukebox and the music was loud. George didn't want to yell, so he leaned even closer.

"Her blouse, Dave. She dropped off a blouse this morning and it had a major stain on it that we couldn't get out. I worked on it myself."

I knew that George took great pride in his ability to get almost any stain to yield under his careful work. "So? What does that mean?"

"You told me that you saw her at the market, right?" Dave nodded. "And I'll bet she had on an off-white blouse with a flower design on the sleeve."

I nodded again. I was sure of that. The scarf around her head had the same floral design.

"Well, the stain is from make-up, but it's not make-up like a woman usually uses. It's more like acting make up."

"Grease paint?"

"Not that heavy, but it was dark, a lot darker than she would normally wear. You know how Tina looks. With her complexion, she'd wear light beige make up if she wore any at all. This was mostly black with some dark brown and some dark blue mixed in."

I looked at George with what I am sure was a measure of perplexity. "Maybe Freud was right, George. Maybe sometimes a cigar is just a cigar."

"It was a big stain, Dave. Nothing small about it."

"You don't think you might be jumping to conclusions?"

"I'll tell you what really got me thinking, Dave. I was over in Eastland last night. My store manager's mother passed away the other day and I went to her wake. I'm standing there at the funeral home looking down at her in the casket when I notice something. She was a black lady, Dave, from Jamaica. Well, funeral directors use tons of make up, Dave. You can ask Bob, but you've been to enough viewings to know what I mean. It's really caked on. On this lady, it was mostly a mixture of brown with some black and a little blue mixed in. And there was just a little smudge on the collar of the dress they put her in, and I swear it's the same thing I saw on Tina's blouse today."

"Get out!"

"No, Dave, it's true. I think Tina used make up to make it look like she was all bruised up. I'll bet Ken never hit her!"

"Holy shit, George."

"Dave, all of a sudden you think Ken's been slapping her around. Why? Because you saw her with dark glasses and a kerchief? So tell me, who's jumping to conclusions?"

I didn't want to clutter my brain with these thoughts and life was complicated enough without wondering about these possibilities. "I'm just going to drink my beer and forget everything for a while. How about you? Want something to drink?"

"I just might splurge and have one of those ultra light beers."

I stood and started towards the bar. The follow up question I had for George (and he probably had for me) was left hanging in mid-air: Where did Tina get the make up, and was Bobby Hayes, our friend and undertaker, somehow entangled in this? No, no way did either of us want to consider the possibilities.

When I sat down again with the two beers, I decided to change the subject. "Is it me, George, or does Phil Marchand look old? I mean, it's been a long, long time and we're all a lot older, but there's something about him that doesn't look right. Did you see him up close?"

George took a sip and savored his beer, his first in weeks. "Looks like death warmed over, if you ask me. His eyes, man. Tired looking. He even sounds tired."

"That's what I thought."

"Maybe life at the top of the heap isn't so great after all. I mean, he's still got a full head of hair and he hasn't put on a ton of weight, but he doesn't look very good to me."

"You mean it's a good thing that we're stuck here in Apsley where nothing happens?"

George smiled at the thought. "And I thought this was the center of the universe?"

"Phil's raked in a ton of bucks, but it's taken its toll, don't you think? I wonder if he thinks it was worth it."

"Maybe it's all this talk about his sister that's got him looking so bad. If it was me, I'm not sure how I'd deal with it."

"Maybe you're right, George, but sitting there talking and listening to him, I wanted to say, 'Look Phil, do you want Catherine's life to matter, or your own.' Know what I mean?"

We left the tavern together and George walked to his car. I decided that the beers I had weren't worth a DUI and opted to walk home. It was during the walk that I wondered why Phil Marchand had never asked me about my life and what had been going on with me for the past twenty-nine years. I wrote the thought off as vanity . . . after all, it was Phil who was changing his life by coming home, not me . . . picked up my mail from the box on the first floor and went upstairs.

Malcolm Prudhomme was worried. He sat at the table in his unlit kitchen and wondered what went wrong. He thought he was being discreet, standing as he was in the deep cover of the trees and shrubs. That girl must have heard something because she stopped running all of a sudden, and before he could react, there she was, looking at him as he fondled himself.

He should have known better. He was older now, and his reaction time was slow. Besides, in the crisp morning air, and as cold as it was this morning, every little noise carried.

He remembered the girl's expression as it changed from surprise to disgust. She was gone in seconds. He just shuffled off to his house and tried to keep himself busy. He didn't want to think about it. He read the newspaper, watched television . . . but now as he sat, alone and embarrassed, he was also getting terrified.

The girl's name? He watched her at different athletic practice sessions over the past few years. Sam something, or Sammy. He watched her as she entered adolescence. He wasn't certain, but he thought she was Max Zenga's daughter. Max Zenga was the guy with the back hoes, front loaders and Bobcats. If that was the case, he was in big trouble. That guy had a temper. For a little guy, he was strong as an ox.

Maybe she didn't say anything. Maybe she just ran home and would forget the whole episode. He hoped so.

Prudhomme made his way to the refrigerator and checked to see what he had there. Not much. He didn't want to venture out in this cold, but he'd probably have to. He'd wait a while, maybe watch the news and then go to the store. It was a short walk to the convenience store. And maybe the girl never said anything. He truly hoped so.

SEVEN

Friday night

Phil returned to his hotel room, sat on the edge of his bed, and poured a glass of scotch neat. He didn't have an agenda for the next day but he thought he'd start with Bob Hayes, maybe stop by the funeral home first thing in the morning. He wanted to learn more about the new Chief; he didn't want to walk in blind. Besides, he needed to ease back into town, to get a feel for Apsley once more, find out what changed and what stayed the same.

Tomorrow he'd also arrange a meeting with a real estate broker at the new condominium complex. Renting or buying one of the units there would serve his needs and get him out of motel living.

The scotch felt good sliding down his throat. Balvenie, twelve years old, the amber fluid warming his insides.

He lay down on the bed and thought about his mission here, and about his sister. For some reason, he recalled a description he'd once given to a psychiatrist many years ago. Getting to a therapist was his wife's idea and he did so with a sense of resignation. Only after four or five sessions did he come to appreciate the value of speaking to someone in a safe place, a continent away from the competitions and judgments that he faced daily at work. He closed his eyes as he replayed the conversation in his mind.

"She was thirteen minutes younger than me, but I always thought of her as much older than me. I mean, she was smart and popular. She was graceful and light on her feet.

"I don't mean she was perfect. I mean, after someone dies, I guess it's natural for people to remember all the nice things. Maybe that's natural. You know how that happens.

"She could be bossy and sometimes she was mean to me. And she used me a few times like I was her servant. I remember when she had a date with this guy, and then another guy called her and she wanted to get rid of the first guy. So she makes me call him up and tell him she's sick as a dog and can't go out. She told me I had to call the guy and tell him or she'd tell everybody at school that I wet my bed until I was twelve. Meanwhile, she takes off on a date with this other guy.

"Small stuff.

"But overall, she was a good sister. A great sister. I miss stuff about her every day, even today. Like wouldn't it be nice to call her up and talk about things? Maybe she would have had some kids and I'd have some nieces and nephews. My two boys would have cousins.

"But mostly I think about her pain. I think about her alone out there at the edge of the swamp and how afraid she must have been. How much it must have hurt to be hit like that over and over, and not being able to do anything about it. How cruel can a human being be to another human being? What could she have done to anyone to deserve that? What kind of animal does it take to just whack at somebody until they just can't take it anymore and they just die?

"I broke my shoulder once and I thought I was going to pass out from the pain. It was incredible. Like someone stuck a hot poker in my shoulder and twisted it around. But I don't think there were many bones in my sister that weren't broken. I just have a hard time imagining what she went through out there, until she took enough smacks in the head that her brain shut down and her heart stopped and she just finally died.

"It killed my mother and father. It absolutely killed them. They were never the same after that. My mother never made it to forty-nine, and my Dad was fifty-one when he died. They never ever got over it.

"Catherine always used to say, 'Carpe diem, Phil. Carpe diem.' Like I ought to be as positive about life as she was. Then she gets her brains bashed in. She's all alone in the woods and somebody decides to bang her in the head again and again until she can't see, can't breathe. And then he leaves her out there to choke on her own teeth and blood. Well, carpe this!"

Phil sat up and looked out the window of his motel room. He took another sip of scotch and looked at the streets, damp with a light rain that fell off and on since he got to Apsley. Once this front passed by, it was supposed to get bone-chilling cold. The streets already looked like they might ice over and in the distance he saw a sanding truck work its way along the street. It was only 8 o'clock but only a few cars were on the streets. The storefronts were dark and it was another quiet night in Apsley.

The damp cold went right through him and he shuddered. Perhaps this was a signal that he never should have made this trip. He was as miserable on the inside as he was on the outside and he didn't think right now that things would get better.

Max Zenga had steam coming out of his ears as he sat in the front seat of his car and waited. The temperature outside was only twenty-eight degrees but Max kept the window rolled down anyway. He didn't want to miss Malcolm when he came out of the store.

"Son of a bitch," he muttered to himself. He'd waited a while since Samantha told him about seeing Prudhomme in the woods, but the anger never left its place right at the surface.

Max spoke with his wife, Antoinette, about that episode, but they decided then that Sam should take a different route for her morning run, and Max would speak to Prudhomme and also speak to Lou Pellerin, maybe even file a criminal complaint. The whole discussion sounded rather measured and reasoned.

Samantha loved running every morning before school. She was in great shape but making the track team in the spring and cross country in the fall had become obsessions. The girl was determined. After she came across Prudhomme, she modified her running routine and avoided cutting through the woods near Squash Pond.

But, just moments later, he overheard a conversation between his wife and his daughter. It was an accident, but Max was in the basement repairing a break in the hot air heating duct when he heard "Mom, I've got to ask you something."

His daughter's bedroom was on the second floor of the house but he could hear the conversation through the ducts as if they were three feet away. His wife said "Ask away", and that's when he heard the story.

"That old weird guy, Mom, the guy who lives in that huge house. The Prudhomme place."

"The one you told your father about? What about him."

Max waited for more and then he heard what he feared.

"I didn't really tell Dad everything. He was so gross, Mom. He was playing with himself, just standing in the woods waiting for me to run by, and he had his thing out and was pulling on it."

So he wasn't just rubbing himself though his pants, which was bad enough. He was exposing himself to his daughter and masturbating right out in the open.

Max dropped what he was doing and went to the porch to smoke a cigarette and try to control his rage. It didn't work, and he got into his car and drove to Malcolm's neighborhood. On his way, he spotted the old man toddling along the sidewalk in the direction of the convenience store. Max pulled over down the street and waited.

The conversation he overheard took place almost forty minutes earlier, but the voices echoed through Max Zenga's brain as if they'd just been uttered. His cell phone rang and he picked it up from the tray next to the seat. It was his wife and he knew she'd be wondering where he was and why he had taken off without telling her. He turned the phone off and put it back in the tray.

In a few minutes, a man stepped out of the store with a bag in his arms. Even in the neon glare, there was no disguising the slow shuffling walk, and Max knew that Malcolm Prudhomme was now his. The route home for Malcolm would take him by the old Federated Shoe Findings warehouse, long derelict and with no exterior lights.

Max got out of his car and closed the door without slamming it. He stayed about fifty feet behind Malcolm and he flexed his hands, made fists and stretched them in anticipation.

Malcolm was approaching the gravel driveway next to the old factory and Max made his move, shoved the bag of groceries from Malcolm's hands and laid a clean right cross to his cheek. Malcolm grunted, stumbled, and Max caught him by the collar and pulled him upright. He slapped him hard across the face and Prudhomme slid to the ground without a sound and Max bent low and hissed in his ear. "Listen, you old perverted bastard, you stay away from the young girls and you can go on living for a while. But if I ever hear that you're spying on these kids, even just sniffing around, I'm going to make you hurt real bad. I mean it, you sick piece of filth."

Malcolm was having difficulty focusing, his glasses on the ground next to him. He felt around for them and slid them on. His voice betrayed no trauma even though he'd just been punched hard by a man thirty years younger. "What did I do? What do you mean?"

Malcolm had been a mumbler most of his life and tonight his words were even more difficult to comprehend. Max didn't care if he knocked out the few teeth Prudhomme had left in his mouth.

"You know damned well what I mean, Malcolm. You're pulling your pud and these kids can see you doing it. Even my daughter saw you whackin' your haddock. They were right. They should have locked you up when Catherine Marchand was killed and they should have thrown away the key."

Malcolm appeared to regain his senses. "I'm sorry, I'm sorry!"

"They should have lit you up like a Christmas tree for what you did to Catherine Marchand, and then the whole town would be a lot safer

"I'm sorry about today. I don't know what happened. I'm sorry! But that wasn't me with that Marchand girl. I never hurt her!"

"Right, just like you don't play with yourself in public." Max started to pick Malcolm up by the collar, not sure if he was going to slug him once more or let him go.

"I know, I know, I'm sorry. But I never hurt that girl, Catherine, I never did."

"You sick bastard." He cocked his arm and made a fist.

"Please! Don't punch me again."

And what Malcolm Prudhomme said next caught Max Zenga mid-swing. It was as if Max himself had absorbed a gut punch.

* * *

Ken Gladwell had worked late at his office, but not because there was any particular need. When he finally switched off the light on his desk and left, he took his time getting back to Apsley and drove almost aimlessly through the town's neighborhoods just to pass the time. He drove by Dean's Town Tavern and kept on going, in large part because he'd be bound to find familiar faces there. Any ensuing conversation would inevitably lead to one of two subjects, both of which he wanted to avoid at the moment: His separation from Tina and the return of Phil Marchand to town.

Ken's efforts at diverting his attention met with limited success. Memories of Catherine Marchand's murder weighed heavily on his soul, especially as he neared the area of Squash Pond. He stopped his car at the point where the path from the street to the pond began and parked at the edge of the road. If his personal demons had rested dormant for decades, they now sought their way to the surface. He understood his own current state of emotional fragility better than his closest friends might imagine, and he determined as he sat, alone in his car and late at night, to face those demons that haunted his waking moments and gnawed at his core.

He stepped out onto the tall damp grass and looked in every direction. No sounds came from the nearest houses or the nearby school, his mind reconsidering the prudence of this visit, sure that greater wisdom resided in those nearest homes, their inhabitants warmer, dryer and more secure than he on this autumn evening. Nevertheless, he felt drawn to come here. He moved forward with a degree of confidence that even he was certain was feigned. The wind was just starting to pick up and a few thin clouds skimmed across the sky, occasionally obscuring the opalescent wedge of moon and the pale glow it provided.

He took a few moments to adjust his eyes to the darkness and walked on the grassy path worn flat by foot traffic. The air

was dank and the grass slick with evening dew, the moisture
clinging to the cuffs of his trousers as he walked. In a few moments he turned off the path and took tentative steps into the
taller weeds and ferns, sure in the blackness of the destination
he sought if unclear in his reasons why.

A passel of crickets in the meadow kept him company with
infrequent chirps as he made his way to the exact spot he remembered. A larger animal, perhaps a raccoon he thought,
made rustling noises as it traversed another path on its own
solitary quest. He stopped when he reached the spot he sought,
inhaled deeply and studied the ground. He hadn't been back
here in twenty-nine years and it still bore recognizable remnants of his last visit. Directly ahead of him where once stood a
tall oak and a lower stump was now a low mound of brush,
moss-covered and fed by the thick carpet of rotting leaves. He
took two more steps, careful that he didn't slip on the slick
growth, and surveyed the area in every direction, his senses absorbing the scene and recreating for him the events decades past
when he came to this same stark and irrevocably sad place. Ken
Gladwell was as alone as a person could be in Apsley.

One more footfall and he recoiled, stepping back, suspicious
and suddenly filled with fear, bile rising in his throat as if he had
stepped on a grave, the pupils of his eyes at their widest, his
nostrils flaring like a feral animal on full alert, searching with
every sign for the threat, the hairs on his neck erect, his ears
tuned in to every subtle sound. The wind was still too low to
create much more than a slight rustle, but a low howl rose sin-
uous from the dank earth and whispered to Ken a silken alarm.
He breathed short breaths and tasted a metallic tang that
touched his lips and reached far down his throat. He stepped
back again, retracing his steps until he reached the main path
and the surreal sense of dread was lessened if not entirely van-
ished. More quickly than he came, he strode back to his car,
fumbled for his keys, started it, and was gone. He looked in his

rearview mirror more than once as he drove off, no cars behind him but still wondering if he was being watched. He touched his brow and it dripped salty beads of sweat on this cold night.

The event in question, the reason for Ken Gladwell's night-time visit and for Phil Marchand's return to Apsley, the one where an alluring young woman with so much promise was crushed and bludgeoned into another realm, and where so much local lore and speculation but no solution was ever pro-duced, happened in this area of marsh and trees not far from the high school and on the damp edges of Squash Pond. Now, the school was used as middle school and a new high school sat in a field four miles away in another part of Apsley.

No one ever recorded the reason for naming the pond 'Squash' and it was never so officially named. It was really just a wide area in a brook that traversed a bog and it assumed a long, slim shape. In the winter, because of the slow moving water, it froze into an ideal ice skating area. The high school used it for hockey practice and the Apsley public works folks would occasionally auger a hole in the ice and pump water onto the surface during the early morning so the hockey team had a smooth surface after school hours and on weekends. Still, noth-ing official. That's just the way it was.

There was a path of sorts that wove from the high school, beside the so-called pond and over to a neighborhood of mod-est, nicely kept homes. In more recent years, Max Zenga bought one of these homes and it was across this same path that his daughter, Samantha, cut through the woods on her morning jaunts.

There was a peculiar fetid odor in the area of greasy swamp land that surrounded the pond. It was a great place for salaman-ders and bull frogs, and for ferns and moss to flourish along with skunk cabbage, that malodorous broad leafed weed that favored bogs and the rotted carcasses of old vegetation. The trees there were mostly scrub oaks and pines, suckers from the roots and stumps of ancestors that somehow found purchase in the muck and overspread their canopy near the water's edge.

When the high school was first built nearby, the area developed into a favorite hang out for the teens who wanted to escape the eyes of their neighbors and parents. Few adults, save for the hockey coach and a few other parents, and then only in winter when the ground was firm, would venture into the area. There were too many tales of snakes and vermin, even though the teens suspected the stories were overblown.

Once, in the dappled light of an afternoon twenty-nine autumns past, Catherine Marchand walked this path next to Squash Pond. She was alone and walking slow, head lowered and deep in thought. She'd left her textbooks and homework assignments in her locker and was using this alone time to visit the deepest and darkest corners of her mind.

For the few days prior, she'd been facing ghoulish specters, ogres and demons, afraid and alone, certain that she'd earned every shiver that her fears and her guilt and her shame delivered to her. Only today, as the last leaves clung, drying and desperate to their branches, had she found her way from dread to resolution. The terrors disappeared, replaced by determination. She made some important decisions and understood that she must make but one more.

Momentarily surprised and shaken briefly from her reverie when a pair of freshmen boys came around the corner near the neighborhood end, Catherine ducked behind a thick clump of vegetation and stood in silence and stillness. The two boys walked by, one bragging to the other that he saw a "nudie magazine" that his father kept hidden in a closet. "Cool," the other said upon the revelation. "What did you do?"

By the time Catherine heard the answer, they were too far away. She could guess the answer anyway.

She stayed behind the shrubs and found a stand of oak trees that had a peculiar low twist on one trunk that could serve as a seat. Catherine wanted to sit and think and decide, and this place looked as good as any.

She's been sitting alone there for just a few minutes when she heard some rustling coming from her right. Whatever was making the noise, it was big, and she started to get up and leave. That's when, in a rush, she first saw the shape of a large man appear in a flash and accost her. The smell, of bad teeth and body odor, was pungent and sour and Catherine tried to twist away from the man's grip. His skin was oily and she couldn't get a good grip, so she tried to face her attacker and give him a knee in his balls. She'd heard about that tactic from other girls, but her attacker was too strong, and he held her, pinned against the tree as he grunted and moved against her. She thought she was going to be sick.

Then she heard the sound of a zipper and the rhythm of the grunts increased its pace. This was a human being who was rubbing against her backside, masturbating against her, more feral, more primitive and crude, Catherine thought, than rutting beasts. Then a second sound, a younger voice, a young man's voice, pierced the air and the attacker stopped abruptly. He was panting in her ear and she could feel his spittle and maybe his snot against her neck. The young voice said only a few words. "Hey!" Then "What do you think you're doing?" Then something else she couldn't make out. Whoever called out had yet to appear but her attacker suddenly bolted away, shoving her hard to the ground when he took off through the woods and the swamp.

She was recovering and, in truth, had not been harmed beyond a minor scrape on her wrist when she fell. She was sure that her attacker was the infamous local pervert, Malcolm Prudhomme, the same man of foul habits and reputation who always seemed to materialize at the shadowy edges of girls' sporting events. The old joke about sniffing little girls' bicycle seats was written about Malcolm Prudhomme, she was certain.

She was collecting herself when she heard some panting from several feet away, presumably from the young man who ran up and interrupted Malcolm. Her hero. She had no idea who it was, and she turned to look in the direction of the quick breathing. But dusk was coming on fast, and the rusty glow of the remaining sun was barely sufficient for her to see ten feet in front of her. She ran her fingers through her hair and sat back on the spot she occupied before Malcolm came along just four minutes ago. "Thanks," she said to the disembodied hero. Just as quickly had the sound of panting appeared, it disappeared.

She glanced around, still straightening herself out after the attack. Her blouse had been pulled from the waistband of her skirt. "I must look like a mess," she thought to herself. She started to regain her composure and took some deep breaths.

She opened her purse and removed a cigarette and a lighter. She sat on the stump and inhaled, enjoying the calming effects of the nicotine, almost content now.

That's when the first blow caught her. There was no warning. It was just a ferocious slam to the back of her head, just below her left ear. She didn't even have time to scream, and only a small hiss escaped her lips when the second blow struck, this one just at the top of the shoulder line in the center of her back and delivered with such force that it crushed her spine. She fell to the damp, musky earth and ended up face up and eyes wide open. She had a clear look at her attacker this time and could do nothing, could raise no hand, utter no sound, as the third blow came across her forehead and punched in a two inch segment of her skull.

For some reason, she felt no pain, and knew she was alive just the same. She could see just barely and from only her right eye. Then another blow caught her on the shoulder and she sensed her left arm flip up quickly in a wide arc, actually touching her attacker momentarily, and flop down across her chest. Then another blow and another.

She could taste her own blood and, oddly, smell her own torn flesh and exposed bone. She quivered several times, her body obeying some primal urge she couldn't understand. She finally felt the lights dimming. It was gradual, not sudden, which struck her as odd. She never would have guessed it. Then the lights went all the way down, flickered once, and she lost all consciousness.

Only forty-seven seconds elapsed from first blow to eighth, the last one of which Catherine was aware. Her death had been assured by the third blow. But for the killer, another eleven blows and seventy-one more seconds were required to finish the task.

Nancy Easter parked her car in a dimly lit space behind the library and hurried along the sidewalk, her long wool coat buttoned all the way down, her crocheted hat a cocoon for her hair, and a long scarf wrapped twice around her throat. The wind had continued to stiffen after sunset and was now sharp and biting. She pulled the scarf over her nose as she walked. No one else was out walking, and for this she was grateful. Besides, she thought, no one would be able to identify her all covered up the way she was.

She turned the corner from Main Street and the wind gained strength and purpose. She almost ran the rest of the way to the empty factory. The door she wanted was on the side, the second one from the end. She reached her destination and removed a set of keys from her pocket and a small flashlight from another. Getting the keys took some negotiating, but she knew she'd win out in the end; besides, she promised, I'll get them right back to you; no one else needs to know I'm there. She was less self-assured right now, cold, alone and agitated. She fumbled with keys, dropped them once in the dried leaves that gathered in the corner of the doorway, and cursed when she picked them up. Of all nights to do this, she thought.

She unlocked the door and pushed it open, its rusty hinges complaining. She stepped in, kept the flashlight on, and closed the door behind her. In front of her was a large open space, littered with construction debris and dust. To her right, at the very rear of the building were huge openings almost ten feet high and fifteen feet across, now covered by sheets of plywood, but soon to have enormous multi-paned windows overlooking the river.

She stepped to her left and shined the flash light along a brick wall that climbed halfway to the ceiling. A loft above was once a storage area and the space in which she stood was a loading platform, a large hook suspended on heavy ropes and looped though a block and tackle near the edge. Years ago, cartons and crates would have been hoisted by the hook, swung from one floor to the next. This was a center of commerce in Apsley at one time.

The air was as cold inside as it was outside, but here there was no wind and she loosened her scarf. The uninterrupted space looked to Nancy to be about ninety feet long and perhaps forty feet deep. She looked up at the loft and panned her flashlight back and forth over the area. She considered going up the narrow staircase in the corner, but thought better of it. The steps were old and if she fell she might not be found until the workers returned in the morning.

She panned the area twice more, her eyes absorbing the dimensions and her imagination ignoring the debris, calculating and reinventing until the space transformed and her face adopting a broad smile in response. Brittle dry cold was now warm and aromatic, the silence replaced with soft sounds of conversation and sweet music, her flashlight now supplying an ambience of repose and beauty only she could recognize and appreciate.

She caught herself before freefall. Alright, she thought. I've seen what I came to see. She retreated to the doorway, snapped off the light and made her way out, making sure the door was locked behind her. She walked quickly back to the front of the building and took one last look before she turned back in the direction of Main Street.

She hadn't yet re-wrapped the scarf fully around her face and neck when a pick up truck came out of a side street. She turned away and avoided the headlights but I was certain I'd just seen Nancy Easter standing in front of the old Kerrigan Mills. What was she doing out so late on a night like this, and alone? And why did she turn sharply away, as if she didn't want to be recognized? I wanted to stop and ask Nancy if everything was OK or if she needed a ride, but she almost broke into a run down to Main Street, the ends of her scarf rising and falling like a thoroughbred's tail. Nancy Easter, I concluded, wouldn't welcome my questions right now, and I drove home.

EIGHT

Saturday

I signaled for two more coffees and Gordon Jefts and I walked together to a booth far from the diner's counter and away from the chance of being overheard. I set the cups down, and we sat. That's when the dam burst.

"I was in the office late last night prepping for a case," Gordon began, his voice urgent and just above a whisper. "I've got an insurance company lawyer coming in Monday to talk about a case and I wanted to get ready. Those bastards are a different breed. I've come to believe that it's not a sin to lie to an insurance company, and it shouldn't be a crime either. Those pricks start out every conversation with a lie, and then they build from there. So my advice, lie first before they get a chance to lie to you, because I guarantee you, they will."

He adjusted himself in his seat, looking around the diner to make sure there was no one else close by. Even on a Saturday, Gordon was still dressed in clothes that were perhaps three times as expensive as my entire wardrobe.

"Anyway, I was going through my notes when I heard a door open and close. It was Mike and he was just leaving for the day. He said good bye on his way out and then I was alone. I couldn't get something out of my mind, though. Like I told you before, I saw Malcolm Prudhomme in Mike's office before. I wondered if he had a file on Malcolm. So I looked out my window and saw Mike get in his car and drive away, and then I took a chance that his office door wasn't locked, and it wasn't."

"Isn't that kind of stupid? Don't you lock your doors before you leave?"

"I sometimes forget and so does Mike. It's stupid, but the outer door to the office is always locked at night, though, and I hardly ever go into his office when he isn't there. Sometimes I'll grab his phone if he's out and take a message and leave it on his desk, but that's about it. I'm sure he's done the same thing when I've been out and there's nobody out front to take the call. It's never been a big deal. Plus, we both have file cabinets where we keep extra-sensitive files, and I always lock mine before I leave. I'm guessing he does the same.

"So I looked into his office and I could see a file with Malcolm's name on it sitting there." He took a sip of his coffee before he went on.

"I shouldn't have, but I took a look at the file."

"You what? Do you want to get disbarred?" It's one thing to be daring, another to be reckless.

"Hold on. I just saw a file there; I didn't look inside the damned thing. Besides, Mike had it all wrapped up in rubber bands. But it was Malcolm's file, and it's a will."

"I thought you said you didn't look inside."

"I didn't. Mike always uses the same color files just for wills, so I know that's what it was."

"Look, Gordon, this may come as a surprise, but even Malcolm Prudhomme, sick bastard that he is, is entitled to have a will. In fact, since he owns the family house up on the hill and he's the last Prudhomme in the area, he probably needs one more than most people. So what was the big deal?"

Gordon remained silent and his face told me there was more to come.

"OK, Gordon, what is it?"

"There was a post-it note attached to the file, and it had two names on it. It was in Mike's handwriting and it had Ken Gladwell's name on top, then an arrow down, and then Tina Gladwell's name below that."

I sat in silence while Gordon waited for this bit of news to sink in.

I couldn't find anything more intelligent to say than, "Holy shit!"

"Yeah. Holy shit. What connection does Ken or Tina have to Malcolm? I couldn't think of a thing."

"Me either. Ken's family moved here when Ken was a baby and his father took a new job here. Malcolm's family has been here for a hundred years, maybe more."

"And Malcolm never married and all his sisters and brothers are either dead or long gone from here."

Malcolm had been one of a passel of Prudhommes. As far as anyone knew, Malcolm was the last one of the family to stick around. He was alone and had no descendants, at least not nearby.

"So what do you think this means?"

"In my opinion, Dave, and remember I didn't see anything inside the file, there's some changes pending on Malcolm's will. My guess is, Ken is somehow in the will as a beneficiary, and it's being changed to Tina."

"Why?" The idea of putting Ken Gladwell on the same document as Malcolm Prudhomme sounded offensive on its face. I couldn't think of any good reason why that would happen, but I could think of a few bad ones.

"You want to guess?"

"I have my own guess, but I'd rather hear yours first."

"Malcolm Prudhomme is being blackmailed."

"Shit. That was my guess." We sat in silence while that concept washed over us.

Nobody likes to think the worst of a friend, especially one of long standing, as Ken Gladwell was to both of us. I shook my head, an expression of disgust that I knew was shared by Gordon. Ken might have his own idiosyncrasies, and there were many times over the years when Ken's temper had been aimed in my direction. More than once, Ken's anger got the best of him and he'd get belligerent and say something that he'd have to take back later.

But Ken was there when he was needed. It was Ken who was first to volunteer when I got divorced and had to move out on short notice. Ken lugged furniture up and down stairs from my house to my upstairs apartment. He was there to help repaint the walls and ceilings, there to provide a shoulder for me to cry on.

Ken Gladwell had been a friend since grammar school, the one who arranged the surprise party when Gordon passed his bar exam. Ken was generous with his time, even if he was short-fused. When Ken got a big promotion and could have easily moved to a finer home in a nicer community, he'd told me that he loved Apsley and the people in it.

Gordon broke the silence first. "So what's the reason for the blackmail?"

I was still deep in thought when another question came. "I don't really want to know. But if you were asked to name all the people in town who'd be subject to blackmail, who would you name?"

The list was short. "Malcolm Prudhomme. With his history, he's eminently blackmail-able."

Gordon nodded his head in agreement. Neither of us was particularly pleased with this knowledge. He did ask a follow-up, though. "Assume that's the case: Why would Malcolm be changing the beneficiary to Tina?"

I sighed. "My guess is that there's a divorce coming along sometime soon, and this is going to be part of the financial agreement."

Gordon considered this for a moment, cocked his head at an angle, and glanced upward toward the dingy ceiling. "I hadn't thought of that." That was a lie; if anyone considered all the contemptible possibilities before the conversation began, it would be Gordon. We were both aware that Ken and Tina Gladwell were having marriage problems. In spite of the rumors of physical abuse, founded in fact or contrived by Tina, neither of us doubted Ken's temper. It was an indictment of the level of unbridled rage of which Ken was felt to be capable.

Gordon said, "I saw Tina a few days ago and she had dark glasses on. It seemed to me she might have been covering up a shiner."

"I saw her too," I added. "I thought the same thing. I'm not so sure that Ken's responsible for that." I didn't mention that the doubt I had about Tina's bruises had been planted by George Wessel.

"But that still doesn't answer the bigger question, Dave. Why do you think Ken or Tina have anything to do with Malcolm Prudhomme? It doesn't make sense to me."

"And you can't ask Mike Moura."

"Shit no!" Jefts almost spilled what was left of his coffee. "If Mike knew that I was in his office and looking at a client file, he could have my balls. This has got to stay with you and me."

"I understand."

"But I can't help but wonder. Especially with Phil Marchand back here and digging around. It just drags up the whole thing about Malcolm and Catherine." Gordon put his cup down. "Tell me the truth, Dave. Do you think Malcolm had anything to do with Catherine's death?"

I released a heavy sigh and sat back in the booth. "Who the hell knows? I really don't think Malcolm is that violent, but I really don't know. I mean, Catherine's head was split open and almost severed from her neck. That's violence brought to a whole new level. Whoever did it was out of control."

"I remember hearing somebody describe it as an 'ambitious' beating, but what do I do with this information about Malcolm's will? Anything?"

I leaned forward and stared into Gordon's eyes. "Nothing." I was emphatic for good reason. "Stay away from anything to do with this. First of all, you've put yourself in a bad position as it is; you could jeopardize your license. Second, if you ever said anything to Ken, he'd know exactly where it came from, and you'd be a dead man. Third, this is just idle speculation; you haven't seen the will itself, and there could be some other reason for that post-it note. I know, it puts us both in kind of a shitty position."

Gordon nodded in agreement if not with satisfaction. He hated not knowing the truth behind the case of Malcolm Prudhomme's will only slightly less than he hated the thought of an official bar proceeding and the potential forfeiture of his license to practice law. He left me at the diner and went home.

On the way out the door, Gordon saw Max Zenga getting out of his pick up truck and heading to the diner. He looked like a man with a purpose and when Gordon waved to him, Max didn't even see him. Max was focused on the door and Gordon started getting curious once again. He paused on the sidewalk and considered going back. How he hated not knowing what was going on inside! Eventually, his common sense told him to stay away.

Max Zenga strode through the door, looked around, saw me, and walked directly over. I was still fretting over Gordon's revelation, barely had a chance to get out of the booth. "Dave, I need to talk."

I slapped my cap and gloves on the table and said loud enough for everyone inside to here, "Everybody wants to fucking talk! What the fuck is going on in this fucking place? Am I a fucking priest? Go tell somebody else your problems!"

I was loud enough that everyone in the diner turned in my direction. I'm not known to be terribly excitable and my outburst surprised me as much as anyone else.

Max put his hands on my shoulders and said in a low voice, "Relax, Dave, three minutes. I need to tell you what happened last night. I couldn't even sleep."

I considered telling Max to go to hell when I saw the seriousness in Max's eyes and said, "Let's walk and talk OK? I've got to get over to the hardware store. Do me at least that favor."

Together, we walked along Main Street with Max leaning in like a conspirator, giving me a full description of last night's events and what led up to them.

"So Malcolm comes out of the store and I walk behind him. The poor sonovabitch can hardly walk and I deck him. Makes me feel like a real man."

"After what your daughter said, I'm surprised you didn't do a lot worse."

"I told him he should have been put away when Catherine Marchand was killed. That's when he starts almost crying. I got so pissed, I started roughing him up some more, but he says, 'Hold on, hold on!' And I'm wondering why I'm even paying attention and he says, 'I never hurt Catherine . . . It wasn't me!'"

I stopped walking and looked Max in the eye, waiting for the rest.

"Then he says, 'Ask Kenny Gladwell. He'll tell you.. Kenny knows I didn't kill Catherine.' I thought I was going to shit my pants right there. I dropped him and just left him there, and then I picked up his groceries, helped him up and sent him on his way."

"A real boy scout, Max."

"It freaked me out."

I resumed walking and Max stayed at my side. My head was blurred with this morning's information and I didn't need to hear anything more. If someone walked up to me at that moment and told me that Ken Gladwell was just arrested for being a member of a terrorist cell, I would not have been any more shaken.

"Look, I feel bad enough as it is, and that's why I'm telling you this."

"You should talk to the police, Max. They've got some good people working there. Maybe you should tell them about this."

"Tell the cops that Malcolm is bringing Ken Gladwell into that mess? Are you shitting me?"

"On second thought, don't do anything right now."

"I heard Ken and Tina are splits, huh?"

"Just let me talk to Ken and don't say anything else right now. And how's Samantha?"

"She's doing fine. And I don't think Malcolm's going to be whacking his haddock in public for a long time."

"That's one good thing."

"Dave, thanks. And we passed the hardware store back there, just in case you want to know."

At lunchtime, Phil Marchand brought the sandwiches to the table and handed me a Diet Coke. For a moment I thought I noticed that Phil's hand shook a little as he drank his soda. I chalked it up to stress. Here was my old friend after a long solo drive to Apsley. I'd be a little shaky too. Add in the stress and the memories that surrounded the purpose of the trip and there was plenty of reason for the tremor.

"So tell me. What made you just quit a big job like yours at that financial services place?"

"The stench. It just got to me." I noted a bit of a slur in Phil's voice. Had he been drinking already?

He took a long drink from his glass. I saw the tremor again.

"The CEO is one of those flamboyant little assholes who expect fawning from the people around him. His jokes? Raunchy, bigoted and pathetic, but everybody around him laughs like he's the funniest guy on earth. He's got the big newspapers all wrapped up and there's never an unflattering word printed about him. They won't even print a picture of him with anyone that makes him look short."

"Sounds like a charmer, Phil."

He took another swig and I was sure I detected some slurring. Phil Marchand was already half in the bag.

"There's an old saying that the most important thing in business is integrity, and once you've learned how to fake that, you've got it made. Spend a little time with that asshole I worked for and you'll learn just how true that is."

Phil leaned closer and said, "Look, I don't think profit is a dirty word, but this guy would run over his mother to make sure he got his bonus before he let her stand in his way. I was CFO, so I'm spending a lot of time with this stinking worm, and after a while, the smell clings to your clothes."

"So what happened?" My personal experience with the evils of business was limited to the occurrences of petty fraud and small-minded charlatans I'd come across in Apsley. It was somehow comforting to hear that life was just as sordid and contemptible in the plushest executive suites.

"My last year there, he put together a merger with another company. Not that we were forced into it, because we were doing pretty well. Our stock price was up and profits were up."

"So why merge if there wasn't a good reason?"

"The year before the merger, the CEO made three million,

which is great money and right in line with companies our size. But after the merger went through, he pulls down over twenty-one million. A thousand people are out of a job, but he's got twenty-one million reasons to think this is all a great idea."

This was the kind of thing I read about in the financial pages. Here was someone who was right there in the vortex. "How did you make out?"

"He made sure he spread some of the wealth around the executive floor. It has a funny way of curing any outbreak of ethics. I got two million."

I never knew anyone personally who made that kind of money. "On top of your salary?"

"And I had a contract that paid me a big chunk when I left. Want some?"

"No, it's not that. I'm just amazed at the size of the numbers."

"It's giving me a chance to do stuff that I couldn't otherwise. I mean, I almost tried to keep going in the business world, but I think I bailed at the right time."

"So you're not planning on going back into any other sort of business?"

"Never say never, but I'll probably end up doing my own thing, starting my own business. Maybe back here in Apsley. I'm going to check out some opportunities."

"Like what? The town is doing OK, but it's not a real hotbed for a business start-up."

"You seem to be doing alright for yourself. You've got a bunch of apartments, and they have to be worth something."

Bruised knuckles and sore knees came with the rent checks. "Most of the time it sucks, but it's building up and I should be able to do pretty well when the time comes. Besides, I'm looking at a building right now, maybe do some commercial stuff instead of just apartments"

Phil thought this over for a while, chewed on the words.

"I'm going to see if the Chief has a few minutes to see me, Dave. I want to talk to him about maybe reopening the case on Catherine. Maybe even get that sick old Malcolm Prudhomme to finally confess like he should have done in the first place. And if the police won't put the squeeze on Malcolm, then maybe I will. I'll catch you later."

He pushed his plate aside and left.

The Chief was looking over some paperwork when Phil Marchand was shown in by the dispatcher at the front desk. After some handshaking and congratulating, Phil explained his mission while Wetman took notes.

Wetman paid close attention to Phil Marchand and didn't ask many questions. While he was expecting Phil to come in ever since Lou Pellerin got wind of Marchand's pending return to Apsley, he didn't want to be spending a lot of time looking into a cold homicide this early in his new career. After fifteen minutes of note taking, they parted ways, Wetman remaining non-committal. He did agree, though, to discuss the matter with assistant chief Pellerin.

"What about talking to Malcolm Prudhomme?"

"Look, Mr. Marchand, I'm brand new here, but I've heard that name. I'll look into this with the Assistant Chief. If there's a reason to rethink the investigation from twenty-nine years ago, we definitely will."

When Phil Marchand was gone, Wetman reread his notes. If there were any files in Apsley on this case, Wetman would be among the last to know where they might be. The basement? A locker somewhere? He had no clue. Who knows? In a town as small and as tightly knit as Apsley, maybe the case was the subject of local folklore. Maybe Lou knew the details already. In any case, he went back to his paperwork and set the matter of Catherine Marchand aside.

* * *

Before the business day came to a close, George Wessel sat at his desk with a can of diet soda. The store would close in another five minutes. George saw Betty Forman rummaging through a shoebox that served as her collection of random items. She'd toss stray pencils, paper clips, elastic bands, nails and other such items in the open shoebox under the counter. When it got sufficiently full, she'd attend to the task of sorting through the contents and returning them to their proper places: pens in with the pens, paper clips in the paper clip jar, etc. There was no set schedule for this little routine and George just figured that the time had come.

"Betty," he said, with a question. She looked up from her task and waited for him to continue. "Do you have a minute?"

"Well," she looked down at the shoebox. "I'm in the middle of something, but I can take a break. What's up?"

George went to the front door, locked it, hung his "closed" sign and came back to his desk where Betty was already waiting. George smiled when she walked over and took a seat. He knew that Betty didn't stop her sorting without some regret, so he felt blessed that his questioning was sufficient motivation. "Malcolm Prudhomme. You must have known him all your life."

"Malcolm is a pathetic creature, George. Take a close look at that man someday and you'll see what I mean."

"Not Mr. America. I'll give you that." That was an understatement. He was the antithesis of personal attraction. Malcolm was perhaps five-foot seven and had a face that looked like it had met more than one angry fist in his lifetime. Most of his teeth were gone. George wondered if they were knocked out, pulled out, or just escaped of their own volition. What few he had left were crooked yellowed stumps. "He's got a reputation as a sort of . . ." He was reaching for the least offensive way to say it to Betty.

"Degenerate. A freak. That's Malcolm. We always thought

he was a weirdo, even when he was just a youngster. What about him?"

"It's just that. Was he always like that? I mean, all his life?"

"Pretty much. One thing you could always count on if you were going to see young girls playing tennis, or basketball, you'd find Malcolm. Usually pretty harmless, but I've heard stories."

"Did you ever hear of him actually hurting anyone?"

"Like I said, usually pretty harmless, but there were always rumors about him grabbing a girl and trying to touch them. No stories about him ever getting to the point of, you know, actually causing physical harm. Don't think he could, truth be known. My guess is he caused a lot more psychological damage to some young girls in this town over the years."

"Was he ever arrested? Was he ever in jail? I mean, what he's done can be serious. It's assault, even if he was never successful."

"He's been in and out of the police station dozens of times, usually when parents complain that he was ogling their little girls. When that Marchand girl was murdered, Malcolm was a suspect and they kept him in jail for a while. But nothing ever happened and they had to let him go."

"But he was never put in jail?"

"Never went that far. I do remember that he was sent away one time to some sort of funny farm years ago. Might have sent him there more than once, for all I know. I think they tried medicating him or something. But I can't tell you much about that. Just rumor."

"And no family?"

"Now that's the funny thing, George. Malcolm comes from a big family. I think he's got four brothers and five sisters. Poor as dirt farmers, the Prudhommes. But I give those kids credit; they were hard workers. The old man was a drunk and so was the mother. The kids took care of each other, all except Malcolm, and nobody could help him. But they all moved away long ago and Malcolm is the only one left."

"And the house? It's his?"

"Oh, yes. I remember one of his sisters, she used to come in here way back before you bought this place and before she moved away. Jeanette, I think her name was. She was sort of the mother hen of the clan, and she told me that all the brothers and sisters agreed that Malcolm couldn't make it on his own and they all signed over their interests in the house to him. Then she moved away just like the rest of them. I've wondered more than once if they kept any contact with him. I wouldn't blame them if they didn't."

"Thanks, Betty. I knew you'd know the story. You know everybody around here."

"I should be paid for all the information I got stored up here. I swear I've gone to that historical society museum they have at the library and I'm always finding mistakes. Instead of doing all their research, most of which is just plain wrong, they should just ask me. What's with all this interest in Malcolm, by the way? Something to do with Philip Marchand coming back? Or that rumor going around about him stalking some young thing over by the pond?"

"You should have been a newspaper reporter, Betty. You know everything that's going on."

"And Malcolm's been walking around with a big bandage on his jaw. I can still put two and two together, George. Some father caught up with Malcolm. It's happened before. You'd think at his age he'd finally learn a thing or two."

"I'll bet."

"And if this new Chief knows what's good for him, he'll get to know Malcolm Prudhomme. Remember Claude Raines who played the policeman in *Casablanca*? Well I'd put Malcolm on my list of 'the usual suspects.' If that new Wetman guy does his job, he'll get to know Malcolm real soon."

NINE

Sunday

"So, Lou, is this the whole thing?"

They were standing in the basement of the town hall in a locked storage area for old police department files. Lou Pellerin, as Wetman suspected, knew where the Catherine Marchand files were as soon as Wetman asked. It was Pellerin, as well, who insisted that he come in on this Sunday morning to help the Chief start sifting through whatever they found.

Wetman and Pellerin were looking at two large dusty cartons, cardboard evidence boxes. In black marker on the ends of both cartons: "Marchand, Catherine", plus a case number and the date of her death.

"That's everything we have, Chief."

"You know, if this murder took place today, we probably wouldn't have much evidence here to show for it. The District Attorneys today usually bring in their own State Police investigating team, especially in a small town like Apsley. Most of the evidence would end up in some county or state office building."

"I know. Back when Catherine Marchand was killed, it was a different story."

"Well, let's take a look." He started to open up the box nearer him. Inside were six thick files of documents. He picked them up one by one and read the labels before stacking them on an old desk. The first one read: Statements of family members. The second one was marked: Interviews with neighbors near murder scene. The third contained medical and lab reports as well as autopsy photographs. The fourth was labeled Photographs—Crime Scene. The fifth was Interviews—Suspicious Persons. Finally there was a file marked Time Line, Statements, Miscellaneous—Clippings, Etc. This last one was bound with a thick rubber band that crumbled into a dozen pieces when Wetman picked it up.

"Want me to open the second box?" Lou was reaching for the second box as he asked.

"Sure. Let's take a look at both of these. Let's make sure we don't get too wrapped up in this right now, though. There's a ton of stuff I need to go over upstairs, and, sad to say, Catherine Marchand isn't going anywhere."

Lou agreed. He knew about these cartons but had never opened them up in all the years he was on the force. He knew he could get absorbed in these cartons very quickly, and he suspected he'd recognize most of the names in the files that were assembled twenty-nine years ago.

"Lou, is anybody still around who was on the force back then?"

"Anybody who worked here then is either retired or dead by now. I think Bill Turner is still alive, but he must be ninety by now. I'll bet we see his name on a bunch of this stuff because he was the detective on the force when I was just a little kid."

"I'll bet our buddy Mr. Philip Marchand hires some detective agency to come in. I get a sense he thinks his sister was short changed when nobody was charged or tried. He'll pull something, I'll bet on it."

"He's got the money to do it."

He looked at his watch and Wetman noticed.

"What do you say, twenty minutes?"

Lou nodded. So far, Wetman was looking like a decent guy. He wasn't going to pass full judgment on the new Chief just yet, but so far so good.

They looked inside the second carton. Inside were clear plastic evidence bags with assorted clothing. The labels indicated that these were the clothes that Catherine Marchand was wearing when they found her. One was labeled simply "Top". In it was a polo-type shirt, yellow and stained heavily with brown spots, dried blood. Many of the spots had circular holes, most likely from investigators at the lab testing blood samples.

Others bags were labeled Shorts, Underpants, Brassiere, Hose and Shoes. Several smaller bags were labeled Kerchief, Earrings, Belt, Barrettes, Watch, Purse, Contents of Purse, and Other Evidence Photographs. Another larger plastic bag held several smaller ones. Visible inside were such things as a nail and some small pieces of glass.

"Ever seen this stuff, Lou?"

"Never. This is the first time. I've heard a lot about it but never saw any of this."

"Well, let's each grab a file and start looking through them. We can use that table over there."

Wetman pointed to a plain metal table at the side of the room. Side by side, the two sat and started the task of reading over everything that had been written and documented about the murder of Catherine Marchand.

In twenty minutes, Wetman had to nudge Lou to get his attention. "Let's call it a day right now and thanks for coming in on a Sunday morning, Lou. We can go back to this tomorrow."

Lou, though, was caught up in the case already and asked if he could keep at it for a while longer. The case had captured his attention and he wanted to learn more about it.

Lou Pellerin examined the contents of several clear plastic envelopes that represented items collected from the scene. He spread them across the metal table in the storage room in two rows of three. The first held a Coca Cola bottle cap and the notation on the envelope indicated that it was found five inches from the left foot of the victim and that no fingerprints were found. A second contained a wrapper from a piece of Juicy Fruit gum; a single print was found but never connected to any person. Pellerin made a note to locate that print and submit it to the national data base. There was a slim chance that it belonged to someone whose prints had since been added in the past twenty-nine years. A third held a cigarette butt, a Tareyton filter, not crushed.

The fourth envelope held a rusted nail about three inches long and the notation indicated it had been found eighteen inches from the right shoulder of the victim. A fifth envelope held a white plastic button that had been identified as matching a missing button from the victim's top.

A sixth contained a broken Timex watch with a gold-colored case and a black leather band. It also contained several small pieces of thin glass. The notation on the envelope said that the watch was attached to the victim's left wrist and that the face of the watch was broken, probably in a defensive motion by the victim. A clear partial print appeared on the watch but it matched the victim. The pieces of glass appeared to match the smashed crystal from that watch.

The seventh and final envelope in this package held four photographs. One was of a lady's pin in the shape of the letter "C" and holding several jewels identified as red and clear rhinestones. Alongside the pin was a ruler to indicate the size of the pin. A second photograph was of the back of the pin. On the rear of the photograph appeared a handwritten notation that the pin was shown as found, with the clasp closed. It was found under the victim's left shoulder. Blood on the pin was identified as the victim's. No discernable prints were found.

A second pair of photographs showed an Apsley High School class ring, also shown with a ruler adjacent; a second photo showed the back of the ring. A note on the back indicated that the ring was on the victim's ring finger of her right hand, that the victim's initials appeared on the inside of the band along with trace amounts of blood identified as Catherine's.

A piece of yellowed note paper clipped to this group of photographs indicated that the pin and the ring were cleaned and returned to the victim's parents on December 16, some weeks after Catherine's murder.

Lou stared at the items on his desk top and wondered what, if any, information he might gain from them. There were few murder investigations in his background, but he knew that almost every criminal act left a trail of evidence; in his experience perpetrators weren't smart. The challenge was sifting through the evidence. The clues existed somewhere; he'd just try to assemble the evidence and look for them.

The light from the single bulb over the table cast a sallow glow across the surface of the table. Lou stood, rubbed his eyes, and then slipped on a pair of latex gloves. Removing a penlight from his shirt pocket, he took out the evidence from the plastic bags, peered at each piece of evidence on the desk and studied them.

The bottle cap, he felt, was unlikely to yield anything of value. The area where Catherine was found was not far from the path past Squash Pond and this was likely some litter disposed of by someone earlier. Besides, there were no prints. Even if Catherine or her murderer had drunk a bottle of Coke and tossed the cap, there was no bottle and no prints. He could have the cap checked for DNA, but it would be a long shot at best. And any DNA would have to come from scraped skin by whoever removed the cap, surely degraded by now. Besides, the murder took place before every soda bottle had screw-off caps; this one was bent by a bottle opener, so the chance of finding any DNA was between nil and nothing.

The nail was just as likely a discarded item, and again, no prints were found and no nail marks were found on the victim. It was just another item collected at the scene and could have been there for years before the murder.

The gum wrapper might yield something of value, but that was surely another long shot. He'd have to wait for a response from the print database in any event. The white button appeared to hold no promise as it matched a missing button from Catherine's blouse. It likely was torn off during her struggle and simply landed there.

The watch and the pieces of crystal were intriguing if only to show that Catherine most likely tried to fend off a blow from the murderer. The hands of the watch, smashed flat by the blow, were set to five seventeen and that matched the medical examiner's approximate time of death.

Lou then paid close attention the photographs of the jeweled pin and the class ring. The pin was the kind of bling you'd find at any jewelry store or a mall kiosk. Probably twenty dollars more or less at today's prices. A gift from her parents or a boyfriend. Or maybe Catherine bought it for herself.

The ring was standard issue. Lou Pellerin's class ring from several years later had the same design and the same deep garnet colored stone.

Lou looked at the photographs and wondered how the pin happened to be found on the ground near Catherine. Torn off during the struggle, probably. Her watch was smashed; a button was torn off. Most likely, since the clasp was closed when it was found, the pin was ripped from her clothing during the same battle as she fought for her life.

If the clues were here, he couldn't see them. He'd by now seen the crime scene photos with the twisted wreckage of the young girl, plus the gruesome autopsy photos. He'd read the summaries from the medical examiner who performed the autopsy. He'd sifted through the two cartons of evidence. Frustrated, he replaced everything in their plastic bags, stripped off the latex gloves and sat at the table, thinking.

Phil Marchand sat at the desk in his motel room and flipped though his Blackberry looking for a number. When he found it, he picked up the phone and dialed.

Most mortals would have a difficult time getting direct access to the governor, especially on a Sunday, but Phil had developed precious connections over the years. He'd met the governor several years ago when Phil was CFO of a chemical firm and the governor was chief counsel at a competing company. They struck up a friendship and Phil kept track of everybody; the practice served him well. When the governor answered his private line at home, there were good wishes all around.

"Jack, I need some help and I think maybe you can give it to me." Phil's first-name familiarity was practiced. He wondered, one time long ago, if he might have been better served had he chosen politics instead of finance as a career.

The governor was only too happy to hear Phil out. Yes, he could make sure someone on his staff checked the situation out. Yes, he'd get the State Police involved. And yes, he'd be happy to have a drink with Phil now that he was moving back to his home state. "If you're back in Apsley, then you're officially a constituent, Phil. I need your vote, and I just may call on you sometime for help myself."

Phil Marchand knew what that meant in politico-speak. Fund-raising was never too far from a politician's mind. Phil, with his personal wealth and his contacts with the rich and powerful, could be useful to the governor in the future.

When he hung up, he wished he could be a fly on the wall when the Apsley Police Chief found out that the State Police would be brought in to the case, and perhaps even lead the investigation. After years at the top of the corporate hierarchy, Phil was used to exercising his authority. This was no different. He'd get these bumpkins reassigned to traffic duty where they belonged. Malcolm would be brought in for some serious interrogation, and a confession would result. Phil Marchand had come to demand and expect results over the course of his career and was not about to modify his habits now.

When he hung up, he noticed that his right hand was trembling. He wanted to assign this to stress and excitement, but he knew better. He reached for his toiletry kit and found the bottle he wanted, uncapped it and took out a large white tablet, swallowing it without water. Only four left, he thought as he fumbled with the bottle to replace the cap.

Chief Wetman went home that night with a note pad filled with questions. He tried being good company for his wife at dinner, but she could tell he was preoccupied.

"What's wrong, Jerry? Something happen at work?"

"Just an old case we're reopening, Mary Alice." He gave her the details. Murder twenty-nine years ago of a young girl. Only one suspect at the time, but he was exonerated. No good leads. And the victim's brother, a big corporate guy, has just retired and come back to town asking questions and almost insisting that everyone drop what they're doing and jump on his sister's case.

"And here's the deal. Almost everybody that was close to this victim is still right here in Apsley, even the old perverted fart that the police thought they had for the murder. Everyone else was someplace else, as far as we can tell."

He sat down at his desk after dinner and tried to assemble the facts as he knew them, and they were sparse. This was a new place for him, and he didn't know all the characters yet. Lou Pellerin filled him in on the personalities of the people who were there at the time and the circle of friends that surrounded Catherine Marchand, but it wasn't making sense to him yet.

He looked at the list Lou drew up for him:

Nancy Easter, scholarship to Columbia but dropped out. Never married. Works at the Apsley library.

Lourdes Freitas, got a full scholarship to Brown, then med school in Chicago, and now a physician and working at a New York teaching hospital.

Tina Kerrigan Gladwell, from a prominent family that used to run some factories in town, used to own and run a health club in town, married to Ken Gladwell.

Ken Gladwell, engineer, partner at a large firm, well-known, has a bad temper, rumor that he and wife might be getting a divorce.

Dave Blondin, divorced, used to date Catherine, owns some apartment buildings in town.

Malcolm Prudhomme, elderly, reputation as a pervert, still lives in town, was a suspect in Marchand murder but never charged.

Philip Marchand, left Apsley after graduation, became a corporate exec, separated recently from wife, just returned to Apsley. Wetman had his own notes on him.

George Wessel, owns a dry cleaners, good rep.

Max Zenga, hard worker, good rep, also known to have a temper.

Bob Hayes, funeral director, good rep.

Elissa Summers went to school at Berkeley and never returned, publisher of an alternative lifestyle magazine on the west coast.

There were thirty-one names on the list. Pellerin knew details on just about everyone in town and Wetman was glad to have him as the number two guy on the force.

Wetman studied the list and made notes. Most of them were accounted for during the time the murder took place. Nancy Easter was at a math meet in another town but returned around the same time as the murder; Dave Blondin was out of town at the time of the crime visiting a relative with his parents at the regional hospital and didn't return until later; Tina Gladwell was at the high school where she was cleaning and organizing athletic and sports equipment. Lourdes Freitas was with Gordon Jefts at Lourdes' home. Elissa Summers was at home at the time. Ken Gladwell was seen at six o'clock at the diner where he bought a milkshake. All had been checked out by the detective at the time, Bill Turner.

If these people had committed this horrible crime, there'd be some evidence, some stray hair, some skin, some blood stains on their clothes. No weapon was ever found. Everything appeared to have been checked with no results.

Except for Malcolm, whose alibi was weak. He was known to walk the same path on occasion by Squash Pond. No one saw him that day in the vicinity, but he wasn't seen anywhere else either.

He was getting nowhere, but he felt like he was getting to know the machinations of the community a little better.

Then he looked at the crude map that Lou sketched out of the murder site. Squash Pond was between the high school . . . now a middle school . . . and another neighborhood. It was a swampy area and there was some higher ground with a well worn path that was used as a shortcut from time to time, especially by the kids who went to school there. Catherine Marchand's home was in that adjacent neighborhood, and it was likely that she was using the shortcut to go home when she was attacked.

Catherine's activities on the day she was killed intrigued the chief. She was described by some witnesses as preoccupied the day she was killed. She had met with her cheerleading coach after school and said she wanted to quit. The coach was surprised; after all, Catherine was the captain. The coach asked Catherine to rethink her decision and they'd talk about it the next day. Of course, for Catherine, there was no next day.

She also was seen walking downtown after school, and the pharmacist at the drug store where Catherine worked part-time said she had stopped in that day and quit. Too much going on in her life, with sports and college applications, and cheerleading; she'd have to give up her job.

Curious behavior for a young girl with her life ahead of her, Wetman thought. Something was bothering this girl. He'd do some more digging tomorrow and hoped that Pellerin could fill him in some more.

From another room, he could hear his wife, Mary Alice, shuffling about as she put some things away. There were cardboard boxes everywhere and he wanted to move into something permanent soon. He walked over to one carton and opened it up, removed his small stereo from it and set it on a bookcase. In a few minutes, the strains of the aria *Habanera* from *Carmen* flowed through the apartment. When he went into the kitchen to see if he could help Mary Alice, she was at the stove cooking and smiling. He wrapped his arms around his wife, kissed her neck and swayed with her to the music.

TEN

Tuesday, the following week

Lou Pellerin walked into police headquarters this morning expecting a comparatively uneventful day. Monday had been spent doing routine duties before he settled in with the evidence reports of Catherine Marchand's murder. He didn't find anything that he didn't expect, but the ordeal was exhausting and he was looking forward to setting the file aside for a while.

His expectations were dashed when Officer Henry Bruno, the oldest and most senior member of the force stepped into Pellerin's office and closed the door. "Hank the Tank", as he was known in town, was red in the face and Lou Pellerin thought he saw smoke coming out of his ears.

"Look at this bullshit," Bruno said as he waved a sheet of paper in front of Lou's face. "This is going to the union, you can trust me on that!" Bruno's enormous bulk, stored largely in his gut, was shaking.

Lou, who'd barely settled into his swivel chair when Bruno

appeared, rose in place and took the paper, saying, "Go back and open the door, Hank. I'll look at this, but no one closes my door unless I ask them to."

Bruno did as he was told but his boiling rage remained on the surface. "Fire me. I don't give a shit. Fire me, Lou. But don't treat people like this."

"Take a deep breath, Hank, and relax. Let me look at this." Lou waited until Bruno stopped fidgeting and took a deep breath. Lou took his reading glasses from his pocket. When he'd finished, he put the paper down on his desk. "Where did you find this?"

"On the bulletin board in the squad room. Right in the middle where everyone could see it."

The bulletin board usually had notices that included shift schedules and general announcements. Wetman, apparently, found another use for the board when he posted the notice this morning:

FOR SALE
Officer Henry Bruno's Smith & Wesson Semiautomatic Pistol
Never Fired, Only Dropped Once
See Chief Wetman for Details

Lou tried to remain deadly serious. Bruno was the only officer who failed to show up at the pistol range for mandatory practice. This notice was Wetman's not so subtle way of advising the department that he meant business. Bruno earned this embarrassment, but he was also a brave and loyal police officer; if you were going into a dangerous situation, you wanted Bruno at your side. Right now, he just needed a little guidance.

"Hank, Hank, Hank. Don't you see what he's doing? You're the only one in the department who didn't get to the range yet for practice."

"I don't care, Lou. This is downright nasty."

So Hank the Tank is a sensitive guy, Lou mused.

"So what are you going to do about it, Hank?"

"I'm calling a union meeting, that's what I'm going to do. You better let your boss know that I'm not putting up with this stuff. No way."

Lou walked around to the front of his desk and sat on the edge. "Grab a chair, Hank. Let's think this over." Bruno moved to a seat and parked his rump on the front edge.

"You've got what, thirty years on the force?"

"Almost thirty-two."

"And when was the last time you went to the range? Two years ago?"

"That's not the point, Lou. You know it isn't." But Lou could see a sense of embarrassment cross over Bruno's face.

"Let's just say you go out to the range after your shift today and do what everyone else did. Let's say that you go down there and actually fire your weapon, shoot your rounds and clean the weapon. Let's start there before you run off to the union. What do you say? No reason to get all bent out of shape over this right now. After all, in another year or so, you're going to retire and you're going to turn in your badge and your weapon and go fishing, right? Don't you have a cabin at the lake?"

"Right, Lou, but . . ."

Lou cut him off. "I'll go see the Chief and this won't happen again, Hank. But please, make sure there's a firing range report on my desk the first thing in the morning. You're too valuable a police officer to let this get in the way of your career. Come on, Hank."

He put his arm around Bruno's shoulders, barely reaching half way around, and walked him to the door, never stopping at the doorway. Bruno had settled down and was heading back to the squad room. Lou made a straight path to Wetman's office.

"Hank Bruno just talked to me."

"Don't tell me, he didn't like the want ad, did he?"

"Not a bit. His feelings are hurt. He's afraid what the other guys are going to say. "

"They won't say a word, Lou, because the only ones to see it were Henry Bruno, you, and me. I waited until I saw him coming in before I pinned it to the bulletin board. Then I went out the door before he saw me in there."

Lou nodded, appreciating the game.

"And unless you or I or Officer Bruno say anything, nobody's going to know a thing." Wetman looked back at the paperwork on his desk. "So what else is on your mind?"

Lou said nothing and started walking back to his office, a half-smile on his face. On his way, passing the front desk, he saw an elderly woman holding a thick file and talking to the receptionist/dispatcher. He thought she looked familiar but couldn't connect a name with the face. When he got back to his office, the light bulb in his head went on: Mrs. Poore, the doctor's wife. He thought to himself: I wonder what she's doing here.

Twenty minutes later, Wetman was perusing the file that he'd just received. He got to a section that caused him to gasp. He read the section again, then put his hand on the intercom and said, "Lucy, tell Lou to get in here on the double."

In a few moments there was a knock at the door and Lou stuck his head around the corner as he opened the door. "You wanted to see me?"

"Come in and close the door. Grab a seat and tell me what you think." He slid the page over to the other side of the desk so Lou could read it.

When he sat down, Lou slipped a pair of reading glasses from his shirt pocket. He hunched over the document and read every word. Wetman, meanwhile, rose from his seat and stared out the window of his office. After a few minutes, Lou let out a low whistle. "Holy suffering cats. Holy shit! This is unbelievable."

Catherine Marchand, the notes said, was pregnant at the time of her death.

"So you never heard anything about this before? No rumors? Nothing?" Wetman returned to the desk and sat.

"Never," Lou said, still looking at the doctor's notes. "This is the first time. Where did these notes come from?"

"I got it from the files of that doctor that died about a month ago."

"Doctor Poore? I thought that was Mrs. Poore at the front desk a while ago."

"That was her. She was clearing out his papers, sending files on active patients to other doctors around here and she saw a file on Catherine Marchand. She said she was surprised he kept it all these years and she called here. She said she knew that Philip was back in Apsley and figured we'd be interested. Her husband did the autopsy at the hospital, but apparently he didn't put this information in the autopsy file. Instead, he kept them himself under lock and key at his office. He'd been sitting on this ever since."

"Holy crap? Why? This is serious! This could have changed the whole direction of the investigation."

"I talked with Mrs. Poore few minutes ago when she dropped off the file. Seems like a nice lady. She told me that her husband was devastated by the girl's murder. She and her husband were close friends of the Marchands, went to the same church and socialized together."

"But what if Catherine's boyfriend, the father of this child, knew about the pregnancy and killed her?"

"That's what I'd like you to look at, Lou."

"Do you think she looked at the file? Do you think she knows about Catherine's pregnancy?"

"I got that impression, and I even asked, but she's a coy lady. She didn't admit it, but she danced around the question. I think we have to assume she knows that Catherine was pregnant."

Lou put his glasses back in his pocket. "I'll call her right now."

"Wait a second. After you talk to her, check the records at the hospital and see if they kept any records of the autopsy, especially any slides. Maybe there's something we can use."

"Like DNA? Catherine Marchand's murder took place way before those tests were around."

"I'm not sure. They can do incredible things with one little drop of blood today. I just want to get a better idea of what's available to us."

Lou stood up and moved the paper back in front of Wetman. He didn't move immediately to leave and asked, "Chief, I know this is a huge deal, this pregnancy, but how much do you think we ought to make of it?"

Wetman looked up at Pellerin, puzzled.

"Look, I understand that Phil Marchand wants to find out what happened, and so do we. So now we find out she was pregnant when she died. This information could have been huge back when she was killed. It's probably not going to get us a murderer after all this time, I don't know. But maybe it's going to make things worse. For Phil, I mean."

Wetman looked down at the report and back up at Lou. There was a prolonged silence. "I understand what you're thinking, Lou, but there's no statute of limitations on this. Somebody killed a young girl and we still don't know who. If we find out something about this pregnancy, it could lead us down a different path. And maybe we learn something else. But I understand. This is just between us right now. Nothing goes to Phil Marchand on this unless we find out a lot more. OK?"

Lou nodded. It's what he wanted to hear. He made an appointment to see Mrs. Poore in an hour and left the office. He'd drive to the hospital later to see if there was anything at all still there that might help.

Mildred Poore had managed her husband's office until he retired and both she and her husband were fixtures in the community. When she greeted Lou Pellerin at the front door of her home, she took his hand in both of hers and welcomed him into the living room where they both sat. After a few minutes of condolences and a few memories, Pellerin got right to the key questions.

"Mrs. Poore, first of all, both the Chief and I are grateful that you dropped off the file on Catherine Marchand. But why do you think your husband kept this information to himself for all these years?"

She nodded her head as Lou asked the question, understanding its importance. "Sure. You're right. There was important information in that file that might have been considered helpful at the time. And believe me, when I read the file myself, I was stunned."

Lou had his notebook on his knee, pen ready, but took no notes for the moment. He waited for her to continue.

"We were very close to Catherine's parents. I'm sure Chief Wetman told you that. My husband would not have wanted to cause any more pain to that family than they had already suffered."

Lou nodded and was about to ask a follow up question, but she continued.

"And I believe he knew more than he wrote in that file. I've given this some thought, of course. It wasn't like my husband to do something like this. After all, he was the Medical Examiner for this area besides running his own practice, and he worked with the police on many cases over the years. He knew its importance. That's why I think Catherine told him who the father of her child was."

"Why do you think that?"

"Well, two reasons. First of all, it was like my husband to ask. He was known to be discrete, of course, but I think he would have asked. If nothing else, he'd want to know if this was the result of a rape. It's been known to happen, you know, even in Apsley. Incest is no stranger here, either, unfortunately. But the second reason is, my husband would have said something to the police as soon as Catherine was murdered . . . unless . . . and that is a big 'unless' . . . he knew for certain that the father of the child couldn't possibly have been involved in her murder.

"That's why I believe he must have known that, known that the father was clear of suspicion . . . probably another case involving close friends in this small town . . . and decided to remain silent about it."

Lou was quiet for a moment as he considered this.

"You think he did his own investigation? That he decided that the father of this unborn child couldn't have murdered Catherine?"

"I wouldn't use those same words and say he did his own investigation. But if he knew the father and knew that the father couldn't have possibly been involved in her death, then maybe he reached that conclusion: Making that information known would not have enlightened anyone involved with the investigation, and would cause great grief to the families for no worthwhile reason."

"And he never said anything to you about this?"

"My husband and I were very close. He shared information about patients with me that would be considered illegal in today's world of medical privacy. But no, he never told me anything about Catherine's pregnancy. I was as astonished when I leafed through the file as you were."

Apsley still had a small hospital, even though the population really didn't warrant such an investment. It served mostly as an emergency room and walk in clinic now, and more serious cases went to the regional hospital fourteen miles away.

But years ago, it provided a greater level of in patient hospital care: Minor surgery, X-rays, a maternity ward, and the like. A small room downstairs served as a morgue and functioned as an autopsy room on occasion. Dr. Poore did Catherine's there, and Lou Pellerin asked at the front desk about getting access to the old files. Agnes Norgaard had been at the front reception desk for as long as Lou could remember. She pointed down the hall and said, "Ask Linda. I think she's in her office."

It took Linda Gariepy, the administrator, twenty minutes to make her way through the cartons in the basement with Lou Pellerin at her side. The room was surprisingly bright and clean and there were stacks of boxes neatly piled as high as they could go against one painted concrete block wall. It was air-conditioned and there was one wall with a refrigerated case where the body of a recently deceased could be placed until it was picked up.

"There used to be an autopsy table right in the middle." Gariepy was trying to figure out which box might hold the information Lou wanted. "We're going to have to find a place to put this stuff someday. Almost everything we've done for the past seven years is on film, tape or disk, but I don't think anyone's going to want to spend the money to digitize all this stuff. Some of this goes back to the thirties."

She and Lou were trying to makes heads or tails from the markings on the ends of the cartons. There was little order that Lou could understand. They looked like they were just randomly stacked. Linda moved a ladder from the wall to one stack of boxes and went up to the second step. "I think we're getting warm. These are from the right period. See?"

She explained the numbering and lettering system as she scanned the boxes. She tapped one and said. "Here. This should be it." The carton was three down from the top and she started to slide the top carton off and pass it down to Lou. "It's not too heavy, but be careful. You can just set it on the floor." She slid the second box out, passed it down, and reached for the third box, the one Lou wanted to pore through.

When she stepped off the ladder she said, "Bring that with you and you can use the empty office down the hall to look through it." He did as he was told and found a clean table top and a chair in the otherwise empty space. "Let me know when you're finished and I'll arrange to get everything put back where it belongs."

Lou thanked her and sat down with the carton in front of him. He opened it up and saw a neat arrangement by date of files on every death that occurred in the year at the hospital. Some had just a page or two in their folders; others were in red pressboard folders thick with documents and envelopes containing, he hoped, slides and other test results.

It took Lou a few minutes to put his hand on the correct folder and he removed it from the carton, double checking the box to make sure nothing had slipped out. He put the cover back on the box, placed it on the floor and set the Catherine Marchand autopsy file in front of him. Taking a deep breath, he opened it up and began to read.

The body was that of a well-nourished female, Dr. Poore wrote in a hand that was remarkably readable by M.D. standards. She appeared to be approximately seventeen years old and was brought to the hospital morgue at 9:50 the night before. The time was now 4:25 AM. The clothing was removed and placed in plastic sterile bags for testing of the blood and fluid stains by the county's crime lab. They would be delivered to the police.

The lower limbs were intact and had superficial abrasions only. The torso was severely lacerated and showed signs of crushing injuries, especially in the area of the shoulders. The arms were similarly lacerated and crushed. Dr. Poore described Catherine's skull as having suffered multiple catastrophic injuries.

He noted lividity in the jaw, buttocks and feet, and noted that his prior night's estimate of the time of death was approximately two hours before his arrival at the crime scene, or about 5:00 pm.

So far, Lou didn't see anything that he hadn't seen before. This looked like the same sort of paperwork he saw in the file at the station. He flipped to the second page, then the third, scanning every page for more details.

In twenty minutes, Lou completed his examination of the written report but curiously there was no mention in the report file about a fetus. So far, the only mention was in the file that Chief Wetman had on his desk, and that was from the file that Dr. Poore kept at his office, not in the autopsy file where it should have been. Pellerin made some more notes.

Then he opened the file of autopsy photos. They were gruesome, to be sure, but he'd seen most of the same things in the police file. Nothing new. He closed the envelope and set it aside.

There was a third envelope, a thick padded one affixed to the file and that's where he found individual sealed plastic bags. Pellerin assumed these were slides and sealed vials of tissue samples, along with some vials that appeared to once contain liquids, now all turned to powder and scale. One held some brown and grey material and was tagged "Fingernail Scrapings." He set that aside.

The slides were all labeled clearly: Lung, Heart, Liver, Brain, Sputum, Vaginal Smear, Cervical Smear, and finally one that told Pellerin he'd completed his search. One plastic bag held two slides: "Fetal tissue, approx age eight weeks." Along with the slides was a plain sheet of paper, folded up tightly. On it was written: "5/8, no sex determined." It also contained the date of the autopsy.

Why did Doctor Poore leave the incriminating slides here if he didn't include the information on his report? Lou Pellerin wondered at this. Did he want to leave some trail, even if it was almost hidden? Did he simply forget the slides were in here?

The slides were intact, but Lou had no idea if any of the material would be useful to the technicians of a crime lab. He placed the test results and slides back into the padded envelope, restored the balance of the file to the carton and put the cover back on. He put the carton back in its place in the storage room, replaced the other two cartons that were sitting on the floor, shut off the light and left. He'd stop by Linda's office and let her know that he was removing the padded envelope. Then he'd sit down with the Chief and have a meeting about what he found.

Phil Marchand sat in his Mercedes and watched. Directly across the street was the home of Malcolm Prudhomme. The house was probably painted white at one time, but almost all evidence of that last paint job was long gone. The clapboards were weathered gray and the downspouts that remained were sagging or gone altogether. A front porch apparently once had a railing and balusters at one time, all of which had disappeared.

Marchand had been parked in this same location for an hour, a Nikon camera with a telephoto lens on the passenger seat.

There was no movement from inside the Prudhomme home save for the movement of a curtain about forty minutes ago.

The postal delivery truck went by seven or eight minutes ago and Marchand was hoping to see Malcolm step outside to retrieve his mail.

Patience was not Phil Marchand's strong suit and he flipped open his cell phone and punched in a series of numbers he'd memorized earlier. He waited for the call to be answered, which it was on the third ring.

"Hello, you perverted old man. Do you remember me? Philip Marchand? Remember? You killed my sister, you bastard. Come on out, Malcolm. Come out and get your mail. Let me get a good look at you."

The phone was hung up and Marchand pressed redial. It rang without answer.

A few minutes later, the front door to Malcolm's home opened and the old man appeared. Dressed in a plaid flannel shirt and rumpled jeans, he carefully stepped down from the porch and walked with a pronounced limp to the mailbox.

Phil was quick to grab the camera, open his car door and start taking pictures. Malcolm looked up once and then averted his gaze, and walked back as quickly as he could manage to the safety of his home with his mail in hand.

"That's it, you old bastard. Walk away. You murderer! You murderer!"

Malcolm slammed the door.

Phil returned to his car and left.

I took the call on my cell phone. This was no small feat as I was twisted like a pretzel inside the base of a kitchen cabinet trying to handle a wrench and a flashlight when the phone rang. It was Gordon Jefts.

"Hi, Gord. What's up?"

Gordon Jefts sounded nervous. "Dave, I need to talk to you. As soon as possible."

Gordon had a history of high drama, but this time he

sounded genuinely anxious and upset. "I'm just fixing a sink and I'll be out of here in ten minutes. At your office?"

"Jesus, no! Someplace else. Your place."

"Fine," I said. "I'll be there as soon as I'm done here."

The phone went silent. I wondered as I finished installing the new drain what might be bothering my friend. I finished the job, wiped down the pipes and crawled out from underneath the counter.

I was putting my tools back in the case and wondered what the hell I was doing here at my age getting all twisted up and cramped to save a few dollars. This was becoming a common refrain for me, especially after finishing a job that taxed my creaking bones, like this one. I eventually dismissed my complaints as whining and in a few minutes I was approaching the driveway to my apartment and saw Gordon standing near the front door.

"Christ, Gordon, what's got your shorts in a knot?"

Gordon didn't smile but made a hurrying motion with his hands. "I need to fill you in. Let's get inside."

I opened my apartment door and set my tool kit on the floor and out of the way. "Let me have something to drink first. My back hurts and my shoulders ache, and I'm getting old, Gordy. I need to sit down for a second. Want a soda?"

"OK. OK." Something serious was on his mind.

We sat down at the kitchen table and Gordon spoke in earnest. "I looked at some things this morning and it bothers me. It bothers me a lot."

"What?"

"I'm not supposed to have done this and I could get into some trouble if it ever comes out that I did. So make sure this stays here."

"Of course. Is this still to do with Malcolm's will?"

"I saw Malcolm's entire file on Mike Moura's desk this morning."

"I held up my hands. "Didn't we have this conversation already? How badly do you want to lose your license?"

Gordon acted as if I hadn't said a word. "I went in to see Mike about an estate I'm working on and he's the expert on a lot of tax things. But he wasn't there. I checked his calendar and found that he was at superior court today and that can take hours. He likes to bunch up a lot of work and then spend three or four hours at court to try to wrap everything up at once. Anyway, he wasn't expected in and I looked around to make sure his car wasn't in the parking lot or anything. That's when I stood at his office door and saw the file. Dave, I'll tell you, I couldn't help myself."

He paused and waited for me to react. I was tired and sore and not in the mood.

"Just get to the point."

With Gordon, every story seemed to evoke a Shakespearean urge to lead the listener through a series of dramatic high points. A little bit of information here, and then another piece there.

"So I checked with Lois, the secretary, to see if she knew when Mike would be in, and she said that Mike called and was going to be later than he expected and she had to make some phone calls to reschedule today's appointments."

"And the point, Gordy?"

"So I walked around the corner away from her desk, went back in and picked up the file. It wasn't all wrapped up in elastics this time, and I looked inside. Mike had a record of every will that Malcolm ever executed. It goes back to before Mike took over John Rynne's practice, so the oldest one was way before Mike took over."

That struck me as a bit odd. Malcolm didn't seem like the kind of person that would have had a will when he was young. But what did I know? I'm not a lawyer, and maybe Malcolm had a will since he was eighteen.

"The estate isn't huge, but it's worth something. Maybe a half million, maybe a little more."

"Shit, Gordy. You're walking on thin ice here."

"You bet your ass. That's why this stays here. But let me tell you what I found."

"God forbid."

"Twenty-one years ago, there was a change in the will."

This was classic Gordon. Say a couple words. Wait for the anticipation to build, and then come through with the coup de grace. I said the only thing that Gordy was waiting for so he could continue.

"So what?"

"And what we guessed before was right: Ken Gladwell is mentioned in the will as a beneficiary and it's being changed to Tina."

"Oh no." The air came out of me like a leaking balloon. I didn't want to know any more.

"Wait, wait. The best part is, the absolutely sole beneficiary for the last twenty-one years has been Ken Gladwell."

It struck me like a slamming door. It took me a while to process the news and consider the ramifications.

"So what do you want me to do about this, Gordy?"

Gordon just shook his head. "I don't know, Dave. But it doesn't look very good to me."

"So you think I should talk to Ken about this?"

"Shit, no! He'll be able to trace it back to me and I'll be screwed, not to mention disbarred, sued and out on the street. Maybe you could just feel out the situation. I don't know."

I could tell Gordon was worried. Even beyond Gordon's usual hyperbole, he was worried that he was knowledgeable about the fact that Ken Gladwell stood to benefit from Malcolm's demise; that Malcolm Prudhomme and Ken Gladwell had no familial connection, and in fact no connection at all beyond the fact that they happened to live in the same town; and that Ken Gladwell was a person with an unpredictable and sometimes violent temper.

"Look Gordon, if Malcolm made him the beneficiary of his will, what am I supposed to say? 'Hey, Ken, how are you and Malcolm getting along lately?'"

Gordon had a look of frustration on his face. "No, no, no. Just try to find out if there's any connection here that I'm missing."

"Why? When we talked about this before, the only possibility that came to mind before was blackmail. If there was no other connection between Ken and Malcolm, maybe that's exactly what it was. Not a kind or generous thought, but what else could it be? I can't think of anything."

Gordon took his time thinking this over. He didn't want to be a nag, and he wanted to have a legitimate reason for probing into the situation. "Something just isn't right here. There's another agenda I can't figure out, but it's there anyway."

I nodded my head, agreeing with him.

"Dave, I know this is tough, but if there's some way to find out what's behind this, maybe there's a way we can help. Ken's been a friend for a long time, but you know him better than anyone."

I nodded again and just sat there. How was I going to raise the subject? Should I even raise the subject? What business was it of mine?

Gordon rose from the chair and headed out. "I'll be around, Dave. Let me know what you find out. This is really gnawing at me, and I'm sure it's got to be killing you."

We said our good-byes and I returned to the kitchen table and sat alone with my thoughts. They weren't very good company.

Before Ken got back to my apartment, I did a load of laundry and vacuumed the carpets. The laundry was due to be done, but the rugs were perfectly clean already. I just needed to keep busy. I decided to order some Chinese food from the new shop down the street and also decided to wait for Ken to see what he'd like.

Around six thirty, Ken walked into the apartment and put his briefcase by the front door. His tie was already off. I was in the living room trying to keep my mind distracted by watching the news on TV. "Hi, Honey. I'm home."

I smiled in spite of myself and went into the kitchen. Ken had already popped open a beer and was holding a fresh one out for me.

"What's the haps, pardner?"

"How about some Chinese for supper? From the new place."

"Whoa. Let me have a minute to compose myself. I need one beer before I make that kind of decision. Besides, I've got some other stuff on my mind. Like a wife who has now officially booted my ass out, a constable who served me separation and divorce papers, at work no less and in front of my colleagues, and a contract for seventeen million dollar job in Malaysia that went belly up just before I came home." Ken took a big gulp. "What's happening here, Dave? I'm not sure there's any more bad news to be had."

I popped open my beer and remained silent, still lost in my thoughts about my conversation with Gordon Jefts about the Prudhomme will.

"What?" Ken could see the black cloud over my head. "What other bullshit news do I have waiting for me here?"

I shook off the gloom for a minute and tried for a change in mood. "Nothing, Ken. Just a bunch of piddle shit problems of my own. Nothing like you're facing."

"Well, I got the gift-wrapped news about Tina from a stubby little guy named Constable Reginald Dredge. What a freaking name, and it fits the little twit to a tee. He walked in, asked me if I was Kenneth Gladwell, handed me a manila envelope, and said I should have a nice day. I told him not to tell me what to do; if I wanted to have a completely fucked up day, I would. He just sort of frowned and kept walking out." Another gulp and the beer was drained. He opened a fresh one and started in on that one. "I'm in a meeting with my boss and two other guys and that shit happens."

I didn't say anything. I'd experienced this part of the divorce process myself, and I understood the pain and the humiliation all too well. I drank some of my beer and nodded.

"Look, Dave. I know you're a veteran of the divorce war, but this is all new to me. I don't want a divorce. She wants to cut the cord and she won't talk to me about it."

Another gulp, this time a big one.

"And the kicker is, the kicker, Dave? The divorce papers claim that I've been physically abusive. That I've struck Tina on repeated occasions causing extreme emotional and physical harm. She's got a restraining order and I can't go within a hundred feet of her without getting arrested."

I said nothing.

Ken looked over at me, glaring. "You don't still believe that shit, do you?"

"Listen to me for a minute before you go ballistic." I told him what George Wessel told me, that Tina's blouse had dark make-up stains on it. Ken face told me he was startled and confused. Welcome to the club.

"You know, Dave, I've never seen any evidence of a black eye or a bruise. It's not like she fell or anything. Not that Tina lets me get very close."

Ken looked beaten.

"Tina's setting you up, Ken."

"It sure looks that way, buddy. Tina's going around looking like a whipped puppy."

I didn't want to get into the balance of his conversation with

George, the part about the funeral home make-up. There was no sense getting Bob Hayes' name drawn into this mess if Bob didn't know anything about it.

There was a prolonged silence. Ken finally started talking.

"If someone wants a divorce, why not just say so? Hey, we never had the perfect marriage to begin with, but this is just bullshit!"

He swallowed the last of the can and grabbed another from the refrigerator. I was still nursing my first can and waved off Ken's offer for a fresh one.

"Here's a big difference between you and me, Dave. I know you went through a bad divorce and I appreciate that you want to help. But have you ever heard of serendipity?"

"Sure. Why?"

"Because things just sort of went your way for so long without your having to really try. Even back in school, you got decent grades and did well, but you didn't even crack a book. It just came to you. For the rest of us, getting a good mark meant we had to really study. You know that."

"I did study, Ken."

"Yeah, but what took me five hours took you ten minutes. You just 'got it' really quick, but not the rest of us."

Ken went to the refrigerator and pulled out some cheese to nibble on. It hadn't taken him long to settle right in to my place.

"You graduated and had the world by the tail. Went to school, got your degree, went into the service, got a good job, got married to a nice girl, then the house and the two kids. It all just happened for you the way it was supposed to. And then, fifteen, twenty years go by and KA-BOOM! Here's good old Dave Blondin whose life is lived entirely in the key of C, and then bad shit starts to happen and everything goes to hell faster than he can keep up. It's all chaos, and he can't deal. And when the dust settles, here he is. No wife, kids who don't care if you live or die, job down the toilet, living in a dinky apartment and driving a pick up that looks like it's got the clap. Go figure."

I listened to my friend with bile rising in my throat. Ken had no right to present a one-minute analysis of my life. But, I acknowledged silently, it was a truth I'd pondered many times. I just didn't realize that my life was so transparent.

"Me, on the other hand? I had to scrape a lot more. Life sucked when I was growing up. You were there plenty of times, and my parents weren't exactly Ward and June Cleaver. I mean, we didn't live in the rough, but I had to bust my balls to do well. Then I come back and get married to Tina. We have a beautiful son and then we find out he's got some severe mental issues. Then he does himself in with carbon monoxide, and ever since, Tina and I have been living in an ice palace. Silence, anger, and followed by loud arguments. I tried taking her away on nice vacations, but she just keeps her distance, like I'm not even there."

I wanted to add that I thought Ken added to the problem.

"Remember when I was hospitalized?"

I nodded. A few years ago, Ken spent some time in the hospital. He'd been close-mouthed about the reasons and Tina's only comment at the time was that it was "stress".

"It wasn't my idea, but I was seeing a psychiatrist for a while."

"I thought you said you'd never go to a shrink. You told me that yourself."

"Well, I did. And apparently my shrink thought I was about to do myself in. That was about four years ago."

"I remember, Ken. It was a year or two after Eric died."

What I remembered was a Ken Gladwell who had gone from athletic to a shriveled skeleton in the space of about six months. The death of his son made him understandably depressed, but after a few months, he seemed to be back to normal. Then, another year went by and he was withering like a leaf, drying up before it finally fell to the ground and turned to dust.

"The shrink had the pink paper all set and signed on his desk when I showed up for an appointment at his office in the hospital wing. I never had that same feeling before or since, like I had stepped over the threshold into the twilight zone."

I never heard the whole story before, but I knew that Ken was in the hospital for a couple weeks. We never discussed that time, making it sort of off-limits, too sensitive for the bright lights of examination. Ken appeared to want to talk about it now, and I listened.

"I should have suspected something when this big goon was standing in the hallway outside my shrink's office door. He turned out to be the muscle that was supposed to grab me if I made the great escape. I was screwed."

I saw that Ken was reliving each moment. He had that faraway stare like he wasn't here. I've seen that stare in other people a few times, especially in the buddies who'd been in military battles and talked about their experiences there. It seemed best to me that Ken just keep going; when he wanted to stop, he would.

"I knew I was depressed. Hell, the doc had me on some pills for almost three months by then. He thought I was bipolar for a while, but it was good old unipolar depression. But Tina called him and told him she was worried about me, and that I was acting strange. So the doc set me up for a little stay in the loony bin."

I interrupted only to say, "C'mon Ken. That's not what it is."

Gladwell cut me off before I could go on, and he was suddenly angry. "What do you know, Dave? It's a damned loony bin! I know! I was there!"

So much for an effort to soften the experience, I thought. I just nodded and let him go on.

Ken seemed to settle back down in an instant. "It was group therapy three times a day. After a few days, you just get in the routine. Like it was becoming normal. But I'll tell you, I got into the group stuff. Found out I wasn't alone with this thing. Most of the others were really messed up. Manic-depressive, drugged out, severe alcoholics, a woman with paranoid schizophrenia. My depression was pretty lame stuff compared to everyone else there."

He stopped and seemed to be looking up towards the ceiling, zoned out. I waited for his eyes to come back down in my direction.

I finally said, "I remember you started to put some weight on again after you came home." In fact, I recalled that Ken zoomed right back up to his fighting weight and kept on going for a while.

That seemed to get him out of whatever zone he was in.

"Shit, I was down to one-sixty-three when I went in. And I'm six-six! That's almost forty pounds below what I was. When I came out, I was on different medications and started to feel a lot better. I got to two-o-nine and I told the shrink I must be feeling too good and he made a few adjustments."

He was smiling now, as if he'd got past the screwed up part of his life. He wasn't off in space any more.

"Did things get better between you and Tina?"

"For a while, maybe. I'm not sure. We just coexisted. Look, Tina has her own issues to deal with. I had a hard enough time dealing with myself to be able to do anything for Tina beyond suggesting she see a therapist."

"Did she?"

"For a little while. Then she stopped. She just kept insisting that I was the one who was messed up, and who was I to argue? After all, I was certified crazy by a psychiatric professional."

I put my hand on Ken's arm. "What about Tina? What are you going to do?"

"I really don't know. See a lawyer, I guess. I'd like to find out from Tina what the hell she's up to, but the restraining order keeps me away. I want to know why she's doing this."

ELEVEN

The Same Day

Lou Pellerin, out of uniform and off duty, sat at the end of the bar where he ate a packet of potato chips and drank a glass of diet Coke. He wasn't an infrequent visitor to Dean's Town Tavern, the "Dean" in the name being married to his first cousin, Lucille, who also happened to be the receptionist at the police station. In fact, on particularly busy nights, Lou was known to bus some tables and load the dishwasher to help Dean out. Because of that, customers were accustomed to seeing the Assistant Chief occasionally help Dean out behind the bar doing clean up and other chores.

Today, though, things were different. He'd taken Dean aside and let him know that he needed some help in an ongoing investigation, and that the tavern was an ideal place to conduct an important part of that investigation.

"Just bring me the glasses I tell you, Dean. I'll mark names on a napkin and you'll use the napkin to pick the glass up. Just put the glasses on a tray and leave them at end of the bar. I'll take it from there."

Dean, whose reputation as a hard worker was never questioned, was not particularly bright, but he knew better than to ask Lou Pellerin any questions. If Lou wanted him to pick up some glasses with a napkin and put them on a tray, then that's what he'd get.

"Just try not to get your prints on the glasses, Dean."

Dean's only complaint was that he could run short of glasses while this investigation was going on. Lou gave him a folded pair of twenty dollar bills to get him over that hump.

Chief Wetman wasn't thrilled with this primitive method of collecting sputum samples, but went along with Lou's suggestion anyway. "It's the whole 'chain of evidence' thing, Lou. It's got to be maintained. If the glass is out of your sight for a moment, then it's out. You've got to keep your eyes wide open and clearly identify who drank out of which glass."

This evening was the second of Lou's effort, and so far he had four used bar glasses in sealed, marked plastic bags. With mine and Gordon Jefts', the total would be six. With a little luck, he could get nearly every glass he wanted in just one or two nights. Both Gordon and I were frequent customers and he expected us in later tonight or tomorrow.

Tomorrow, when he had every glass he wanted, he'd put the glassware in a carton and arrange to have them delivered to the State Police Crime Laboratory where they'd be tested for DNA. There was certainly enough saliva on the glass rims to test, and with a little luck, he might even get some results within a few weeks.

Bob Hayes checked the caller ID on his phone before he answered. The practice helped him develop his "all business voice" (for calls from the hospital morgue), or "sympathy

162 / P.D. LaFleur

voice" (for those calls most likely to be from families of the recently deceased). This call said George Wessel was calling, so he put on his "warm friend" voice. "Hey Georgie, whassup?"

George Wessel hated caller ID and didn't like to check it when he took incoming calls. He just couldn't get used to it. "Hi Bob. It's George Wessel."

"I know that, you putz. What's happening?"

"I was wondering if you were going to be around tomorrow morning. Say around nine?"

"I should be here. But don't you open your place at nine?"

"Betty can handle it for a while." In truth, George knew, Betty could take care of things for a long long time. "I just wanted to stop by and talk about something."

"Whatever you say, Georgie. Want to give me an idea about what?"

"Not really, Bob. Not over the phone."

"Sure, George. Is there a problem?"

"Well, it could be a big problem. I'd rather not say right now."

Bob knew how to play George Wessel. "OK, tomorrow morning. You're feeling OK, huh? I mean. It's not a professional thing is it?"

"No, no. Nothing like that. It's sort of ..."

"C'mon, Georgie. Don't keep me in the dark. I'm a big boy. What's on your mind?"

"It's, it's... there's some rumors going around, Bob, and they're not good."

That stunned Bob Hayes to the core. "About me? What are they, for Chrissake?"

"It's about you and uh, Tina Gladwell."

OK, thought Bob. This was what George wanted to warn him about, to tell him in person. The news sucked the oxygen out of his body for a moment. After a few seconds, he recovered.

"Listen, thanks for the warning. I'll say this to you right now: Tina's started hanging around once in a while and I didn't stop her. But I never slept with her, George. Never! And I'm going to make damned sure that she doesn't come around here again. You can take that to the bank. OK, George?"

George was planning for a long, uncomfortable session tomorrow morning, but here it was, all out in the open and done with. He wasn't sure how it happened, but he felt better. "Sure, Bob. Absolutely."

"And George, this is between you and me, right? I never heard anything, and you didn't either. It's just done, right?"

"No problem, Bob. Done. Finis."

"OK, George. Thanks for the call. Maybe I'll see you down at Dean's later on."

George answered, "Your welcome, Bob, and I'll see you down there," but the phone line was already dead.

Sitting at the desk in his study, Bob Hayes looked at the phone as if it was on fire. "That damned Tina," he thought. He'd be absolutely certain that the message would be delivered in clear terms: Stay away and don't try to change my mind. Bob, in truth, considered Tina's recent attention delightful, but dangerous.

She was, without question, a stunning woman in fabulous physical condition. But she was as well a deeply troubled one.

He saw the lust in her eyes and her manner, and it made him ill at ease. Not so much that he wasn't tempted to fool around a little. But Ken was a long-time friend, and he didn't screw around with the wives of friends. Don't shit where you sleep, was the adage he's heard a hundred times. All those times, though, it was just an adage. Now it made complete sense.

He'd tell her straight out. Stay away, Tina. No more. Then he'd go down to Dean's and have a beer or four.

*   *   *

I had been thinking about the old Kerrigan factory for a while. I'd walked around the property a few times, almost like kicking tires.

At the moment, a developer from out of town was doing some demolition and reconstruction on the rear portion of the building. As far as I knew, the front section where Tina had her health spa was still available. Gordon never got back to me with that information.

Going through Gordon would be the best way to get a closer look since he was handling the building for the Kerrigan Trust. Until I heard from him, though, I was left with just looking at the outside. It was three stories tall and the walls had to be two feet thick, but I wanted to see it up close, inside and outside, before I pitched an offer.

I took a ride over on the off chance that I could get inside. After all, the back of the building was open and there were some tradesmen working around there. If I looked like I belonged, I just might be able to make my way to the inside of the building and get the up-close look I wanted.

It was from this same building that I'd sworn I saw Nancy Easter almost sneaking away down the street. Maybe I was mistaken; there didn't seem to me to be any reason for Nancy to be there, especially late at night and all alone. I parked on the street and took a flashlight from the glove box.

The spa that Tina Gladwell operated still had its exterior sign in place over the front entry but the large windows facing the street were covered with brown paper so I couldn't see inside. I recalled it as a large open area with some separate rooms on the periphery for massage rooms, showers and lavatories. A wide set of stairs in the back of the central space led to Tina's office and a storage loft. The office and the loft were part of the building in the rear and that space being renovated by the developer; it would not be part of the space I was looking to buy. The second and third floors directly above the spa were accessed, I thought, from another staircase near the front of the building as well as a small passenger elevator. I walked around the back of the building where a dozen workers were busy measuring and cutting and sawing. An open overhead door stood in the center and I strolled in. Nobody paid me any attention.

The rear of the building was going to be commercial space on the first floor with a floor of offices above that and a third floor devoted to small loft apartments. These units would overlook the river with the developer hoping to attract young professionals as renters. I looked around the first floor and saw the second story loft area with a hook suspended above. In its days as a working factory, crates and bales would be lifted to and from the storage loft with that hook. I recalled being here a few times when I was in high school. Warren Kerrigan, Tina Gladwell's late father, let the school's athletic department use the loft to store off-season equipment.

I walked to the back of the first floor space and saw a narrow wooden staircase leading up to the open loft. It didn't look entirely safe but I made my way carefully up the stairs, testing each tread as I went. When I reached the loft, I saw at my left the wide staircase leading down to the front of the building and Tina's old health club. I bypassed the remnants of Tina's old office in the loft and walked down the wide staircase to the front.

When the spa was open, I was a regular customer, using the workout equipment and the weights to give me at least the illusion that I was staying in shape. The equipment was now long gone as well as the odor of sweat that permeated the space in its prime. I paced out the space and guessed it to be over two thousand square feet. I used another narrower staircase on the far side of this space to reach the second and third floors and was amazed at the pristine condition of the building. If I could buy the front portion of the building at the right price, I could handle the remodeling with a minimum of expense and generate some serious revenue. I mentally ran through some numbers and figured I could recover my capital costs in about seven years. From that point on, I'd be in terrific financial shape. *If* I could buy it from the Kerrigan Family Trust at the right price.

I returned to the first floor and then went back up the broad staircase to the loft so I could make my way out the same way I came in. I wondered when I reached the top how this space would be blocked off if and when I acquired the building. I took a moment to look around. To my left was a large open area and an enormous solid oak table stood roughly in the center. Unlike the rest of the building, the surfaces here were oddly dust free and I noted a set of wooden shelves on the far wall. On one of them were dozens of votive candles. On other shelves were assortments of other items, some sports paraphernalia, including baseball gloves and a basketball. A few framed photographs occupied a shelf by itself, although I was too far away to recognize the people in them.

That's when I heard one of the workers calling up to me from below. He didn't sound very happy with me and let me know that I wasn't welcome on an active work site. "I'm just leaving," I said, and took the shaky stairs down and walked out of the building. When I climbed back into the front seat of my truck, I called Gordon Jefts' at his home number and left a voice message. I wanted to make sure I had a chance to make an offer.

Nancy Easter was upset. She'd been calling all day from her desk at the library and leaving messages. Keeping her voice low was a chore and by the time she left the library at the end of the day, her blood pressure was high and rising.

Finally, as she sat alone in her apartment, her telephone rang.

"Listen," she said to her caller. "Did you get the keys I dropped off in your mailbox? I think somebody saw me at the

Kerrigan place the other night. Dave Blondin. I don't know if he recognized me, but you've got to move fast."

Nancy didn't want to listen to excuses and interrupted her caller.

"I'm telling you, we've got to move fast. I've heard that Phil Marchand is already nosing around looking for some investment property and I don't like it. He could screw up everything. And Dave Blondin's his best friend. I don't care what it takes. Just get going and get this done."

She slammed the telephone down on its cradle. She'd waited too many years and toiled too many hours to let something get in her way. With Phil Marchand back in town, things could go haywire.

She bit her lip and went to her refrigerator where she removed a bottle of Chardonnay. She removed the cork and poured a glass. As she sat alone in her living room, she contemplated her next move.

Business was slow at Dean's when I walked in. Only a few people sat at the bar and one of them was Phil Marchand. I walked over and took the seat next to him.

"Sure, I'll have one if you're buying."

Phil didn't say a word but clapped me on the shoulder and signaled Dean for a beer.

On the way back to me, Dean started pouring the beer into a glass.

"Whoa, Dean. I'm a bottle guy, remember?"

"Oh, man, what was I thinking?"

"No problem. It's probably just a touch of Alzheimer's."

Dean brushed the suggestion off with a smile.

Phil turned to me and asked, "What's happening, Dave? How's Ken Gladwell doing?"

I told him that Ken was upset about his marriage breaking up.

"I wasn't his best buddy when I was a kid, but I feel sorry for him."

"What got you two to be such enemies, anyway?"

"Who knows? I beat him out for starting shortstop one year. Maybe that's it. We never got into a fight, but we never got along either. I don't know exactly why, because he got along great with Catherine."

"I remember. He talked about asking her to the prom, but she'd already said yes to me. Besides, if he did ask and she said yes, I think that would have pissed Tina off."

"Man, Tina wanted him to herself, didn't she."

The door opened and Ken Gladwell stepped in, looked around quickly, and stopped.

"Pull up a stool, Ken." It was Phil extending the invitation.

Ken stepped forward, removed his jacket and pulled up a stool, never smiling. Dean had half of Ken's beer poured into a glass when Ken said, "Dean, it's me. Just a bottle."

"Crap! Where's my head today? Sorry about that, Ken."

I felt I was in the presence of two gladiators, pheromones wafting through the beery atmosphere of the tavern. Ken lifted his glass and clinked with me and Phil. "Cheers."

If I wanted to be in a place with less cheer, I couldn't think where I'd go.

"We were just talking about high school Ken. Remember the prom?"

"Sure." One syllable, said in a near grunt.

"Dave here went with my sister and you went with Tina, right?"

A nod, nothing more.

"Five dollars says you can't name the girl I took."

"Dotty Bertram."

Phil was stunned that at the quick response. "You remembered?"

Ken had his hand out.

Phil took his money clip out and said, "Shoot, Ken. All I have are fifties."

"Yo, Dean. Get this big man some change."

Dean came over and Phil passed him a fifty. When Dean came back with smaller bills, Ken grabbed his arm and removed a five. Dean, not a party to the conversation, saw no objection and gave the forty-five dollars to Phil.

Ken then drained his beer, put his glass on the bar, grabbed his jacket and was gone.

"My good buddy Ken Gladwell."

"You dared him, he won."

"Another?"

"No thanks. I've got to catch up with Gordon tonight about a deal."

"Which one?"

"The old Kerrigan Mills. I'm looking to make an offer on part of it. I think the back is already taken."

Phil turned away and faced the bar.

"Well, good luck."

"Ciao." I was glad to be gone.

I parked my truck and decided to walk to the next block and ring Gordon's doorbell to see if he was home. Gordon came downstairs and let me in.

"Hey buddy. Didn't see you down at Dean's. Get my call?"

"Dave, I think I'm going to quit being a lawyer and go into something like men's suits. Fewer headaches."

We walked upstairs and into Gordon's loft apartment. I was always taken with the taste that Gordon had in designing and decorating his space. The place always looked like it belonged in some trendy section of New York City. My place, by comparison, reflected common utility.

Where I had a white Amana kitchen range and a dented Whirlpool refrigerator, Gordon Jefts had a Viking six burner restaurant range and an enormous Traulsen stainless steel commercial refrigerator. I kept my few bottles of wine in either my refrigerator (for my supermarket whites) or a small wooden rack (for my supermarket reds). At least, I thought, I'm sufficiently sophisticated to know what goes where. In Gordon Jefts' place, one entire wall was dedicated to built-in wine storage with proper temperatures set for every type, and there were many, mostly French or Italian.

"So what's with the long fez, Abdul?"

"Too many people to keep happy, Dave. Sometimes none of my clients are happy, and I get the backlash."

"Poor puppy. But speaking of keeping people happy, tell me you can do a decent deal on the Kerrigan building."

"Are you kidding? It's already gone."

"Not the whole building. Isn't the front section still available?"

Immense relief showed on Gordon's face. "Oh, that part. Yeah, I think it's still open. They'll want a number that comes pretty close to theirs, though."

I took a note pad and pencil from my pocket and jotted down the figure I had in mind. I tore it from the pad and showed it to Jefts."

"Not too bad, Dave. I think they'll at least talk about it. Will that work for you?"

"Yup."

"Sure?"

"Why? What's going on?"

"Let's just say that the developer is probably going to unload part of the building real soon and they've already got a lease with that high tech company for the entire second floor on the rear. The Kerrigan Trust already has its money from that deal, so Tina's mother is even richer than rich right now. The trust isn't under a ton of pressure to make an incredible deal for the piece you want. It's probably a good time to pitch this."

"Who is the developer going to sell a piece to? Maybe I'll be interested in that, too." In for a penny, I thought. I must have been feeling like a financier when I said this.

"Please, Dave. Don't complicate things right now. Let's just see what happens with your offer."

Gordon's reluctance to divulge any further details meant that he probably was in the middle of the transaction right now. Otherwise, he'd be Gordon Jefts as usual, kibitzing about the possibilities with any willing audience.

Just then, his phone rang and he picked it up.

"No! Who told you? When? I'll find out and call you later."

When he put the phone down, Gordon Jefts had a look of dread.

"What's up, Gordon?"

"Like I said, men's suits might be my best bet. That was the developer himself. He just got a huge offer for the back of the building from another potential buyer. I've got a client who's going to pitch a royal fit."

"Sorry, Gordon."

"Good luck to whoever made the bid, but he's offering twenty percent more, and I've been close enough to the financials on the place to know that those numbers just won't work. Whoever is making this new bid can't make money at that price."

"So why make a stupid bid?"

"Who knows? I'm sorry I can't grab a beer with you tonight, but I got to get onto this right away."

"At this hour?"

"It's not men's suits. I can't just close the shop and go on my way. Yet."

TWELVE

Monday, two weeks later

The woman standing at the door of his office looked in to see Wetman munching on a tuna sandwich and struggling with a crossword puzzle. He was murmuring to himself, unaware that anyone was watching him. "Seven letters ... Tempestuous monster." She remained where she stood, wondering if she should tap at the doorframe to announce her presence. She checked her watch, and she was fifteen minutes early for her appointment with the chief.

Finally, Lou Pellerin walked up and stood at the door just behind her. In a whisper, he said, "I wouldn't interrupt him mid-clue. Puts him in a foul mood."

Wetman heard or sensed the presence of the pair at the door and put his newspaper aside. Without any sense of embarrassment, he stood and said, "Come in, come in. Grab a seat. I'm Chief Wetman and I guess you've already met Assistant Chief Pellerin."

"Not formally, no. I'm Angela Kim from the DA's office."

She shook hands and took her seat, resting her briefcase on her lap. Wetman guessed her to be in her late thirties, maybe early forties. Straight dark hair framed an oval face of olive skin that suggested a combination of Asian and maybe Mediterranean heritage. She was probably an inch or two taller than Wetman.

Lou explained her presence to the Chief. "Ms. Kim is here to talk about the investigation into Catherine Marchand's death."

"Please. It's Angela, and I'm just trying to gather some basic information so I can follow it along with you as you make progress. If and when you need our office, we want to be ready for you."

"You're jumping the gun a little, don't you think, Angela," said Wetman. "Lou, here, can tell you that there's not a lot happening."

"That's right," said Lou. "The victim's brother moved back to Apsley after a long absence and he's asked us to take another look at the case. I wouldn't say the case is officially reopened or that we have new leads, but we want to see if there might be anything that was missed back when it happened. That's about it."

Angela Kim had a pad of paper on her lap with some notes on it and referred to them when she spoke. "But you did develop some additional information, correct? At least enough to submit evidence for testing at the State Police Crime Lab, yes? Some DNA work?"

Wetman cursed under his breath. He should have surmised that the DA would have its contacts at the State Police lab. Someone there was making a fuss about getting the case assigned to his people. Angela Kim must be here as a result of some discussions about that.

She looked down and checked some other notes.

"The victim was pregnant at the time of the homicide, is that correct?"

Wetman answered, "Yes, but we're not sure that has any bearing on her death. At least not now."

"Motive, maybe?"

Wetman had enough. "Look, Miss Kim, we are looking into the case and we are trying to develop new information, but we don't really see a need to get the DA's office involved just yet. If we get some more information, maybe we can get in touch then."

He smiled, knowing that it was a smarmy smile, but it was the best he could come up with at the moment.

Angela Kim wasn't ready to be put to the side quite yet, though.

"There was a suspect wasn't there at the time of her murder? And I understand he's still alive and living here in Apsley."

"Where did you get that information?"

"I'd rather not say, but Chief Wetman, people do talk."

Lou Pellerin wanted to end this conversation and wipe the coy smile off the face of Angela Kim, esquire. He jumped into the conversation.

"There was never a clear suspect in the death of Catherine Marchand, not then and not now. There was one local character who was placed under suspicion for a brief time back when it happened, but he was released for lack of evidence. There was no other suspicious person at the time, and there's still none."

Angela Kim put her pen down and turned her attention back to Wetman. "Well, perhaps someone was jumping ahead of themselves at the county level. Maybe even at the state level. That happens from time to time. I can understand how having me here might prove a little cumbersome for you at this time, so I'll just leave you my card and ask you to call me at any time."

She stood and gathered her briefcase before shaking hands and moving towards the door. Lou followed her out and she turned to him and said, in a low voice, "Caliban."

Lou leaned closer and said, "What was that?"

"Just tell Chief Wetman it's 'Caliban'." She spelled it for

him. "He'll understand. And is there anywhere around here where I can get a good cup of coffee?"

"Damn it, Lou. Reilly should have been back by now. Where can he be?" Wetman was pacing across his office and chewing on an unlit cigar.

Lou Pellerin shrugged his shoulders. "I'll try him on the radio again, but he's in his own vehicle. This is his day off and he only offered to pick up the results because he was going to take his mother shopping in the mall and it's only a few miles from there to the lab.

"Shit. Doesn't he have a cell phone? "

"I've tried, sir. No answer. It goes right to voicemail. We need more cell towers around here. A couple of solar flares and we lose cell service here. Happens all the time."

Wetman grunted. He'd already heard this explanation twice before. Hearing it a third time didn't help him overcome his anxiety. He pulled the cigar from his mouth and said, "And that little miss from the DA's office. She's got to show up today and try to get her nose under our tent. I don't like this, Lou."

"She sounds like she's only doing her job, chief. She didn't seem to press too hard when you shot her down."

Wetman grunted again, as if in grudging assent. "Maybe. Maybe. But I just hate it when the state starts sticking its nose into our stuff. Like the locals don't know what they're doing. Like we need their wisdom to find our way out of a paper bag. I've dealt with those jack-offs enough to know that the only thing they can run efficiently is a gigantic cluster fuck. I just need their lab; that's all. Just show us the lab results and we'll go from there."

"I don't disagree, chief. But we can't run around bursting blood vessels while we wait for Reilly to show up. C'mon. I'll take you out for coffee. When we come back, chances are the report will be sitting on your desk. C'mon."

*   *   *

Chief Wetman and Lou Pellerin were gone for only ten minutes when Detective Reilly showed up with a sealed envelope
in hand. He also had the carton of the tested glassware, also
sealed. Both the carton and the envelope had his dated signature across the sealing tape. He placed both items in the evidence locker and left a note on the chief's desk as to their
whereabouts.

THIRTEEN

Tuesday

"Tell Reilly to come in, would you?"

Wetman was holding a manila envelope when he spoke to Lucy at the front desk and walked into his office. The seven-to-three shift was just starting its day when Wetman arrived. He understood that in the old days, meaning before Wetman's appointment as head of the department, the old Chief rarely showed up before nine, and then he was out for coffee at ten. He placed the envelope on the edge of his desk and took a seat in his chair. There were several pink message slips next to his phone and he picked them up, sorted them into piles . . . *must* return call . . . *maybe* return call. . . . And *no way will I ever* return call.

He had just finished his sorting when a fresh-faced Officer Jimmy Reilly knocked on the door frame to announce his presence. Wetman looked up.

"Come in, Officer Reilly. Take a seat."

Officer James Patrick Reilly did so gingerly. He'd rarely

been in the Chief's office in his three years on the force and the last time he was here he suffered a tongue lashing for wearing mismatched socks. It was a uniform violation and a note had been placed in his file. So this office carried some bad memories for Officer Reilly and he wasn't quite sure how to take Wetman.

He'd seen the Chief's postings on the message board in the squad room and knew that several of his colleagues were less than pleased with some of the new rules put in place by Wetman. He took his seat and looked at the Chief with a question. Am I about to get yelled at again?

The Chief looked at the young officer and smiled. Reilly had a face full of freckles and his red hair was clipped in a crew cut. I'm looking at Opie, he thought.

He could read the uncertainty on Reilly's face and decided to put him at ease, even if his stern expression betrayed him.

"Two things, Reilly." The officer sat at attention. "First of all, thank you for this report."

Wetman pointed at the envelope that still rested on the desk corner.

"It's straightforward, clear and concise. It had all the relevant information right up front and explained every finding in detail. It was, young man, perfect. Thank you."

Reilly didn't respond. He completed the report late yesterday and was surprised that the Chief had already read and digested it. So far so good, Reilly thought. But he didn't want to do or say anything to screw things up. He looked at the Chief and waited for the other shoe to drop.

Wetman let his praise sink in for a second or two.

"Now, here's what I want to make absolutely sure of. This report you submitted . . . have you mentioned the findings to anyone?"

Reilly found his voice but his response cracked with nerves. "No sir."

Wetman bored in on him. "No one? Not a fellow officer, not your wife? Not anyone?"

"No sir. I just brought back the results from the State Police Crime Lab yesterday and prepared the report. No one else knows. And I'm not married."

"Good. I mean, I'm glad you didn't reveal anything to anyone else here, and I didn't know you weren't married, and maybe that's a good thing. I don't know."

He paused and let Reilly consider this for a moment. "Is it?"

Reilly wondered at the question before answering. "I think so, sir."

"Girlfriend?"

"Yes sir."

"She live with you?"

"No sir."

Reilly, raised a Catholic and fully aware of the cosmic punishment for living in sin, was willing to risk certain eternal damnation if Lisa Camara would move into his apartment with him, but his parents, especially his god-fearing mother, would be apoplectic. She didn't even want him to get his own place, never mind live like a married couple without first taking the sacrament. To Reilly, his personal happiness simply wasn't worth the hassle.

"Good. I'm glad. First of all you've done a good job, and second, you haven't told anyone. That's two good things to start the day."

Wetman went back to scanning his phone messages. Reilly thought this was his signal to leave but didn't want to presume. He sat rigid, waiting.

Wetman didn't wait long. He didn't look up and said, "That's all."

Reilly stood and started to leave.

Wetman kept his focus on the dozens or so slips of paper in

front of him when he said, "And just so you know, Officer Reilly . . ."

Reilly stopped in his tracks, not yet out of the office. He could taste the freedom from fear that lay in the hallway mere inches in front of him. This was the other shoe, he was sure. He turned to face the Chief and braced himself.

"I'm putting in paperwork for you to attend a training program at State Justice Headquarters. It starts next month and I'll make sure you get the details before the end of today. It's on evidence handling. I expect you to do well."

Reilly wasn't sure how to react. This was great news, but he didn't want to presume anything yet. His gut was still in knots and he just said, "Yes sir. Thank you sir." And started to leave.

"One more thing." Reilly knew it. He could sense the bad news coming and here it was.

"That mention in your file about your uniform violation? It's been tossed."

Reilly was still digesting this news, another in a steady stream of good news items so far, when Wetman added, "A single guy who can't match his socks? That report must have been written by a married guy. So forget about it. That's it. And nothing leaves this office about this report. Dismissed."

Reilly stepped into the hallway and took two deep breaths. He felt like he'd just stepped into the lion's den and came out intact. In fact, better off than when he went in. He started slowly back towards the squad room and by the time he reached the door, he felt just great, his chest full of pride.

Assistant Chief Lou Pellerin, just entering the station's front door, watched him enter the squad room and wondered why he was practically strutting. Reilly was a quiet cop who kept to himself and did a decent job. He wasn't one to get puffed up. On his way to his office, he removed his rain coat and stopped at the dispatcher's desk to grab the handful of phone messages.

He stopped at Wetman's door to let his boss know he was around.

"Morning, Chief."

Wetman was reading a file on his desk and didn't look up when he answered, "Morning, Lou. Come in and shut the door."

Lou Pellerin did as he was told and sat, waiting for Wetman to finish what he was reading. When he did, he looked up, wiped his face with his hands and said, "Sorry. This stuff is good reading and I want you to look at it." Wetman then sat back in his chair so far that Pellerin thought the chair might fall over.

The pages remained in front of Wetman and Lou didn't want to presume to simply slide them over in his direction, so he said something off the point.

"You look like shit, Chief, no offense."

Wetman leaned back upright. "Yeah. Thanks. You look like a sack of warm dog turd yourself. And by the way, I'm signing Opie up for classes over in Mount Pilot. Have you seen him yet?"

"Reilly? He looks a foot taller. No wonder. He'll eat that stuff up. Which class?"

"Forensics. Serology. Crime Scene Security. Basic stuff, but I like the kid. And the whole thing about the socks? I shredded it this morning."

"Good idea. I'm sure he's on cloud nine."

Wetman slid the pages around for Lou.

"Now, what you are about to look at is *not* going to be cloud nine. This is more like a terrible explosion deep beneath the surface of the earth. Let me know what you think. I've got to go to the men's room, then make some phone calls."

Wetman rose from his chair and added, "But read this in here and keep the door closed. This stuff can't leave this room. At least not yet."

Wetman left and closed the door behind him. Lou put on his reading glasses and started the report.

When Wetman returned, the pair sat down and digested the contents and formed a plan. Wetman would handle the initial contact, today if it could be arranged. Reactions would be carefully scrutinized for inconsistencies.

"This could blow up, you know, Lou. He could flip out. From what I've seen of him and from what people have told me about him, that's not very likely. But still ..."

Lou agreed and offered to back up Wetman, an offer the chief refused. "I need to meet him somewhere other than the station, someplace more comfortable. I want to see his reaction. The only people who know about this are you, me and Reilly. Until I have a chance to talk with this guy, I want to keep it that way."

Wetman's message to Lou was clear: He was being trusted to keep this information absolutely quiet.

Wetman made one more phone call to arrange a meeting. When he hung up, Wetman said, "4:00 this afternoon, out by Squash Pond." Lou repeated his offer to stay at a distance, just in case, but Wetman waved him off and said, "Thanks. I'll need you at my back someday, but I think this will work out OK." He paused for a second and added, "And if I'm not back by 5, then you know where to find my body." They smiled at each other and went to handle their day's work.

The wind was blowing hard now. It had been expected all afternoon, but it hit later and harder than expected. The rain was supposed to come after the wind died down, but here it was, pelting and well ahead of schedule. I grabbed a poncho from behind the driver's seat of my pick up and headed over to the unmarked blue sedan where Chief Wetman sat reading by dying sunlight. The Chief was already dressed in his Columbo-style trench coat and immediately exited his car as soon as he saw me approach. He held out his hand in greeting and then extended a large umbrella that came reasonably close to keeping us both protected, even though he had to struggle to keep it from blowing away.

"Thanks for coming, Mr. Blondin. Sorry about this weather."

"It's Dave, and there's nothing you can do about the weather. What did you want to show me?"

Wetman stood a few inches shorter than me and he craned his neck to look over his shoulder at the pick up. "Nobody with you?"

"Nope," I said. "You told me to come alone and I did. So what's up? Or do we just stand here and get soaked to the bone?"

Wetman was focused entirely on my face and I felt uneasy at the attention. Chief Wetman was actually studying me, looking as if for some reaction or some 'tell' that would give him some clue about me. He shrugged after several moments and turned towards a stand of trees near the edge of the pond. "C'mere. Follow me."

The pond was over its banks with the wet weather we'd been having for the past week and the ground was saturated and soft. My work boots sank into the matting of leaves and ooze with every step and made a sucking noise whenever I lifted a foot. For some reason, Chief Wetman didn't seem to sink at all into the muck, which was good for him because he was wearing loafers. He was much lighter than me, probably no more than 145, and that certainly helped his cause.

We reached a stand of pine and oak trees where the cover was thick enough to keep most of the rain from hitting us directly, and Wetman pointed to a spot about forty feet to the right. "See that?" I followed his line of sight. Some scraggly oaks were clumped in a rough circle and there were several fallen trees whose rotting stumps dotted the area. I nodded.

"You know what happened here?"

This was where Catherine Marchand was killed. Everyone in Apsley over the age of thirty-five knew this. I nodded again. I wanted to be somewhere else, anywhere else that was not so stark and utterly sad.

"You were questioned at the time?"

"You know I was. You also know what they found out."

I didn't appreciate Wetman's question, the answer to which he knew full well.

Wetman shook his head as if to say, "Ah, yes, I do know." I would not have enjoyed this little trip to the woods in wonderful weather, but under these circumstances, I was starting to seriously dislike our new Chief of Police.

I asked him, "Have you been here before?"

"Once," he said, eying the spot. "It's pretty soggy over there right now with all the rain. Think you want to see it again?"

"No. I've seen it plenty of times already."

"You know, Dave, when I was younger, I used to like getting into the mind of every victim and perpetrator, right down to reenacting every scene. I'd lay down in an alley trying to feel what the victim felt, or climb a fire escape during an ice storm to see exactly what a shooter did. I just had to experience everything for myself."

He pointed at the clump of trees and continued. "At one point in my career, I would have been sitting right there in the muck where those trees are, even in this rain. Then I'd try to get into the scene with my whole body and soul. Try to imagine what it must have been like at the time of the crime, you know? Like the Stanislavski Acting Method. Get right into the whole thing, you know? I thought it would help."

"Did it?"

"Maybe. A little."

"But you don't do that any more?"

"Not if I can help it. I think I've become more cerebral with age."

"So there's some reason why we're out here. Give me a hint."

"Come on back to my car. It's dry, and I'll tell you." We slogged through the swampy mess to the chief's sedan. His was a dinged up former police cruiser with plenty of miles on it. On the side was the emblem for the town of Apsley and the words "Chief of Police" stenciled in black

I opened the passenger door with a tug and it creaked as I tried to shut it. I had to reopen it and slam it to get it closed.

"Why not get a better car, Chief? It was in the budget."

The town's Finance Committee voted in favor of a brand new vehicle but Wetman set that aside. The new vehicle was the old Chief's idea, not his, and as far as he was concerned, a used cruiser was fine by him. Apsley is only twelve square miles, he reasoned, and brand new wheels would be a waste on him. At least that's what he told the newspapers.

"Would you be more impressed if I had a new car?"

He turned the ignition key and started it up. It was a little loud, but it started just fine. He adjusted the heater fan and then inserted a CD into a slot on his dashboard and all of a sudden, some soft concert music came through the speakers. "This is the only thing I wanted," he said, indicating the CD player. "Beethoven, Dave. Symphony Number Seven. I put the CD player in myself."

I waited for Wetman to give some indication for his wanting to meet here in a driving rain storm. Nothing was happening yet. He adjusted the speakers until most of the music came from the rear speakers and then sat back and turned his to face me. "Wait until we get to the horns, Dave. It's just like magic. They absolutely soar."

I wasn't sure what to think. I was sitting in the front seat of a beat up cruiser with the new Chief listening to Beethoven. I was trying to make some sense of the scene when Wetman did it for me.

"Dave, I need to ask you a few questions that were never asked before in the original investigation."

"OK. Did something new come up? Some new evidence?"

"Sort of," he answered, and I could tell he was reluctant to explain. "Tell me about Catherine. Was she beautiful? Plain? Prim? Sexy? Stuck up?"

I didn't expect this, but I did my best. I thought the question over for a few minutes before I began to answer. The Chief didn't seem to mind the wait. "Catherine was beautiful. Stunning. She really turned heads." Wetman was attentive, nodding. "And I wouldn't call her either prim or stuck up? She was friendly and outgoing. Everybody loved her."

The Chief looked out the windshield as if assessing the weather. "'Everybody loved her.' I hear that from just about everyone, Dave. Catherine had no enemies. She was beautiful. Bright. Funny." He stopped and turned his attention back to me.

"And dead, Dave. They don't say that, but she sure is. Cold and dead. Violently dead. With plenty of pain and torment, if you believe the medical examiner's report about her injuries, and I do.

"So, even though you say everybody loved her, I have to tell you, Dave, somebody really didn't like Catherine Marchand one bit. I've seen plenty of murder victims in my time, and I've spent some time looking over the pictures from Catherine's murder. Whoever did what was done to Catherine Marchand didn't just dislike the girl. This beautiful, funny, loveable young woman was savaged. This was intense, well-formed, horrible loathing."

He let that sink in. Of course, he knew, I and everyone else who knew Catherine all believed that. Why was she murdered when she was so well liked?

Wetman reached for a manila envelope that was wedged into the cushions of the front seat.

"So, Dave, she was beautiful. She wasn't plain or prim or stuck up. But you never mentioned sexy. Was Catherine sexy?"

The question seemed a bit over the top, especially when the person you're discussing has been dead for so many years. But I tried anyway.

"I guess you'd say Catherine was sexy. She was pretty and guys found her attractive."

"And she was attractive. You said that already."

"Very attractive. Look, you've seen her pictures, I'm sure. She had great figure and she was very pretty. So yes. I'd call her attractive and sexy. For someone seventeen years old, she was great looking."

"Nice figure?"

I thought the conversation was getting perverse.

"Yes."

Wetman was still holding the manila envelope in his hands and appeared to be debating with himself as to what he was going to do with it.

I asked him point blank. "What's in the envelope?"

"That's why I asked you here. Nobody except for Officer Reilly, who wrote the report, and Assistant Chief Pellerin, and me, of course, know what's in here. Well, the lab that did the testing also knows, but that's fifty miles away and they don't give a rat's ass what it says. Besides, they just had numbers to work with, not names. You know, like 'Sample #31, Victim #63.' The lab techs didn't know what they were looking at, except that it was human DNA material from sleepy little Apsley and that it was connected to the Catherine Marchand murder case. But me? I care a lot. Officer Reilly? He's just a young police officer doing his job, but I think he's a discrete sort of a guy. Know what I mean? He just did his job and did it very well. He'll make a good detective someday. Nope, Jimmy Reilly's not the kind to kiss and tell."

"You didn't mention Lou Pellerin."

"You're right. I didn't."

Wetman looked as if he was weighing how much he could take me into his confidence.

"I like Lou Pellerin and he's a fine Assistant Chief. He's been very helpful too, I'll tell you that. But you've known him a lot longer than I have. He wants people to like him and respect him, and if he makes mistakes it's probably because of that. Maybe it's just basic insecurity. Some people in town tell me he's never been the smartest guy in the world, but he's got some measure of power and prestige, so he uses what he has to accomplish that. I'm not a shrink, so I don't know. That's just opinion. What do you think?"

"I think if what you're going to show me has been seen by Lou Pellerin, and if it's important for you to keep it close to the vest, then Lou needs to understand the penalty of spilling it."

"You think he likes to act like the big shot? You think he'd blab stuff around town?"

"No, not that. I know he wanted the job you ended up getting. Maybe it's just as well that he's kept on a short leash."

Wetman thought this over and eventually handed me the envelope.

"Read this and tell me what you think."

"Now?"

"It's not leaving my presence and I need you to read through it, so yes, now."

So I started to read. It was a brief report with a heading that included Catherine's name and date of death. The first paragraph detailed the purpose: To determine if any of eleven samples of human saliva supplied to the lab matched the DNA profile of a tissue sample supplied to the lab approximately one month earlier.

The second paragraph described the testing process that was used by the laboratory. I didn't understand or even recognize a single word.

The following pages had charts and other test results. It was still Greek to me. And then I got to the last paragraph where the laboratory's conclusion appeared.

"In the opinion of the following signatories, no single saliva sample presented a profile that matched the DNA profile of said tissue sample. However, sample #5 indicates a parental relationship to the said sample. That is, the individual noted as #5 bears a direct parental relationship to the fetus from which said tissue sample derived."

When I finished reading, I sat staring at the paragraph. I reread it, not sure precisely what this meant, but I knew I was number 5. Otherwise, what was the purpose of Wetman meeting me here? I read it once more before I looked up at the Chief.

"Saliva sample? From who? How?"

"Not important right now. It's enough to say that it was collected legally."

"And the tissue sample? It came from Catherine?"

Wetman nodded. Yes.

"She was pregnant?"

He nodded once more. Yes.

"Holy . . ."

"Catherine Marchand was pregnant when she died. Just a month or two along."

"And it was . . . ?"

Wetman just nodded.

"My child."

Wetman let my words reverberate and then dissipate inside the confines of the car for several seconds before he asked the next question.

"How long were you and Catherine involved?"

I looked up from the papers and directly at the Chief. In spite of the rain and the humidity, my mouth was as dry as dust and I had trouble getting the words out.

"Just a few months. I'd see her at her house after school, or at my parents' place. Our parents had full time jobs."

I knew I must look like a guilty teenager as I said this, and that's exactly how I felt.

"Did Philip Marchand know you were sexually involved with his sister?"

I shook my head no.

"No chance that Catherine would have said anything to him?"

I shook my head again and added, "She was close to her brother, but I don't think she'd say anything to him. It's not the kind of thing you tend to talk about with your brother."

Wetman said nothing for a while as I sat staring at the report, not seeing anything but a blur.

"It's probable that Catherine would have had some morning sickness. She never said anything to you?"

"She never mentioned anything to me. I didn't know."

I held up my hand to keep Wetman from asking any more questions for a minute. I needed some more time for this to sink in.

Eventually, I went on.

"If I had known, I don't know what we would have done. We were seniors in high school. There's no way we could have taken care of a kid."

Wetman consulted some notes on a small pad he'd had on the seat.

"She was about seven weeks along. Too early for a young athletic girl like Catherine to show. I'm not a doctor, but she would have missed at least one or two periods, don't you think? Still in the first trimester, though."

I looked at him when he spoke.

"I don't remember if abortion was legal back then. If it was, I would guess a girl would have to go into the city to get one."

I tried to recall that time and remembered a few instances

where girls became pregnant in high school. There were usually rumors about convenient miscarriages, and there was talk about 'knowing somebody' who did abortions. If a girl knew the right people, then the pregnancy could be stopped.

Wetman said, "Back when I was in high school, if a girl was pregnant she'd be sent by her parents to visit an 'aunt' someplace until the baby was born. That's the way it was usually done. I remember a few places in the city, usually run by nuns. They ran places for young girls to finish their pregnancies. Then the baby would be given up for adoption. Do you remember that?"

Wetman was right, I thought. That's the way things were done back then.

"Then the girl would come back to school, and hopefully the whole thing would just get forgotten."

I handed the report back to the Chief and he tapped the pages into a neat stack and slid them back into the envelope. He looked up at me and said nothing.

I asked him, "Where does this go from here?"

"It stays right in this envelope for now, but I have to tell you that we're going to be looking at this case a little different."

He closed the clasp on the envelope and placed it on the seat between us.

"I'm not saying that you're a suspect in Catherine's death, but you have to agree we need to look at this from a different angle maybe."

"And Phil?" I wondered if he'd be told about this, and who would do the telling.

"If he hears anything, it won't be from me. At least not yet. If there comes a time when he has to be told, I'll let you know in advance. How do you think he'd react if he found out his best friend was sleeping with his sister?"

"I'm not sure. She was up on a pedestal for him. If he knew that I was the father of her child, I don't know."

"OK, Dave. That's it. Thank you for coming out here on a crappy day like this."

I nodded, exited the car and walked back to my truck. I just sat in it for a few minutes. When I tried to put the key in the ignition, my hands were still shaking. I eventually regained some control and made it back to my apartment where I sat at the kitchen table and opened a can of beer.

I had heard the news with my ears and saw the report with my eyes, but it was still sinking in to my being. Catherine was pregnant with my child. She was murdered and so was the child. I felt a new sense of loss as I sat alone wondering what kind of person this child might have become.

How life would have been different had Catherine lived. More likely than not, she would have gone to visit the 'aunt' somewhere and had the baby, then returned to school. She might even have to repeat senior year, but she was smart and probably would take her classes and do her tests by mail. Then she'd graduate and go off to college. I would have been a father to some child I never knew. Phil and his family would know about Catherine and me and our sexual experimenting.

In real time, the excitement of the moment was overwhelming. Catherine was not only a lovely creature and sought after by any number of boy-men at Apsley High, but she was willing and eager. We never truly discussed this before that day, but there was a tacit acknowledgment as we stroked each other on the living room couch that we wanted to go further. "I think it's safe today," she whispered in my ear. She rose from our embrace, took my hand and led me to her bedroom. I could picture those moments as clearly as if they'd happened yesterday.

There, the very first time, with the shades drawn, Catherine was the one who unbuckled my belt and slid my jeans down to my ankles. She unbuttoned my shirt and slipped it over my shoulders so I stood there, clad only in my white briefs.

She placed my arms on her shoulders and used her body to

crush up against me, her mouth open and her tongue seeking mine. I tried to slip her jersey over her head and it caught on her bra strap. Our efforts were clumsy but we ended up naked in each other's arms on her bed. In minutes, I was joined to her, feeling the heat inside, and emptying myself in vigorous but diminishing measures. When I heard her moan, my happiness was as complete as I could ever imagine.

Had she become pregnant that very first time? Over the next several weeks, we repeated our performance three more times, once nearly caught by Mrs. Marchand who returned unexpectedly early from her job as a principal. We barely made it into our clothes and back into the living room where Catherine turned on the stereo and we pretended to be fully engaged in our study of gravitational pull of the various planets before her mother walked in, the air still musky and our skin still rosy with lust. If Mrs. Marchand suspected anything, she never said a word.

When did Catherine first learn that she was pregnant? What went through her mind when she first missed a period, or the second time, if there was one? What if Catherine had lived? Would we have gone to college as we planned? If the child was given up for adoption, where would he be now? Or she?

I was trying to sort through all these thoughts when the phone rang.

The rain let up by the time Wetman returned to headquarters. A State Police cruiser was parked at an angle in front of the station. Probably not good news, he thought. Instead of using the front door, he used his key to the rear entrance, entered his office and called Lucy at the front desk by telephone to report that he was in his office.

The two State Troopers stood in the lobby of the Apsley Police Headquarters, eyes straight ahead, as erect and as stony as the statue of the town's founder on the front lawn of the Town

Hall, with their pants tucked into their tall black boots. Lucy peered around them when Chief Wetman stuck his head out of his office. She winked and made a quick head and eye motion in the direction of the two troopers as if Wetman couldn't see them standing there. He signaled with his hand: Send them in.

When the Troopers came to Wetman's office they identified themselves as John Clancy and Mark Terrebonne, both assigned to the Clanton barracks where the State Police Crime Laboratory was located. Clancy stood a half pace in front of Terrebonne and was obviously in charge.

"Chief Wetman, we are here to advise you on behalf of Captain Blackwood of the Clanton barracks that you are to turn over all evidence your department has in connection with the homicide of Catherine Marchand."

Wetman ignored Clancy's rude introduction, looked closely at the officer's name badge and said, "Well, good day to you, too, Trooper Clancy. Thank you, I'm fine. And how are you today?"

This took Clancy by surprise and he took a few seconds to recover, glancing at Terrebonne once and then again for support. In the end, his only option appeared to repeat himself, this time a bit louder.

"Chief Wetman, we are here to advise you on behalf of Captain . . ."

". . . Blackwood of the Clanton barracks, et cetera, et cetera. I heard you quite well the first time."

Terrebonne decided to make a supportive effort. He took a half-step forward and said, "Sir, we want all your files on the case. It's an order. From Captain Blackwood."

Bayard Blackwood was assigned to the Investigative Unit and was familiar to Wetman. He always reminded Wetman of a zucchini. His neck was thick and unusually long and his small head perched on top like a swelling. Even the texture of his face was evocative with its various lumps and bumps. Wetman had a difficult time looking at the man without snickering. He had no intention of turning over the files on Catherine Marchand to Bayard Blackwood, no matter what influence and authority he might have as State Police Captain.

Wetman stood at his desk and nodded before he responded as if he was considering their advice.

"And you have written documentation from this Black-wood fellow?"

"Yes sir," Clancy replied in clipped military fashion. "And it's Captain Blackwood, Sir." He turned to Terrebonne whose left hand immediately shot out with an envelope that he laid on the Chief's desk.

Wetman looked at the envelope but made no motion to reach for it. He looked at Clancy and then at Terrebonne and thought: Two good reasons why I never wanted to join the State Police force.

The Chief coughed into his hand once and said, "How far is the Clanton lab from here, where I assume Captain Binky Blackwood is at the moment?"

"Twenty-one miles, sir," said Clancy, his face reddening at the mention of the Captain's loathed nickname.

"And how long did it take you two to drive here from Clanton?"

Clancy looked at Terrebonne who glanced at his watch. Terrebonne responded to the question. "Approximately thirty-eight minutes, sir."

"Good," said Wetman. "So I can expect a call from the Binkster in approximately forty-five minutes."

Clancy looked at Wetman, his head canted a bit, and said, "Sir?"

"You can drive back to Clanton, tell the Captain that I send my regards, but not my evidence, and suggest that he call me, which should take just under forty-five minutes. I think that's fairly clear."

Wetman sat at his desk and began to peruse a stack of paperwork on his desk, ignoring the Troopers.

Several seconds passed while Wetman engaged in scanning the latest state crime statistics, a matter of absolutely no interest to him whatsoever. He looked up when he didn't hear the sound of footsteps leaving his office. Clancy and Terrebonne were fixed in place.

"Sir, we will relay your message, but I'm sure that the Captain won't be happy about it. Our orders are to pick up all the evidence and return to Clanton with it in our possession."

Wetman looked back down at another report and waved the pair off with his hand.

"Then I guess you're going to have to tell the Captain that he will not get the evidence."

Clancy and Terrebonne stood motionless and silent for several seconds, unsure of themselves. Clancy's face was reddening. Most of the Troopers were assigned to highway duty, but this pair must be running errands for Blackwood. State Troopers were not accustomed to being denied. Clancy, the more senior of the two, was also certain that Captain Blackwood would blow his stack when they returned empty-handed.

"Sir," Terrebonne started, "we are going to return with the evidence in our possession. That was an order from the Captain and we intend to carry it out. Where is the evidence, Chief Wetman?"

With that, Terrebonne struck an impressive pose, legs slightly apart and right hand on his holstered weapon.

Wetman remained apparently more concerned with the papers in front of him, some kind of budget memorandum from the Town Accountant's office, and said nothing. He made some marks in the margins of another memorandum, this one concerning a Finance Committee Hearing schedule, before he looked up and said, "Gentlemen, you're dismissed."

The jaws of both Troopers were rigid. Clancy looked at Terrebonne and they both did an 'about face' and left the Chief's office.

Before they reached the doorway, Wetman said, "Watch your speed on our roads, gentlemen. We take our limits seriously. And unless you are on your way to a mission of demonstrable imminent danger to life or property, you're going to keep your lights off and sirens silent as you leave our community. And no cheating. I'll know. And I'll have you pulled over and ticketed. And believe me, I mean it."

Wetman saw Clancy's eyes narrow, but he said nothing and they were gone.

As soon as he heard the station's door close, he buzzed for Lou Pellerin. The Assistant Chief was in the office within thirty seconds.

"Lou, I just had a visit from two fine members of the State Police who insist that they are going to collect the evidence on the Marchand murder. Apparently, Captain Bayard Blackwood, who has never been encumbered by either ethics or common sense and is one of the most miserable shits to ever wear a badge, thinks that he's going to take the case over. What do you think gives?"

Lou thought for a moment. "I know Blackwood, Chief. I was in school with him a few times over the years. It must have been the lab, Chief. When we sent a few things over for them to check out, word must have gone up from there. What did you tell these guys?"

Wetman stood up and sat with one buttock on the edge of his desk.

"I said they could not have our evidence. And in a little while, their boss is going to be on the phone giving me hell. What do you think I ought to tell him, Lou?"

Lou's forehead creased and Wetman could see he was deep in thought.

"I think I ought to take the call, Chief." Lou, who usually kept criticisms to himself, added, "Is it me, chief, or does Blackwood look a little like a light bulb? I mean, his head is just sort of a bulge at the end of his neck."

Wetman glanced over and said, "I had some other image in my mind, Lou, and besides, a light bulb suggests some brilliance."

"OK, I'll agree with you there. But I still think I should take the call. In fact," Lou looked at his watch, "you've got an important meeting to go to. There's an emergency over at Lafferty's Diner."

"And what emergency is that, Lou?"

"Your coffee's getting cold."

Wetman didn't need any more convincing.

"You're right, Lou, you're absolutely right," said Wetman as he slipped on his coat.

"And what are you going to say to Captain Blackwood in my place?"

They walked together to the front door of the station. Wetman slipped on his trench coat, even though the rain had abated, and Lou accompanied him down the front steps.

They stopped and Lou said, "First, I'll remind Binky Blackwood that I'm the one who beat the crap out of him in a boxing match several years ago, and then I'll suggest that he take his shiny black boots off and shove them up his ass."

Wetman stopped and looked at Pellerin. "Blackwood must have three inches on you and thirty pounds. How'd you do it?"

"He's slow as a musk ox and he's got a glass jaw. He never laid a glove on me and it was over quick."

Wetman nodded and sauntered off in the direction of the diner and nodded.

"You understand, Lou, that I expect a full report when I return."

When he was clearly out of earshot, Wetman kept his head down and mumbled, "And you really should be nice to Captain Blackwood, Lou."

Lou Pellerin had plenty of experience over the years with State Police and its command staff. They considered themselves the elite of the state's multiple law enforcement agencies and treated local police officers, especially those in smaller towns like Apsley, as if they were annoyances, like hemorrhoids. In Lou's experience, some of them were outstanding professionals, but others threw their weight around and were generally successful with their tactics when they took cases over from local forces. This was usually done under the guise of "bringing in expertise" but it amounted to simple bullying.

If Catherine's murder happened today, the Apsley police would likely have little control over the matter. The D.A.'s office handled all capital crimes directly from its office, except in bigger cities where there was a sizeable investigative staff and considerable experience.

This was a very cold case, though, and things were considerably different.

Success in taking over cases didn't necessarily translate into success at solving cases, Lou knew. Certainly, the State Police had the labs and the equipment, but their ability to close actual cases was not a record that Lou Pellerin would be proud of. The State Police tended to get puffed up and make a lot of noise on the high profile successes, but they never uttered a word about their failures. In fact, the low percentage cases were never sought out in the first place.

The fact that Blackwood and his staff knew some of the recent developments in the Marchand case only confirmed for

Lou that Apsley's police department investigation was headed in the right direction. But the fact that Apsley did not have a full-time detective was a plus for the other side. Blackwood was sure to be keeping that in mind as he plotted the takeover of the case; it was ammunition when he went to the D.A.'s office in his attempt to assume control.

When the call came in from Blackwood, Lou enjoyed taking the phone call in Wetman's office. He stared out the window at the tree lined Main Street and listened to Blackwood rage and spew invective in his direction. There wasn't even a calm start to the conversation; Blackwood began to rail as soon as Lou picked up.

"Don't pretend that you have the staff to handle this, Lou. I know Apsley. You guys should stick to what you do best, like directing traffic, and leave the tough jobs to the professionals."

Lou could picture Blackwood's jaw in front of him and wanted to smack it.

"Here's a case that's decades old that you haven't solved yet. I have an experienced special Cold Case squad that deals *only* in cases like this and unless I get those files, I'm going to the D.A. today to let him know what kind of cooperation I'm getting from you peckerwoods. Just so you know, the Governor personally called the Attorney General on this case, and the A.G. called the District Attorney, so you guys should expect to see my same two Troopers back to visit your Chief real soon. Tell him that! And tell him that when they show up, I expect to have all the files and all the evidence ready for them to take back with them. Do you hear me?"

When the steam finally lifted and there was a pause of some length, Lou suggested to the Captain that he would personally drive over to Clanton the next morning and slam Blackwood in the nose like he did the last time.

"You fell like a leaky sack of wet manure, Binky. I'd like to see that again if you don't mind."

Lou knew that his comments would get a response and Blackwood seethed. Lou waited again until a gap appeared.

"Save your gas money, Blackwood. If your guys show up here again, they're going to get the same treatment they got today."

The call ended abruptly when Blackwood slammed the telephone down. Lou felt vindicated but the D.A.'s involvement could hurt. The Governor's interest in the case didn't help either. He'd let Wetman know about this and see what developed.

FOURTEEN

The next morning

Wetman was sitting in his office tilted back in his chair. Pellerin put a cup of coffee on the Chief's desk and opened his own.

Wetman never looked up. "What's a seven letter word for Dubai?"

Lou thought about this for a few seconds before he said, "Damned if I know?"

At that moment, Officer Jimmy Reilly came into the office and stood, a little sheepishly, near the doorway. Wetman glanced over the top of the paper. "Reilly, what's a seven letter word for Dubai."

Reilly looked up at the ceiling for a second or two before he said, "Emirate."

Wetman filled in the squares, leaned forward and put the paper on his desk. "You da man, Reilly!" He smiled and motioned for Reilly to take a seat.

Wetman waited until Reilly was settled and put a serious expression on his face for the occasion. "Reilly, Assistant Chief Pellerin, has something to say to you."

Lou turned towards Reilly who had no idea whether this meeting was good news or bad news.

"Officer Reilly, we have been looking over your file and we're impressed with your diligence, your intelligence and your persistence."

Reilly's mouth had gone dry as soon as he heard he was being called into the Chief's office. He was glad he wasn't being asked to respond verbally.

"Chief Wetman has just created a new position in the Department and we'd like you to consider applying for it. In fact, we are suggesting strongly that you do."

Reilly's face took on an air of confusion. His brow furrowed and he glanced back and forth between Wetman and Pellerin in an unsuccessful attempt at getting clarification. He tried to ask a question but his lips were stuck together.

Wetman saw the distress and bailed him out.

"Relax, Reilly. We want to have a full-time detective on staff and we want that detective to be James Patrick Reilly. If you accept, you've got the job."

Reilly said nothing, just absorbing the news.

Lou coughed slightly, "Ahem. Chief."

Wetman went on. "It's an official position within the department, but until the next budget revision goes in, there's no extra money for the time being. When that happens, in another sixty days or so, we're going to have to do some paperwork. I'm hoping we can get you a good raise for the work we're asking you to do."

Lou jumped back in. "No promises, Jimmy, but we're going to try our best. Meanwhile, we'll need a decision from you pretty quick."

Reilly couldn't think of any reason why he'd ever consider saying no. Nevertheless, he knew he should never look too eager; it makes it too easy for superiors to take advantage of you.

A few seconds went by, during which Wetman shifted from one foot to the next.

Lou saw the quandary on the young officer's face. "By 'pretty quick', Jimmy, I mean right now."

Reilly nodded vigorously up and down, violating his own advice about appearing overly eager.

Wetman let out a long sigh.

"Lou, take Detective Reilly into your office and give him a briefing on the Marchand homicide."

He turned back to his desk and said as he sat down.

"And Reilly, congratulations. It took me nine years to make detective. It's a job I loved and did well. I expect you're going to do a great job."

I was sitting alone in my apartment looking over a spreadsheet I created for the bid I was making on the smaller portion of the Kerrigan Mills, but I was having trouble maintaining concentration. My mind was filled with conflicting images of parenthood with Catherine, of an entirely different life direction, or a living, breathing Catherine Marchand growing into adulthood and parenthood. I was filled with sadness and regret. I may have felt sorry for myself at other points in my life, but never like this. Nothing was making good sense when I heard my doorbell ring.

When I went downstairs and opened the door, I was surprised to see Tina Gladwell standing there. She'd been drinking and I could smell the gin. Without asking if she could come in, she entered and took the stairs to my apartment. Her eyes were just a little glazed over and when she walked in, she took solid, sober strides. She sat down at my kitchen table, removed her knit hat and scarf and folded them neatly.

"I know. I probably shouldn't be here, but Ken isn't around

and he won't be back for at least an hour. So. No scenes. No yelling."

I took a seat at the same table and Tina reached across and covered my hands in hers.

"I need to talk. Stupid, I know. You're my husband's friend and I've just had him served with divorce papers. But I need to talk."

I thought I saw a tear appear at the corner of her eye. It may have been the cold.

"This is probably something I should talk to another woman about, but hey! No women friends, know what I mean?" Tina was smiling but it did nothing to cover the pathos that I saw and felt.

"You and Ken. You talk, right? I mean, besides football and cars and good looking women. You talk sometimes, right?"

"Not a lot, but sometimes. It's not really a guy thing."

"Even when one of the guys is going through a divorce?"

"No. But we talk sometimes."

"Well, Dave Blondin, I need to talk, too. Do you have a drink for me somewhere in this place?"

I stood and went to a cabinet before I asked, "Are you sure?" She was already well into the bag.

"Hell, yes. Gin and tonic if you've got it. Hold the tonic."

She took her drink and sipped. It was smaller than she wanted but about what she expected. Then she smiled.

"You wanted to talk, Tina?"

"Sure. That's why I'm here. I'm so-o-o fucked up, Dave. You just can't believe."

She suddenly caught herself. "Oh, I know you've had your own problems over the past few years. I don't mean to tell you that my life is lousier than yours. I didn't come here for a contest or for sympathy."

She took another sip and glanced out the window. She looked disconcerted, and I sensed that she was locked in a study not of the gray trees that rose bare branched into the sky. More likely, she was staring into darkness and seeing some ugliness staring back. I waited for her to return.

"A few years ago, I had a good business that was booming, remember? I was working out every day and my body was so-o-o tight. The health club was just going great. I loved it.

"I had a beautiful son, and a very tall, very handsome husband who loved me. Now, here we are. My beautiful son is dead. My husband is so self-absorbed that I don't even know him any more. And my business is closed down because I couldn't stand being nice to customers any longer."

"You've had a rough patch, Tina."

"I see people I've known all my life and they look at me crooked. Sometimes they stop me and ask, 'Is anything wrong?' "

She took another sip.

"My question, Dave, is anything, anything at all . . . Is anything right?"

I shrugged my shoulders. When the world is crumbling around you, how do you just go on as if everything's fine? "You and Ken have been through a lot."

"Know something, Dave? When Eric died, I never saw his body. I never saw him at the hospital or at the funeral home. I don't know what he looked like. Like, was he grimacing when he died? Were his eyes open? Was he pleading to be found? To be saved?

"I'm his mother, and he was only a few feet away at the hospital morgue, lying cold and under a sheet on a table, but I couldn't do it. I couldn't look at my own son. How sick is that?"

"No one can blame you for the feelings you had. It was an awful time. Don't blame yourself."

"Whew. There's a word for you, Dave. The 'B' word. You're

right. I blame myself for not even looking at my son, my little boy."

"Would looking have made you feel better? It wouldn't have changed anything."

"You're right. I know that. But I still blame myself. And like a lot of people, I figure I deserve it. That's what I read once. Some people feel guilty and absorb all kinds of blame because they feel they deserve it."

"You didn't deserve that. No one ever does."

"You should have been a therapist, Dave."

I was feeling like a therapist at the moment, and didn't enjoy it. I didn't like the responsibility and I didn't want to say anything that would make matters worse. Tina, like Ken, was extremely fragile at the moment. Anything might set her off. I was trying to be careful.

"Want to know something? One time, a few years after Ken and I were married, I cheated on him. I screwed my boss at the bank for about six months. On his desk, on the floor, in his bed when his wife was visiting relatives."

I held up both hands to indicate 'stop'.

"What? Don't want to hear my confession? I screwed him as much as I could before I got tired of him and he got tired of me. Do you remember him? Charles Cox. Great name. He left Apsley a long time ago and took a job someplace else."

"You don't need to tell me this."

"Hell, if confession is good for the soul, then I ought to feel better, right?"

"Tina. You need to speak to someone. A professional. Not me."

"Not you, Dave? But you're the best buddy anybody could have. I hear that from everybody. Good old Dave Blondin. What a guy!"

"Tina, please."

"Don't worry, Dave. I'm not going to tell people I screwed you. There was a time, though, when I would have jumped all over you."

"Tina."

"Lately, I'm feeling like I need to screw somebody, Dave. I'm trying, but the poor guy just can't bring himself to do it. He likes Ken too much. Imagine that? I'm offering him a good roll in the hay and he feels too much loyalty to take advantage. I'm pretty good, too. I'm not in perfect shape any more, but hey, I've still got a decent figure, you know. No surgery, either."

She pointed to her breasts as she continued. "These bad babies are one hundred percent natural. I could show this guy a great time, but no. I even tried surprising him in the middle of the day. Snuck in, got naked, and got under the covers. But no way. He wanted to, I could tell. Even felt me up for a minute before his guilt motor got revved up."

"Tina."

"Poor Bob. Oops. You knew it was Bobby Hayes, right? I mean, I know you know. Poor guy."

"Look, Tina, it's none of . . ."

She cut me off. "You're absolutely right. It's my guilt we're talking about and nobody else's. You're just going to have to go and get your own."

She rose from her chair, wrapped the scarf around her collar and slipped her hat back on.

"I'm thinking, Dave, that all I want is one safe little place where I can go and relax and feel safe. I've tried to do that but it doesn't always work. What the hell, I've got nothing left to lose, right? The battle's over. I've paid my dues. Don't I deserve just one safe little place?"

I didn't know how to answer that.

"Yeah, Dave. That's what I thought. I'll see myself out. Thanks for the drink."

When she was gone, I looked out the window. Tina Gladwell was walking away. She must have sensed me looking at her because she waved at me over her shoulder without looking back or breaking stride. As sorry as I felt for myself before Tina showed up, I didn't know when I felt worse for another human being.

FIFTEEN

Monday, the Following Week

"So you're the famous Dave Blondin. The way my husband spoke of you, I figured you'd be at least eight feet tall." She shook my hand with a firm grip, confident.

I wasn't expecting Jacqueline Marchand so early and I was yet to shave and get fully dressed. When she called yesterday, she told me she'd stop by my apartment sometime in the morning. To me, that means 'after nine o'clock', or what I consider a civilized way to interpret the suggestion. Right now, my watch read eight twenty, well over the bounds of polite society. Nevertheless, she looked very nice for such an early hour, and I readily forgave her this breach of etiquette.

Phil's wife was clad in tan slacks, probably camel hair, an ecru silk blouse and a light brown cashmere cardigan. She carried a belted trench coat in taupe leather and a silk scarf from Hermès in shades of green and orange. She wore a cameo pendant around her neck and gold hoop earrings. I'm not sure if I ever saw a woman who was dressed with more class than this one before me, at least not in person. I, on the other hand, wore a hooded gray sweatshirt, torn at one elbow, a pair of faded Wranglers and scuffed brown work boots. If anyone walked by right now, we would make an improbable pair.

"Come in, come in," I said, dumbstruck for a moment while I still absorbed my first cup of coffee and the situation at hand. I held the door wide and said as she passed, "I'm upstairs and to the right. Go right on up."

She smiled and said as she walked upstairs, "Sorry if I called a little early for you. I guess I'm a morning person. But if you have hot coffee, I'd love a cup."

I describe myself as a coffee snob, fussy about the type of bean and the degree of roasting. I grind and brew my coffee every morning and use an air pot to keep it fresh and hot for hours. "You happen to be at the right place for good coffee."

We entered my apartment and I pointed the way to the kitchen table. "Sorry for the mess. Let me get you a cup. Cream? Sugar?"

"Thanks, but I take mine black."

"My kind of woman." I poured a cup and she savored the aroma. I took the seat opposite her at the table and we gave each other appraising looks.

She took a sip and smiled. "My but that's wonderful coffee. We have six Starbucks in the town where we . . . *I* live . . . and they insist on over-roasting every bean. You lose the snap of a Kenyan coffee or the roundness of a Sumatran. Everything tastes the same."

"I call it 'Char-bucks,' the emphasis equally on the 'char' and the 'bucks'. I'm glad you like this."

We were still evaluating the other when she broke the brief silence. "Phil spoke so highly of you. You must have been very special friends."

"I guess we were. It's been a long time." I was studying her as I spoke. Lovely bone structure, long sculptured nose, heart-shaped face, thick brown hair going to gray, a slightly crooked smile. Not beautiful, but handsome. Comfortable with herself.

"To hear Phil talk about you two, you were joined at the hip."

I took a sip. I needed my coffee. "Maybe Phil is making more of the friendship than it really was. We were good buddies. We hung out at each other's house. We played baseball together. We dated some of the same girls."

"And you were at the Marchand home when the police came to tell them about Catherine."

I was a little surprised that this would have made such an impression on Phil that he'd keep that information filed away for easy retrieval. "Yes. I was there. I went home, but I knew something was wrong. Phil parents were obviously crying. I thought maybe his grandmother died or something."

"But it was Catherine."

I had replayed the scene in my mind more than once in the past several days. "Yes. It was Catherine." I was staring into my coffee cup when I answered. When I looked up, I saw a woman who was serious, intent on learning more. "Jacqueline . . . do people call you Jackie?"

"Not really. My mother's idea. If she heard someone call me Jackie, she'd be horrified."

I could just imagine the mother. "Then I'll call you Jackie."

"Thanks."

"Jackie, why are you here?"

"It's Phil, and yes, there's still something there. There's everything there." She shifted position in her chair and leaned forward. "Did Phil tell you about the break up of our marriage? That we'd become estranged? That I was cold? Or that we argued? Did he talk about us?"

"He didn't say much. Nothing at all really. I just guessed

that there'd been some sort of breakdown. That's what usually happens, isn't it?"

"Like your marriage? Phil told me you were divorced a few years ago."

"I guess."

The shift in focus caught me off guard. I tried to neutralize the shift as well as I could. "Everybody has his own story, but sure, like my marriage. Have you talked to Phil lately?"

"Only once since he's been up here, and not about you. No, before he ever considered moving back here, he hired a private investigation agency where we live and got a detailed report on just about everybody he knew up here. I saw the reports on his desk."

"Creepy."

"He'd probably say he was thorough, but I know what you mean."

She didn't say anything for a while and the silence was getting uncomfortable, at least for me.

"Dave, did Phil tell you that I love him? That I've always loved him? That I asked him to stay? That we could go to counseling? That he insisted on coming here alone? That I want him to come home? That I'll follow him here if that's what he wants? Did he say any of that?"

Jacqueline Marchand was a pistol. Strong and opinionated and not afraid to speak her mind.

"No. He never said any of that."

"I don't expect Phil or any man for that matter to share his feelings as much as women do around each other. But Phil? He really clammed up. And I don't think he's been looking his best lately. He won't tell me what's wrong, and I'm worried about him, Dave."

I didn't want to be dragged into the middle of a husband-wife confrontation and tried to extricate myself from the arena as quickly as I could.

"I'm sure he's OK. Older, sure, than I remember, but still Phil. But you should be talking to him directly. I mean, I'd like to help, but Phil is the one who needs to hear what you have to say."

She smiled and kept eye contact. "Smooth, Dave. Very smooth."

Like a man falsely accused, I straightened up and raised my hands, palms to the front. "Me? What do you mean?"

"It's OK. I want to see him and talk with him. Face to face."

She studied me carefully before she continued.

"I found a note in his pocket once. Incriminating, if you know what I mean. We rarely escape cliché on the essential matters of life, isn't that so?"

"Incriminating note?"

"Phil? A philanderer? Maybe. At least I thought so once, especially after that silly note."

She finished her coffee and reached for her coat.

"When I look back on it, the note was juvenile and probably meaningless. Just a note. Maybe he dismissed it. Maybe he didn't. Maybe he disregarded it as an advance from some cute young thing. Maybe he plunged right in, pardon my choice of words."

"Look, I don't know about any note, and I don't know anything about another woman. And, Jackie, I don't want to know. Stuff like this is between you and Phil."

We faced each other at the table.

"Thanks for your time and your coffee, Dave. And thanks for listening. I hope we can speak again soon."

I put my hand on her arm in a gesture of understanding and agreement. "I'm sorry. I just blew you off. Have another cup of coffee." She didn't look certain that she wanted to stay but shrugged her shoulders and laid her coat back down.

"OK. And that's exactly what you did. It was ham-fisted, don't you think?"

"Probably," I said, pouring more coffee for both of us. "But like I said, Phil hasn't said much of anything about you or the divorce. At least not to me."

"And you're the one I would expect he'd be most likely to speak to," she said quickly.

I thought about what I was about to say before I said it and my pause caused Jacqueline to cock her head in anticipation.

"Honest, guys might sit around in a bar and complain about their wives or their girlfriends, but we're not much for sharing innermost feelings. When men get together, there's usually a macho thing going on, even though we would never admit it. I'm not saying that's good; it's probably terrible. But that's the way things are."

"I understand, Dave. Really, I do."

"So tell me about the Phil you know. How do you think he's changed over the years?"

"He accomplished a great deal in his career. But you know that."

"We spoke about his work. He did very well, didn't he?"

"Did he tell you he was fired?'

My bewilderment showed.

"He really believed he was going to be named the top banana at the firm. Honestly, he never saw it coming."

"He never said a word."

"Am I surprised? Phil reveals himself very carefully. Getting canned shook him to the bone. He was there for a long time and they brought somebody in from the outside. It happens."

"He doesn't act like someone who got fired. He still swaggers like he did back in high school. Cocky, like the old Phil I knew a long time ago."

"That's Phil. He was always a tiger when it came to analyzing a company's financials, but personal inadequacies don't exist if you ignore them long enough. I've given this a lot of thought. Phil's experiences over the past twenty or thirty years in the business world might have been illuminating and rewarding, but I don't think he ever found that nicely wrapped package of self-realization. After you look at all his accomplishments, he's still the same self-centered Phil that I met many years ago and that you probably knew just as well."

"If that's the person you're fighting for, why are you trying so hard?"

"Because I acknowledge that we're, all of us, imperfect, and some are more imperfect than others. Because this is a guy who used to have a lot of power, and he used it; I'm not sure he'll do well back here on his own. Because . . . because he's generally thoughtful and kind, a good lover, a wonderful friend; we're fond of many of the same things; he's my husband, the companion with whom I've shared so much that is history for us . . . just because."

I recalled something I'd read or heard many years earlier.

"To live is like love: All reason is against it and all instinct is for it."

"Marvelous, Dave. Did you think that up yourself, or did someone else say that?"

"Someone else, I don't know who. But maybe it fits."

I sipped and was finally feeling awake. "I meant what I said earlier by the way, too. He doesn't look bad. He looks a little intense sometimes, but I think I would too in the same circumstances. I notice he's got a little twitch once in a while, like he's got a case of nerves. He's probably had his share of ulcers over the years. He's also thinner than I would have expected. Most of us have a little paunch on us after all these years."

"He's always been vain about his looks. He's a handsome man, but he can be as superficial as a matinee idol. Maybe more so. As sharp as a tack when it comes to business, but as thick as two planks when it comes to things like relationships. In any event, poor Phil never walked by a mirror without glancing twice."

I found that amusing. I'd probably say the same thing about

Phil. As a teenager, Phil was always conscious of his looks. Just the right jeans, the hair combed just so.

"And he has had his share of ulcers. Phil was highly thought of at his company, you know. The firm always made its projections by a penny or two, never more. And it never failed to at least meet the analyst recommendations. That caused a lot of stress, but that's his M.O. Reliable in matters of numbers; totally at sea in every other respect."

"Is he that bad?"

"I saw it at his work more than once. Honestly, I thought of it as a sort of homosexual trait that he kept repressed. He was always on the look out for the sharpest dressing man in accounting or finance and he'd groom him for a bigger job and keep advancing him. They had to be apostles of profit, but they also had to 'look the part', as Phil would say. Those are his words: 'Look the part.'

"Whenever he found one, he'd make sure the young buck moved ahead, have lunch with him at his club, have private chats. He'd explain the mystique of the business world to the youngster and push him ahead as fast as he could, sometimes to the chagrin of all the other people in the department who weren't as 'clean cut' but who were just plain capable and efficient. That's Phil. He's bright and generous, but shallow as a saucer of cat's milk."

She shifted in her chair. "Look, Dave, I don't expect Phil to drop everything that he's doing here, but I want him to be safe. He might have the look of a captain of industry, but he's a babe in the woods in terms of real life events. I don't want him to get hurt and there's something in the air, something in the stars that tells me he's in trouble."

I was paying attention. "What kind of trouble?"

"I'm not sure. He was acting a little strange. Before he told me he wanted a separation, he wasn't himself. I'm not sure I can describe it. His nervous twitches, as you've probably noticed, they got a little worse. He was pale. Then he told me he needed to get away from us. That's how he put it. Get away from 'us'."

"Strange way to put it. Was he depressed? Not sleeping? I told you I thought he was thin, maybe losing too much weight?"

"Maybe. I wanted us to go to a counselor but he wouldn't hear of it. Said his mind was made up."

"Your kids? What did they say?"

"They were as shocked as I was. They're both incredibly busy, but they both took time to come home and try to talk with their father. Nothing."

Dave was thinking. Silent. Then, "Is he ill? Do you know?"

"Nothing I'm aware of. I asked him once and he said no. It was just something he needed to do. Get away from 'us', like 'us' was the big problem. I have to tell you, I never saw it."

"How about your parents. Just as shocked by all this?"

"They're both quite elderly now, and frail. When Phil left, they were devastated."

"Your family is very wealthy. Was that a problem?"

"It was an issue with Phil, especially early on. Wanted to make sure he made it on his own and didn't have to rely on my family's money, and he did do very well financially. We have a comfortable life and we have always been entirely self-reliant."

The phone rang and I answered it in the living room. When I returned to the kitchen, Jacqueline was already standing, her coat on her arm. "I really should go."

"No, please. It's all right. That was a friend of mine. I told him I'd meet up with him later on."

She looked quizzical. "Not Phil?"

"No. Another friend. In any event, we have time. You don't have to go."

"I'm staying at that motel downtown for a few days, maybe more. I'm planning on sticking around for a while, so please call me when you can. I'd like to talk some more."

She started towards the door and stopped suddenly. "One thing, Dave. Did Phil ever mention the box he found? It was Catherine's."

"No. I can't say he did."

"When Phil's parents died and he was cleaning out their things, he found it. I've never seen it myself because Phil treats it like the Holy Grail. You might ask him about it."

I nodded and she walked off. I watched her from my front steps as she got into her car and drove off with a wave. I could imagine how Phil was enthralled with her. I just couldn't figure out how and why he became so unenthralled so suddenly and why he had to make the cut so quickly and completely.

Today must be divorce day, I thought. I was seated in Lafferty's Diner waiting for my BLT and onion soup when Chief Wetman invited himself over and sat down. We ate our lunches . . . open-faced turkey sandwich and a cup of coffee for the Chief. I told him I met Phil Marchand's wife earlier today and that got the Chief started.

"When I got divorced, I was shattered," Wetman said. As it happens, the diner's television was on; another pop star was separating with her husband . . . of almost eighteen months in this case.

"We were married for almost twenty-three years when she came to me and told me she wanted out. Same story I'd heard a hundred times from other guys."

"What do you mean?" I was curious to see how closely Wetman's experience matched my own.

"You know. Like she hadn't been happy in the marriage for years . . . we had grown in different directions . . . she loved me, but not as a husband . . . it was time to make a clean break and move forward. How many times have you heard that?" Wetman sipped the last of his coffee and signaled for a refill.

I had, indeed. The words were always used euphemistically.

The departing partner either had a lover, or just got bored, or had never really been in love with the other, marriage was something they'd fallen into when marriage was expected of them. How could you tell? What did it matter?

Wetman took a sip of the fresh cup and continued. "After we split, I started making the rounds. When you're a cop, your buddies are always ready to fix you up with somebody. Most of them have been through this thing before. Then along comes Mary Alice, and I think . . . whoa, not for me. She wasn't my type. She's from this big Italian family and I know from one of my buddies that her brother is really connected. Like, I need that crap, right? Besides, in my mind, I'm looking for this nice sweet little thing, and Mary Alice . . . well, she's sort of broad across the beam, know what I mean?

"But I give it a little time because I'm lonely and she's nice enough, and we go out to eat once in a while. And I think, what is it with this woman that keeps me coming back, besides the fact that she's a maestro in the kitchen? And I talk to my therapist over and over about this. Mary Alice isn't pushing me into anything, but I keep thinking that here's a human being who has an enormous heart, a wonderful sense of humor, beautiful values, and she's the person I want to spend the rest of my life with."

"You had a therapist?" The thought struck me as unusual. Here was a hardened city cop admitting openly that he needed help and found it.

"I still have one. I go to him once a month to keep my head on straight. I'll give you his name if you want a good one. Guy almost became a priest years back. Good guy. Anyway, I keep calling Mary Alice to ask her if she wants to go out, and she keeps saying yes, and we just like each other so much, and I think about her when I'm at work, and she thinks about me. And I like her soul and her smile and her family, even the connected brother, and I finally get up the nerve to ask Mary Alice if she ever gave any thought to getting married . . . after all, she'd been dumped by her first husband, and we all get kind of gun shy afterwards. Or we don't, but we should.

"And she says, 'What? Are you freakin' crazy?' And I sort of had my feelings hurt; it took a lot for me to ask the question, and she's blowing me off. I was so pissed off I just walked out and left her in her living room and drove home, and my message light is blinking. And I press the button and it's her.

"And she says, 'Look you little Jew asshole' . . . a term of endearment if I ever heard one . . . 'you must have rocks in your head. We've been seeing each other for only a couple of months, so let's give it some time, huh?'"

"And then what?"

"And I gave it about a week and I couldn't stand it, and I gave her a diamond and she said yes and cried. And we got married, and I love her like crazy, and she loves me, and we love being together. It's one of the good stories that comes out of a divorce."

"And she didn't have any problem with moving to Apsley? I mean we say it all the time here: It's not exactly the center of the universe."

"Not at all. We love it here, and she told me I needed the change. And Dave, for Jerry and Mary Alice Wetman, Apsley *is* the center of the universe."

"But what about missing things in the city?"

"The only thing we miss is opera. No, wait a minute. Opera and a good Jewish deli. Just can't get good pastrami on rye with a half-sour anywhere around here. Anyway, we'll probably go back into the city once in a while to take in an opera. But outside of that? We don't miss the traffic and the smog and the noise. Apsley has been good to us so far, and we have each other."

"I never figured you for an opera guy?"

"My wife, Mary Alice, she always wanted to be an opera

singer. She even sang opera on the radio for a while when she was in a chorus in New York. She's been on stage in the city, too, as a supernumerary . . . an extra. She has the voice of an angel."

"Do you know what they're singing? I mean it's all Italian, isn't it?"

"Or German, most of the classics. But I wouldn't know what to do if they sang in English. There's was a guy one time . . . I forget his name. He said he didn't care what language opera was sung in, so long as it was in a language he didn't understand."

Wetman had nearly finished his second cup and he signaled the waitress for two more. I begged off, thinking I'd be wired for the twelve hours and urinating hourly for the next six. Wetman, it seemed to me, drank the stuff all day with no ill effects.

"You know, my wife and I, we talk a lot to each other, and she knows as much about my work as I do. I'm probably violating some confidentiality rule somewhere, but I need to talk to someone, and Mary Alice is the best listener I know. Plus, she wouldn't break a confidence even if you put her in Abu Greib and stretched her on the rack. She knows the people I deal with, even if she's never laid eyes on them, even you.

"And last night she says something that really catches me off guard. She says, 'Jerry, this guy David Blondin, I think he's fifth business in Apsley, isn't he?'"

"What? What's that mean?"

"Well, in opera, there's a hero and a heroine and a villain and usually a confidante. Usually, the hero is a tenor, the heroine is a soprano and the villain is a bass. The confidante is usually an alto, but these are just generalities. But one of the keys in an opera is a character called fifth business. He's not listed in the program that way, but he's usually there. He's not a hero, but he's not the villain either. He's there . . . get this . . . to keep the story moving along and to keep it from running off the rails. He's involved without being involved. He's crucial to the whole drama, but he's not the star of the show. He just pays attention . . . fifth business guys are always good listeners, by the way . . . and moves things along. So what do you think? Is Mary Alice right?"

He looked at me for his answer.

"Not exactly how I thought of myself. I mean, what's so great about being the guy that doesn't really do anything but move the story along?"

"Ah, Dave, that is one of the cruelties in the theater of life; we all like to think of ourselves as stars, and we don't appreciate finding out we're just supporting characters."

I thought about this, but not with any sense of pleasure.

"You're thinking about this, huh?"

I turned to Wetman, almost scowling.

"Well, remember, it's an essential role, even if no one remembers the names of the players. Without fifth business, there's no opera."

"I guess I should say thanks. I just don't feel like it."

Wetman smiled, toasted me with his cup, and finished his coffee.

Phil Marchand was trying to take a nap but couldn't get to sleep. He was exhausted and had taken some pills to relieve the tremors he'd been experiencing. Maybe that kept him from slumber.

He lay back on the bed and closed his eyes. Just some rest, some peace and quiet, would do him good.

The telephone rang.

Marchand considered letting it go to his answering machine but decided on the third ring to take the call.

"Mr. Marchand? It's Chief Wetman from the Apsley Police Department."

Marchand sat upright. "Yes, Chief, have you found out anything about my sister's murder?"

Marchand didn't trust the small Apsley force to accomplish anything, hence his call to the governor. But who knows, he thought, maybe they'll surprise me.

"The only thing we've found out is that the State Police would like to relieve Apsley of its duties in this case. Maybe you know something about this?"

Marchand should have expected this call earlier than it came, but he was prepared.

"Look, Chief. It's been close to thirty years since my sister was murdered. Maybe you can understand my frustration."

"Oh, I understand. I also understand that you came into my office all peaches and cream only to leave and make a well-placed call to one of your buddies. A man, and I mean a man, would more likely speak directly to my face instead of sneaking out the side door."

"It wasn't like that!"

"Oh sure it was. If you had your mind made up after two days back in town, then fine. You're rich and smart. Good for you. But if you want to go around my back, then be a man."

Marchand wasn't used to being spoken to like this and his blood was boiling. But before he could lash back, Wetman said, "And by the way, if I hear another report that you're parking across the street from Malcolm Prudhomme's house, I'm going to personally put the cuffs on you for obstructing an investigation."

"Now you listen to me, Chief . . ." But the line was dead.

SIXTEEN

Later that week

Detective Jimmy Reilly was at his desk at 9:30 AM peering at photos of evidence collected at Catherine Marchand's murder scene. He'd already cleared a breaking and entering case from the day before and scheduled four witness statements on a hit and run accident before he picked up the envelope with the Catherine Marchand photos. His day was going to be a full one.

He grabbed his Diet Coke and took a sip as he studied every facet of every photograph. Something was there that he wasn't seeing. Of that he felt certain. He just didn't know what he was looking for.

Assistant Chief Pellerin told him the same thing a few days ago when they looked over the evidence together: "They missed something twenty-nine years ago, and we've been missing it ever since. There's something here and we're not seeing it. You've got a chance now."

His wristwatch beeped. It was a gift from his girlfriend on

his promotion. It was a lot more than she could afford, and he didn't think he'd be using all the various functions on the watch, but already he was accustomed to using it to keep his appointments. He checked his calendar and saw that he was due to meet a complainant on an alleged theft case. Then a walk over to the cleaners to pick up his dry cleaning before lunch.

He also wanted to use that time to talk to Mr. Wessel at Apsley Cleaners and ask some questions. Catherine Marchand had been classmate of his back in high school, and Reilly wanted to get a better picture of the dynamics that occurred back then. Mr. Wessel could give him a first-hand account.

Like, did she date a lot? What kind of reputation did she have? It was a small group . . . only eighty-one kids in the graduating class . . . how did she get along with her classmates?

Reilly also did some research and found that at the last reunion for that class, thirty-four showed up. Seven had died, and thirty two others did not or could not attend. The rest were unaccounted for. He didn't know what this data would show or if it would help at all. It only helped Reilly get a better grasp of the Apsley High School Who's Who of twenty-nine years ago. All the effort of reconstructing things like this might just be for nothing.

He tried to consider other possibilities, but could not find anything else that might give him a hint. There were, for example, no strangers sighted by anyone in the area before or after the murder.

Reilly was also privy to the Catherine Marchand pregnancy matter. But Dave Blondin was out of the area at the time of the murder; that was confirmed several times by as many witnesses.

Further, the thought that Blondin would arrange to have someone else dispatch Catherine was considered and dismissed. This was a passionate murder, not a quick hit. According to Chief Wetman, Blondin exhibited absolute surprise when he heard the news of Catherine Marchand's pregnancy. No, that scheme didn't fit.

Reilly looked over the numerous pages of interview notes when Malcolm Prudhomme was brought in, but that yielded nothing of either great value or interest. There were neither witnesses nor any physical evidence to link Malcolm to the scene. Still, thought Reilly, something isn't right.

Then he placed a telephone call to a retired police officer, William Turner, and asked if he could stop by for a visit.

Bill Turner was almost eighty-nine years old, but he still had a higher degree of mental acuity than most people half his age. When Detective Reilly stopped by his house to ask him some questions about the original investigation into Catherine Marchand's murder, Turner was raking leaves from between the yew shrubs in his front yard.

"So you're the new detective? Come in, let's talk. I should hire some young kid to do this outside work, but it just seems like a natural thing for me to do. I put those yews in fifty-five years ago when they were twigs, and cleaning them out every year just seems like something I should be doing myself."

They sat at the dining room table and drank hot cocoa with marshmallow.

"So you drew the short straw."

Reilly wasn't sure what Turner meant.

"I mean, you've been assigned to find the killer of Catherine Marchand. That's the short straw. I know, because I drew that same straw twenty-nine years ago."

"Why do you think you couldn't find the killer, Mr. Turner?"

He wiped the marshmallow from his lip before he spoke.

"Well, first of all, very little physical evidence. I'm sure you've looked at the same things. Not much, is there?"

"You're right. There's not much."

"Now maybe with DNA tests and all, there might be something new that shows up. Have there been anymore tests?"

"Some, but nothing that shows anything new." Reilly decided not to reveal the pregnancy or paternity issues to the retired police officer.

"The second thing was, no motive. We didn't have any indication of anyone who wanted her killed. Now that doesn't rule out a motive-less crime, a crime of opportunity where she just happened to be in the way. But still, we had no evidence, no witnesses, nothing incriminating to anyone. Sure, there was Malcolm Prudhomme, and the Chief back then, Al Moncton, he wanted to put Malcolm away. Probably a good idea, but we'd never win a conviction."

"What about jealousy?"

"Ah, did you ever hear the stories about Catherine and the other girls they called the princesses."

"I think everybody in Apsley knows about them. It's part of the local folklore."

"There was plenty to be jealous of. Catherine was beautiful, smart, and had great future ahead of her. Captain of this and that. She had the world by the tail for such a young thing. But who was jealous enough to kill her? My goodness, the other four princesses could have been targets of jealousy as well; they all had so much going for them. Anyway, I did look at that angle, and you've probably gone through the same notes I wrote down."

Reilly didn't feel comfortable revealing names, but Turner knew the stories anyway.

"I'll give you one name that came up at the time, young fellow. Nancy Easter. When the Marchand girl was killed, Easter had the most to gain. She took over in Catherine Marchand's absence. Became captain of the cheerleaders for example. She also ended up graduating first in her class. You already know that Catherine was tops in her class when she died. So there's a possibility, right?"

"You interviewed her."

"I certainly did. Several times. She didn't have a great alibi, as I recall. But nothing came of it. No physical evidence. The same story we had with everybody."

"Anybody else?"

"The young fellow, David Blondin."

"Why?"

"That was his girlfriend, at least for a while. In cases like this, you look at the people closest to the victim. There were rumors that she wanted to dump him for another guy. Maybe that got him angry enough to do it."

"But he was out of town at the time."

"You're right, but the timing was close. The difference between the presumed time of death and his return home was just under an hour. That's awfully close."

"But nothing?"

"I'll bet we spoke to that kid three times, leaned on him fairly hard, but nothing. And Dr. Poore wouldn't go back and change the time of death. He was darned certain of the time within fifteen or twenty minutes either way."

Reilly was frowning. This was taking him nowhere new.

"And Ken Gladwell. That's an interesting one. He had a bad alibi, too. I didn't believe him, frankly, but there was nothing connecting him to the scene. No blood on his clothes, no motive that we could find. As I recall, he was sweet on the girl, too."

"How about Tina Gladwell?"

"Tina Kerrigan back then. But yes, I thought about her too. Lousy alibi and nobody to back her up. But again, no motive that we could pin down, unless you call coming in second as prom queen a motive for murdering the queen. And no physical evidence. No blood spatters, no nothing."

"George Wessel?"

"Sure, I spoke with him, but he was never considered a suspect by any means. Didn't have a great alibi, but nobody really did. One of the strangest came from that kid Gordon Jefts, the one who became a lawyer and Lourdes Freitas, that girl who became a doctor."

"Why is that?"

"Well, I probably didn't put every detail in my notes, but they were at her house doing the old dipsy doodle before her parents came home. I had a hard time getting that information out of them. They were real upset that I might put something in the official notes, which I didn't, but I needed some better evidence of their whereabouts than just their word for it. So the Chief interviewed the girl and I interviewed the boy and we had to get absolutely every detail, including size and shape of their body parts and the color of the wrapper on the rubber he used. I'll tell you, that was a weird interview. But they corroborated each other's statements on everything. You never saw two more relieved kids when we let them go."

"I think your notation in the file said only that they were checked out and cleared."

"That sounds right. I spoke to everybody that knew her. Bobby Hayes, Max Zenga, all of her teachers, her coaches, the pharmacist she worked for. Interesting thing was, she told her cheerleading coach she wanted to quit the same day she was killed. Same thing with the pharmacy; said she wanted to quit. That struck me as very odd. You too?"

"It does seem strange. She also put all her school books back in her locker and left it unlocked. It's almost like she knew she was going to die."

"That's what I thought. I forgot about the locker. But nothing else seemed to fit. You know, things weren't as tightly scheduled as they are today. There were no cell phones to keep track of people, and there were only so many scheduled activities for kids after school. Not like today. So kids hung out in different places, unless they had a practice or something, and then they wandered home. Shoot, there weren't that many school buses back then. I'll bet there weren't that many kids that even wore wristwatches. It was tougher back then to build a refined time line."

"You never found a weapon, but you said in your notes you thought it was a baseball bat or something similar."

"There were small particles of wood in her wounds, but that's all in the autopsy report. That and the shape of the wounds. We canvassed the whole area and nobody saw anybody carrying a baseball bat or anything that might come close."

Reilly started to stand. "Thank you Mr. Turner for taking the time to speak with me. I appreciate it."

"Look, there's nothing I told you that wasn't in the files, and I'm sure you read them over and over. You didn't have to come to my house to speak to me."

"You're right. I did read everything you said, but I wanted to talk to somebody who was there."

"Son, I was there and I wish I wasn't. It was awful what happened to that girl. I drew the short straw then, and now it's your turn. I hope it works out better for you than it did for me."

Reilly was getting into his car when one more thought crossed his mind.

"The pin, Mr. Turner, the one shaped like the letter 'C' that was found at the scene. Any thoughts on that?"

"I remember that pin, but no, I thought maybe she was carrying it when she was struck. We all did. I don't think she was wearing it because we would have seen where it was torn off. I remember going with the Chief to the Marchand's house to ask about it. Nobody had seen it before. Why? Is there anything new?"

"Not at all. Just wondering."

In another room in the department, Wetman and Lou Pellerin were discussing the officer scheduling sheets. There were three patrol shifts and a pool of twenty three officers. At any given point, since a given officer couldn't work seven days a week, there were about sixteen available officers working a given day. Allow for vacations and illness and you're down to fourteen on the streets.

There was also one sergeant per shift, so the total went to seventeen or eighteen. A fourth sergeant was available but usually served as the prosecutor when there was a court case. One of the regular officers served as a juvenile officer and spent most of his time in the schools.

Then there was Detective Reilly, who'd work twenty-four hours a day if Wetman would let him. Add the Chief and the Assistant Chief, and the sheet listed a total of thirty people. There was a civilian dispatcher and two people in the office to take care of the routine clerical duties.

"And I'm supposed to do what?" Wetman was incredulous.

"Ask for a staffing increase. They expect it." Lou Pellerin was giving the Chief the routine.

"Like, how many?"

"It's always been three or four, every year. Then, maybe once every five years, they spring for one."

"And we do this every year?"

"Absolutely. And then there are the vehicles. We always need new vehicles."

"How many do we ask for?"

"Lately, I'd guess maybe replace four and add one. They usually replace two or three and never add one."

"But we do this anyway?"

"Right. You were scheduled to get one this year but you really screwed the pooch when you declined."

"But I don't need it. The old one runs fine."

Lou was having difficulty holding a straight face.

"Are you pulling my leg with this bullshit?"

"See, Chief, you've always been one of the guys, one of the wandering herds of nobodies who wear blue. Now, you're the Chief and you get to handle all this financial crap with the Board of Selectmen. Believe me, they'll expect you to posture and threaten and go to great lengths to argue for your department. It's part of the job."

"Nobody told me. I mean, I understand the paperwork, but the way I figure things, we need maybe one replacement vehicle this year, with two next year. The juvenile officer can use the one we replace until the wheels fall off. Next year, we'll do the same for the detective and the court officer. At least that's my thinking. And we need some new equipment, like some new vests, maybe $8,000 worth by my count. Other than that, I think we're in OK shape for now."

"But you're depriving Apsley of the high drama and the emotion that comes with budget hearings. If you go and ask for a modest increase, they won't know what to say. There won't be any raised voices or threats of recriminations. We sort of like this theatre and we expect it to come around every year."

"What's this about threats? I'm supposed to make threats?"

"Of course. Do you realize how many kids are going to get run over next year on Apsley's streets, or get hooked on heroin because the Selectmen didn't give you two more officers and two more vehicles?"

"But that's bullshit!"

"Of course it is, but it makes for a good show."

Wetman retreated to his office to ponder the political realities of being a Chief at budget time, while Lou left the station and drove to Apsley High for a session with the freshman class on drug abuse.

When Lou Pellerin returned, Wetman was out of the office.

"He had a dentist appointment, Lou," Lucy at the front desk told him. Should be back in a little while. When he turned to go into his office and check his messages, Reilly was standing there.

"What's up, kid?"

"Sir, I've been thinking about this case and going over and over the details and I have a thought."

Lou motioned him over and said, "So what is it?"

Reilly began to tell him when two other police officers dashed by on their way out the front door. Lou called after them, "What's up?"

"Hank Bruno just radioed in that a man is on the bridge and says he's going to jump."

The pair raced to a cruiser and drove off, lights flashing and siren blaring. Lou grabbed his coat, trotted out to his car and radioed the cruiser that he was on the way. When he pulled up on the bridge he saw the two officers approaching a man who was straddling the metal railing above the cold waters of the river below. The bridge was only about thirty-five feet above the surface of the water, but the waters were extremely cold and running swiftly. The fall might not kill the jumper, but the fast waters would sweep a person along very quickly. If that didn't kill the jumper, hypothermia probably would.

Lou radioed for two officers as backup to keep vehicles and pedestrians off the bridge and used his cell to call the county's Department of Mental Health. A psychiatrist was always on call at DMH for emergencies like this and the receptionist advised Pellerin that Dr. Hairston would be on the line shortly.

While he waited, he noticed that the man on the bridge, the man desperate for help and threatening to end his life, was Malcolm Prudhomme. Hairston came on the line and listened to the description of the situation. The man needs to be kept talking, Hairston advised Lou; he'd be there in twenty minutes.

Lou made one more call, to Chief Wetman.

Wetman was on his way back from his dental appointment when his cell phone rang. His jaw was still numb from the Lidocaine injection and his words were slurred. Spittle dribbled from the corners of his mouth but he managed to make his point to his Assistant Chief: Remain on scene at the bridge and wait for the psychiatrist to show up; Wetman was going to call on Mr. Philip Marchand. He didn't like this coincidence and suspected Marchand might have something to contribute to the discussion.

Without returning to his office, Wetman walked to his car and drove to the condos at the far end of Main Street where Philip Marchand lived. He wanted Marchand to stop interfering, and he'd do whatever it took to make sure he stopped.

As he pulled into the lot, he saw Phil walking to his own vehicle. Wetman tapped on his horn and pulled up directly behind the black Mercedes. Marchand smiled and extended his hand but Wetman just stood at his open car door.

"So tell me about your conversation with Malcolm Prudhomme." The Chief's jaw was still half-numb and it didn't come out exactly like he'd intended. Nevertheless, Phil got the point.

"Just come from the dentist?" Phil was smiling as Wetman used a handkerchief to wipe his mouth.

Wetman nodded and waited for an answer.

"You told me to stop visiting his house, so I did."

"Non-answer. Did you call Malcolm?"

Phil held his hands up as if defending himself. "Look, I stayed away from that bastard just like you said. I figured a phone call wouldn't hurt."

"When?"

"When? Yesterday. I just encouraged him to come forward. Tell the truth about Catherine. That was all. Why? Did Apsley's model citizen file a complaint?"

Wetman walked up to Phil Marchand and stood inches away, intentionally invading his space.

"Look, Mr. Marchand, if something bad happens to Mr. Malcolm Prudhomme, as much as you or I don't like him, then I'll be back to arrest you. I want you to stay away from that man, no visits and no phone calls. If you see him on the street, you're going to cross the street and avoid any chance meeting. You're going to do this or I'm going to come down on you like you don't want to see."

He hissed the words and sprays of spit hit Marchand on the face. Wetman didn't care and Phil wasn't smiling any longer.

Lou Pellerin waited at the end of the bridge for Dr. Hairston and motioned Hank Bruno to come closer.

"Hank, call the Fire Department and arrange to launch their boat with a diver down river and wait. Also, tell them to send an ambulance and use the back way so Malcolm won't see it. They can park it around the corner. And tell them to run it quiet. We've got a sensitive situation here and I don't want any more commotion."

Then he took a few tentative steps towards Malcolm Prudhomme.

"Malcolm, remember me? Lou Pellerin?"

"Leave me alone."

"Malcolm, that water is awfully cold. You don't want to end up down there.

"I just want to die. I just want this to stop."

"I understand, Malcolm. I really do. But this isn't the way to do it."

"I just want to be left alone."

Malcolm's speech, always difficult to understand precisely, was especially garbled today. The cold weather was making him shiver.

"Who's bothering you, Malcolm?"

"Everybody."

"Everybody's bothering you?"

"The kids are pointing at me and calling me names. Another guy punched me and pushed me down on the ground."

"When was that, Malcolm?"

"I don't remember. Last week. No, the week before."

"Do you know who did it, Malcolm?"

"Yes. It was that girl's father."

"What girl?"

"And another guy keeps calling me and taking my picture."

"Who's that, Malcolm?"

"He calls me a murderer. I never murdered nobody."

"Lou. Lou." It was Hank Bruno trying to catch Lou's attention without shouting."

Lou backed up in Hank's direction, never letting his eyes leave Malcolm Prudhomme.

"Lou, the Fire Department is sending the ambulance but not the boat. The engine's in the shop and it won't be fixed until tomorrow. I'm going to try Sam Silverman."

"Good thinking. Go!"

Sam Silverman at Apsley Provisions was the only man Pellerin knew who used his fishing boat every day except those where the ice covered the rivers and lakes in the area. With a little luck, Sam would be put off by the cold weather and was still at the store. Rachel Silverman answered the phone and Pellerin found that Sam was just coming back from a morning on the lake and holding a string of three trout. He hoped Sam's luck

238 / P.D. LaFleur

continued when he told him he needed him and his boat down by the bridge.

In fifteen minutes, Sam pulled in a quarter mile away at a landing near the old belt factory. Pellerin brought another police officer with him, dressed in a wet suit and holding his scuba gear. He explained the plan to Sam and the officer; just idle in the river about fifty yards downstream in case Malcolm jumped. If that happened, get him out fast and bring him to this landing. The Fire Department would have an ambulance at the scene in a few minutes, standing by.

Pellerin walked back towards Malcolm and was pleased to see a short, bald, odd-looking man who was apparently Dr. Hairston already approaching. The psychiatrist, dressed in jeans, a light blue shirt, bright yellow Loony Toons tie and a worn navy blue blazer nodded at Lou and said, "Thanks. I'll take it from here. Do we have an ambulance around, just in case?"

"An ambulance and a boat will be here."

"Great. Try to keep everyone as far away as possible, OK?"

Lou Pellerin motioned his officers to back people further away. He stood at the very end of the bridge and watched the interaction between Malcolm and Dr, Hairston. There was still a distance of fifteen feet between them, but Pellerin could see that Malcolm was listening. He couldn't hear the conversation but Malcolm looked engrossed. Then Hairston walked over to the closest police officer on the bridge and asked a question. The officer turned and trotted down the sidewalk of the bridge and reached Pellerin.

"Malcolm wants a cigarette."

Pellerin waved in the direction of the gas station and told the officer to make it quick. After the officer returned and handed a package of cigarettes and a lighter to Hairston, the psychiatrist placed them on the bridge and invited Malcolm to light up. In a few moments, Malcolm was inhaling a Marlboro deeply and Dr. Hairston was standing within eight or ten feet of him.

They seemed to be making progress and their conversation appeared relaxed and amiable. Malcolm was no longer straddling the railing but was on the street side of the rail and leaning back against it. He looked more composed and Lou hoped the tension was winding down. He stayed by his cruiser and watched the scene. To his left, he could see Sam Silverman's boat holding its own in the churning waters down river and hoped this was a precaution that would not be needed today. Clusters of people formed at each end of the bridge and he thought he saw the local newspaper reporter, camera and note pad in hand.

Lou remained about forty feet away and strained without success to hear the conversation. Whatever Hairston and Prudhomme were saying, their voices were too low for Pellerin to discern anything beyond a few syllables. But if the volume was low, so was the apparent tension. Hairston used his hands as he spoke and gave no indication of any stress. Prudhomme was listening, attentive, curious even, moving only when he removed or replaced the cigarette in his mouth.

In the distance, sirens could be heard approaching, and Pellerin grumbled, reaching for his cell phone. The Fire Department was supposed to be running quiet. Before he could make the call, Pellerin saw a State Police cruiser crest the hill behind him and head towards the bridge at some considerable speed. What?

Lou stepped back quickly as the cruiser squealed to a stop just a few feet away. Two State Police officers exited their vehicle, lights still flashing, and stepped towards him. The pair was familiar; Clancy and Terrebonne. Clancy had his Taser drawn.

Lou stepped in front of them and held his hands up. "Whoa, boys. What do you think you're doing with that thing?"

"We're here on orders from Captain Blackwood. We'll take over from here." Terrebonne did the talking today as Clancy surveyed the scene being played out on the bridge.

"Uh, not so fast. This is Apsley and you're in my jurisdiction. We've got things under control. And how in hell did you even know about this?"

"Dr. Hairston. He's got to check in with us before he goes out on any call. So he's part of our team, not yours. We've dealt with these situations before, so step aside and we'll take care of things. Terrebonne made a move to proceed when Lou caught him by the sleeve and yanked him back.

"Get in your cruiser right now and leave. Otherwise, I'm going to draw my weapon and order you placed in handcuffs for obstructing a police action. Do you hear me?"

Lou kept his voice low so as not to cause any distraction for Hairston or Prudhomme, but he made his point clear.

"Back off, now. And put that Taser away before I jam it right up you ass."

Terrebonne shook off Lou Pellerin but made no move to retreat. Instead, he turned to Clancy and said, "These hayseeds think they can handle this? Do you hear that?"

Lou didn't move.

Terrebonne pointed his finger at Lou and leaned into his face. "Listen, Barney Fife, put your bullet back in your shirt pocket. You're off this scene right now. You hear me? We've got cuffs just like you and I don't see any reason why we can't put you in restraints right in front of your officers and these other folks standing around."

Terrebonne's voice caught Hairston's attention and the doctor turned abruptly and stared at the scene of the disagreement.

Hairston almost growled. "Gentlemen, take your discussion somewhere else."

Lou reached behind him and removed a set of cuffs from his belt. With his other hand, he unsnapped the cover of his weapon and prepared to remove it. Clancy saw what was happening and pointed the Taser at Lou's chest.

"Don't make a move or I'll have to fire. It won't be pretty, I assure you."

Lou knew that was true. The electrical jolt would incapacitate him for ten seconds while he rolled around on the ground in convulsions. Lou, Clancy and Terrebonne stood frozen in a tableau filled with adrenalin. A few Apsley police officers moved closer, aware of the increased tension.

Suddenly Clancy sensed pressure at the base of his spine that made him flinch. "Holster your Taser."

It was Wetman and he held his hand close to Clancy's waist.

"Nice and slow. My weapon is loaded and the safety's off. And I'd hate to see your blood all over our nice bridge."

Clancy did so without turning in Wetman's direction. Terrebonne turned and stared Wetman in the eye. A camera flashed and Wetman said, "This is the scene that will be in the papers tomorrow morning. How do you think that will look?"

There was no response.

"Now, gentlemen, you're both going to smile for the cameras and walk nice and slow back to your cruiser. Then you're going to leave immediately. You're going to leave at normal speed, no tires squealing, no lights flashing, and no siren. Is that clear?"

Terrebonne and Clancy stood mute. After five seconds, they made slow deliberate moves in the direction of their state police cruiser. Clancy, scowling, looked at Wetman's hand and saw that it was holding only a radio transmitter.

"Son of a bitch," Clancy said, and he raced to the edge of the bridge where he drew his Taser and fired directly into Prudhomme's chest. Prudhomme's arms shook violently with the jolt and the cigarette fell out of his mouth. Then he arched his back over the bridge railing and did a double tumble into the icy waters of the river.

Hairston was just as stunned as if he's been the one shot by the Taser. Clancy leaned over the railing and watched Prudhomme flailing as he bobbed to the surface. In moments he was being carried downstream, tumbling through the swift waters.

Terrebonne remained standing near Wetman and said, "We took action that needed to be taken," he said to Wetman. "If someone doesn't care about their own life, you don't know if they're going to take you with them."

Wetman bared his teeth and snarled as he grabbed Terrebonne's arm and snapped a pair of cuffs on one wrist.

"We can do this the easy way or the hard way, but you are going to spend some time in our jail."

Wetman signaled to Hank Bruno who ran up and held Terrebonne's other hand so Wetman could attach the other cuff. Wetman disarmed Terrebonne of his service revolver and Taser and marched him over to an Apsley cruiser. He didn't bother handling him gently as he stuffed Terrebonne into the back seat and slammed the door.

He said to Bruno, "Hank, have that State Police cruiser towed someplace and make sure it's far away and in the muddiest field you can find."

Clancy, seeing the commotion, ran to Wetman, Taser still drawn, and started to object when Lou grabbed the weapon from behind, slammed the officer into the side of the cruiser and attached a pair of cuffs. Cameras were flashing all the while. Clancy, face bloodied and missing two teeth, joined Terrebonne in the back seat of the cruiser.

Lou said, "Chief, they've got Malcolm in the boat and the ambulance is going to get him over to the hospital right away. Son of a bitch."

"Right," Wetman added, "Son of a bitch. I want all the weapons from these two boneheads brought to the department and put on my desk. Blackwood's going to be here sometime today and I want to present them to him. Minus firing pins. If the barrels get twisted and the weapons rendered useless, well, c'est la vie."

He stormed off in the direction of his own vehicle.

* * *

An hour later, Wetman sat at his desk while Captain Blackwood stormed around his office.

"You have no goddamned right, Wetman!" Blackwood was sputtering. "The Attorney General is going to be on your department like flies on warm manure!"

Wetman said nothing and tried to think of anything but a zucchini. He casually reviewed some budget paperwork and some manpower and training schedules while Blackwood fumed. Eventually, Blackwood stepped in front of the desk and swept every paper from Wetman's desk on to the floor.

Wetman watched calmly and turned to the intercom. "Lucy, send two officers in here please, and make sure they have a set of cuffs with them."

"You're an idiot, Wetman. You're going to be out of a job and on your ass before tomorrow morning."

The officers appeared and Wetman instructed them to place cuffs on Captain Blackwood and arrest him. Without questioning the Chief, one officer moved forward and Blackwood pushed him away, but the pair quickly grabbed Blackwood by the arms, twisted them sharply behind his back and cuffed him. Blackwood growled as they removed the service revolver from his holster, walked him out of the Chief's office, and followed the full arrest protocol at the booking desk.

Wetman was enjoying the ensuing silence when his phone rang. He glanced at the caller ID and opted to take it, calling out "Bring the prisoner back for a moment, officers."

Blackwood was standing in the doorway with an officer on either side when Wetman reached for the phone. "Yes, sir," Wetman said into the phone. Blackwood stood and shifted his weight from foot to foot, impatient and angry, and anxious to put Wetman and all of the Apsley Police Department right where they belonged.

"Yes, sir. Yes, plenty of photographs. I'm sure there will be photographs in all the papers. The statement from Dr. Hairston? Yes, I have that." Wetman looked at Blackwood. "Yes, both officers are confined to our cells here. And the Captain himself is just being booked as we speak." Blackwood could hear a voice coming through the line.

"Certainly sir, I'll tell him. He's standing right here in my office. I would say so, sir." Another pause while Wetman listened. "Well, he did throw everything from my desk onto the floor. Official police files, reports, and so forth." Blackwood's curiosity was heightened.

"Do you want to wait while I tell him, sir?" Wetman put the phone on his desk and said to Blackwood, "I wish to advise you that you are to be conducted at once to the office of the Attorney General where you will surrender your badge until an official investigation is completed. As you are a prisoner of the Apsley Police Department, I'll arrange to have you personally escorted to the Attorney General's office."

Blackwood just stared at Wetman who picked up the phone and said, "I advised him, sir. No, he's still here. Do you want to speak with him? Ok, sir. It's good to talk with you too. And please say hello to Martha for us. Mary Alice is always asking about her. And thank you." He hung up.

He looked at Blackwood and said in a mild and controlled voice, "That was the Attorney General. He'll be waiting for your arrival."

Blackwood's eyes bulged from his head and Wetman said to his officer, "Take Captain Blackwood to the Attorney General's office. He'll be there waiting for him." Wetman turned to pick up some of the papers that Blackwood had tossed to the floor when he spoke once more. "And do not under any circumstances remove the cuffs."

Wetman finished organizing all the papers on his desk and decided to make one more call. For this, he used his police radio. "Assistant Chief Pellerin, please come to my office and bring Detective Reilly with you."

While he waited for their arrival, he reread the report from Dr. Hairston based on the events earlier at the bridge. Hairston did, as protocol required, notify the State Police office of the request for his services in Apsley. But the detailed account of his conversation with Malcolm Prudhomme at the edge of the bridge showed that he'd succeeded in convincing Malcolm to accompany him to the psychiatric ward of the hospital for an evaluation and possible treatment. He was simply waiting for Malcolm to finish his cigarette when Clancy used the Taser. He was still reading Hairston's words when Lucy from the front desk buzzed him.

"There have been four calls from newspaper reporters in the past half hour. They all want your comments about the events at the bridge. What should I tell them?"

Wetman considered some options and asked Lucy to return all the calls. Tell them, he said, to contact the State Police for details. They should ask for Captain Blackwood who ordered the use of the Taser. Lucy's smile came through on the line and Wetman made one more request. Call that young reporter from the local paper and tell him to come in before six tonight. Wetman would wait.

Lou Pellerin showed up with Reilly in tow and they took seats in Wetman's office. The instructions were brief and clear. They were to call Philip Marchand and arrange to meet with him, preferably at the hospital where Malcolm was taken. They were to instruct Marchand that he would be charged with criminal mischief for pushing Malcolm into such a desperate situation that he threatened to jump.

Hairston would be there to confirm this. They were to arrange to have Marchand's Mercedes towed to the same remote and muddy location as the state police cruiser and escort Mr. Marchand back to the station for processing.

Pellerin offered an objection. "That's pretty thin, isn't it?"

Wetman nodded in agreement. "Just go through the motions and make life a little pissy for Philip Marchand for a few days. We have some information to develop about the murder of Catherine Marchand and I don't want him butting in. He'll have to spend a night here before he posts bail, and then he'll have to get his car back. Let him sit and stew for a little while and maybe we can do some digging."

Reilly pointed out that the cells were filled already with the two State Policemen, Clancy and Terrebonne. "Fine," said Wetman. "Put Mr. Marchand in with either one and let him find out what it's like to have to share a cell and a toilet with one of those cretins for a few hours. I don't know if it'll teach him anything. Maybe humility, but I'm not hopeful. Maybe that we consider his stupidity to be worthy of a criminal complaint. But so what? I just want some time to relax, clear my head, and maybe even have a cold beer."

In another part of Apsley, Ken Gladwell was drinking heavily and there was plenty of time left in the day for him to drink a lot more. He was on his way back to Apsley from his office when he heard the news on the radio about Malcolm Prudhomme's adventure at the bridge. The thought of Malcolm on the bridge and then being stunned over the rail and into the water made Gladwell sick to his stomach.

He decided to stop at Moynihan's Bar, a seedy joint on the very edge of town, where he downed three drinks right away. His throat burned and his eyes watered. The drinks tasted terrible, and that was fine with him. His shoulders rose and fell with a pulse that made him want to lash out. His muscles flexed and his arms stretched and he wanted to find Phil Marchand and beat the crap out of him.

He knew he could do it if he wanted to, and he'd stayed in shape, so to speak, as long as he wasn't hung over. He also knew that he needed to talk before he took that kind of action.

His few weeks in the "loony bin" taught him that, and the lesson stuck.

He made a call on his cell phone and waited for me to answer. After a few moments of conversation, he hung up, ordered a fourth drink, and waited for me to arrive. He had to speak with somebody about this whole mess and I was his best shot.

Odd, though, that I would be his choice. I was the one friend he had to whom he was able to pour his heart out, the single most trustworthy soul he had. But Phil Marchand would likely say exactly the same thing about me.

Phil Marchand stayed as far away from Trooper Terrebonne as he could, but it wasn't far enough. The cell was only a few feet wide and only a few feet longer. A single stainless steel bunk with a thin mattress and no blanket was suspended along one wall. A single stainless toilet, waterless, sat at one end of the short wall, with a small sink that dispensed only cold water adjacent to it. No matter what he did, Marchand could only manage to be four feet away from the ranting Terrebonne.

Marchand never let on to the Trooper that he was familiar with Malcolm Prudhomme, and was silent about the connection between his conversation with Malcolm and the suicide threat on the bridge. By midnight, a representative of the AG's office showed up with paperwork that effected the release of the two Troopers and Marchand finally had the cell to himself. He placed a call to an attorney, the only one he knew in Apsley, but Gordon Jefts was still not answering his page. Marchand finally resigned himself to a lonely uncomfortable night in the Apsley jail.

When I arrived at Moynihan's Bar, Ken Gladwell was standing next to his car with his jacket off and doing jumping jacks. My expectations leaned more towards a drunken Ken Gladwell slouched over the bar snoring, so I was pleased with the sight. I beeped my horn and Gladwell stopped his exercises, grabbed his coat from the hood of his car and opened the passenger door. "Mind if I sit here for a bit? I can't drive like I am, but I might be able to in another half hour or so."

I waved him in and drove off, telling Ken I'd drop him off at his car in the morning. We went to my apartment and I filled him in on the news about Malcolm's fall from the bridge; between local radio and a phone call from George Wessel, I had the best news sources in the world.

By one in the morning, after five hours of a far ranging conversation, a cold pizza and a six pack of club soda, Gladwell was sound asleep on the couch.

I sat at the kitchen table, stunned and mouth open, still trying to comprehend what my friend had told me:

"I remember that day as clear as if it was yesterday, Dave. It was a fabulous day, getting a little cold, but still filled with sunshine. I went to football practice but I had a wrenched knee and the coach told me to lay off from contact drills. So I did a few pattern runs and spent the rest of practice doing stretching exercises. Then I went back to school, took a shower, got my books out of my locker and started heading home.

"I decided to cut down by Squash Pond because it would save me about ten minutes. I was carrying my duffle bag with my football gear and I had my books stuffed in there with everything else. I was all alone. Most of the other guys had already left and gone home, so no big deal.

"I walked along the path and the trees were changing colors but they were still on the trees, you know? In another few weeks, they'd all be on the ground. But it was beautiful, all different colors. Then I heard something from the woods, not far from the path. I thought I recognized the voice, but I wasn't sure. It sounded a little like Catherine Marchand. I figured she was with some guy, you know? So I just walked along. Then my curiosity got me. I'm not sure if I wanted to see Catherine doing the nasty with somebody, or if it was her voice that got my attention. Anyway, I dropped my duffle bag on the edge of the path and started to walk towards her voice.

"Then she started to yell, but it was muffled, like someone was covering her mouth. By then, I knew it was Catherine's voice. She had the nice mellow voice, remember? Really distinctive. I started moving a little faster and then I saw what was going on.

"It was Malcolm Prudhomme and he had a hand over Catherine's mouth telling her to be quiet. 'I won't hurt you. I won't hurt you. I promise.' Him and his speech impediment. I remember what he said just like it was yesterday.

"He was rubbing up against her like he was getting off, you know? Like a real pervert, and he's grunting and telling her to be quiet, that he won't hurt her, and I must have made a noise or something because Malcolm stopped and turned around real sudden. He couldn't see me; it was getting close to dusk by this time, but I saw him looking around, still holding his hand over her mouth, and he just drops her and runs off like a jack rabbit. Not that Malcolm could move fast at all. He was so flat footed. But he took off and ran away.

"I saw Catherine start getting back up on her feet and I was going to say something but she reached into her purse and took out a cigarette and lit it. She just stood by the tree and watched Malcolm run away. And then she laughed, sat down and smoked her cigarette.

'That's when I left. I mean, Catherine looked fine when I last saw her. She was smoking a cigarette and laughing.'"

I sat quietly trying to absorb all this. My friend was relating events from nearly three decades ago, a story I'd never heard and never suspected. Ken was sober now, leaning with his elbows on the table. I asked, "So Malcolm didn't have anything to do with Catherine's murder?"

"That's right. I told you what I saw. Malcolm left her in the woods by the pond and ran off."

"How do you know he didn't come back?"

This question seemed to catch Ken off guard. He didn't want to answer, that was clear. I prodded him. "So how do you know? Maybe Malcolm came back and bashed her head in."

"He didn't."

"How do you know? Were you there?"

Ken stared at his hands when he answered. "I followed Malcolm out of the woods and saw him heading up the hill towards his house. He was moving fast. Well, as fast as Malcolm could move. I watched him. He never turned around. I'm sure he went to his house."

A prolonged silence ensued. I asked another question. "Did you see anybody else? Maybe you saw someone and that person is the killer."

"No. Believe me, I'd like to be the one who points the finger and says I saw the whole thing. But I just told you everything I saw. I can't tell you who killed Catherine, but I can tell you it wasn't Malcolm.

"When I left the woods near Squash Pond, Catherine was laughing a little and looked fine. She was pissed off at Malcolm, but she wasn't hurt and she actually looked a little relieved, almost relaxed. I'm not sure of the exact time I left, but based on what I read, she was probably dead within a half hour. Maybe even less. At that exact same spot."

It was time to ask. "You never told this to the police, did you?"

Ken stood up and walked around the small kitchen, on edge. "No. I never did."

"Even though Malcolm was brought in for questioning? Even though he was the major suspect? Why?"

Ken didn't say anything until he sat back down at the table.

"I was going to, especially when the police brought him in and said they had a suspect. I thought about it, but I didn't. I think . . . I think I would have if they ever arrested him and charged him, but they never did. A few days later, they let Malcolm go home."

My mind was spinning. How Ken could sit on this information for so long? "Were you afraid the police might suspect you?"

"Of course. You remember how we all interviewed two, three, four time by the cops. I thought about it a few times, but I knew there'd be no evidence to tie me to the place. I was never closer than maybe twenty feet."

"So why not tell the police about Malcolm? It would have saved him a lot of aggravation and all the accusations ever since."

"Because . . . because I figured I could use him. That's why."

Things started to make sense. From Gordon Jefts, I knew that Malcolm's will named Ken as his beneficiary of his estate. Seeing Malcolm gave Ken a chance to blackmail him.

I didn't want to believe the worst of Ken Gladwell but I was seething. "So you took advantage of Malcolm's situation."

Ken nodded.

"And you looked at Malcolm as your meal ticket."

"Whoa, I wouldn't go that far! What did I get? A used car worth maybe a thousand dollars at the most?"

I blew my top. "Don't lie to me, Ken!" I slammed my fist on the table.

"I'm telling you the truth. I mean it."

I wanted to shriek but I couldn't. I couldn't let on that I knew about Malcolm's will or the recent change in the will from Ken to Tina. That could sink Gordon Jefts' legal career. So I bit my tongue about that. I looked deep into Ken's eyes and said, "You're a bastard, Ken. I didn't want to believe that you could stoop as low as you did, but you are a first class bastard. And all for money."

Ken tried to defend himself. "It was years ago, Dave. I was a kid and I was broke. And all I got was a car, that old Chevy that I got when I went to school."

"Don't keep lying, Ken. Please."

"I'm not! I know what I did was rotten and wrong, and I'm telling you now exactly what I did. Why do you think there's more to the story than that?"

I didn't say anything. I just stared and held Ken's gaze, doing my best to assess the truth of his words. There was no reason for Gordon to make up anything about Malcolm's will. It didn't make sense. But I thought I knew Ken and I would bet my life on the assumption that Ken was speaking the truth right now. I chose another approach.

"So what are you going to do now? Go to the police and tell them what happened?"

Ken didn't know and just shook his head.

"You've got to do something, Ken."

Ken had a pleading look in his eyes. "I was hoping that maybe you'd talk to Phil, maybe tell him that you know for a fact that Malcolm didn't kill his sister. Malcolm might be the biggest loser in town, but he doesn't deserve to have Phil hounding him like he's been."

We both knew that Phil was doing everything he could to make Malcolm's life miserable. If Ken was speaking truthfully, then Phil needed to know and he needed to back off. I said, "Let me think about it. Maybe I can talk to Phil tomorrow."

"Any word on Malcolm? How is he?"

"I'm sure he's a mess. He was taken to the hospital. Jesus, he's got to be eighty years old. He's lucky he survived at all."

Ken was despondent. "I'm sorry, Dave."

"Maybe you need to tell that to Malcolm."

SEVENTEEN

Early evening, the next day

Doctor Hairston rapped on the jamb of the door with his knuckles and Wetman looked up from his desk.

"The lady at the front desk told me you were waiting for me."

Wetman was, in fact, waiting for a few people. One was Philip Marchand; another was David Blondin; this had to be Doctor Hairston, although he defied Wetman's usual perception of a physician.

Doctor Donald Hairston was short and slight, not unlike Wetman himself, but that's where the similarities ended. He looked to be in his early forties. The top of his head was as shiny and smooth as an egg and the remaining fringe of reddish brown hair hung to his shoulders in thin wisps. His face bore a crooked nose, probably broken more than once, flanked by cheeks that were pock-marked and scarred. This was not a handsome dude.

Nevertheless, the smile was broad and genuine. And the eyes, wide set, were deep blue and penetrating.

Clad in jeans, worn tennis shoes, faded blue chambray shirt, navy blazer with shiny elbows, and a silver tie with ducks on it, he appeared completely at ease with himself. There was a curious comfort level with this small rumpled man that defied explanation.

When they were both seated, Wetman asked the psychiatrist the opening question. "How is Mr. Prudhomme?'

He was fine, Hairston said, albeit with some serious bruises on his right side and a nasty cut on his head. No broken bones. No lingering effects from the electric shock of the Taser.

"The major fractures are all emotional. He's going to be there for a while. Maybe with some therapy, we can come up with a diagnosis and determine where we go from there. Right now, I'd like to see him get stabilized, inside and outside. By the way, he gave me a waiver to talk to you about him. Otherwise I couldn't tell you much. But he seems to like you, maybe because he read the paper this morning. That was quite a thing you did."

Wetman brushed off the compliment and asked, "What have you heard from the brass back at headquarters? Blackwood must be pissed."

"Not a thing. They're not quite sure what to do with me and they sort of leave me alone. Blackwood's on leave, if you didn't know. It seems he had a meeting with the Attorney General and it didn't go well."

Just then, Lucy appeared at the doorway with me and Phil Marchand in tow; Phil was being released and I was supposed to make sure he stayed out of trouble. After the introductions and when everyone was seated, Wetman addressed Marchand.

"I trust you enjoyed your stay as our guest with us last night."

Marchand was still smarting from the experience and wasn't letting it go. He scowled at Wetman but said nothing.

"And Mr. Blondin here is a friend of Mr. Marchand, Dr. Hairston. Maybe you'd like to say a few things to these gentlemen."

Hairston started by describing the events of the day before. Then he described his meeting with Prudhomme in the hospital.

"Here's a man, Mr. Marchand, who felt so threatened and so minimized that he thought that taking his life might bring some relief, not only to him but to everyone else. That was a serious low point. He's severely depressed, along with the injuries he sustained."

Marchand interrupted. "Don't blame me for the injuries. That was the fault of the goofball Troopers."

"I agree, Mr. Marchand. The Troopers used bad judgment, and if it makes you feel any better, they are likely to be relieved of duty very soon. But the reason why Mr. Prudhomme was at the bridge in the first place, that's a different story."

"You call him Mr. Prudhomme like he deserves some respect. The guy's a dimwit, a pervert, a drunk, and a murderer. And if the Apsley police did their job when they were supposed to, he'd be off the streets right now and in jail where he belongs."

Hairston asked, "Are you convinced that he's responsible for your sister's death?"

Marchand leaned forward and spit out his words.

"You bet I'm convinced. Malcolm's got a long history in this town, and the cops could have sent him away for what he did to Catherine, but they let him go. He's been walking the streets for the past twenty-nine years while my sister is in a grave. I have a right to be pissed off."

Hairston waited patiently until Marchand was done. He was

about to respond when I interjected: "Malcolm didn't kill your sister."

Phil turned to me and said. "What? What are you saying?"

Wetman leaned forward to make sure he heard every word in the scene being played out.

"I said Malcolm didn't kill your sister. I don't know who did, but it wasn't Malcolm."

Phil slammed his fist on the desk. "What are you saying? Like *you* know all about what happened. What's up with you, Dave?"

I looked at Phil and spoke as if there was no one else in the room.

"I can't say. Just that Malcolm didn't do it. Oh, he was there alright, but then he left. Catherine was killed after he left."

"You know what the hell happened and you won't tell anyone. What are you hiding? Who are you protecting?"

I waited. The silence was filling the room. "Leave Malcolm alone. He didn't kill Catherine. That's all I can say."

Marchand rose from his seat and stormed out of the room, slamming the door to Wetman's office on the way out.

After a few moments, Wetman said to me, "We have to talk, don't we?"

I looked at Wetman and said, "Like I said to Phil. I can't tell you anything about who killed Catherine. I can only tell you that Malcolm didn't do it."

Wetman studied my face and said finally, "I'll be in touch."

I left quietly, leaving Wetman and Hairston alone in the office.

"I don't know the entire background of this case, Chief, but Mr. Prudhomme insists that he had nothing to do the murder of the girl. I know I don't have any evidence to support the feeling, and believe me, I've been wrong before, but I believe him."

"So did the Chief who had the case then. He let Malcolm go, even though he wanted him to be guilty. You've seen him. He's an oddball with bad habits, poor personal hygiene and a propensity for young girls. That's apparently been his M.O. his whole life. But there was never any evidence to put him at the scene. No witnesses, no physical evidence, nothing. And the guy has always been non-violent."

Hairston asked, "So what do you think is motivating this other fellow to say what he did?"

Wetman said, "I think Philip Marchand said it: He's hiding something or protecting someone. I need to speak with the guy."

Hairston said, "I'd like to speak with him, too, if you don't mind."

"But you're a shrink. You're not a cop. He needs to be interrogated."

Hairston reached into his pocket and removed a black leather wallet, flipped it open, and revealed a badge.

"I'm officially part of the State Police force. Well, sort of. So I can try to talk with him. Informal, of course."

"He goes to Dean's Town Tavern for a beer now and then." He checked his watch. "My guess is, that's where he is right now."

Hairston stood, shook hands and left. On his way out he said, "I'll be in touch."

When Hairston was out of hearing range, Lou said, "Who is Dave Blondin protecting? Any ideas."

Wetman rubbed his jaw and gazed out the window of his office. "I'm not sure. He knows everybody involved, knows everybody in town. I think he's telling the truth, but I still get the feeling that the road to Catherine Marchand's killer goes through Malcolm Prudhomme somehow."

Reilly asked, "What if he did it himself? I mean, he and Catherine had some history."

"You're right, but I don't think he did it. The guy would have some other signs of pathology somewhere, and I don't see any indication of that at all. He's protecting somebody. Maybe Hairston will come back with something."

Wetman was right. Hairston found me sitting alone at the end of the bar at Dean's. He went to the bar, ordered a beer and asked if he could join me. I nodded my approval; I wasn't looking for company, but I expected something like this.

"You really lit a fire back there."

I didn't respond.

"Your Chief is a studious type, I think. He'll be planning his questions for you right now. Your friend, though, Mr. Marchand, I'm afraid he's much more impulsive. Probably belting down a couple fingers of Jim Beam as we speak."

"Balvenie."

"Ah, likes good Scotch. But I see you're a beer man, like me."

I said, "Sometimes beer, sometimes wine, sometimes scotch. I don't limit myself."

"I used to like the hard stuff but it didn't like me. Metabolic thing, maybe. Me and Scotch or Bourbon . . . not a pretty thing. Wine? Once in while, usually with a nice meal. But beer? Beer and I seem to get along OK."

I started to smile but suppressed it. I took another sip. "I don't know if beer is my friend or not, but Phil Marchand? I don't think he's my best friend right now."

"Yes, you're probably right. Can I buy you another?"

"Sure. Why not. I'm walking home."

"Actually, so am I. Staying at the Apsley Ritz Carlton down the street."

I couldn't suppress a smile at that one.

"Well, maybe I have the name wrong." We touched beer bottles and said "Cheers" before tipping our second beers.

I suppressed a burp and asked, "So, am I being interrogated by an officer of the law? Or am I being analyzed by a shrink?"

Hairston looked up at the ceiling. "Perception is everything, Mr. Blondin. It's whatever you want it to be. What do you prefer? The thumb screws or the couch?"

"I get a choice?"

"You get to *feel* like you get a choice. Personally, I'd go with the thumb screws. Self reflection isn't all it's cracked up to be. Rots the brain."

"Like beer?"

Hairston clinked his half empty bottle against mine. "Touché."

I sensed a camaraderie with Hairston in spite of the little man's profession, his association with law enforcement, and his unusual looks. "So before you bring out the rack, tell me about yourself."

"Certainly. Donald O. Hairston. Forty-two. Third of five children, father a plumber, mother at home. Got a scholarship to college, majored in poetry and drama, played guitar, then got into medical school. I don't really know how. Residency in urology. That was the plumbing background coming through. Wasted a few years looking at wee-wees and prostates, then changed to psychiatry. I love it. Took a job in a clinic way up north on a reservation. Then saw a chance to work down here. Admittedly, it's with a state agency, and I'm assigned to the State Police, which is run by your basic Neanderthal types, but I'm closer to what's left of my family, and I have a chance to start my own practice. How's that in less than forty seconds?"

"Married?"

"Once. An R.N. Russian lady. But she almost killed me. It lasted seven months. Annulled, on the principal that if at first you don't succeed, destroy all the evidence that you even tried. You?"

"Born and raised right here. Married once. Divorced, about seven years ago. Two kids. Boys. I live alone in apartment building I own."

"I've been looking for a place somewhere around here. Something a little more permanent than the apartment I've got right now. What do you think of Eastland?"

"Small town, a lot like Apsley but even smaller. Poorer. If it's property you want, it's not going to get much cheaper than it is there."

"Cheap is good. Poor is OK."

"I would think that the poor are the most neglected when it comes to health care, especially psychiatry."

"You're right. Poor people, poor teeth, poor everything. Unfortunately, in this country, it stands to reason."

I caught a hint of some anger and cynicism in Hairston's response. "Political?"

"Political? Me? I guess so, if thinking that a country that has more wealth than any other on the planet can hold its head up when most other countries . . ." He stopped talking and smiled. "OK, you got me. It's political and it pisses me off."

"I'm glad. It pisses me off too."

"So were you telling me that Eastland is more humiliating than Apsley?"

"What?"

"You make it sound that Apsley is fairly well beat up. Lost its place in the battle for prosperity. But Eastland was never in the race. Am I wrong?"

"That's not a bad metaphor, or comparison, whatever."

"So either town sucks?"

"No. Not at all. It's just that here, we sort of had a feeling that we were going someplace. But when it happened, it happened to somebody else, someplace else. So maybe we feel, as people, like we look when you drive through town. A little beat up, worn around the edges. But humiliated? No, that's going too far. Even for Eastland."

"Wrong choice of words. But between the rich and poor, psychiatric problems don't respect economy. But poverty contributes to the symptoms of things like depression. Suicide goes up, too."

"We've had our share here in Apsley."

"I'm sure you have. And there are usually a lot more than get reported."

"Really?"

"Take the elderly. Some old duffer comes back from the doctor after he's found out he's stage IV colon cancer. He's seen some of his buddies go that way, so he knows what he's got to look forward to. He says to himself, 'Fuck that!' And he takes his bottle of gin and gets hammered, and then swallows a handful of sleeping pills. End of story. Happens more than we'd like to think."

"I suppose. I'm not sure what I'd do if it was me."

"Not pleasant to consider, but I've seen a lot of these kinds of things and I've reached my decision."

"What? Take the booze and the pills?"

"If I had no kids? Maybe. But if I had kids? No. Just the opposite. Suicide is a curious thing. When a person commits suicide, he leaves a legacy to his kids; the chances are much higher than average that his kids will do the same thing someday. When it's an older person with kids, he robs his children of their right to learn compassion. I know that puts that old duffer in a spot . . . he's the one that gets to suffer after all. But compassion is so precious, and it's terribly difficult to teach secondhand."

I waved Dean over for another two beers. As maudlin as the conversation was getting, I enjoyed this chat with the doctor.

Hairston took a long sip and set his glass down. "Been a long time since I did this. Feels good."

"So, no thumb screws tonight."

Hairston chuckled. "Afraid not. But I do want to know about what you said in the Chief's office. I think you're protecting somebody who knows what happened. Not Catherine's killer, but someone who knows the circumstances. It makes sense."

I had my antenna up. "Why?"

"Because you're a straight shooter. And according to the Chief and the few other people I've met here who know you, you make friends with people who will never be friends to each other. That's why the Chief wanted you there with Marchand. This guy comes back to Apsley and pisses off a lot of people in a real short time; doesn't have a ton of friends. But you? There are some important people around here who think that you're usually the good guy."

I said nothing.

"Maybe you learned compassion from someone in your family. Or is it magic?"

I sat poker-faced.

"And as far as I . . . the detached professional observer . . . can tell, you even displayed a little compassion for the infamous Malcolm Prudhomme. And I get the sense that there are very few people in this town who'd object to his slipping this mortal coil."

Still no response from me.

"But I don't think it was Malcolm you were defending. He might have been the beneficiary of your compassionate largesse, but only because you were defending . . . 'protecting' is the better word . . . someone else."

I turned to look at Hairston but held my silence.

"So I'm right."

"Bullshit."

"No. It's not bullshit. I'm a shrink, remember? I can read

minds." He smiled broadly, clinked glasses and let the subject drop.

We were both silent for a while. Then I spoke up. "What's with the hair and the clothes?"

Hairston almost spewed out a mouthful of suds but contained himself. It was my turn to smile.

"Nice segue, Mr. Blondin. I just tell you how compassionate you are and then you cut me to the quick. What a prick! But I'll try to answer: Leftover from an earlier age; a rebellion against my urological period; doesn't put me in a superior position with my patients; sends a message about the pointless nature of outward appearance; disdain of fashion allows more time for loftier thoughts; cheap enough to squeeze a nickel until it shits two dimes; poor as a church mouse; doesn't really give a shit. Pick one or more. They've all fit from time to time."

"Honest?"

"Absolutely. Why? You think I'm lying?"

"Maybe. You could have your reasons. Maybe you need to give it some serious thought."

"I told you, too much introspection only rots the brain. Just tell me something interesting, Mr. David Blondin. Tell me something about this place. Just don't talk about me and I won't talk about you. Fair enough? No couches here."

Over the next ninety minutes, we consumed too many beers, agreed to meet the next day . . . nine o'clock at the earliest for coffee at Dunkin's . . . and staggered our separate ways home.

EIGHTEEN

The next morning

After a quiet cup of coffee the next morning with Hairston, I pulled into a parking spot at the Pompicott Village condo complex. It's a presumptuous name for the luxury development. It has the cachet that comes with a Native American name, even though there is, I'm sure, no such tribe. Further, the buildings are of Spanish colonial architecture, something more suited to the southeast or the southwest. Finally, it's built on the site of the now dissolved Saul Schindler junkyard enterprise. There's probably as much petrochemical product below the surface here as there is in Saudi Arabia. On hot days, in spite of the new buildings and the lush green carpet of grass, a discerning nose can identify the peculiar odor of unburned fuel.

I stepped out of my pick-up truck and looked around. The cars in the lot were almost all late model foreign jobs, all in good shape. The upwardly mobile were moving in, and I mused that this was just one more bit of evidence that Apsley was forever changing. My dented pick up looked like a poor country relation coming to visit its prosperous city cousins.

This was the visitor lot though, and Phil Marchand's Mercedes would be safely behind the doors of his two car garage. I walked in the direction of Phil's place and noted that the morning paper was still on the front stoop. This was not a meeting I wanted to have, but I knew it must happen. I picked it up and rang the bell, calling, "Paperboy, Mr. Marchand."

Phil opened the door after a short wait and welcomed me in. "Grab a chair, Dave. I'll be right with you."

Phil had obviously just stepped from the shower. He hadn't buttoned up his shirt or combed his hair when I arrived and it brought to mind my condition when Phil's wife, Jacqueline, showed up at my door.

I used the few minutes alone to scan the headlines. There was nothing in the paper about Prudhomme or Wetman or anyone else involved in the whole Catherine Marchand affair, and for that I felt relieved. I checked the sports pages but there was nothing of sufficient moment to distract me from the seriousness of my mission.

Phil came into the room and took a seat opposite. "Coffee? It's fresh."

I waved it off and said, "I just met somebody for coffee at Dunkin's a few minutes ago."

"Oh, yeah?" I could tell that Phil was more than mildly curious. "Who?"

"Oh, that guy we met at the Chief's office. Dr. Hairston."

"The shrink?"

"We had a couple beers yesterday and we thought we'd get together this morning over something more sensible, like jelly donuts."

Marchand almost smiled at the thought but was still alert to the fact that Dr. Hairston and I were advocates for Malcolm

Prudhomme at the moment, and that put him squarely in the opposition.

"And I suppose I was the subject of your conversation? How nice."

I reacted sternly. "You give yourself an exalted level of importance. It's not always about you, Phil. Although I won't deny your name came up."

Phil looked chastened and he asked, "So why did you call me this morning. You just had to see me, you said. What am I missing?"

"Because you're bound to hear some information coming out, and I'd just as soon you heard it from me first."

"OK, so what's this information that just can't wait? "

I inhaled and braced my body to say everything at once, fully and completely. I held Philip Marchand in eye-to-eye contact when I spoke.

"When Catherine died, she was pregnant and I was the father of the unborn child."

I waited for the reaction but Phil held my gaze, immobile. Neither flinched. After a while, I noticed the corners of Marchand's lips curl upward in the start of a smile, a response I didn't anticipate.

"You asshole, Dave. You are such an asshole."

I was frankly bewildered by his words.

"I know she was pregnant and I've known for a long time. And I know you were the father for just as long."

"But how? I just found out myself."

"Because . . . because Catherine told me."

I was at a complete loss and shook my head, dazed. "How? When?"

"That's not important, Dave. If it's any consolation, my parents knew, too. Knew everything. And they were . . . none of us were . . . ever angry with you."

"Catherine told you? She never even told me!"

"Catherine, in her own way, told us everything. About you, about the baby, and nobody ever thought any worse of you. I mean that."

"How did she sound when she told you? I mean, I never knew that she was pregnant, never knew how she felt. Was she upset? What did she say?"

Marchand said nothing.

"Tell, Phil."

"She was upset, OK? Very upset."

"She actually told you? I can't believe it. How did she break the news?"

"Look, Dave, it was a shock to everybody. My parents . . . you remember how strict my father was. It was a shock."

Marchand watched me digest this revelation and said, finally. "Now get out of here and get to work. You must have something better to do."

On the way back to my truck, I remembered what Jacqueline had said about a box and that I should ask Phil about it. I'd try to remember for the next time.

Jimmy Reilly sat down in the overstuffed chair in his cramped apartment. The chair was one of the 'gifts' he'd received from his mother when he moved out of his parents' home and out on his own. It smelled faintly of cigarettes and sweat but it was comfortable and, best of all, free.

On the side table lay a stack of photocopies and books and Jimmy began paging through the material. Occasionally he used a black handled magnifying glass that his parents bought and engraved for him when he was made Detective for the Apsley Police Department. At first he thought it was a thoughtful, if impractical symbol of his new position. Now he was putting it to use as he tried to get a clearer view of some of the small photographs. In one, a copy of an old newspaper, he found a grainy photo of the queen and her court at the Apsley High School homecoming football game. It was dated just a week before Catherine Marchand was killed.

In front was Catherine herself, smiling broadly for the camera. Behind her were the three members of her court: Nancy Easter, Lourdes Freitas, and Tina Kerrigan.

"Princesses," he said to himself.

They were shown standing in front of the convertible that took them around the football field at halftime. Catherine wore a crown and a sash while the members of her court all wore small tiaras and sashes. All of them held small bouquets, probably from Rindy's Flowers, which was still supplying flowers and plants for most of the weddings, funerals, graduations and proms in Apsley. Behind the group could be seen the school principal, Mr. Bert Shacklefield, whose son, Bruce, was the current principal.

Reilly didn't need a magnifier to see every tooth in Catherine's brilliant smile that appeared in her class yearbook. He turned to that page once more. Given a page to herself, in memoriam, the caption below her photo read:

> Catherine Lee Marchand
> *Forgive our grief for one removed,*
> *Thy creature, whom we found so fair.*
> *We trust she lives in thee, and there*
> *We find her worthier to be loved.*

Reilly wondered about the source of the poem that was used. It sounded familiar in some way, as if he'd read those same words in class a long time ago. He made a mental note to look into it.

Catherine's photo showed a spray of freckles, high cheekbones, wide set eyes and a dimpled right cheek. She was a lovely girl to be sure, the kind who'd get a second and third look as she passed by. He flipped back to Philip Marchand's yearbook photo and saw the same dimpled cheek but no freckles and a less toothy smile. He looked more serious, more determined than his sister.

Reilly set the stack of newspaper copies and other papers down on the table and yawned wide. It had been a long day and he felt like he was getting nowhere. He had a better feeling about the case of Catherine Marchand earlier when the paternity of her unborn child was determined. It seemed like an important fact, one that could lead to motive for her murder. After all, there were all kinds of possibilities.

Maybe, he thought, Dave Blondin got upset and lost his temper when he heard the news. Or maybe Catherine had another boyfriend who lost his temper when Catherine told him the child wasn't his. Or maybe Catherine's father lost his temper. Somebody, to be sure lost his temper, for the beating and the brutality that was visited upon Catherine Marchand that early fall evening was full of anger and malice and hatred. Surely, a 'lost temper' only began to describe the seminal moments of that episode.

But that turned out to be a dead end, or at least it appeared that way.

Then, when Malcolm Prudhomme talked about jumping off the bridge, he thought this was it. Malcolm was doing this because of the enormous burden of guilt he'd carried all these years, magnified by the reappearance of Catherine's brother, Philip. It would be a nice way to tie up the case with a bright red ribbon. Unfortunately, it didn't work out that way. Not only was Malcolm *not* jumping out of guilt for Catherine, but he was practically exonerated from all consideration, if Dave Blondin's statements were to be believed.

That left fewer options, but one stuck in Reilly's mind. Among all the photos he'd been poking around at for the past two hours was an interesting set of photos that appeared both in the yearbook and the newspaper. At the prom in May, just a few months before she died, Catherine was chosen queen. She wore a form fitting gown with spaghetti straps that would still be in fashion today. Reilly wouldn't call the gown provocative, but it certainly showed the young woman's figure to advantage.

The photos were black and white, but the gown was light in color. Off white, maybe pink or light blue. Catherine struck a model's pose, one foot pointed to the front, the toe of her shoe poking out from beneath the hem of the gown. But what struck Reilly was her companion, the king of the prom that year.

Ken Gladwell was very tall and had dark eyebrows and wavy hair. He wore a black tux like someone who was accustomed to wearing one, even though Reilly knew that Gladwell didn't come from a moneyed family. His smile was as broad as Catherine's and he was as photogenic as his companion. It was a movie star shot. Both of them looked stunning and comfortable with each other.

Another shot in the same grouping showed the couple dancing together. Gladwell had to be nearly six and a half feet tall, and Catherine, five foot nine, Reilly recalled from her autopsy measurements, looked like she was made to be wrapped in Ken's long arms. They were smiling at each other in the shot, and the smiles certainly didn't look forced on either's part.

In a conversation with the Chief earlier, Reilly suggested the possibility that Ken Gladwell's involvement in Catherine's murder was more than they knew. But Chief Wetman, without dismissing the idea entirely, said no, he didn't think so.

"I've been wrong before," the Chief said, "but there's something about this guy that tells me he's not the one we're looking for."

He wanted to check into this a little more before he dismissed this as a hopeless exercise. He remembered that someone told him . . . he couldn't remember who right now . . . told him that Gladwell had been dating Tina Kerrigan in high school. He couldn't remember who Catherine's date had been for the prom . . . maybe Dave Blondin? He'd check this out another time. Right now, it was time for Reilly to get some sleep.

Ken Gladwell was just leaving George Wessel's business with his shirts and suits when Chief Wetman saw him and engaged him in conversation.

"Got time for a quick coffee?"

Ken wasn't in the mood for a cup of coffee, and certainly not one with the Chief of Police, but he acceded. He knew there was a cloud over him, and he didn't want to appear reluctant. They walked together to the diner.

"So, Mr. Gladwell, I imagine you've got some issues in you life that are presenting some problems." He said it almost as a question.

Problems, Ken thought? Issues? Half the people around me think I've been beating my wife, and the other half think I had something to do with Catherine Marchand's murder. He studied Wetman's face for some clarification. He hadn't planned this encounter with Wetman and was on guard, leery of making some mistake that could only make matters worse. "You know I do, Chief." Wetman was waiting for Ken to open up and said nothing.

"Can I call you Ken?"

Ken said, "Sure," as if there was nothing to lose. It was a meaningless gesture.

Wetman acknowledged that with a nod. "Thanks. I'm Jerry, then.

"Your buddy, Dave Blondin, you know he told us that Malcolm couldn't have killed that girl, Catherine."

"That's what I hear." Gladwell tried to cover up his anxiety with nonchalance.

"He really stuck his neck out for somebody, I'll tell you.

Really put it on the line, and with Philip Marchand sitting right there in the room at the same time."

The silence was powerful and Ken could feel his blood pressure rising, the heat going to his face.

"When Dave left, we sort of agreed that he must be protecting somebody. That's what we think anyway."

They were getting close to the diner and neither said anything more until they had their coffees and sat at a booth.

"Who do you think Dave Blondin is protecting, Ken? Any ideas?"

"I guess it could be anybody." Ken held the cup to his lips, wariness in his eyes, the scent of distrust and betrayal overwhelming the aroma of the coffee.

Wetman fixed on Gladwell's eyes and Ken turned away and looked at his watch.

"Oh, shit! I forgot. I'm supposed to be over in Marlton for a meeting." Ken stood up abruptly, turned around and walked out of the diner. Wetman wasn't surprised at Ken Gladwell's discomfort and sat alone with his thoughts.

Moments passed as Wetman's mind considered various possibilities, and the voice of Lou Pellerin broke the reverie. "Want some company?"

Wetman glanced up and nodded, gesturing to the seat opposite like a good host.

"You look lost in thought."

"I am. I just had a little meeting here with Ken Gladwell before he escaped the difficult questions."

"I saw him getting into his car on my way over here. He looked a little upset, if you ask me. Did he say anything?"

"Not really. But I still don't see him as a killer. He strikes me as more confused and hurt than angry."

"He does have a short fuse, though. I've seen him lose it more than once over the years."

"But nothing serious, right Lou?"

"A lot of heat and smoke but not much fire."

"He's got some good friends here, and I think they keep an eye on him so he doesn't run off the rails. I just don't know if he recognizes that."

The pair sat in silence for a few moments when Wetman asked, "Lou, do you mind if I tell you a story?" I haven't said this to anyone here before."

Lou nodded.

"You know that I was a major crimes detective in the city before I applied for this job in Apsley."

Lou listened. He knew this fact full well.

"During my interview for this job, one of the Selectmen asked me why I'd want to give up a higher paying, higher-profile job to take this one in Apsley. After all, I already had a good job making good money. Why would I uproot myself and my wife for a job here?

"I told him them that I was tired of the horror that I saw every day as a homicide cop, and wanted a change. I'd been divorced and remarried and saw Apsley as a place to start fresh. The papers picked that up in a story the next day. Do you remember that?"

Lou said, "I do. Your answer made sense to me."

"And to the Selectmen, apparently. They offered the job and I took it. And I'm glad I did. I like the town, I like the people, and my wife is enjoying the hell out of it. Plus, she sees me a lot more now than she did when I was in the old job. Nicer, you know? For everybody."

Lou said, "I'm glad for you." He wanted to get through his cup of coffee and get out of there. The conversation was getting uncomfortable.

"I'll tell you. There was a different reason why I left my old job. Not a nice reason. I've told my shrink, and of course my wife knows, and a few buddies know. But that's it. Nobody else. I'll tell you about it if you want. In fact, I'd like to tell you. Do you mind?"

Lou was unsure, hesitant to disagree. Wetman was offering to share a confidence, and confidence, he knew, is a sort of gift. Once you accept the gift, you're in a box, obligated. He was learning to like Wetman, but losing out on the Chief's job still smarted. Wetman waited patiently for Lou Pellerin's answer.

It finally came with a considered nod and the words, "Go ahead." Lou was ready to unwrap the gift.

Wetman sat back in the booth and began. "All right. I needed the change, and I wanted it. That was absolutely true. But I didn't say anything about the partner I had for the past six years named Collins. Enormous guy, filled a doorway, blacker than black, and as gentle as a lamb. He was 'good cop' and I was 'bad cop' whenever we had to interrogate somebody. He was thoughtful, and I was the action guy, you know? Ready-fire-aim, that was me. We fit well and I learned more from him than I did anybody else, even though he was a lot younger than me. I loved the guy like a brother."

Wetman shook his head as he remembered Collins and continued.

"One day, he was following up on a lead in a homicide case we were working. It was one of those drug deals gone bad where the buyer got killed. Collins got a call to meet with a guy who claimed to have some information, even though I told him not to go alone. I was on my way but he wouldn't wait, said everything would be OK. And the son of a gun got shot. Three times. Two gut shots and a head shot. He was set up. It was all arranged ahead of time. No witnesses."

"I'm sorry to hear that." Lou was becoming intrigued that Wetman would share his personal past.

"I was angry out of my mind, then depressed, real seriously depressed. But I wanted to lead the investigation into Collins' murder. My bosses didn't think it was a good idea, but I wouldn't let go and they finally gave in. I dug in and dug in and finally found the connection." He paused, smiled at Lou.

"What happened?"

"The drug unit bagged a guy who was dealing and distributing coke, pounds of it a day, and in his stash they found one bag with a piece of an official police evidence sticker still on it. They traced it back to another bust four months before."

"There was a cop involved?" Lou was deep into the story by now.

"There was, and the dealer eventually gave him up. The truth was, Collins was set up by another cop, a dirty cop, who got into the drug business and made a small fortune. In fact, I was supposed to be with Collins at the time, and if I was there, I'd be dead too. When I found out, I tracked the bastard down. I was going to kill him with my bare hands. I found him in the locker room at headquarters and told him what I found out. Then I went for him, but two of my buddies were there and they jumped in front of him and protected him, told me they couldn't let the guy plead 'police brutality', but I was out of my mind. I beat the crap out of those two buddies, sent them both to the hospital. One with a broken shoulder, broken jaw and internal injuries. He's still out on disability. The other guy ended up with two broken ribs."

"What happened to you?"

"Here's what. The dirty cop went to trial and got life in prison, no parole. My two buddies never filed a complaint against me, even after what I did to them. Claimed they fell and never changed their stories. I walked. Nothing in my jacket. Not one thing. If they did tell the truth about what happened, I'd be out of a job and wouldn't ever get back in to police work. The guy who's still on disability? He's the one who showed me the ad for the job in Apsley."

Wetman looked deep into Lou Pellerin's eyes, waiting for some response. Lou frowned, not knowing what to say. Wetman had revealed himself, had exposed a vulnerable underbelly. He didn't have to.

"So that's the story. But it's not the whole story. Because it taught me something I'd forgotten until I was sitting here thinking about Ken Gladwell."

Lou leaned forward, understanding in some part of his being that he was being manipulated, but anxious nevertheless to hear everything.

"Friends. That's what the whole thing taught me. Friends are good to have."

A long silence ensued. Lou considered the story, the trust Wetman placed in him, and the unwrapped gift of confidence. This was new to him, something he didn't expect. He stood and extended his hand to Wetman. "Thanks," he said. They finished their coffees in silence, then left the diner.

I was looking forward to a quiet night alone for a change. Ken was going to be staying at a hotel in the city tonight after some business meetings, and I didn't want another beer, another frantic meeting with a nervous friend. I was dead tired after a long day that began with a cup of coffee with a shrink, then a visit to my friend Phil, followed by a visit from an anxious Bob Hayes in the middle of trying to replace a water heater.

I didn't welcome Hayes' visit, but it was mercifully short and to the point.

"Look, Dave, Tina Gladwell has been all over me lately, and I'm putting a stop to it. Believe me, nothing happened, but she's nuts, man! I don't want any part of that. If you've heard differently, then you've heard wrong, Dave."

All I could do was try to hold the copper supply line clear so I could slide the replacement heater in place. I had trouble keeping my focus.

Hayes kept rambling.

"She came over one day right in the middle of an embalming. Remember Elsie Morse? It was what, about three weeks ago? I'm putting the fluid in and there's Tina standing right next to me, rubbing my thigh. Christ! She wanted to do it right there in the same room. Nuts!"

I let him talk. In a few minutes, Hayes' emotional bucket was empty and he moved on, giving me some silence to finish my task. Now, I could look forward to cooking the piece of cod I bought yesterday, along with some steamed vegetables. Maybe even a bottle of wine. Then a good book, some tunes on the stereo.

When I opened the door to my darkened apartment, I noticed one potential source of trouble. My answering machine light was on. It would have to be a personal call since my property calls all went to a separate business number. I turned on the overhead light and approached the answering machine warily, debating for a moment the wisdom of ignoring it.

I hung my jacket in the hall closet and removed my boots to give me time to consider my options. In the end, curiosity won out and I pressed the 'play' button.

"Hello, Dave. It's Jacqueline Marchand. I'm sorry to call but I wanted to tell you that I got a call today from a doctor back home. He was calling Phil and he didn't realize that Phil had moved.

"The man's a neurologist. He was concerned that Phil missed an appointment without calling and asked if Phil was OK. When I told him that Phil wanted a divorce and had relocated to his old home town, he clammed up. With all the privacy laws, he wouldn't tell me anything, but I got the distinct impression that Phil is ill, and it's serious. I've left messages for Phil but he doesn't return them. I was hoping you could say something to him, or at least tell him to call his doctor. I'm sorry Dave for bringing this up, but I hope you understand. Thanks. Call me when you can."

So the slight shaking and the pallid complexion; they weren't just the result of normal aging or my overactive imagination. I saved the message and decided I'd done enough that day. Phil Marchand wasn't planning on going anywhere for a while, and I needed to spend some quality 'alone time' inside the sanctuary of my small apartment. Tomorrow and the next day would be here soon enough.

NINETEEN

The next evening

"The box?" Phil turned abruptly at my mention of the word. He saw that I knew much more than he'd counted on. We were in the living room of his condo.

"The one you found at your parents' house. It was Catherine's."

His glanced up quickly. "Who told you?" There was a flash of anger, but it cooled quickly. "Never mind. It was Jacqueline, wasn't it? "

"So what? You never said anything about it. What was in it?"

Phil got up from his seat and walked over to the window where he stood silently and stared out at the snowflakes falling thicker now. His lips pursed before he spoke.

"Private stuff. Just a bunch of private stuff."

"No, Phil. It was a lot more than that. There was more than just some private stuff, right?"

"Memories, that's what's in it. Some of her personal things."

Phil remained in place and stared vacantly out the window. I waited, every passing second felt like minutes. A reasonable person would observe that only two people were in the room, but I would not ever doubt the presence of Catherine Marchand standing with us in every real sense, coaxing her brother, giving him the permission to go on. It was time.

"It was like a kit, Catherine's kit." I heard his voice choke when he started again. "Like a goodbye kit to all of us. What a nightmare she must have been living."

"A goodbye kit?"

"A note saying goodbye. A doctor's test results. A stash of pills. She even had a list of songs she wanted at her funeral."

"Test results?"

"From Doctor Poore. That's how I knew about Catherine's pregnancy."

"And her note said I was the father?"

"Yes."

"So when you told me yesterday that Catherine 'told' you about her pregnancy, this is what you meant?"

"Yes. Although, in retrospect, I should have guessed. She was throwing up every morning before school for a couple of weeks. I just never put two and two together."

"And pills? What kind of pills?"

"Remember, Catherine worked at Howard's Drug Store? She must have been sneaking some pills from the stock room. It was a mix of pills . . . Seconal, Nembutal, some others . . . all barbiturates. I think she probably snagged a few here and there from the pharmacy. It was plenty to send her into a coma and kill her."

Phil walked back and sat down and I could see that there were tears on his cheeks. Marchand took a long drink, swished it around in his mouth and sat back looking almost relaxed.

"But it was the note and the other papers that really took the cake." Another drink.

"The real clincher was the goodbye note ... beautifully written in long hand. She had beautiful handwriting, you know. Graceful, never using those cute circles and hearts when she dotted her I's. Her handwriting was just so ... her. I wish I had it here to show you but it's in a safe deposit box downtown. But it is absolute poetry. A long, sad poem by a very sad girl."

I was afraid to ask for details but they weren't long in coming.

"She never mentioned you by name, you know. Not that there was much room for doubt. Even though you and Catherine weren't officially going out all the time or anything, you'd been close, real close for a while before that. I should have known, Dave. But she did talk about being in love and being caught in a vortex because of everything. She was so, so ..."

"Afraid to disappoint?"

Phil looked up when I said the words. They caught him by surprise, as if Catherine's fear of disappointing people was something of which only he was aware.

"It was that obvious?" I said nothing.

"And here she was, beautiful and kind and confident and smart and knocked up. She couldn't face her mother or her father or her brother, or even you apparently, and just talk about it. She just couldn't do it. And remember when girls got pregnant back then? They went away. They just went away, wherever the hell that was, and they had the baby and came back. But she couldn't do that? She was so damned afraid."

He started weeping in earnest now, choking back tears as he spoke. "Imagine that, Dave? A person as good as Catherine, someone so damned beautiful inside and out. And just too damned afraid to talk about it or to disappoint anyone."

"We didn't have therapists back then like we do now. We

were raised to be strong and handle all our personal bullshit on or own. That's just the way it was."

"I know what you're saying. We weren't supposed to be weak and we were supposed to solve our problems on our own. Self-reliance. Anything else, and you were a weirdo, a fruit-cake."

There was silence for a while as we each pondered the thought of life back then. Truly, I thought, any hint of emotional fragility, just the simple need to reveal personal fears, identified a person as a mental cripple.

When I broke the silence, I did so very softly. "She didn't commit suicide, Phil. Catherine might have been thinking about it, but she never reached that final point. That has to mean something, Phil. She couldn't do it."

Phil took a sip from his drink. His hand had a more pronounced tremor now, and a few drops spilled before he got the glass to his lips. He looked at me as if in apology.

"Sorry. Nerves. I've been doing that a lot lately."

I nodded, dismissing the need for the apology, but neither accepting of the explanation.

He took a breath and exhaled before he started.

"Here's something you might not know, Dave. Catherine quit cheerleading right after she found out that she was pregnant. Then she brought all her schoolbooks back to school and put them in her locker and left it unlocked. After that, she went to the drug store where she worked and told them that she was quitting her job. That's when she finally started walking back home. And that's when she took the shortcut through the woods near the pond."

"That was the day she was killed?"

"The note she wrote? It was dated that night before. Dave, Catherine was on her way home to take her barbiturates and go to sleep."

I didn't know what to say, my mind trying to plumb the thoughts of a young woman I thought I knew so well.

"What irony, huh Dave? Whoever killed her only shortened her life by about an hour, maybe two. If the killer had just waited a little while, Catherine was going to take care of the job herself, and she wouldn't have had to go through all that agony. All those broken bones and her face mashed to a bloody pulp. She would have gone, nice and quiet, and on her own terms."

I stood and approached my friend, putting a hand on his shoulder.

"The fact remains that she didn't kill herself. Sure, she had a plan and she had the pills. If someone didn't attack and kill her in the woods, those notes and pills might still be in that box. She might have dealt with her situation a lot differently than you suspect."

Phil patted my hand. "Thanks. I'd like to think you're right. I hope you're right. I just don't think so."

I asked, "Mind if I pour one for myself? I've changed my mind."

Phil smiled and I poured two fingers, neat, into a paper cup. I turned back to Marchand and said, "What's with your shaking, Phil? Those tremors you're having . . . have you seen a doctor?"

Phil was caught off guard by the change in subject. "I told you. It's nerves."

"Sure, Phil. It's just that you're so thin and you look sallow. Then you're shaking a lot. You ought to check that out."

"I did, Dave. It's nerves. I'll be fine."

"Are you taking anything? Do you have a prescription?"

"Look, asshole. I'm fine. Knock it off."

"No way, Phil. You're sick. Very sick, and a lot of people don't want you to get any sicker. Do you have a prescription? Have you seen a doctor?"

"Look, I ran out of my medication, OK? I'll get it refilled tomorrow."

"Good. Give me the empty bottle. I know the pharmacist and I'll get it for you as soon as he opens."

"Dave, knock it off."

"No. You knock it off. What's wrong, Phil? Tell me."

Phil walked to the window of the condo and looked out. "I've got a medical condition, OK? It's not one of the better conditions to have. Huntington's. Ever hear of it?"

"I think so. I'm not sure."

"It's a genetic thing. Starts with tremors, gets steadily worse, and you die a bad death. I'm not sure which of my parents had it, and maybe Catherine had it too. Whichever parent had the trait, they were both dead of other causes before any symptoms appeared."

"Do the medications help?"

"Some. They tend to reduce some of the tremors. Eventually, they won't work any more."

"And there's no cure."

"None."

"Phil, I'm so sorry."

"Me too, Dave."

"Is that why you left Jacqueline? Why you came here?"

"Dave, Jacqueline doesn't need to take care of a guy with Huntington's. Do you know what that's like? The spasms are the easy part. But wait until I can't do anything but drool and mumble and can't even remember my name? Wait until I become violent. That happens in a lot of cases, too. Wait until I can't feed myself, or even swallow on my own, or until I piss myself all the time, and shit myself. That's what Jacqueline had to look forward to if I stayed around. Who wants that?"

"Ask her, Phil. You may find this hard to believe, Phil, but some people actually love someone else more than they love themselves. That's probably an alien concept to somebody like you whose whole life is filled with himself. You remind me of that old joke: 'Enough about *me*! Let's talk about what *you* think of me.' You're so damned self-obsessed you can't dream that people might have a different view of the important things in life and of themselves."

"Screw you."

"Jacqueline told me that underneath the façade, you're still the same shallow little shit you always were. She's absolutely right. But that's beside the point: Jacqueline loves you as you are, and she wants you and she wants to be with you. No matter what. Why deny her that?"

"You don't understand."

"And your two sons . . . it's very possible that one of them has this same genetic trait. Maybe both do."

"I know. I know."

"So what's your brilliant alternative to facing the rest of your life with your wife and family? I understand your wanting to settle Catherine's murder once and for all. I do. But there's more to your returning here than that. Why come back here? Piss everybody off? Settle some old scores? Stick your nose in everybody's business? Who gave you that right?"

Phil's eyes bored holes in my face

"I know you lost your job, by the way."

"Who . . . ?"

"Why does it matter? You got the axe, just like millions of other people before you. Does losing your job mean so much that you have to come back here and wield your power, even if people get hurt? Because you got hurt? Because you can't be the big fish in the big pond any more, so you jumped into to a small pond? And while I'm on the subject, somebody came out of nowhere and made a huge offer on the Kerrigan factory block, and when I think of who would possibly do that, frankly, you come to mind. Am I right? Are you the one who contacted the developer?"

Phil looked away.

"I thought so. For what? Because you have Huntington's? Because you feel sorry for yourself? Because you resent somebody else's happiness so much that you have to screw it up? Why? You won't be able to manage it if your offer gets accepted; you can't run that business, and you know it. Is your ego so great that you have to feed on everybody else around you? You know, Phil, I have no way of knowing how you intend to die . . . maybe you have a gun and you want to take that way out. But honestly, who gives a rip? On second thought, don't give me your prescription bottle. Don't call your wife. Buy the damned Kerrigan building so you can ruin somebody else's dreams, no matter how legitimate they are and how illegitimate yours are. Wallow in self-pity. If that floats your boat, then you deserve it. I'm sure I'll see you later, but I'm not looking forward to it."

I went to the door and opened it before Phil called out, "Wait! Don't go!"

I was trying to control the rage I felt, but I took a cautious step back and waited for Phil to say something.

"Dave, you're right. I'm sorry. Thanks for reminding me what I'm like. You always did that with me."

I listened, nodded agreement. I was only half embarrassed about my angry display, and hoped Phil would give me some word, some signal that he paid attention. I didn't wait long.

"The prescription bottle, Dave. It's on the kitchen counter. If you can get it filled, I'll appreciate it."

I looked on the kitchen counter and took the empty pill bottle with me.

"And Dave, I'll call Jacqueline tonight."

Phil walked to the door, tears coursing down his cheeks and hugged me.

I patted my friend on the shoulders.

"Phil, I'll drop off the pills tomorrow. I've got to go. I met a beautiful lady the other day and we have a seven-thirty dinner reservation."

Phil backed away. "Really Dave? Who?"

"A very nice, very attractive lady that I met at the coffee shop a few weeks ago, and I'm meeting her at the diner for whatever the daily special is. I'll see you tomorrow."

After a dinner at Lafferty's Diner, where we both enjoyed the creamed salmon and peas on boiled potatoes, Angela Kim and I retired to Dean's Town Tavern for a nightcap.

From there, we went to my apartment where we spent the next hour and a half ripping each other's clothes off and making . . . lust.

Eventually we got around to exploring each other in less physical ways. I learned a lot about Angela Kim, like her early years in rural California, her scholarship to Stanford, her difficult marriage to an ambitious marketing executive, and her daughter, now eighteen years old and away at college.

I also learned that becoming a lawyer was almost an afterthought. Angela graduated with a degree in accounting and worked for an insurance company as an assistant in the tax department when an opening came up in the law department for a financial investigator. After a few boring months poring over reports and accounts looking for fraud, she decided to try law school at night, with part of the cost paid for by the company. Angela did well, graduated with honors, and passed the bar on her second try.

She spent two years handling routine legal matters for the insurance company, and decided she wanted courtroom experience. She applied for a job with the district attorney's office.

"I learned to love my job. When my marriage finally fell apart, and with my daughter in college, I asked for more hands on experience, and Catherine Marchand's murder is the first one I've ever supervised."

"Does this mean that the DA doesn't have a lot of faith that the case will end up going anywhere?"

"You mean because he assigned it to a rookie? That's a hell of a way to put it, Dave, but you're probably more right than I'd like you to be."

"How do you feel about that?"

"So far, it's not going as I expected. The job is political in a lot of ways and I'm being assigned to this case as a favor. I'm not sure who the favor is for, but it's true just the same. Nobody else wanted it, but it gives me a chance to work with a case on my own. It's just that I'm not getting much cooperation here."

"But it's not all bad," I said. "Look at the side benefits you're getting."

Angela raised herself so she leaned on a shoulder and rested her hand on my chest, sending a pleasant shiver through me.

"So tell me a little bit about Apsley. Like, what was it like when you were a child here? How did you get to be such a close friend of Philip Marchand?"

"I met Phil on my tenth birthday at Lake Crocket. I was just starting swimming lessons to get my Intermediate certificate when the instructor plopped a new kid in line right behind me. I was all arms and legs, totally uncoordinated. This new kid actually had shoulders and a defined waist, even at ten, and he went directly into Advanced as soon as the instructor saw him do the Australian crawl non-stop for a hundred yards. I hated him.

"Catherine, was a different story. There was nothing to hate and everything to love about her. If Phil took after his mother's side, with the olive skin and sharp features, Catherine was her father's, with thick golden hair and freckles splattered across her nose and cheeks. I loved her and imagined us married with a flock of beautiful children from the first moment I set eyes on her.

"The Marchands lived in Apsley for a few generations but Phil and Catherine didn't start attending Apsley schools until fifth grade. Their mother was a teacher at St. Martin's, a private academy about eighteen miles away, and that gave them free tuition there. When she took a job as an assistant principal in Eastland, the kids started attending public school in Apsley."

Angela was twirling some of my chest hairs through her fingers while I spoke. She slid her hand down and under the sheets and gave me a squeeze.

"I'm sorry that Philip Marchand made you feel so inadequate. Let's see if we can help you overcome that ego-crushing sense of worthlessness."

I leaned into a long kiss. "I like you, David Blondin," she said when we came up for air. "I like you a whole lot."

When the telephone rang, Nancy Easter was almost asleep in her living room chair. She checked caller ID and took the call. This could be the call she was waiting for.

"What did you find out?"

She listened and looked for a pencil and paper. She wrote down some numbers and said, "I'm going to make my move soon, and if this gets in the way, then I swear, I'm going to handle the problem myself and in my own way."

She listened to the response and slammed the telephone back on the cradle.

"I'll kill that bastard. I swear I will."

TWENTY

Saturday morning

Officer Reilly stepped into Wetman's office and saw the desk covered by stacks of paperwork, all organized into separate piles. This was budget time, and Wetman was scrutinizing two sheets of paper, glancing at one and then the other, a frown creasing his forehead. The wrinkles were deep and without humor. He was in no mood for amusement or a waste of time. Immersed in this process of budget and spending comparisons, he remained unaware that Reilly was standing there until the "Ahem" caught his attention. Wetman looked up sharply, laid the two sheets of paper down, waved Reilly in and pointed to a chair.

Wetman's brow was still creased in concentration. "I got your message. What's so urgent that it can't wait until Monday or can't be put in writing?"

Wetman, Reilly saw, was in a foul mood. But he pressed on.

"Sir, it's about that pin that was found at the crime scene. The one with the rhinestones."

"This would be the pin shaped like the letter "C" and encrusted with some inexpensive red stones? It was given back to the victim's parents if I remember right. There's a color picture of it in the crime file. What else am I supposed to know about it?"

Before Reilly could answer, he sat back in his chair, put his pencil down and said, "I'm going to give you a little bit of advice Reilly, as a new detective. Don't try to read too much complexity into every situation or piece of evidence or you'll end up making things more confusing than they need to be. That's a rule I tried to keep when I was a detective, and like Sherlock Holmes said, all things being equal, the simplest solution tends to be the best one."

"Occam's Razor, Sir."

"What did you say?"

"That was Occam's Razor, not Sherlock Holmes, Sir."

"That was Sherlock Holmes, I'm sure of it."

"Whatever you say, sir. But sir, here's the thing. I went over to pick up my dry cleaning and I was going to ask Mr. Wessel some questions, just as background. He went to school with Catherine and he seems like a nice guy, so I thought I'd ask him some questions."

"What did he say?"

"Well, he wasn't there, but Betty Forman was, and she knows everyone in town and everything that's going on. When I was there, she said something that stuck in my mind. She's known the Gladwells, Ken and Tina, since they were little kids. She always liked Ken Gladwell, even if he flies off the handle sometimes. I guess his father could fly of the handle once in a while, too."

"I've heard the same thing, so tell me something I don't know."

Reilly shifted in his seat.

"It's what she said about Tina that made me think. First of

all, she said that Tina was determined when it came to Kenny; she wanted to get married to Ken Gladwell, and there was nothing that would keep that from happening. Tina hated it when they went to different colleges because she couldn't watch over Kenny like a hawk. Tina dated a couple other guys when she was at Smith, but that was just for show. That's what Mrs. Forman said."

"There's a point here, Reilly. Let's see if you can get to it."

Reilly cleared his throat.

"Yes sir. I guess Ken Gladwell didn't exactly share the same feelings as Tina. He liked women in general, even if he was dating Tina. I'm not absolutely sure about this, but I think he might have even had an eye for Catherine Marchand."

"The girl was gorgeous, Reilly. What guy wouldn't have an eye for her?"

"Well, it's what Betty called Tina Gladwell. She referred to her as 'Christina'. That's her real name, the one she was baptized with. I never knew that, and even the phone book says 'Kenneth and Tina Gladwell.' So I thought I'd mention that.

"The file said that nobody in Catherine's family was familiar with the pin that was found at the scene, and then I heard this, about Tina's real name, and thought I'd mention it to you."

Wetman just stared at Reilly as in a stupor. His head was still cluttered with remnants of budgets and debits, and Reilly's discovery took a few seconds to make its way through the tangle of synapses before it registered. Finally, he uttered two words.

"Fuck me."

"Sir?" Reilly wasn't sure he heard correctly.

Wetman stood up and pumped Reilly's hand. "Good work. No, great work! Get Lou in here. Find out where he is and get him in here. Now!"

Reilly had seen the Assistant Chief about twenty minutes earlier finishing a training session with two new officers in the conference room. If his pattern of behavior held true, then

Reilly suspected that Lou Pellerin would be having coffee at Lafferty's Diner a block away. He raced out the front door of the police station and saw the Assistant Chief Pellerin walking in the direction of the diner.

Reilly raced down the steps to intercept the Assistant Chief. "Sir? It's the Chief, sir. He wants to meet right away in his office."

Reilly was almost blubbering and it came out crooked, but Pellerin got the point. He trotted back to the station entrance and rushed to Wetman's office, Reilly trailing behind him. Wetman was pacing like an anxious father-to-be when they came in.

"Lou, wait till you hear what our new detective has to say. Grab a seat and listen to this." Wetman signaled Reilly with his eyes to go ahead.

"Well, sir, it's just that I spoke with Betty Forman and she told me a story about Mrs. Gladwell, Tina Gladwell."

Wetman was impatient. "The point, Reilly. Tell him what she said."

"Well sir, she said that Mrs. Gladwell's real name was Christina. She's used the name Tina all her life, but her given name is Christina."

Lou was trying to make sense of the revelation but wasn't yet in on the fully assembled concept. Wetman and Reilly both said at the same time, "The pin!"

Wetman went on, "Lou, the pin that was recovered at the scene of the Marchand murder. It wasn't Catherine's."

Lou looked back and forth at Wetman and Reilly and said, "Fuck me."

Reilly went to work making copies of the photographs of the pin that was in the Catherine Marchand homicide file. Then he called Philip Marchand at his apartment. Did Marchand have the pin, Reilly asked? Marchand said that the pin was in a safety deposit box at the bank. Could he get to the bank and retrieve the pin right away? Reilly needed to bring the pin back as evidence and would meet him at the bank.

Before he left the station, Reilly went next door to the Town Clerk's office to search through birth and marriage records. It would be nice to have some confirmation, something official, of Tina Gladwell's given name from someone other than Betty Forman.

The Clerk's office had a note taped to the door: "Back in ten minutes," which baffled Reilly. Ten minutes from when? One minute ago? Nine minutes ago? He pulled out his cell phone and called his mother and found that her repository of information was almost as reliable and certainly more readily available that the town clerk's. Christina Gladwell was indeed born Christina Kerrigan and her mother was still alive and living at the family home on Harrington Road. On his way to meet Philip Marchand at the bank, he called Lou Pellerin and made arrangements to pick him up in about forty-five minutes. Together they'd pay a visit to Tina Gladwell's mother; Lou Pellerin agreed to call Mrs. Kerrigan and set it up.

Philip Marchand was only too eager to share with Reilly his knowledge of the pin. Yes, he remembered when a police officer dropped off the pin with his parents some months after Catherine's murder. No, he never remembered seeing Catherine wearing it, never knew she had such a pin, although it was possible. It wasn't particularly expensive or well-made; any boyfriend might have given it to her, or she may have even bought it for herself.

Reilly gave him a receipt for the pin, placed it in an evidence bag, and drove to the police department to pick up Lou Pellerin.

"I don't think I ever met the woman," Lou said when he

joined Reilly, "but she's got a reputation, I'll say that. Always considered herself better than the unruly masses, if you know what I mean. Awash in money from her husband's factories."

Reilly asked, "Didn't those factories close down a long time ago?"

"Not before Kerrigan sold his equipment to a company down south, and he invested a lot of money in those new places, too. That's what I heard. Then he either sold off some of his property here or converted them into apartments or offices. That huge four story mill on River Street, where that high tech company has its headquarters? That's one of the Kerrigan buildings."

Reilly knew the building well. Once a noisy factory with hundreds of people manning the machinery, it was now quiet, upscale corporate offices for maybe eighty people, with high ceilings, brick interiors, and lots of modern art and diffuse lighting. Adjacent to that, another factory was converted to up-scale condos called "The Haven at Riverfront," a pompous name by Reilly's standards.

"When the old man died, everything that was left went into a trust."

He asked Lou Pellerin, "Does the family still own the Kerrigan Mills?"

"I heard that part of it was sold to a developer. He's doing the rehab and he wants to parcel it out. I think the only part the Kerrigan Trust still owns is the smaller section where the health club was."

They reached their destination, the Kerrigan home, a mansion really, at 97 Harrington Road. The nearest neighbor was two hundred yards away and the massive structure sat high on a rise with an expansive front lawn, extensive plantings, and a columned portico that was barely visible from the street.

Lou Pellerin and Reilly got out of the cruiser and stepped into shadows of the covered portico. The light snow that had fallen the night before never fell through the dried twigs of the wisteria that covered the frame overhead and Lou stomped his shoes on the slate flooring of the portico to rid them of the mud and muck they'd collected on the way here. Reilly did the same.

Lou said, "Let's see what she has to say about Catherine Marchand and everybody else before we show her the pin. When I say we're going to leave, you bring it out. Let's see what kind of reaction we get."

Reilly nodded.

"Try the bell. She's probably in," said Lou Pellerin. "I didn't see any tire tracks in the driveway." Reilly did so and a series of chimes could be heard through the walls.

Several moments passed before they heard latches being undone on the doorframe. The door opened and neither Lou nor Reilly could tell if there was anyone there, given the brightness of the outside light and the darkness indoors. Only a thin voice told them that Grace Kerrigan was there. "Yes? You must be the fellow who called. And this is?" She stepped into the doorway and the appearance was one of caution. Grace Kerrigan was reed thin and squinted to get a better look at her visitors.

"I'm Assistant Chief Pellerin, Ma'am. This here is Detective Reilly. May we come in?"

There was a silence as she appraised the pair. She turned away and said, "Oh, all right, but please stay on the carpets in the hallway. The wood floors are expensive, you know."

They followed her inside and Reilly closed the door behind them. Their eyes adjusted and Reilly couldn't contain the urge to glance around the foyer. He'd never been inside the house although he'd been by it countless times. There was a kind of hush, a kind that hangs over a place after everyone is gone. Reilly felt a chill, struck by the irony that he felt warmer outdoors where the thermometer reading would have to have been forty degrees colder.

Grace Kerrigan didn't offer a hand but stood, leaned slightly forward. She was dressed in a simple dress of cornflower blue, probably cashmere and matching the blue of her eyes. A large gold broach in the shape of a spear was clipped near the shoulder. She was a picture of well-tailored and elegant old wealth. Reilly supposed her closets would have been full of clothes to match her eyes. Only her soft matching flats indicated that she sought some degree of comfort over form.

The foyer was decorated, if that's the correct word, with old statuary and paintings, all old and obviously expensive. A winged figure holding a globe sat on a tall cherry pie crust tripod table. A set of three miniatures, all portraits, of what were likely to be the ancestors of the household, were perched on a narrow shelf. In the corner, an enormous grandfather clock chimed the half hour in tones so dulcet as if apologizing for the passage of time. There was a spell cast by Mrs. Kerrigan and the space and Lou Pellerin broke it with his opening comments.

"Mrs. Kerrigan, we're investigating the death of Catherine Marchand."

"A bit late, aren't we?" The irony was laced with bitterness and sarcasm.

"Yes, well, we've reopened the case and Detective Reilly and I wanted to ask you some questions."

"Questions? I can't imagine why. Yes, I did hear that young Philip Marchand managed to stumble back into our community to seek, I suppose, some 'closure'." She drew out the word. "But I don't see the relevance to me. I hardly knew the tart."

Lou glanced at Reilly and continued. "Yes, well, we're trying to assemble a list of all of Catherine's friends and acquaintances and we understand that she spent quite a bit of time here, with your daughter Tina. Is that correct?"

"Quite a bit of time. An interesting turn of a phrase, isn't it? I suppose she was here more than once but I suggested, firmly, to my daughter, Christina, that she associate with some other young ladies. Catherine, you see, was not a good influence."

Reilly raised an eyebrow and followed up. "Why is that, Mrs. Kerrigan?"

She turned her attention from one to the other in slow motion. "Because Catherine was, I learned quite by accident, someone whose habits and character were less than honorable. As I said, Miss Marchand was a tart."

Reilly wanted more detail. "Why do you say that? Most people who knew her have gone on record as saying she was popular, bright and someone they truly liked."

"Popular, perhaps. But that's not always an admirable trait, is it?"

Reilly said nothing but held her gaze, encouraging her to say more.

"Young men, like dogs chasing a bitch in heat . . . you might say the bitch was popular, wouldn't you?"

Lou Pellerin was stunned by the remark and flinched at the characterization. Reilly pressed. "That's rather severe, Mrs. Kerrigan. She was attractive and had boyfriends, I'm sure. But so were many of her friends. That's what we're hearing, anyway."

"Your hearing is impaired, then. Or your sources questionable. Catherine Marchand threw herself at the boys, and they, like all young men in good health and proper inclinations, responded as one would expect."

Grace Kerrigan reached for a cane that was propped against the dark wood paneling. Lou nodded to Reilly and said, "Thank you for seeing us, Mrs. Kerrigan. If we have any more questions, we'll call you." That was Reilly's cue.

Mrs. Kerrigan started to respond when Reilly took a plastic bag from his pocket and asked, "Before we leave, Mrs. Kerrigan, would you please take a look at this and tell me if you've ever seen it before."

He removed the pin from the plastic bag and held it out for her. She took it from his hand and squinted as she held it so it captured the best light. "In spite of my years, young man, I have excellent vision, and I can tell you that I've never seen this before. It's rather cheap looking, if you ask me. One can tell that it's just some sort of base metal and rhinestones thrown together." She handed it back.

"Nothing, Mrs. Kerrigan?"

"I wouldn't wear such a thing and my daughter would never do so either. If she did, I would tell her to remove it. It's a trinket, if you can't tell the difference. Why do you ask?"

"Just following up, Mrs. Kerrigan. You understand."

Pellerin added, "If we have any other questions, we'll let you know, Mrs. Kerrigan."

"You'll be wasting your time if you want someone to attest to the fine character of Catherine Marchand. The individual I knew by that name was not, let me assure you, one of fine character. Good day."

With that, she tipped her cane towards the front door. When the door closed behind them, they could hear the same latches being thrown.

"Delightful woman, that Mrs. Kerrigan," Lou Pellerin offered as they trudged back to their vehicle. "What a charmer."

"You've never met her?"

"I've lived here my whole life and I don't think I saw her more than five times in my life. She lives inside that mansion and never comes out."

"Imagine what it must have been like to be Tina Kerrigan growing up in that place."

Gordon Jefts' phone rang and he reached over from his easy chair to answer it. He was exhausted and half-hoped he'd be able to nap for a bit, even with the load of files on his lap.

He listened to the caller and the conversation was brief and enlightening.

"Thanks," he said. "I've got some calls to make and I'll let them know about this. I appreciate a little good news now and then."

He flipped through the pages of his phone directory and was about to dial when his phone rang again. He checked his caller ID and it was Mike Moura.

"Hi Mike, what are you doing working on a Saturday?"

Jefts listened to Mike describe still another telephone conversation. Mike related a stunning conversation he'd just had with Malcolm Prudhomme who called from his hospital room. Malcolm wanted some major changes to his will and he wanted them all completed and ready for signature early Monday morning. Mike was in the office making the changes right now. But since Mike was already scheduled to be at a meeting in the city on Monday morning, would Gordon handle the signing?

"Sure," he said, his mouth dry as toast, wondering if Mike suspected him of snooping in Malcolm's file. He decided to ask a follow up to test this.

"What's the change by the way?"

Mike explained and Gordon was astonished and relieved simultaneously. When the call was over, he was barely able to contain himself. All the news was good and he dialed before another call could interrupt him and possibly spoil the moment.

"Look," he said when his call was answered, "We got the go ahead from the seller. We can drive into the city together Monday around noon and we can get the documents signed Tuesday morning. It'll be yours."

He listened to one objection.

"Not before ten or eleven on Monday morning. Something's come up and I have to cover something for Mike Moura at nine. I'll call when I'm done and we'll take the ride together."

He listened again.

"Great. We can have dinner at the nicest restaurant in the city. It's going to be your last moment of peace because the press will be there on Monday and it'll be all over the news by Tuesday morning."

Great, thought Gordon as he hung up.

Now to make one more call and share his bit of good news.

Gordon tried my apartment but got my voice mail. "It's Gordon. Got some great news on the building you looked at. And I've got some better news, too. In fact, I've even got some great news on top of that. Give me a call. I think I want to have a toast later on to celebrate."

It was time for Lou Pellerin and Reilly to meet with Mr. Kenneth Gladwell and speak with him. Both considered the chance very high that Ken Gladwell, who was dating Tina Kerrigan at the time of the murder, bought the pin for her as a gift. But before the pair sat down with Ken Gladwell, they wanted to speak with Chief Wetman. Lou called the Chief on his cell phone.

"Nothing, Chief. She never saw the pin before. But this Mrs. Kerrigan is a woman with a lot of opinions, and none of them are good."

The Chief agreed that a call on Kenneth Gladwell was in order and he wanted to be there when that happened. Lou explained that Ken Gladwell was living at a friend's apartment since he separated from his wife.

"I keep thinking, Lou," Wetman said. "If Gladwell bought that pin for Tina and hadn't given it to her yet, and then met up with Catherine in the woods . . . I don't know."

"Maybe he bought it for Catherine for that matter."

"Possible."

"But why would Ken Gladwell beat the life out of Catherine?"

"Rejected love? Maybe Catherine even planned to break

things off with him. After all, she was pregnant with someone else's child. There were rumors, according to the file, that Ken Gladwell had a thing for Catherine, even though he was dating Tina. He might have snapped if he found out that Catherine's relationship with his best friend was more than it seemed."

"Maybe, but why take it out on Catherine? Why not go after Dave Blondin instead?"

"If he was in the vicinity at that time, maybe he would have. You've heard about the famous Gladwell temper."

"Possible. Look, I've got a call from Dr. Hairston on the other line. Come by the station and pick me up and we'll go see Gladwell together."

Hairston greeted Wetman over the phone and said, "Chief, Mr. Prudhomme is sitting here with me right now and we've had a conversation about some things that deal with parts of your investigation of the Catherine Marchand case. I'd like to put him on the line, if you don't mind."

Wetman listened to Prudhomme's story and took notes simultaneously, and almost ferociously. The conversation took thirteen minutes and Wetman had five pages of notes. When Lou Pellerin and Reilly showed up at the station, he called them into his office and closed the door.

"Here's what the guy said. He admitted to me he was at the pond when he saw Catherine Marchand. He thought she was the prettiest girl he'd ever seen and he was always going to the football games just to see her lead the cheers.

"Anyway, he said he 'lost himself' that day. Those are his words. He saw her at the pond, alone, and he went up behind her and grabbed her. He was 'getting a climax' . . . his words again . . . by rubbing up against her. Then he heard somebody yell at him and he stopped, ran away and went home.

"About a month later, he got a knock at his door and it was

Ken Gladwell. He told Malcolm that he was the one who saw him with Catherine at the pond, and he was going to tell the police what he saw. The police didn't like Malcolm and would have loved to have a witness or some other evidence that he was at the pond. The police knew nothing about this assault, as you know.

"Anyway, if Ken Gladwell talked, it was going to put Malcolm at the scene, and he told Malcolm that he wasn't going to tell the police anything about him running away. In other words, the finger would be pointed directly at him for the murder, and there'd be an eyewitness to put him there.

"But then Ken Gladwell told him he'd make a deal. He needed a car, and Malcolm could help him get it. Just give him one thousand dollars and Gladwell would never call the police. Malcolm was happy to pay him."

Reilly interrupted. "Ken Gladwell was interviewed several times back then and he never said a word."

Lou added, "If he did say anything about seeing Malcolm at the scene, he would have been placed there as well. He probably decided that he wasn't going to tell the police about what he saw with Malcolm, no matter what. But Malcolm couldn't be sure of that. So paying some money to Ken was easy."

Wetman continued.

"Here's the rub, though. A few years went by and all of a sudden, Malcolm gets a letter from Ken Gladwell. He's married and broke, and he needs money. Another thousand gets paid."

"But Tina's family was loaded. Why blackmail the guy?" It was Lou Pellerin's question.

"Pride? I don't know why. But less than a year later, Malcolm Prudhomme gets another letter, this time threatening to go to the police unless Malcolm makes Ken Gladwell the beneficiary of his estate. Malcolm was afraid. Ken Gladwell wanted a copy of the will, all notarized, or he'd go to the police and Malcolm would be hauled in."

Wetman let that sink in for a moment.

Lou said, "What a bastard Ken Gladwell is, if we want to believe Malcolm Prudhomme's story."

"Right," said Wetman. "That's the way it was drawn up and it stayed that way until a month or two ago. Malcolm got another letter saying that the beneficiary should be changed to Tina Gladwell, and Malcolm was to get the change made and send a copy of the updated and notarized will to Gladwell's house. Malcolm's not going along with it, though. He said he's too old and too tired to keep running from Ken Gladwell and he already called his lawyer to make some other changes. Ken and Tina Gladwell will be out of the will entirely."

Reilly made an observation. "Ken Gladwell must have told the story about seeing Malcolm in the woods to Dave Blondin. That's why Dave was so determined to let Philip Marchand know about Malcolm. But Dave didn't want to put his buddy Ken Gladwell in the crosshairs, so he just gave us part of the story to protect his friend."

"I agree with you up to a point, Reilly," Wetman said as he slipped on his jacket.

The trio of police considered various possibilities as they drove together to my place, a short hop down the street from the station and around the corner. There was no answer at my apartment and neither my pick-up nor Ken's Impala was in the parking area in back. Lou Pellerin trotted down the street a few doors down and knocked on Gordon Jefts' door. A few moments later, Lou returned with my cell number and it was Lou who placed the call.

I had blocked out some time this afternoon to help Ken move some things out of his house. Tina agreed earlier to be out of the house so Ken could collect some clothes and a few pieces of furniture. I was on my way over to the Gladwell house when my phone rang.

"Ken? Sure, Lou. He's over at his house right now. He was going to pick up some things while Tina's out for the day. What's going on?"

"Just need to ask him a few questions, Dave," Lou Pellerin said, but I wasn't convinced.

The three left my place in one cruiser just as I pulled into the Gladwell driveway. I wanted to get to Ken first, to warn him. Now was not the time for Ken Gladwell to explode, not with three armed policemen in the same place.

TWENTY-ONE

The Same Day

"I'm royally screwed, Dave. Royally screwed." Ken sat in an overstuffed recliner in his living room and all the shades were drawn. The only light came from a table lamp on a side table. Next to him sat a glass, half-full, and a bottle, also half-full, of Johnny Walker Black. On his lap was a pistol, a revolver with a dull gray finish and a brown cross-hatched grip.

Ken's eyes were glazed, but he didn't appear to be drunk. I'd seen him drunk plenty of times, and this was more of a look of stunned amazement. In light of the events of the recent past, I could understand and appreciate that sensibility.

Ken looked up at me as I stood at the doorway. "I'm not going to shoot you, you know. Grab a seat."

I stepped into the room and sat in one of the wing backed leather chairs. I turned it slightly to face my friend.

"So what's with the gun, Ken?"

"This? It's my old Smith & Wesson I've had for years. It's

one of the things I came here to pick up. I have another one, a little Glock, but only this one was in my bed stand. I've been looking all over the house for it. By the way, I'm only going to take some clothes and a few things with me. Tina can do what she wants with the rest."

"Ken, Lou Pellerin just called me. The police want to talk to you."

"So, you heard about Tina? And that asshole Bob Hayes?" It was as if Ken either didn't hear me, or just didn't care. "Perfect, huh? My wife was trying to screw the undertaker. I guess I'm supposed to understand?"

"Tina isn't herself, Ken. You know that."

I watched Ken take a swallow. "Not herself? That's precious, Dave. Not herself, Dave? You know, I wonder sometimes what normal really is. I'm beginning to doubt everything."

"You're a good guy, Ken. It's just been rough. Especially since Eric died."

"Right. Eric. That really messed us up. Eric, poor kid. He'd be, I don't know, twenty-three? Maybe he and I would be sitting down having a drink together and laughing about some stupid shit like guys do." He took another swallow.

"Eric's death also screwed up Tina."

Gladwell studied me now as if he was seeing me for the very first time. He tilted his head, curious, and looked into my eyes.

"Look, Dave, you know as well as I do that the Ken and Tina Gladwell story isn't exactly Romeo and Juliet. We were plenty screwed up even before Eric ever came along."

"Who's got the perfect marriage, Ken? Certainly not me." I leaned forward. "Ken, do me a favor and put that gun out of sight before the police show up. Don't ask for trouble. You've got enough already."

"Right."

"They're going to be here soon, Ken. Please. Put it down on the floor and let's walk out there together when they show up."

Ken started to laugh and caught himself, ending almost in a sob.

"What do they want with me? Are they still hopping around because of Phil Marchand? Do they think I killed his sister?"

"I have no idea, Ken."

"What I told you about Malcolm . . . you didn't tell them, did you? Besides Tina, you're the only one I've ever said anything to about that."

"Malcolm told Max some stuff, that you can prove that he didn't kill Catherine."

"That dumb old bastard."

"He's still in the hospital. After what he went through at the bridge, he might have told others."

"So you think your good buddies are on their way to talk about me and Malcolm?"

"I don't know, Ken. They probably have questions and they think that you have some answers."

"OK, good buddy, old pal. Tell me what you really think happened. You're so damned smart, you tell me What-You-Have-Figured-Out. Go on, tell me."

"Come on, Ken."

"No, please tell me. I'm all ears."

"OK. You saw Malcolm and Catherine; he was roughing her up and you interrupted him. He took off and you used that information to blackmail him. And now, with Malcolm as sick as he is, you stand to rake in a huge windfall."

That caught Ken by surprise. "What are you saying?"

There'd be no going back on this if I opened his mouth. I just hoped it wouldn't blow up in Gordon's face. "Malcolm's will. I know you're the beneficiary."

That took the wind right out of Ken Gladwell. He leaned forward as if checking himself to see if he had what he thought he heard.

"Fuck you, Blondin."

"You end up with his house, the land, maybe some money in the bank."

"Who's telling you this horseshit?"

"I can't say. I just know."

"Well what you know is absolute horse shit! I'm in Malcolm's will? Are you shitting me?"

"So that's wrong? Even though it's in black and white and filed with the court?"

"No way! Look, I'll admit I did ask for a grand total of one thousand dollars from Malcolm so I could buy my first car. But that was it. Finis. No mas. I admit it was a shit thing to do, but I was broke and had no way to get back and forth to school, so I did it. Shoot me for a thousand dollars."

"You really don't know? About the will?"

"No fucking way. Where are you getting this shit?"

"And you never saw what happened to Catherine after that?"

"The last thing I saw, I told you, Catherine was fine." Ken's eyes filled up. "You have no idea, Dave, how much I wish I stayed there with Catherine. No idea."

He looked gaunt, his shoulders sloped.

"Ever since I heard that Phil Marchand was coming back, I've been reliving those moments over and over. If I had only stayed there, by Catherine, she might still be alive."

We sat in silence. The only noises were from a ticking clock on the mantle.

"But honestly, Dave, the last I saw her, she was a little shaken up but she was perfectly fine. I followed Malcolm with the dumb bastard zipping up his pants all the way to his house. I didn't even mention anything to him about what I saw until maybe a month later."

My cell phone rang. I checked caller ID. It was Gordon Jefts and I let it go to voicemail.

The doorbell rang and we heard the booming voice of Lou Pellerin and a loud banging on the front door. "Police, Mr. Gladwell. Please open up."

Ken Gladwell put the pistol on a side table and went to the door with me not far behind. He opened the door and was greeted by Chief Wetman, Assistant Chief Pellerin and Detective Reilly.

Lou spoke for three of them. "Mr. Gladwell, Ken, we have some questions for you. We'd like to go down to the station. What's this?" Lou saw Ken's revolver on the side table.

"It's my old revolver. Here, take it if it worries you. It's not loaded."

"Any other weapons in the house?"

"I have another pistol but I can't find it. Tina must have moved it. Why?"

Wetman stepped forward as Pellerin collected the revolver. "Look, Ken, we need to talk. Let's take a ride downtown."

"No way. Unless you're arresting me, you can talk to me right here."

"If you insist."

Wetman suggested they go to another room. Ken led the way to the dining room in the rear of the house where he and Lou Pellerin and Wetman took seats. Reilly and I remained standing by the doorway.

"We have a question for you, Ken. Detective Reilly, can you show Mr. Gladwell the pin?"

Reilly stepped foreword and showed Gladwell the pin that was found at the scene.

"Christ, what do I know? I've never seen it."

"You're sure? It would have been a long time ago."

"Is this to do with Catherine Marchand? Dave has been telling me all kinds of bullshit about that and here you are talking to me about it. Some coincidence, huh?"

My cell phone rang again and I checked caller ID. It was Gordon again and Lou Pellerin looked over and gave me a not so subtle hint to step out of the room.

When I stepped away and took the call, Gordon started with a rush.

"I tried reaching you at home, Dave. Two things: Your offer on the front section of the Kerrigan block was accepted. I'll work out the details and get everything ready for signing Tuesday morning. But it's yours, baby, so go shop the banks for money. Second: The will I told you about. It was going to be changed and Mike told me all about it today. The beneficiary of the will was amended to read Tina Gladwell alone, but Malcolm changed his mind. Ended up telling Mike to change it to the Salvation Army and wants it all done for Monday morning. I'm handling the signing. Weird or what? There's a third thing going on, too. Big news, but I can't talk about it until Monday night or Tuesday."

I don't think Gordon took one breath when he told me all this. Then he stopped and waited. I didn't say anything. "Well? No comment? Are you there?"

There was too much for me to process and Ken was still sitting in the next room being questioned by the police. I said, "Gordon, I'll have to call you back."

"But Dave . . ."

I closed his phone and stepped back into the dining room.

"Take a close look at it," Wetman insisted. "Did you buy a pin like this when you were in high school?"

Ken was getting angry. "I'm supposed to remember something that I might have bought back in high school? Are you nuts?"

I stepped closer and looked at the pin in question. The memories came back in an instant.

"Ken, didn't you buy a pin like this once for Tina? We were in Marlton, I think, at that little shopping center."

Ken studied the pin again.

"Yeah, it could be." He considered that possibility and nodded. He turned to Wetman. "OK, it looks like a pin I bought Tina back in high school. Why?"

"Did you actually give her this pin? Or a pin like it?"

"I must have. I think I gave it to her after a dance we went to. So what?"

"And have you seen it since then?"

"No . . . I don't think so. I figured she lost it somewhere, you know? It wasn't expensive. Just junk jewelry, really. What's the big deal?"

Chief Wetman, Lou Pellerin and Reilly looked at one another, each reaching the same conclusion.

"Where is Mrs. Gladwell right now?" Wetman asked.

"I guess she's probably doing some shopping. I don't know. I'm just here picking up a few things to . . ."

Lou was already moving away and using his radio to call in to the station. Wetman and Reilly raced past, leaving me and Ken mute and alone in the dining room.

George Wessel decided he'd go off his diet a little bit, pulled on his jacket, and walked to Eubanks'. There, he picked up a Sky Bar and a newspaper. He'd been losing so much weight on his diet that he didn't feel so bad about cheating just a little bit with the Sky Bar. He took the wrapper off and ate a bite while he scanned the headlines of the day's paper. Not a whole lot to report except for the recent decision by the Board of Health to close the landfill in three months and open a transfer station.

George liked it better when there was just a plain old town dump, but he understood the problem and accepted that the transfer station might be at least part of the solution. What bothered him about the news was the suggestion at the same meeting that clear plastic be required for household trash bags so some trash police could bust anyone who commits the very serious crime of trying to throw away a recyclable aluminum can. It didn't pass, but George would expect the issue to come back up again.

George turned when he heard a horn and saw Max Zenga, bundled up in his parka and wool cap, driving by in his new front end loader and waving. George waved back and heard Max yell something that he couldn't distinguish over the engine roar. When he turned back, he saw Tina Gladwell walking along the sidewalk across the street. He hadn't seen her in a couple of weeks and thought there might even be some of her dry cleaning hanging in his shop waiting for her to pick up. She looked preoccupied, like she was on a mission, and he decided not to call over to her. She'd be in one day soon.

He paused and looked in the window of the Apsley Dress Shoppe, the one place in the area that carried better quality clothes and shoes for women. It wasn't the same as going into the city or to that fancy mall over in North Bradford, but it did a brisk business. Carla had pointed out a beautiful dress to him last week in the window and he stopped to look at it again. Her birthday's soon, George thought, as he looked it over.

At the register inside, he could see Nancy Easter with a stack of boxes and some long dresses (gowns, he wondered?) being rung up. She must be going to some gala, he thought, if she's buying clothes like that.

He continued down the sidewalk and went back into his store and put the rest of his Sky Bar in his top drawer. He checked the wall clock; another hour until closing. He hadn't even removed his jacket when the police scanner burped to life.

He recognized Lou Pellerin's voice as Lou contacted the rest of the police on duty to be on the lookout for Tina Gladwell. He turned the volume up, just as Lou Pellerin said that Tina could be armed and should be approached with caution. Something had gone terribly wrong.

George immediately yelled to Betty who was just coming

out of the washroom, and told her to call 911 and tell the police that Tina Gladwell was walking east on Main Street. With that, he snagged his cell phone from the desk and bolted from the store to follow her and keep her in view.

George thought he'd lost her when he looked down Main Street and saw a few people, but not Tina. He broke into an easy trot and wondered where she might have turned. He looked into the front of the flower shop and saw one customer, but no Tina. The pizza shop next door was empty of customers. Then the hardware store. He went in, raced across the front and looked down every aisle. He called out to Walt Burke who was sorting nuts and bolts, "Did Tina Gladwell just come in here a few minutes ago?"

"What's up, George? What's your hurry?"

"Was she just here? I need to know!"

"Nope. Saw her walk by a little while ago, but she didn't come in here. You know, she looks darned good for a woman her age, I'll tell you." But by the time he'd finished, George was already out the door.

He increased his speed, huffing a little as he went, and glad he'd been losing weight. He didn't think he could have done this even three months ago. All those extra pounds made a lot of difference.

He was running out of businesses on Main Street and, with them, the reasons why Tina Gladwell would be in the area. He looked down every cross street, knowing as he did so that the likelihood of seeing Tina was slim. Then he took one guess as to her destination.

If George was right, she'd be heading there. There didn't seem to be any other places where Tina might otherwise go. Not in this part of town. He reached the corner and never slowed, and ahead of him he could see Tina Gladwell get to the Kerrigan Mills building, unlock and open a side door and go in.

George reached the door less than a minute later and pulled

on the handle. She hadn't locked it behind her and it swung open, revealing a nearly black interior. He stepped inside and kept the door open with a stray piece of debris that lay on the floor. If the police came by, he wanted them to see the open door and reach the conclusion that Tina was here.

Then he stood absolutely still, waiting for his breathing to settle down and his eyes to adjust to the low light. He listened carefully for any noise that might indicate where Tina might be. In seconds, he heard the clatter of quick steps being taken in the far left corner. Tina was climbing the stairs to the second floor.

George walked in the direction of the footsteps and tried to remain as quiet as possible. He edged closer to a doorway and saw the dim form of a staircase. He moved back toward the doorway, reached for his cell phone and called 911, covering his mouth and the mouthpiece as much as he could.

"I'm calling about Tina Gladwell," he said in a voice barely above a whisper.

"Speak up, sir. I can't hear you."

"Tina Gladwell," he said slowly, hoping the operator would understand.

"Tina Gladwell? Hang on, please."

Another voice came on the line. "Is this Tina Gladwell?"

He could tell that the voice belonged to Hank Bruno and he said, "Hank, it's George Wessel, from the cleaners."

"George! It's Hank. Do you know where Tina is?"

"She's at the Kerrigan Mills. I think she's on the second floor, right over her old health club. I left the door open on the side of the building."

"I know where it is. Look, George, I'm getting this information out to the Chief right now. Hang on."

George could hear some radio communications in the background and Hank reappeared on the line. "Two units should be there in a few minutes, George. No sirens, just in case. George, are you OK? Can you talk?"

"Not now, Hank. I'm just inside the building and I just heard her run upstairs. I'll just hang here until the police show up."

"George, you be careful."

Hank Bruno waited for some response, but George had already cut the connection.

George stayed near the doorway and listened. Nothing. He crept closer and stuck his head around the corner and looked up the stairs. He slipped off his shoes and took one step up, then another. In a few moments he was at the top of the landing and heard some muffled sounds coming from his left. He moved to the doorway and craned his neck around the edge of the doorframe.

Twenty feet away stood Tina Gladwell, her back to George, at a large oak table on which was a photograph and several votive candles all lit and casting a golden glow over the area. It looked like an altar. Tina, he could see, was just blowing out the match she used to light them.

This was an old storage area and was open to the loading platform one floor below. George remembered being here many years ago for this was once used by the high school athletic department to store off-season equipment. Tina at the time was manager of the baseball team.

Suddenly George heard some voices coming from outside the building, probably from the open doorway that Tina and he had entered a few minutes before. The police, he thought.

The noise caught Tina's attention as well and she turned around quickly, only to see George standing there. She raised her right hand and George was stunned by the sight of a pistol.

"George," she said, no hint of anger in her voice. "What are you doing here?" She looked almost serene and her voice was calm and even.

"The police are looking for you, Tina. I saw you and . . ."

"You followed me?" She smiled at the idea.

George nodded. Tina stared at George, never blinking.

"Tina, please put the gun down."

"I like to come here once in a while, George. It's my own private little refuge. Just like a little church, don't you think?"

She turned her back to him and looked at the altar. George could see now that the framed photograph was of her son, Eric. He took two tentative steps forward.

"The police want to talk to you, Tina. Maybe we should go there together. What do you think?"

"George Wessel, you are such a good man. Everybody says so. They call you a stand-up guy, whatever that means."

"Tina, we can go to the police together. It'll be all right."

"They'll want to talk about Catherine Marchand, I'll bet." Tina's voice remained calm and even, almost disembodied, the syllables floating across the space.

"I don't know, Tina, but we can go there together."

"Do you know what I'd tell them about Catherine? George, do you have any idea?"

"No, Tina."

Her voice took on a strained gritty quality and she almost growled her words when she continued.

"That she was a pig and a whore and she wanted my Kenny. And that I knew she was stealing him from me. She was evil. Catherine was evil, George. She wanted my Kenny, I know she did. And she already had everything she wanted. She wasn't going to get my Kenny. No way, George. That's what I'd tell them, George."

George was dumfounded.

"I saw her walk into the woods that day, and a few minutes later I saw Kenny leaving school after practice and go the same way. Catherine was luring him, reeling my Kenny in just like a big fish. I knew what she was after. Kenny was so taken with Catherine, and she told everybody what a great looking couple they'd make. She was setting the trap, George. And I was going to catch her fooling around with my Kenny. Then I saw Kenny running away. He must have heard me coming, but there she was, her clothes all mussed and she's smoking a cigarette. She was such a whore, George. And I just got so mad, George.

"And I had a bag full of baseball bats that I was going to bring over here to the mill. And I used one of them to smash her. Over and over and over and over. And that was it. I'm glad she's gone, George. She wasn't ever going to get my Kenny. I wasn't going to put up with that."

"Tina, let's go. Let's go to the police together." He took a step toward her.

"Don't come any closer, George." He stopped, frozen.

He looked around the space. An upholstered wingback chair was on the left and he could see a bookcase close to the wall. Everything was spotless and dust free, even with the construction that was going on during the week right nearby.

To his right was the gaping space that opened onto the loading platform.

"I come here to be alone, George. It soothes me, even though it's been so noisy around here with all those workers and their drills and saws. I come on the weekends or at night and I keep it nice and clean." She paused, the pistol hanging limply in her right hand.

"I talk to Eric and make sure he's OK, and I sit and think about things. I wish I could see him. But he sounds fine. He misses some of his friends."

She turned back and faced the makeshift altar in a heartbroken fog. "Did you know he'd be twenty-three next month, George?"

The sounds below were becoming louder. George thought that the police must be at the bottom of the staircase by now.

"He'd be tall and handsome, maybe even married. Maybe I'd have a little grandchild." Without turning around, Tina suddenly raised the pistol to her head. "I'd really like to see Eric."

George sprung forward, raced several steps and dove for her ankles, catching her left foot and rolling past her. She squeezed the trigger and the pistol went off, the explosion echoing off the brick walls. The round went into space and struck something metal that made a loud clang.

Tina spun to the side and George regained his footing only to see Tina point the pistol in his direction. He lunged to the side as she fired the weapon and fell fifteen feet to the dock below in a tangle of old ropes and cartons. His ankle, he was sure, was broken and he felt something warm and wet on his left side."

He turned, looked up, and saw Tina lift the pistol with both hands and bring the barrel toward her mouth.

"Tina!"

A shot rang out and Tina was down.

In forty minutes, the pandemonium was over. Lou Pellerin used a flashlight to survey the scene. He systematically blew out the candles that Tina Gladwell had lit and studied the photograph of Eric Gladwell. Wetman came over.

"Is this the son that committed suicide?"

Lou Pellerin nodded.

"Good looking kid. Looks like his mom."

"She kept a picture album on the table next to that chair, and there are some diaries going back to her high school years on the shelf underneath. Obsessive."

"Right. Obsessive and dangerous. George Wessel was darned lucky."

"I suppose. But the image of seeing her with the gun barrel in her mouth will stay with him a long time."

"Well, she was lucky too. You know," Pellerin added in a low voice. "You're probably going to have to give that kid a medal. He saved a life with that shot."

"Reilly? You bet. Good thing he goes to the range, Lou." A

half smile came over his face, but Lou didn't see it in the deep shadows. "Is he OK?"

"I told him to sit down in that chair near the wall. He's never shot at anyone before, but I think he'll be fine."

Just then Reilly called out from the chair he'd been occupying about twenty-five feet away. He had the beam of his flashlight pointed at a baseball bat that was standing against the wall, partially wrapped in tissue paper. "Look at this!"

Wetman and Pellerin stepped closer and looked. It was a Louisville Slugger baseball bat, brown with age. Near the barrel end was the signature of Roger Maris.

The barrel end was darker than the rest of the bat, with what appeared to be dark gray and black stains. The three knew exactly what they were looking at and remain fixed in place as they gazed at it. Wetman finally broke the silence.

"You'll need some more paper. Lou, can you call the station and ask Hank Bruno to bring some here? He can stop by the hardware store and pick a roll. Ask him to bring a couple of cameras, too. We need to get photographs of all this."

Reilly said, "That's it, Chief, isn't it?"

Wetman hadn't moved his eyes from the bat. "I'd say you're going to get a report from the lab that says these stains are of human blood and it's going to match Catherine Marchand's"

"I'd say you're right."

Lou returned. "Hank will be here in a few minutes."

Wetman put his hand on Reilly's shoulder like a proud parent and said, "Helluva job, Opie. You've had quite a day for yourself. Now, hand me your weapon. Standard procedure."

Reilly was turning red, a fact not evident in the low light. He muttered something that sounded vaguely like thanks as he stood and removed his weapon from its holster, checked to make sure the safety was on, and presented it to the Chief. He went back to the corners of the room to check out more of the contents with his flashlight.

On the floor near the altar was some blood spatter that the three scrupulously avoided. It was Tina Gladwell's, whose arm still held the slug from Reilly's weapon. Pellerin was right: Wetman and the whole Apsley community owed the young detective some honorific. A special award, a picture in the newspaper, a letter of commendation.

This was a classic one-two, Lou Pellerin thought. The town's oldest unsolved murder was solved, and a young police officer took a perfect shot to keep the perpetrator of that murder from killing herself.

There was still a lot of work to do to wrap things up. If the case went to trial . . . Wetman suspected a very long committal to a psych facility was more likely . . . the file would be on some sort of active status for a long time.

TWENTY-TWO

Monday

Jacqueline Marchand was studying the frost on the stubble of grass in the small plot of lawn in front of my apartment when I approached. The sound of my footfalls caused her to look up.

"It's amazing to me, Dave. In North Carolina, we have these near perpetual lawns that never have to die back and get reborn."

"I don't take this for granted, Jackie."

"I'll bet you don't. Out for an early walk?"

Just loaned my jumper cables to a guy down the street. In this weather, cars are tough to start. Cup of coffee sound good?"

"Absolutely. How's George?"

"He's coming home tomorrow."

"I'm so, so sorry, Dave. Phil's return caused a lot of problems."

"We had the problems all along. We just didn't know it."

We took seats at my kitchen table while the coffee brewed. "And you? Out for a morning drive and just decided to stop by?"

The aroma of hot coffee filled the room and we sat alone and still, deep in our own thoughts. When the last gasp of the coffee maker was complete, she stood, found two cups and poured.

I sat, hugging my cup and enjoying the warmth on my frozen fingers. "I wish things could have been different."

"But they're not, are they? Phil told me about you and Catherine."

I wasn't surprised and nodded.

"Your kids, your ex-wife, do they know?"

"Not that I know of. Don't know what that would mean anyway. She's off doing what she wants. My sons? I think I should tell them. I'm thinking about that."

"Phil tells me there's somebody else in your life. Somebody named Angela?"

At her name, I smiled. "Yes, there was somebody named Angela. A lawyer, for crying out loud. Saw something in me, can you believe it?"

"You're speaking in the past tense, Dave."

"It's intentional. She wants to stay in the city. And me? I'm sticking here. I should have run away from home a long time ago, but I never did. For better or worse, I'm a small town guy."

"Well, it's her loss. She would have had a winner with you."

"Thanks."

She reached out for my hand and held it when she spoke. "I came by to say thanks. Phil and I are driving back tomorrow morning. He'll see a doctor back home as soon as we get back."

"Will I have a chance to see him? To say goodbye?"

"He doesn't want to see anyone, Dave. Maybe more to the point, he doesn't want to be seen. His spasms are getting worse and he doesn't like to be seen jerking around. He needs to get back to his doctor right away."

"When I talked to him the last time, he was fine. A few spasms, but nothing severe."

"He told me about your last conversation, Dave. It made an impression."

"But not so much that he wants to be seen looking less than perfect?"

"That's my Phil. He's back at the condo. Before we take off tomorrow, he wants to go to the cemetery to see Catherine's grave. Then we're off."

"He'll be in good hands, Jackie."

"He'll be in my hands. Whether they're good or not, I can't tell for sure, but I love the man and I want to be with him, no matter what. "

She stood on her toes and gave me a kiss. "Good by, David Blondin. I'll miss you and Phil will miss you."

"I'll write."

She smiled and left, her perfume . . . was it White Linen? . . . lingering. I watched her from my window as she got back in her car and drove off. Then I took a last sip of coffee, slid into my parka and went downstairs and took a walk downtown.

The air was more than crisp. This was a definite cold snap. I liked the change of seasons, but my knuckles hurt and my knees ached. I could feel every joint creak as I walked up the steps to the library.

Nancy Easter wasn't at her desk and I found her in the stacks putting returned books back on their shelves. She saw me and stopped, then went back to her task. She looked particularly lovely today, clad in a beautiful cream colored dress and with her hair styled perfectly.

I took two steps closer, still concerned that I'd be yelled at for speaking too loudly in a library. Old habits died hard. "You heard?"

Nancy Easter straightened up and met my eyes. "About Tina?"

"That, and Phil, and George. And even Catherine, I guess."

"I did. All in the time it took to have a cup of coffee and half of a bran muffin at the diner yesterday morning. Some people think they need satellite TV? Let them come to Apsley."

"Look, Nancy."

She turned back to face me, a question on her face.

"I was thinking, I got invited over to Chief Wetman's house tomorrow night, and I hear that his wife is a wonderful cook. Maybe you and I could go together, if you're free."

I could swear that Nancy blushed a little.

"Well, thanks, Dave. That'd be nice."

"He's a real nice guy, and if his wife . . . I think it's Mary Alice . . . if she's anything like him, it should be a nice night."

"That sounds terrific, Dave. What time?"

"6:30? You don't mind my pick-up, do you?"

With that conversation, I remembered why I liked Nancy Easter. She was still a reserved human being, probably with good reason, but there was a gentility and a degree of uncommon tenderness underneath that I saw when she was fifteen and sixteen, and even later on when she returned to Apsley and took her job at the library. I saw it in her smile and in her deep blue eyes with the silver flecks. And I found that I wanted to know her better.

When I left, Nancy went to another section of the library and removed the copy of *What's All the Screaming About* from the shelf. If she was going to be visiting people who loved opera, a fact that traveled through Apsley within moments of its revelation, she wanted to learn some of the basics, and this book was a great place to start. She also took the CD of *Il Trovatore* from another section and was walking to the office to put the items in her purse when she saw me at the checkout desk. After I left, she checked the record and saw that I'd taken out the CD of *Madame Butterfly*.

She looked at her watch: 9:45. She stepped into the office and reminded the head librarian that she would be leaving soon and would be taking the next day off as well. With that, she slipped into the new cashmere coat she bought on Saturday and stepped into the cold air. She buttoned the coat as she walked in the direction of the office of Gordon Jefts.

George Wessel was resting in bed with his foot elevated. He adjusted the bed covers and peeked at the dressing on his side. The wound from the round fired by Tina Gladwell hit soft tissue and skin, and indeed, the ankle was broken when he fell, but not so badly that any surgery was required. Bandages and a pair of crutches would do for now, and he got both at the Apsley Clinic. A cast would go on in a few days. He'd been lucky.

Lou Pellerin stopped by to check on the patient, and George's wife, Carla, who was doting on him, gave him a few minutes alone with Pellerin.

"So, George, you're a hero in Apsley again?"

George smiled. "I just tried to get her to drop the gun. Not very successful, huh?"

Lou took a seat, moving two flowering plants in order to do so. He said, "Well, it was enough to break Tina's concentration."

"She'll be OK?"

"Reilly caught her in the upper arm. Hell of a shot. She'll be in the hospital until this afternoon, then she's going to a locked psych ward at Woodland hospital."

"She's real sick, Lou. She was just so calm, so collected when she was standing there talking to me at that table."

"Tina's been sick for a long time, George. You heard what we found there?"

"Not really. They've been giving me some pretty strong painkillers and I've been zoned out most of the time."

Lou told him about the discovery of the baseball bat. "The forensic guys said it's blood and it matches Catherine Marchand's blood type. We'll get DNA in another week or so and we'll confirm it, but Tina as much as admitted it."

"Holy . . ."

George winced and Lou made excuses. "You listen to Carla, George. Word is, if you give her any problems, she'll break your other ankle." Then he was gone and in four minutes, George was sound asleep.

Ken Gladwell was at the hospital in his wife's room. A policeman stood guard outside the door. Ken didn't say anything and just studied the face of his sleeping wife. Her right arm was bandaged heavily. Even in sleep, Tina's face was set in an angry snarl. No peace, not yet. He had no illusions that she'd ever leave a hospital or a prison based on her admissions to the police so far and upon the evidence the police uncovered at the factory.

Tina stirred in her sleep and started to roll over when a twinge in her shoulder caused her to utter a small cry and open her eyes. She looked at Ken and then glanced at her surroundings, trying to grasp her situation. She tugged at the corner of the blanket and closed her eyes, her lips thin and set in the same scowl.

When he returned to Apsley Police headquarters, Lou Pellerin looked over the day's roster on the squad bulletin board. Reilly's report on the shooting Saturday was due on his desk at noon.

Chief Wetman came up beside him. "Hungry? I'm just heading to the diner."

"Give me a few minutes and I'll join you. Reilly should have a report on my desk any minute. Mind if he joins us?"

"Not at all. I'll get a booth."

Ten minutes later, Lou walked into Lafferty's followed by Reilly and the half-dozen customers and staff stood to clap and cheer. Lou waved it off but smiled broadly. Reilly was blushing and averted the eyes of the patrons. Lou moved towards Wetman's booth and acknowledged the praise with a few "It's part of the job" comments. Reilly said nothing but a broad smile did appear and stayed in place.

After lunch, Reilly went back to the station. Wetman ordered coffees and said, "Thanks for everything you did on this case, Lou."

"I appreciate it, Chief. I'm actually not a bad cop, you know."

"In fact, you're a damned good cop and you'll be a great chief. Just give me a couple years, OK?"

They clicked cups.

Lou asked, "Did the District Attorney's office get in touch with you yet?"

"Early this morning. They'll be sending over a lawyer and a State Trooper tomorrow morning to interview us and collect the evidence we have. They'll take over most of the work on this case from here. By the way, the Trooper won't be Binky Blackwood or Clancy or Terrebonne."

Lou smiled. "How about that woman lawyer? What was her name? Angela something. Is she going to be handling it? I heard that she and Dave Blondin had a thing going?"

"It's been assigned to another lawyer in the D.A.'s office. Besides, that deal with Angela Kim and Dave Blondin is all done. You've got to get better sources of information, Lou."

Lou let out a little chuckle and went on. "How about that Jimmy Reilly? He's really something isn't he?"

"Opie? He's going to be a good detective. I like the kid."

As if on cue, Reilly came back into the diner grim-faced and held out a piece of paper for the Chief. When he finished, he

330 / P.D. LaFleur

handed it to Lou Pellerin. It was a copy of a police report
that had just come in: Malcolm Prudhomme was found dead
of an apparent heart attack on his front porch twenty minutes ago.

"How long was he dead?"

"Not long. The cab driver says he picked up Malcolm at
a lawyer's office and dropped him off at his house at ten-
fifteen."

Gordon Jefts pulled into the parking lot of the state Lottery
Headquarters just after 12:30. He jumped out of the driver's
side and sped to the passenger side so he could open the door
for his VIP passenger. Nancy Easter was looking especially
beautiful today and Gordon could not help but admire the turn
of her ankle and the shape of her long slender leg as she stepped
out of the car.

"You look smashing, Nancy. Absolutely stunning."

And she did. Her coat was calf-length cashmere in a shade of
blue that echoed her eyes. Her hair cascaded to her shoulders,
thick and luxurious.

"You make being beautiful look easy. You look as good as
you did when you were one of the 'princesses' back in high
school."

As soon as he said the words, he regretted them. They had
both been discussing the events of Saturday on the way in.

Nancy overlooked the gaffe and said, "Thanks, Gordon. Let
me tell you that getting to look this good isn't as effortless as it
once was."

"Do you mind if I nibble on your ankles for a minute before
we go in."

"You're a filthy pig, Gordon Jefts."

"And that's why you hired me."

"I wouldn't have it any other way."

"Well, in another hour or so, you're going to have to beat

admirers off with a stick. The difficulty is going to be separating the sincere from the charlatans."

"They will all be charlatans, Gordon, and thank you, I know who my real friends are."

Gordon held the door and Nancy walked into the lobby, about to present her winning ticket and collect her six million dollars . . . although the lump sum cash amount would barely reach three point three million dollars.

After the requisite photo session and newspaper interview after she collected her winnings, the pair would head downtown to the city's newest restaurant, La Ruelle, for an early but elegant dinner.

"Don't get wrecked on the wine, Gordon," she cautioned on the drive in. "And after dinner, you're taking me home so we can both be fresh and ready for tomorrow morning. I'll feel a lot better when the papers are signed."

"It's all set up. Their attorney is coming in at 9:30."

"So when do I get the keys?"

"I'll have cashier's checks for him, so you'll have the keys in your hand by about ten, unless they want to sit and chat. I have an insurance binder already that will go into effect at the same time. You are ready to roll, Nancy."

"I was sweating this, you know. When Dave Blondin saw me at the Kerrigan Mills that night, I was devastated. I know he's been scouting out the building."

"But not the back section that you wanted, overlooking the river."

"I understand that now. Anything to report, by the way?"

"I can't say anything, but I wouldn't be surprised if Dave showed up in my office tomorrow just about the time you're leaving."

"Good for him! He'll do a nice job with that building."

"It's still a crime scene for the moment, you know."

"I'm not too worried. I'll have an architect and an engineer in there next week and the police should be done and out of there by then."

They continued in silence and Nancy said, "It's just so damned sad, Gordon. It was bad enough to lose Catherine, especially the way she died. But Tina as well. She's just as lost."

"Very sad."

"Do you remember when Catherine used to sing? Her voice was part angel, part truck driver."

He recalled the voice clearly, the one that was featured in their high school musical and the one that dominated every performance by the chorus. So melodic one moment, so raw and raunchy the next, as if to say sometimes you power right through your sadness, and sometimes you just keep your fingers crossed and hope for a miracle.

The memories kept them both thinking for a while.

"How about your job at the library? When are you going to turn in your resignation?"

"Maybe in a week or two. I've got time and I want to give the library a chance to get somebody in and I can do some training."

"Do you know Emily Donahue?"

"At the supermarket? Sure."

"I know she's looking for a job."

"I'll remember that."

Early the next morning, I met Gordon Jefts at the diner.

"Nancy's so excited she could just fly."

"I'll bet. She kept her secret about the lottery real well."

"Don't forget me! You have no idea how much keeping that secret that was killing me."

"Good boy, Gordon. Did she ever describe what she wanted to do with the place?"

"A few hints, that's all. The only thing she said specifically was that Apsley needed what she was going to deliver. My guess is a nice place to go at night. Maybe a little café, music, that sort of thing. That would be her style."

"We already have Dean's Town Tavern. Who could ask for anything better than that?"

Jefts said, "I heard Harold Marcus is taking Tina's case, by the way. Good lawyer. Not cheap either."

I accepted Gordon's assessment. "Ken's got money. He can afford it."

"That's the thing, Dave. Ken didn't hire Harold; Tina's mother did."

"Grace Kerrigan?" The news took me by surprise.

"Yup. She's calling the shots on this. What I heard is that she blames Ken for Tina's problems."

"No shit?"

"No shit. My guess is, you won't see Ken sticking around Apsley much longer."

"Maybe it's for the best."

Phil Marchand was at the cemetery that day, and even brought a folding chair. Sitting alone under the twisted branches of an old oak in front of the cold ground of Catherine's grave, he had a long, one-sided conversation. So far, he'd taken the news with little emotion. His tone with his sister was explanatory and clinical.

"She's going to go to jail when this is all done, even if she can't go to trial. The Chief told me she'd at least be confined to a hospital. Tina's sick, Catherine, but you know that."

He spent over an hour sitting there in the bitter cold talking to Catherine. A town worker from the Cemetery Department stopped by to ask if everything was alright. Phil waved him away.

A black Mercedes drove up and Phil turned, looking in the car's direction. Stepping out of the vehicle, Jacqueline Marchand walked to him. He never took his eyes off her.

EPILOGUE

When I started to write this, I knew that making it absolutely accurate would be impossible. I wasn't party to every conversation and I can't read minds. I'm not a reporter either, and I didn't conduct interviews with every single person to cross-check every account. The story, if I ever finished it, was going to be the truth, but only as I saw it. I asked my friends to forgive me if I jumped to the wrong conclusions, which I am certain I did more than once. All of them said they would, but I don't believe them.

Today, when I read histories or biographies that I pick up at the library, I have a greater appreciation for the process writers have to go through when they put their pens to paper. It is not an easy task to make sense out of events, even those we are closest to. To go back hundreds of years and pretend to know what a person really said or meant back then has to be practically impossible.

Speaking of libraries, Emily Donahue did apply for Nancy Easter's job. She got it and left her job at the supermarket where the hours were long and the tasks tedious. She isn't as good at her library job as Nancy was, but she's happy and the head librarian is happy, so that's good.

Nancy opened a coffee house and wine bar in the space she bought from the Kerrigan Mills, and the place is a hit. The new people in town wanted something like this, and the old townies have been coming in to get a taste of good coffee, good wine and good music. It's set up for wi-fi so there are always a bunch of people there during the day doing work and checking email. Nancy and I see each other occasionally, but neither of us is ready for anything serious right now. Maybe someday. I'm not rushing, and I think she's just enjoying running her own place.

The music there is all acoustic, classical guitarists and folk music most nights. One of the regular performers is Dr. Hairston, the psychiatrist. He offered to play for tips, but he's developing a loyal following with a curious brand of blues, jazz and humor, and the café is SRO when he's on the small stage. He's setting up his own office in Eastland and he's only working part-time at his state job, so he'll likely be a regular around here for some time.

I bought the section of the Mills that I wanted and I'm still working on it. Doing it over is going to take me another three months or so, but I'm getting bites on the first floor space, and the upstairs units, the real estate people tell me, will rent up fast. I'm glad I made the move and someday I might even be able to think about retiring before I'm a drooling old man.

No one has heard from Phil Marchand directly, but I get an occasional note from Jacqueline. The notes don't give many specifics, but I can read between the lines; Phil is not doing well. Bob Hayes tells me that he sees a spike in deaths after big holidays like Christmas and New Years, as if people hang on just long enough to get through the important times and then expire in some strange form of release. Phil's return to Apsley was no holiday, but in some sense, I wonder if the same thing happened with him, even if death won't necessarily come quickly in his case.

Ken Gladwell decided to move away, closer to his job, which also happens to be closer to the women's prison and the mental health center there where Tina is going to be living for a long time. People who have seen him tell me that he's gaunt and thin. Tina? No one I know has any idea how she is doing. People here don't talk about her much, as if they expected viciousness to have an ugly and less familiar face.

Everything and everyone else in Apsley remain pretty much unchanged. A few more new houses are getting built on the edge of town and the train line is expected to reopen in another two or three years. We'll see plenty of changes then when people realize they can commute to the city in less than an hour and still live in a relatively small, if growing, town. New families will move in, real estate prices will climb and the old Apsley will be a lingering memory to those of us still left.

That's OK with me. Not all of my memories of Apsley are good ones. There will be lots of new people and lots of new memories to be made. They'll have their own crises to work through, just as my friends and I did.

I'm dealing with the whole Catherine Marchand ordeal in my own way. I stop by her grave once in a while and put two flowers there, one for Catherine and the other for our unknown, unnamed, unborn child. Sick? Maybe. I see Dr. Hairston once a month now and he tells me not to worry about it. I don't try too hard to decode the significance of my actions; I agree with Hairston that too much introspection rots the mind. That sounds to me like a sufficiently honest answer.